I0761777

Detective “Doc” Wiley, an ex-Army Ranger Medic, a veteran of Vietnam and the Nassau County Homicide Squad, no longer knows what he wants, only that what he has falls short. Madeline Maclear, director of nursing at an area hospital, is a widow whose husband was a troubled Vietnam vet. She is trying to reassemble her life. The two rudderless individuals are thrown together when Carl, an untraceable expert assassin with a private arsenal, a fortune in cash, and a perverse sense of humor, returns to Long Island in the spring of 1999. Six former flower children that have all but forgotten an adolescent episode on the road to Woodstock in 1969 are scheduled for lethal vengeance.

Carl’s targets begin to die in rapid succession, along with investigators who accidentally trigger bombs at the crime scenes. Peace symbols branded into certain victims suggest a relationship, but no one can fathom what that relationship is. Doc’s eclectic investigative team plays a frantic game of catch-up, encountering colorful characters and chilling traps along the way. Public hysteria and political recriminations emanate from the case like shrapnel from the killer’s explosives. Only the victims glimpse the twisted reasoning behind Carl’s mission of mayhem. When one corpse turns out to be the buyer of Madeline’s former home, the trail leads to the nursing director…

ACKNOWLEDGMENTS

Special thanks to my good friend, Nassau County Police Department Homicide Detective Dennis P. Aylward (Ret.) for his guidance with NCPD procedures, of which I knew absolutely nothing when I started this book. Anything incorrect in that regard is strictly my fault. Thanks, also, to Ms. Jean-Marie Posner, a former director of the Sands Point Preserve for her kindness and patience with my research. And, as always, thanks to all my colleagues in the writing community for their support and friendship.

THE WOODSTOCK MURDERS

James D. Robertson

A Black Opal Books Publication

GENRE: MYSTERY-DETECTIVE/THRILLER/SUSPENSE

THE WOODSTOCK MURDERS

Cover Design by Jackson Cover Designs

HC Print ISBN: 9781644372128

First Publication: NOVEMBER 2020

Published by Black Opal Books http://www.blackopalbooks.com.

DEDICATION

For Liz.

Chapter 1

The street looked like a practice field for a plane crash. Police cruisers, private automobiles, news vans, and assorted emergency vehicles stood at haphazard angles wherever they had ceased forward motion. A growing crowd of scurrying humanity was gathering in a blaze of artificial light in front of the house at the end of the block. Reporters and cameramen bailed out of their mobile studios like a SWAT team deployment. Doc Wiley's unmarked, brand new, 1999 Ford Crown Victoria nosed into the street in time to let him see two of the network vans jockeying for position.

"Oh shit," he said, "somebody screwed up big time."

Channel 30, a local all-news station, was there. Their van was right alongside the network vehicles. In Doc's experience, the native news vultures could be even more aggressive in their pursuit of a local story than the kids from that other island—the big gray one west of Brooklyn. Not that he preferred the networks. The Big Three would treat a Long Island story as a passing curiosity. Quickly reaching the limits of their attention span, they would soon lose track of events in the burbs to return their focus to whence they had come—the Big Apple—source of the omnipotent media god, Ratings. Unless of course, the Long Island story proved suitably newsworthy, in which case they would all be gargantuan pains in the ass for the duration.

Doc edged his car into the milieu and goosed the siren to move a knot of gawking neighbors out of his way. A light mist began to fall.

He still missed his old Dodge Diplomat with its Police Interceptor engine. Maybe Old Betsy was as unobtrusive as purple granny glasses, but his new, monochromatic white Crown Vic with its plain-Jane hubcaps still screamed "Cop Car" and, in Doc's opinion, the six-cylinder motor was just a waste of good metal. He would have paid for repairs out of his own pocket just to hang on to the Dodge, but image trumped function in modern police work. Gas mileage overshadowed performance. Muscle cars had passed into history. He thought it a shame.

The citizens of Oyster Bay, unaccustomed to such excitement in the middle of the night, in bathrobes and jackets hastily thrown on against the mist, shunned the glare of his headlights and grudgingly yielded the right of way as they shuffled onto the grassy apron.

The flashing red and white lights of police cruisers, the yellow strobes of ambulances, and one blue dash beacon from a volunteer fireman sent a kaleidoscope of spots racing across the facades of the turn of the century homes. The spinning beams sent brilliant sparks speeding along wet, naked, tree limbs, creating something akin to silent fireworks. The crowd, the lights, the tense feeling of expectation were not dissimilar to a celebration. To Doc, it was a circus.

The years in Homicide were beginning to tell. Doc imagined the cynicism he had seen in the eyes of so many cops clouding his. When had the fire of making a difference cooled to glowing embers? He had been searching for something when he left the Rangers after Vietnam. Purpose? Atonement? He didn't know. After separation from the service and a year or so of what now seemed like non-stop drunken anger, he had cleaned up his act and found a job as a Nassau County Paramedic, sliding into the routine as easily as he had into his duties as a combat medic. Two years of that had led to the same frustration he had felt in the jungle: futile, a Band-Aid on a mortal wound.

A friend suggested he try the cops. At least the uniform wasn't green. He made it easily. The gun was the biggest drawback. He had never expected to carry one again. He remembered how it had troubled him. Wearing the thing came too naturally.

It was a statistical fact that throughout their careers most officers never drew their weapon in the line of duty. If it had not been for that bank robbery in Franklin Square, he might have been one of the lucky majority. At least he hadn't killed the guy, and it did get him into plain clothes and undercover. That had led to the Detective Squad and eventually into Homicide. He found a home there, regained an awareness of what he had missed since the Rangers—the brotherhood—corny as it might sound—that only those who have seen the elephant can truly feel, but he still felt like the shovel in the hands of the elephant keeper.

He slapped the gearshift into park and fumbled in his pocket for his cigarettes. Snapping a light from his old Zippo, Doc sucked a lungful of smoke. He looked at the Ranger tab affixed to the lighter, rolled it over in his palm and read the inscription on the back: Rangers lead the way. Charlie Mike.

"Roger that." When he looked up again, the infant beads of moisture populating his windshield were maturing into full-grown raindrops. The newshounds were ducking for cover.

He chuckled, and muttered, "Attaboy, God, piss on 'em."

A passenger jet roared overhead, turbofans screaming on final approach to JFK. An image appeared in his mind's eye, unbidden, yanked from his memory as if by a chain. That sound always did it. He smelled jet exhaust, envisioned a blue and white Boeing 707—a Pan Am R&R bird—taxiing past a backdrop of palm trees and revetments, felt the heat of the central highlands on his face and Berryhill's hand on his shoulder.

"Go have fun," Berry said. "I'll hold down the fort until you get back."

He shivered. The vision evaporated.

A stunning redhead shoved a microphone in his face before Doc had gotten his six-foot frame out of the car and erect.

"Detective Wiley of Nassau County Homicide, Adrienne Boyd, Channel Thirty News," she said, making introductions for her viewers since she was well acquainted with the detective. "Can you tell us who the victim was?"

Behind her, he saw the live-feed antenna atop one of the network vans was becoming pneumatically erect. A bright red hydraulic hose encircling the growing phallus throbbed with the rhythm of the pump.

Doc smiled at the symbolism, and said, "You know as much as I do, Miss Boyd." He slammed the car door and bunched his shoulders against the rain. "Excuse me. I have work to do."

"But, Detective Wiley—" She stood in his path.

Doc's calculated grin told Adrienne she was wasting her time. She stuck her tongue out at him, spun on her heel to face her cameraman, and ran her finger across her throat. The man behind her extinguished the flood lamp, dropped the mini-cam from his shoulder, and threw Doc a disgusted sneer.

"Come on, Doc." Adrienne whirled on the departing detective. Her face scrunched in a pout. "I thought we were friends," she said to his back.

"You too? I guess we were both wrong. And don't stick that pretty little tongue out unless you plan to use it."

"No problem there."

Looking over his shoulder, he said, "Anything for a story." She flipped him the bird. He turned away again, saying, "Not tonight," and kept walking. The sound of her foot stamping the pavement brightened his mood.

On the front porch of a weathered-gray, modest, frame house with Victorian aspirations stood a forlorn, rookie cop. Doc flashed his ID, lifted his chin toward the media mob, and said, "Who's responsible for the photo op?"

"I guess I am," the kid said.

"Called it in on the radio, did you?"

The uniformed cop nodded, awash in self-pity.

"We live in the electronic age, my friend. Police-band scanners are as difficult to obtain as a trip to the nearest Radio Shack. Tow truck drivers are not the only ones who listen. You won't make that mistake again, will you?"

"No sir. Next time I'll borrow a neighbor's phone."

"No doubt in my mind. Now, who's where?"

"Detective Cordova's upstairs with the body. Crime Scene Unit's up there, too."

Doc smiled at the first good news of the night. Tony Cordova had been a friend since the Police Academy. His sharp wit and quick mouth had been the source of many memorable episodes. Their mutual disdain for bureaucracy—some of their superiors would call it arrogance—had gotten both of them in trouble more often than was healthy for a policeman's career. More than a friend, Tony was a brother Vietnam veteran. Tony wasn't a Ranger, not even Airborne, but at least a combat vet, and that was a bond both men could understand if not explain. Most importantly to Doc, Tony was a good cop.

"ME?" Doc asked. The kid looked puzzled. "Medical examiner?"

The cop made an O of his mouth and said, "Not yet."

Doc surveyed the scene in the street. The mob was creeping closer to the house, despite a growing number of officers' energetic attempts at crowd control.

"Keep the vampires out," he said.

"Yessir."

"That's the ticket, Patrolman…" Doc squinted, but could not make out the cop's nameplate. His eyes were still recovering from the cameraman's flood.

"Gallagher. Bob Gallagher." The kid sighed.

"Relax, Gallagher. Your name won't be in my report. At least you didn't use the phone in the house. That's a really big no-no. Anyway, in a hundred years who's going to give a shit?" Doc flipped his cigarette onto the lawn and reached for the doorknob, trying to remember when he had been as naive as the rookie patrolman.

The heat in the foyer hit him like a wave. Another uniform, much older than the first, was stationed at the foot of a flight of stairs just beyond the entryway. His tie was undone and he held his hat in his hand. He gave Doc a bored smile, and said, "Hullo, Doc. Warm, ain't it?"

"Hey, Bill." Doc loosened his tie and unbuttoned his shirt collar. "It's like an oven in here."

"Yeah. Thermostat was set on ninety. We turned it down, but the burner must have been percolating a while. Place hasn't cooled down yet."

"What've we got?"

"Murder most foul."

"I can do without the Hercule Poirot."

"Sorry, Doc. My old lady's PBS junkie. Must be contagious." The cop jerked a thumb at the stairs. "Front bedroom. The lady of the house. Tony C. and the CSU guys are up there. Jack Kobrigian's in the kitchen with her old man."

"What're they doing in there?"

"Jack took hubby in there to calm him down. Guy's a basket case. You want to talk to him?"

"Later. I'll see what Tony's got first."

Doc signed the Crime Scene Log, noted the time of his arrival, and returned the clipboard to the patrolman. With a sigh, Doc mounted the stairs and climbed slowly, taking in his surroundings, trying to get an impression of the victim's lifestyle. Don't just see, feel the terrain—Ranger School 101—the gospel according to Sergeant Blake.

The house seemed to be an ordinary, middle-class home. Judging by the furnishings it might have once been upper-middle-class, but that had been a while ago. Dusty track lighting heads and table lamps with yellowed silk shades lit worn, green upholstery in the living room off the center hallway.

As he reached the second floor, he heard rock and roll music playing from a room at the front of the house. He knew that raspy guitar. Hendrix. Golden oldies.

Sweat had broken out on his forehead by the time he reached the open door at the end of the hall. He stepped into what appeared to be a lady's dressing chamber. The room was a time warp. Day-Glo fantasy posters covered the walls. Lava lamps bracketed a cracked mirror above a Swedish Modern vanity table. A delicate bamboo and cane chair lay on its side. A fluorescent black-light strip fixture on the ceiling gave the place a ghostly cast. Rope rugs were scattered on the hardwood floor. One red and one yellow beanbag chair filled two corners of the room. Strings of multi-colored beads and crystal hung everywhere. Hendrix slid into "The Star-Spangled Banner," drawing Doc's attention to the adjacent room. He moved through the doorway to emerge in a master bedroom decorated in much the same manner but brightly lit by table lamps.

Tony Cordova stood at the foot of a queen-size bed, his back to Doc. Dennis Stockton dusted likely surfaces for fingerprints. Larry Hoeniger snapped photographs. The flash made the figure on the bed even more grotesque, if that were possible. The air was thick. A cloying scent of incense mixed with the odor of marijuana, the coppery scent of blood, and a faint whiff of sex.

Tony Cordova sensed Doc's presence and turned.

"Evening, Doc. How the hell are you?" Tony's smile was forced. Doc could see why.

"Hey, Tone." Doc's eyes were riveted on the corpse. He nodded a greeting to the other cops, who returned it, but continued with their work. "How's your bride and brood?"

"Well enough. You should stop by. Phyllis would love to see you. The kids, too."

"Been busy."

"Anybody I know?"

Doc ignored the jibe as he ignored all of his colleagues' allusions to his sex life. After his divorce, he had gone through women like a man with a migraine goes through aspirin, but like that chronic pain plagued victim, his brand of medication brought short-lived relief. Self-pride and his inherent sense of honor won out after months of boudoir bouncing, but the reputation stuck. Lately, the mantle of the dashing rake weighed heavy on his shoulders, but he let his fellow cops believe what they enjoyed believing. Even faithful, monogamous guys such as Tony got some kind of thrill imagining his sexual exploits. The bubble would burst if they knew of his new passion. In the testosterone-steeped cop world, even if he had been the most talented sculptor since Michelangelo—which he wasn't—he wouldn't stand a chance. The jokes would be unbearable.

He pointed with his chin at the nude, dead woman lying prone on the bed. A pillow stuffed under her hips caused her buttocks to thrust skyward in a lewd manner. The effect was far from provocative. Doc saw total human debasement. The woman's rump was a road map of razor thin slices. Bruises mottled her back with the imprint of knuckles vivid in many. Someone had tortured the lady long and hard. She had a thin, beaded band tied tightly around her forehead. Bleached blonde hair, graying at the dark roots, fanned out across her shoulders as if arranged. One of the padded, uplifting cups of her Victoria's Secret lace bra was stuffed in her mouth with the straps wound around her skull. The apparent cause of death was a length of fine steel wire around her throat, biting deep into swollen flesh—the finishing touch to a labor of unbridled savagery.

Doc grimaced, despite his years of experience with violent death. He had seen much horror as a policeman, most of it in his years in Homicide, but this one was exceptional. Most murders were passionate, sudden, violent affairs. Jealousy, greed, affronted ego—these were the commonplace motives for slaughter. People snapped. They went at each other with guns, knives, hammers, and lengths of pipe—anything handy. He had come to accept mayhem as a byproduct of the animal world. Humans, his theory went, were merely an advanced species whose superiority begot supreme cruelty when pushed over the brink. But the scenario here was no fit of sudden rage. This smacked of a type of malice he had not seen since Vietnam. The headman's wife in that Montagnard village. Raped. Beaten. Mutilated. She must have begged for death before it was over.

He shook it off, and said, "Hit the high points for me, Tony."

"Mrs. Dorothy Kohler," Tony identified the victim. "Her husband, Jason, found her when he came home from a meeting of some local environmentalist group. Committee to Save the Swampland Peckerheads or some shit."

"That's Marshland Woodpecker, Tony," Larry Hoeniger interjected.

"Whatever."

Doc said, "Kind of late for ecological crusading."

"Maybe. I'll check with the committee," Tony said.

"Do that. The guy in the kitchen her old man?"

"Yeah. I tried to question him, but he's coming unglued. Kobrigian was in the squad room when the call came in and came along for the ride. I asked him to try to settle the guy down."

"Couldn't find a better man for the job." Jack Kobrigian's unflappable persona was legendary in police circles.

"The kid who got the dispatch blew his cool when he saw the lady's condition," Tony said.

"I know," Doc said. "He's guarding the front door and having second thoughts about his chosen career. The news-vultures are circling the block. I had to run the gauntlet to get in the place. Adrienne was on me like white on rice."

"The A-lady? Still after your bod? Doesn't she know you're up to—what is it now? M or N?"

"The A-lady? Only if A is for ambitious. That little bitch is too hungry for her own good." Doc was tired of locker-room innuendo. "And I wish you'd get off this alphabet kick. I am not trying to screw one woman for every letter."

"Ooh, aren't we touchy tonight? Hope you weren't too rough on the Gallagher kid. First homicide is something that stays with you. We've all been there."

"He's young…"

"He'll get over it." Tony grinned as he completed the sentence. "Medical examiners on the way—Shapiro. He's all pissed off that we dragged him out on the eve of his daughter's fifth birthday. He called a little while ago for directions. Said he was wrestling with a Schwinn, trying to decipher instructions he swears are in Japanese, when they beeped him. I know the feeling."

"So, we'll wait." Doc wished he'd left his suit jacket downstairs. The others were in shirtsleeves. "What is this? A sauna?"

"Mister Kohler doesn't know why the heat was turned up. Maybe the perp did it," Tony glanced at the body. "Or maybe the poor thing was cold."

"Or maybe the perp was trying to alter the lady's body temperature to throw off the time of death. Dust the thermostat."

"Already done," Stockton said.

Doc moved to the side of the bed. He knelt to peer at the blackened face with the bulging eyes. A crime scene had a way of making him attuned to all of his senses. The vision of horror before him, the sweltering atmosphere in the overheated room, and the cloying stench of death should have affected his mind to the point of overload, but the familiar music pulsating in the background brought back memories, most of them pleasant.

"What's with the tunes?"

A vintage stereo beneath a street facing picture window supplied a rock and roll theme.

"Woodstock Album," Tony said. "It was playing when I got here. We haven't gotten that far yet. Didn't want to disturb any evidence so I let it play."

Doc nodded agreement, wishing for somewhere to throw his coat, but acutely aware of the danger of contaminating the scene. He looked from the body to the stereo and then examined the rest of the room.

"Flower power lives," he said. It was eerie, like stepping back through time. Visions of student protests sprang to mind. The Chicago riots. Kent State.

"Until tonight it did," Tony corrected.

"That a water pipe?" Doc pointed to a Lucite columnar object with a bulbous base in the center of a red velvet throw pillow on the floor. "What did they used to call those things, Tony?"

"Beats me. I'm too young to remember the sixties."

"You mean you were too stoned to remember the sixties."

"Hey, c'mon. I never inhaled."

"Sure, you and Willie of the White House, straight as arrows. Next you'll tell me you've never had a blow-job."

The other cops chuckled but stayed out of it.

"A bong," Tony mumbled.

"Never inhaled, my ass." Doc stood up. "Looks like whoever snuffed her, beat the shit out of her, carved her up, and banged her doggy style before, during, or after strangling her."

"Yeah. A real sweetheart. The husband?" Tony asked.

"Ain't it always? But here's an odd touch." Doc stooped for a closer look at the murder weapon, careful not to touch anything. "Piano wire, wooden handles, and all. An honest to goodness garrote. Homemade, I'd say. Haven't seen one like that since Nam. Cut a head clean off if you use enough force."

"Lovely," Tony said. "Not exactly basic issue, if memory serves."

"Nope. Special ops stuff. Nasty-time tool."

"All's fair in love, war, and pinochle."

"Yup. Let's get the grieving widower in here." Something caught Doc's eye. "What's that on her ass, Tony?"

"Some sicko's idea of fun and games?"

"Look closer."

"I've been trying not to."

Doc cocked his head; his eyebrows arched.

Tony's lips compressed into a thin, white line as he took a step closer to the bed.

"All I see is the aftermath of a butcher gone berserk."

"Besides the cuts. Right there." Doc pointed, his finger an inch from the victim's skin. "Looks like a fresh burn, almost like a brand. There's a shape to it. Larry, get a close-up of this."

Hoeniger shot several angles and stepped back.

"Little bigger than a golf ball." Doc's eyes narrowed.

"Now I see it," Tony said. "Looks like a peace symbol."

Doc's eyes went to the stereo. "What in hell have we got here? Flower children S and M freaks?"

"Let's ask."

Tony went to retrieve Jason Kohler. Doc took the opportunity to shed his jacket and tossed it to him as he went out. Tony passed an irate medical examiner on the stairs.

"There's still goddamn traffic on the LIE," Doctor Eugene Shapiro told Doc as he bustled into the room. "Let's make this quick. My kid's training wheels are still in the box and I've got to finish the damned bike before I go to work in the morning. I'd like to get some sleep tonight, too." He stopped short as soon as his eyes settled on the corpse. "Christ! What the hell kind of animal did this?"

"We were hoping you could tell us something about that," Doc said.

"My God, Doc, what's the world coming to?"

They were discussing the obvious damage to the woman's remains when they heard a scuffle in the adjacent room.

"I'm not going in there again," said a hysterical, male voice. "He butchered her. I told her never to bring them home. My God, what he did to her. I don't want to see her like that again. You can't make me."

"Don't get physical, pal. I'm warning you," Tony's determined tones interrupted. "We just want to talk to you. Hey, Doc. Would you step out here for a minute, please?"

"Wait for me," Doc instructed Shapiro as he hurried out of the room.

Jason Kohler screamed when he caught a glimpse of his wife's body as Doc stepped through the doorway. He swung wildly at Tony's head with his fists. The detective ducked and grabbed at his clothing to subdue him. Doc threw his arms around the man, pinioned Jason's arms to his sides, and lifted him off the floor. He swung the panicked man around, put Kohler's back to the bedroom doorway, and roared, "Close the fucking door."

One of the men inside the bedroom kicked it shut.

"Calm down, Mister Kohler," Doc said, nose to nose with the distraught husband. "You don't have to look now. Relax, okay?"

"Need a hand out there?" someone called through the bedroom door.

"We're okay." Doc looked at the subdued husband. "Aren't we, Mister Kohler?"

Jason Kohler sagged against Doc and wept. Racking sobs shook the big detective. Tony stood helplessly by.

Doc heard Gene Shapiro's muted voice say, "Let's get this show on the road. I got a bike to build." Then Larry Hoeniger said, "Doc said to—"

The bedroom door bulged outward and split along its length. A shock wave blew the three men in the dressing room off their feet. Jason Kohler shot out of his shoes.

Doc thought he heard someone scream, "Incoming!" His ears were ringing. He felt the prickly nap of a rug against his cheek and choked on dust and smoke. An instant before he blacked out, he recognized the voice. It was his.

Chapter 2

Wide tires on warm asphalt hummed in harmony with the adrenaline buzzing in Carl's brain. On a night like this his Jeep Grand Cherokee became an extension of himself, as inexorable and malevolent as a Cruise Missile. The road was his launch pad. There was nothing to hold him down. Carl began to think he might accelerate into hyperspace until COMING SOON in bright red letters on a white billboard appeared in his peripheral vision. Like a drogue chute, it dragged him back to reality.

"Oh yeah, real soon," he vowed. "Right here in River City, boys and girls."

The germ of an idea began to form. Even before the idea took shape, his quick reflexes sent his car off the road as smoothly as if he had planned the sudden turn.

The background music in his head came on loud. Name that tune. Of course. The Twilight Zone. Perfect!

His headlights bounced off a rank of plate glass windows quartered by strips of masking tape slashed across dust-cloaked panes. For Carl, this was much more than a row of empty storefronts for rent. The freshly paved parking lot was as inviting as the yellow brick road to Dorothy. An embryonic strip mall with a vacant, darkened phone booth was a perfect place to do what he suddenly just had to do.

Carl extinguished his headlamps to bathe in beloved darkness, tightening his grip on the steering wheel as the Jeep swayed over the concrete apron. He stomped on the brake, closed his eyes, and willed the skidding vehicle to halt. The plan appeared in his mind's eye even before the four-by-four lurched to a stop. His eyes popped open and he said, "Show time," as he grabbed a satchel from the floor behind the passenger's seat, leaped from the car, and ran behind it. On the ground, he checked the area, confirmed his solitude, and bolted into the booth, giddy with pure audacity.

Dotty's scent filled the tight space. He sniffed his fingers, savored the tang of sex and death, and held his breath to hold her dwindling corporal remnants close.

"One down, five to go. Colonel one, cops zip."

Cars whizzed by mere feet from his glass and steel cocoon. Headlights repeatedly bathed him in brilliance and then plunged him back into darkness as they passed. He was a specter caught in a strobe, invisible as often as not.

"Let's see," he said to the phone, "how to put it?"

He dug in his pocket for surgical gloves, jammed his fingers into the latex, snapped the rolled cuffs against his wrists, grabbed the handset, and went back into his pocket for a quarter. After rubbing both sides of the coin on his shirt to smear any prints, he dropped it in the slot.

"Convoluted manifesto?" He winced. "No, no, no. Old hat. Finesse—must have finesse. A scholarly treatise on the uneven contest of good versus evil?" He shook his head. "The dummies would miss the point." He shrugged. "Skip it and get on with the mission? No! Do it. A mind is a terrible thing."

He laughed, unscrewed the mouthpiece cover from the phone, and attached tiny alligator clips to the wires inside. The music in his head changed tracks. He listened with his mouth agape.

"Bravo! Good choice. Mission Impossible."

The whirring sound in his ear as the phone on the receiving end rang calmed him. He took a long breath and whispered, "Slow down. Post-kill euphoria is a trip, but it can make you reckless. This is going to be a flawless operation. Bathe in the ecstasy, but don't let it rule your actions."

"Nine-One-One," he heard. "What is the nature of your emergency?"

He smiled.

ꕥ

A plump, harried 9-1-1 operator fingered the snack-sized package of Doritos she had been saving for her break. The tiny bag was a bribe for her conscience. Better to taper off. Dieting cold turkey could throw a girl's equilibrium out of whack.

Trapped in a muggy room, two months before the air-conditioning would kick in, the last thing the young woman wanted to do was work. She had what she could only describe as terminal spring fever. If she did not get off soon, she was going to die. Her console had been lit up like Times Square on New Year's Eve since she came on duty. Weekends were the pits.

She wrapped up the latest emergency—an old woman in Bethpage who had lost her cat—and broke the connection. The next call appeared instantly on her monitor.

"Nine-One-One, what is the nature of your emergency?"

She frowned at the monitor display. The call originated from a public telephone in Plainview. She preferred calls from private residences, where the system displayed the name and address of the homeowner. The voice that answered her query sounded like a cheap robot from a bad science fiction movie.

"The tape of this call will prove useless for voice analysis," the thing was saying. "It is being processed through a highly efficient electronic distortion device. Don't waste time dispatching a unit. I'll be long gone by the time the fuzz arrive."

She said nothing but pulled back from the monitor a few inches, as if that would afford her some protection from whatever was at the other end of the call, and depressed a button to summon her supervisor.

"This will be your only warning," the voice continued. Even through the unearthly quality, she detected contempt. She could hear the smirk of superiority in its tone. "All law enforcement and emergency service personnel who wish to survive to retire should stay at home until the coming storm has passed." She heard a sound she could only describe as a computerized chuckle. "I'm ba-ack. Kicking ass and taking names. You can't stop me. Better people than you have died trying. Have a nice day."

The line went dead. She jumped as her boss reached over her shoulder to punch a key sequence to bypass her station.

"Take your break, Carmella," Sergeant Davis said, grinning.

"That was spooky," she whispered.

Davis pulled the headset jack he had used to monitor the call from the console and said, "Some kid with a new toy. A crank case two quarts low. Forget it."

"You're the boss," she sang, vacating her chair. She ripped open the bag of chips with her teeth and waddled toward the break room, munching merrily.

Chapter 3

Shell fragments whined above Doc's head, shredding leaves and lacerating tree bark. The ground beneath him writhed under the continuous slam of mortar round impacts. Smoke choked him. His eyes watered. His weapons were gone. He pulled his arm tighter around Berryhill. Berry fought him as he always did, and Doc smelled the stink of bile in his wounded friend's mouth. The VC were all around them again as he clawed through the underbrush, frantic to alter the outcome of the dream.

Something told him that if they could make it to the LZ, just once, it would be over.

Doc tried to change direction, but the dream wouldn't yield. The ground beneath them gave way. It became a swift flowing stream. Everywhere he looked along its banks there were trip wires, a cat's cradle of booby traps. Berryhill moaned and Doc clapped a hand over his mouth. He heard splashing.

Too late. She's coming.

They were caught in the current's pull, floating toward the VC girl with the bayonet, helpless to do a damned thing about it. Doc tried to swim, but it was impossible. Berryhill was stuck fast to his side like a barnacle. Panicked, he tried to break loose.

"No way, Doc," Berry said. His eyes were lifeless black marbles. "There's nowhere to go. Booby traps or a bayonet, we're going to die together just like we should have."

The VC girl was behind him. He saw her as if he had eyes in the back of his head. The long, four-grooved blade on the muzzle of her AK-47 was poised for the thrust. Doc screamed, "It wasn't my fault!"

"All right, Detective Wiley," he heard a woman say. "Settle down."

Doc saw a white blur and blinked to shield his eyes from the rectangle of light behind the voice. He tried to sit up, but strong hands held him back.

"Behave yourself," she said. "You've had a rough time, but that doesn't buy you groping rights."

He blinked. His vision cleared and he found himself looking into the angry brown eyes of a cute young nurse.

"No more octopus stuff, huh?" she said. "I've never belted a patient yet. Don't break my record." She stepped back to smooth her uniform skirt with her hands. "You may be strong, but I've got a right cross you don't want to sample."

"I'm sorry," he tried to say, but it came out a croak. His throat felt like sandstone.

"Would you like a drink of water?" she asked.

"Please." It sounded like heeze.

"It's the oxygen," she said, "dries out the vocal cords." She poured water from a plastic pitcher into a cup with a flexible straw and placed the end into his mouth.

He sucked the cool fluid greedily and felt immediate relief. "Thanks," he said, as she replaced the cup on the tray. "I really am sorry."

She raised a disbelieving eyebrow, and then let it relax. "People do strange things when they regain consciousness," she said. "You behave yourself and I'll forget it."

She mopped his brow with a cool, damp cloth, and Doc noticed he was soaked with sweat. He shivered with the memory of the dream.

"Are you cold?" she asked.

"No."

She stepped away from his bedside to make some notes on his chart and he followed her with his eyes. She appeared to be about twenty, Jen's age, and moved with the same lithesome grace. She was pretty, like Jen, and focused on her task. Her brows were scrunched, her gaze intent. It reminded him of his daughter's total concentration when she did her homework at the kitchen table with just the tip of her tongue poking out of the corner of her mouth. He smiled.

"Your eyesight seems to be unimpaired, Detective Wiley." The frost was back in her voice. "Maybe I better stay out of your reach."

"What? No. I didn't mean to stare. I have a daughter about your age." It sounded harmless to him, but by her body language he knew he had made her wary. "I guess I'm a little out of it."

His mind had drifted, unguarded. It was a bad sign. The flashbacks would return if he let them. It was the dream. It had been years since it had haunted him. He couldn't take that hell again. At least he hadn't had to see the end. He knew the end, of course. How could he ever forget it? He remembered it now, but remembering the dream was never as bad as being in it. Wakefulness somehow protected him from the horror. It had been his very own private, nightly fright flick for a dozen years after the war. It had ended when his marriage did.

What would Barbara have thought of the dream? Poor Barbara. The shit he had put her through. It was no wonder she left him. But she had no right to take Jen. He shook his head to clear it. Pain made him inhale sharply through his nose.

"That was a mistake," he said, squeezing his eyes shut tight.

When he opened them again, the nurse said, "Lie still." She pointed with her ballpoint pen at his forehead. "You've got a concussion, and you're going to have a headache to go with that egg on your noggin." She made another notation, and said, "Does she look like me? Is she a nurse?"

"Who?"

"Your daughter." The nurse lifted her eyebrows. "You just said you had a daughter my age."

"Oh. No, she doesn't look like you, and I doubt she's a nurse. She's about your age, that's all."

"You doubt she's a nurse? You mean you don't, like, know?"

"I haven't seen her for some time. She lives with her mother."

"Oh. Where?"

"I don't know."

The nurse said nothing, but Doc saw the doubt in her eyes.

He pulled one hand from beneath the sheets, gingerly felt the bump on top of his head, and winced.

"Detective Cordova has one to match," she said. "You guys must have butted heads like bighorn sheep." She came back to stand beside the bed. "If you feel up to it, your lieutenant is waiting down the hall. He just got here. Not the most patient man, is he?" she asked but did not wait for a reply. "First, we'll have the doctor look at you, then I'll send your boss in, if that's all right."

"Tony's here?"

"Um hmm. They brought all of you into the ER. You're the last one to come around. You had us worried for a while, but I think you're going to be okay."

The dream had thrown him into such a tailspin he had almost forgotten the house in Oyster Bay. What the hell happened?

He was in a hospital. He hated hospitals. They were places you went to when the world had gone to shit, places to stand helplessly by while strangers tried to save those you loved from the savagery of the world outside.

Information was what he needed now. Concentration on the present was the way to avoid unwanted trips to the past. He had to force his mind to work on current problems or the old ones resurfaced.

"You said they brought all of us in. What happened to the other cops? Are they okay?"

"There was an explosion," she said.

An explosion? Was that why the Kohler place was so hot? Was the furnace about to blow?

"I'm not supposed to discuss one patient's condition with another," she said. "I'm sure your lieutenant will fill you in on your friends." He saw sadness in her eyes. And then it was gone. She was all business in a snap.

The nurse pulled an electronic thermometer from its receptacle and tore open a sterile plastic sleeve.

"I'm going to take your temperature, pulse, and blood pressure before I get the doctor, Detective Wiley. No grabbing this time?"

"Did I hurt you?"

"I thought you'd break my ribs."

"It's a recurring nightmare I used to have a lot," he whispered without meeting her eyes. "Vietnam. In the dream, I'm trying to drag a wounded buddy out of danger. I was a medic. It hasn't come back in years. I'm very sorry."

"Is that why they call you Doc?"

He nodded, unable to meet her eyes, not knowing why he had told her. He had never told anyone about the dream.

"Let's get this under your tongue now," she proffered the slim white cylinder, poked the probe into his open mouth, and seized his hand to hold the thermometer in place.

Next, she wrapped the blood pressure cuff around his biceps, never meeting his eyes. Once finished, she made more notes on his chart, mumbled something about the doctor and left.

Moments later the door flew open again and a smiling young Asian resident introduced himself as Doctor Chung before shining a pencil flashlight in Doc's eyes, looking into his ears, poking and probing as he asked questions about his general state of being. Lieutenant Schiff slipped in to hover in the background. He was visibly anxious, waiting for the doctor to complete his examination so that he could begin his own. Doc thought of a pit-bull straining at the leash. Schiff always gave him that impression.

An attractive woman in a white lab coat stepped into the room and stood against the wall. She had high cheekbones and smooth, supple skin. Doc would bet it had the texture of rose petals. There were faint laugh lines at the corners of her eyes, the only hint to her age until he noticed a few strands of gray in her tawny blonde ponytail. Mid-forties he decided with the confidence of the trained observer. The open lab coat, as well as the navy-blue suit beneath, did little to hide her neatly rounded figure. As Doc completed his appraisal, her eyes met his. He decided that they were her most distinctive feature—medium brown, flecked with green, almost hazel, but not quite. But it wasn't the color that was so captivating, it was their depth and promise. Sexy had new meaning. He smiled.

She did not return it. He had the impression he had just been evaluated, found wanting, and rejected. It bothered him.

Doctor Chung turned, seeking the object of his patient's distraction, and said, "Ah, Madeline. Do you need me?"

"No, Doctor. I'll come back when you're through," she said and left.

Doc's gaze stayed on the closing door. The astute physician caught the flicker of disappointment.

"Quite lovely our Mrs. Maclear, eh, Detective?"

Doc mumbled an inaudible response.

Schiff said, "Detective Wiley is something of a connoisseur."

Doc gave Schiff a chilling look.

"You seem to have suffered no permanent injury, Detective Wiley," the doctor said. "I'll release you in the morning, but I'd recommend a few days bed rest at home. Concussion can be very serious if not treated with respect," Chung said, more to Lieutenant Schiff, it seemed to Doc, than to himself.

Both policemen thanked the doctor as he left. Tony Cordova entered the room immediately following the physician's departure. Doc correctly deduced that Tony had been waiting in the hall. Tony had two black eyes to compliment the knot on his forehead. The shiners didn't look out of place on the short detective's swarthy mug.

It was the kind of face that expected damage. Tony's smart mouth had attracted more than one roundhouse punch in his forty-seven years.

"You look like a raccoon, Tony. How you feeling?" Doc asked, as Tony took a seat next to the bed.

"Not bad, considering. We were lucky, you and me. If we'd been in that room…"

Doc thought Tony looked more disturbed than he should. They had both taken worse lumps in the past. Maybe it was the forlorn appearance that a hospital gown on a grown man seemed to foster.

"What the hell happened?" Doc demanded.

"Cordova's pretty much filled me in on what went down before the bomb went off," Lieutenant Schiff began.

"Bomb? It was a bomb?" Doc stared, open mouthed, from one man to the other.

"Yeah," Schiff said, "a booby trap from what we've been able to piece together from the wreckage and what the Crime Scene dicks can tell us."

Doc smelled blood. The dreaded words booby trap always caused that odor to bubble up in his memory.

"But," Schiff continued, "let's start at the beginning and go through this thing step by step. I'll tell you what I know and you guys fill in the blanks."

The two detectives nodded. Doc noticed Tony's eyes close in pain as he bobbed his head too suddenly. He felt tightness in his chest. He forced himself to concentrate on his lieutenant's words.

Schiff accurately recited the events of the night as he knew them, pausing occasionally to consult his notebook. Doc swallowed hard, took deep breaths through his nose, and drove the panic back into its hiding place. Tony was as absorbed in Schiff's recounting as the lieutenant was in getting it right. Neither man seemed to notice Doc's distress.

The lieutenant had undoubtedly been rousted out of bed to oversee the investigation. Brutal murders in upscale suburban neighborhoods made the brass antsy. Doc knew he had to do his job, provide as much information as he could, and deal with his own problems by himself.

"Do you know about the burn?" he asked the lieutenant when Schiff had finished.

Schiff frowned. "The what?"

"Oh, yeah. How could I have forgotten that?" Tony smacked his forehead. He groaned, and said, "That was a dumb thing to do.

Anyway, the victim had a symbol burned into her ass. Like a peace sign?" Schiff nodded. "Almost as if she'd been branded. It was fresh. We were bringing the husband in to ask him about it, and he freaked. The next thing I knew, I was here."

"Stockton doesn't know much and he's the only one who can tell us anything," Schiff began again.

"What about Hoeniger and Shapiro?" Doc cut in.

"Let me finish," Schiff snapped. Doc raised his hand in submission and carefully nodded his head, trying to keep it from pounding again. "Dennis says he saw Shapiro start to roll the body."

"I told him to wait for me," Doc interrupted. The lieutenant's sharp look made him clamp his lips tightly shut.

"It's a good thing for you he didn't listen." Schiff pinned Doc with his eyes. "Why didn't he? You were in charge."

"He wanted to get home to put his daughter's bike together," Tony said. "Tomorrow's her birthday. They were going to have a big party."

Schiff sighed. "Stockton says he heard a distinct click, more like a snap, when Gene started to push her over. He remembers a flash, a loud bang, heat, and a shock wave that knocked him into the closet he was kneeling to dust. He woke up here like everybody else. He broke his shoulder when he hit the closet wall. Other than that, and some scratches, he's all right."

"Shapiro?" Doc asked.

Schiff wagged his head as if it were a great weight. "Never knew what hit him."

"Aw, Jesus."

"That's not all," Schiff went on, "Larry was standing on the opposite side of the bed. He got blown backward through the window. Neighbors and the media people say he did a backflip on the porch roof and came down head first on the lawn. Broke his neck. Died instantly."

Tony and Doc stared at each other, too overcome for words.

"Kobrigian volunteered to go see his wife," Schiff said.

"Jack's all right?" Doc cocked his head.

"Fine. Spilled some milk he was filching from the refrigerator, but that's all. You guys got bounced into one another when the door blew open. Apparently, you've both got hard heads."

Doc remembered their witness. "What about Kohler?"

"A splinter from the door—about so long," Schiff spaced his hands eighteen inches apart, "went through his back like a spear. Punctured his pump. He was dead when he hit the floor."

"A fucking massacre," Doc whispered, compartmentalizing his thoughts, consciously taking a mental step back. Grief and anger cloud the mind. His friends were gone. There would be time to grieve later. A disembodied voice from long ago kept repeating in his head, "Charlie Mike." It was radio shorthand for Continue Mission, the Ranger code.

"Yeah, and Eyewitness News got it all on tape," Schiff was saying. "They were filming the house, doing a set-up piece while they waited to pounce, when the thing went off. The media is already calling it the crime of the century. I'll bet they have theme music by the evening news tonight."

"Terrific," Tony growled.

"I wanted to talk to you two before I go any further," Schiff said. "I got a quick look before I came over here. It's a mess. By the time the fire department got finished tearing the place apart, it was impossible to tell what the hell was where. We'll be sifting through the rubble for weeks, if not months. ATF is on the scene with the Bomb Squad, but any evidence they can salvage will be questionable. The rain didn't help. The Kohler woman is splattered all over the joint. We've got a slew of cops canvassing the neighborhood. Our best hope is that somebody knows something to link us to a suspect. Right now, we've got jack-shit to go on."

"I better get out of here and get to work." Doc reached for the call button.

"Whoa." Lieutenant Schiff grabbed Doc's hand. "Get to work on what?"

"This is my case, Charlie. The clock's ticking."

"You heard what that doctor said. I've lost enough people on this already. I won't have you keeling over in the street somewhere. Beckwith and Kobrigian will work this one."

"The hell they will." Doc saw the spark of anger in the lieutenant's narrowed eyes and the bulldog chin thrust menacingly forward. "I mean, the hell they will, sir." The boyish grin Doc used to disarm irate superiors sprang into place. "Come on, Lieutenant. This is a cop killer. A friggin' maniac. You can't sideline me for a bump on the head. I've had worse than this falling off of bar stools."

“Me too, Lieutenant,” Tony chimed in. “This is going to mushroom. Every politician in the county is going to be screaming for this guy’s head. Wiley and me were assigned to this to begin with. It ain’t fair to give it to someone else.”

“The fact that there might be a little glory, not to mention overtime, doesn’t have anything to do with it of course,” Schiff said.

“You know as well as we do,” Doc answered, “those are the bennies to this kind of case. Why should somebody else get the gravy? We’re the ones this asshole tried to blow sky high.”

Schiff looked from Wiley to Cordova with his arms folded across his chest. If you shaved his head, Doc thought, the lieutenant would look like that little Buddha incense burner he had seen on a bookshelf back at that house.

“High profile cases are double edged swords,” Schiff warned. “I want this done by the book. You don’t go charging around up there like commandos in suits. And I do mean you, Wiley. I might be better off leaving you here to chase nurses.”

Both detectives fixed their superior with frozen stares.

“Okay.” Schiff bobbed his head so that half his body swayed with the motion. “Maybe that was uncalled for.” Doc’s glare made him add, “We’re all upset.” He looked from one man to the other, and said, “You’re on it, both of you. But,” Schiff raised one cautioning finger, “if you sign yourselves out of here, I didn’t sanction it. We didn’t discuss it. I assumed you two clowns were staying the night. Anybody drops dead, I don’t know a thing. Clear?”

Both men eagerly agreed.

“Work the chart with Kobrigian and Beckwith. I’ll be in Mineola preparing a brief for the commissioner. Keep me informed. Good night.”

Schiff was playing the percentages. The more seasoned investigators on this the better. Doc and Tony knew the risks.

The detectives found their clothes in a closet, dressed, and prepared to go back to work.

“You sure you’re up to it, Tony?” Doc was having second thoughts about taking his old friend with him. He had a buzzing sound in his head, faint but annoying. Tony had a wife and three kids. He would never forgive himself if anything happened to his old pal because of his haste. Tony looked as bad as he felt.

“Positive.” Tony returned Doc’s appraising gaze. “You?”

“I’ll live,” Doc said.

"How do we get sprung?"

"Why not just walk out?"

"Okay by me, but do you think we might need our guns again someday?"

Doc's hand went into his jacket. His surprised look made Tony laugh.

"Had worse falling off bar stools, huh? Maybe I should hold your bullets for you."

"Hold this, asshole." Doc tugged at his crotch. "I'm a little rattled is all. I'll be fine. Just need some fresh air." He took a breath and changed the subject. "You know, Tony, those black eyes give you a certain mysterious charm."

Tony made no reply, but stared at his friend through puffy slits, waiting for the punch line.

"You look like Batman." Doc grinned. "No, you're too short to be Batman. You must be Robin, the boy who wonders."

"That's Boy Wonder, wise guy, and I suppose you're the Caped Crusader."

"Too young to remember the 'sixties," Doc muttered. He put a cigarette between his lips, and then cursed as he remembered where he was and why. "People we worked with are dead, Tony, not even cold yet, and we're making jokes. Are we that jaded?"

"Maybe. But I like to think of it as a healthy outlet for the tension."

"Humph."

The lab-coated beauty entered the room.

"Where do you think you're going?" She sounded parental.

Doc was momentarily taken aback.

Tony was enjoying his first look at Madeline Maclear. He gave Doc a wink, and said, "Am I interrupting something?"

To the woman, Doc said, "You are?"

"Madeline Maclear, Director of Nursing. May I speak to you privately, Detective Wiley?"

Doc answered Tony's raised eyebrows with a nod.

Tony said, "I'll be right outside if you kids need me," and left.

Doc smiled, and said, "How can I help you, Miss Maclear?"

"It's Misses Maclear," she said with an edge. "Allow me to express my sincere sympathy for the losses you've suffered, Detective Wiley."

"Thank you. Is that all?"

"I understand you're a Vietnam vet."

"Yes. So is Detective Cordova. Shall I bring him back in?"

"That won't be necessary."

"No? Then, this isn't about Vietnam vets in general. You're not looking for some mutual friend of someone you knew in the war or anything, are you?"

"No, nothing like that."

"Then…"

"Miss Tuttle said you had a bad dream."

"Miss Tittle?"

"Your nurse."

"Ah, I see where this is going." Doc raised an index finger, saying, "Before tempers flare, Mrs. Maclear, let me say something. I got blown off my feet tonight, knocked cold by the same blast that killed two friends of mine. I came to here." He gave the room an all-encompassing glance. "I was smack in the middle of a nightmare I haven't had for years when I did. Yes, it's a Vietnam nightmare and, from what your Miss Tuttle said at the time, I must have had her in an arm-lock when I came around. I explained and apologized. That's all there is to it."

"I know a thing or two about PTSD, Detective Wiley. There are several excellent programs for vets on The Island. Maybe I can help you to find one suitable."

"Post-Traumatic Stress Disorder? If jumping to conclusions ever becomes an Olympic event, Mrs. Maclear, you are a shoo-in for the gold."

"Detective Wiley…" Her jaw flapped, but no more words came.

"Mrs. Maclear, we are both trained and experienced professionals. Forgive my sarcasm, please. I have never been accused of being a masher before. It angered me. Perhaps you should have expected that reaction. I don't brutalize women. Speaking of which—while Miss Tuttle is technically a woman, to me she's a kid, and we grownups are supposed to protect kids. That, I take it, is what you thought you were doing. You know, I think I've found something we have in common." He smiled.

It stopped her. Her chin rose again, but this time she took a breath and smiled back. He saw the hint of dimples, and thought, If Leonardo had seen that smile, he would have blown Mona Lisa off like dust on his palette.

"You misunderstand me, Detective. No one is accusing you of anything."

"Perhaps I have misunderstood. What, exactly is this about?"

“Miss Tuttle was concerned for your mental health, so she came to me to relate what had occurred.”

“You mentioned PTSD. Did Miss Tuttle suggest that?”

“My husband.” Her eyes dropped. “He had—problems after Vietnam. I’ve instructed our nurses to be especially aware of veterans’ needs.”

Doc nodded. “Okay. The kid was just doing her job. I understand now and I appreciate your concern, but it’s misplaced. I’m fine. And your husband? Better now?”

She hesitated. He could see her weighing her answer. “It’s behind him now.”

“Good. Some had it rougher than others. Most of us have moved on.”

The smile was gone. She stood staring at him.

“What?” he said.

She shrugged. “Never mind. It’s nothing.”

“You’re sure? I had the impression you were going to say something.”

She hesitated again, and then shook her head.

“If there is nothing else, Mrs. Maclear, I have a killer to catch.”

She argued that he and Tony should get back in bed. She was wasting her breath, and she seemed to know it. Eventually, she let the doctor warn them of the danger they were placing themselves in medically before agreeing to let the detectives sign themselves out. Doc was prepared to recite fictitious statute codes for kidnapping and unlawful detention, but Doctor Chung seemed like a decent guy. Doc suspected the doctor’s and the nursing director’s admonitions were as much to give fair warning as to cover the hospital in the event of malpractice proceedings.

Madeline showed them to a room labeled Security, where they retrieved their weapons. Her silence was disturbing to Doc.

As they prepared to leave, he said, “We okay, Mrs. Maclear?”

She nodded. “Good luck, gentlemen. And be careful.”

She shook their hands formally, avoiding Doc’s flashing blue eyes. He was aware of a strong physical magnetism when she took his hand. He held hers for too long, tempted to pull her close, yearning for more than visual memory, but she hurried away with her hands thrust deep into her lab coat pockets. Tony watched her hips sway as she strode down the hall.

"Looks like the little lady is a bit smitten with a certain sleuth, eh, Doc?"

Doc scowled, mechanically checked his pistol's magazine, and slipped the weapon into its shoulder holster. For most cops, the rig was considered a thing of the past, awkward and impractical. Doc had worn one like it in Vietnam and had found it the best way to keep a weapon close at hand when he was bent over a wounded man. It felt natural to him.

"Come on, Doc. Don't tell me you didn't notice. She was watching you like kids watch Santa Claus. How the hell do you do it?"

"You better have them check your eyes before we go, Cordova." He wriggled the fingers of his left hand. "Didn't you see the ring? The lady is married."

"The lady is a widow," an African-American orderly advised in a basso-profundo voice as he swabbed the hallway with a string mop.

"But she wears a wedding ring," Doc countered.

"That's to keep the wolves away, I expect," the orderly surmised. "Mrs. Maclear is a real fine lady. She got a lot of friends here." The veiled threat was unmistakable.

"What did she say her name was?" Tony asked.

"Who?" Doc frowned.

"Miss bright eyes. Who else?"

"Oh, her." Doc checked the contents of his pockets for the second time in ten minutes. "Uh, Madeline, I think."

"An M? Isn't that what you need to keep on track?"

"Knock it off, Tony."

"What? What'd I say? Just trying to get a little clarification of the rules here. This alphabetical screwing is new to me. A guy can't take an interest in a friend's hobby?"

Doc ignored Tony's rambling and slapped the crash bar on the exit door. The cool night air felt good on his face.

Tony babbled on as they crossed the parking lot, looking for Doc's car. Schiff had had it delivered, "just in case" they were able to go back to work. Tony's monologue told Doc that his buddy was climbing back on the horse, girding himself for what lay ahead, reassuring his pal that he was in control. It was his way. Doc was silently gathering himself for the hunt. Something…he could not say what…told him they were up against someone who would tax their skills to the limit. There was no room for distractions.

Grief, rage, and confusion swirled on the periphery of his thoughts.

And what was this other thing? This lightness in his heart? A barely remembered emotion. It was tied to Madeline Maclear. She was far too attractive to clutter his thoughts now. Doc tried to shrug her off but couldn't seem to get her out of his mind.

Chapter 4

The obese private investigator unlocked his office door and whirled as he felt a presence behind him.

"Jesus, Colonel, you scared the shit out of me," Earl Wannamaker whined, his breath whistling from his lungs.

Colonel was what Carl had told Earl to call him at their initial meeting. He had given him the intentional impression that he was a retired military man and he was certain Earl would have called him General if he wanted him to, or Red Ryder, or Donald Duck. Earl had no code of honor. Anything for a buck.

"Good morning, Earl," Carl crooned. "What's wrong? Afraid of irate husbands?"

"It's a little spooky up here now, you know? What with me bein' the only tenant left on this floor."

Carl was well aware of that. The rundown office building in the shadow of the Port Authority Bus Terminal was almost deserted.

"The rats deserting the ship, Earl?" Carl grinned an oily grin, knowing it gave Wannamaker the creeps. It was not a smile so much as a baring of his teeth accompanied by an unveiling of his eyes, a slow imitation of awakening—a trick he had learned sent shivers cascading down Earl's pliable spine.

"You know," Earl explained, pushing open the door, leading his client into the outer office, "the neighborhood sure ain't gettin' any better. The cops roust the homeless out of the bus station so they don't annoy the commuters and these people got no place else to go. Guess what happens. They start roaming around these office buildings. With the rents we pay, we don't need this kind of aggravation. Lotta folks movin' to Westchester, Jersey, Brooklyn, Queens, even out on The Island. With today's technology, it ain't as important to be in the city as it used to be." He fiddled with his key ring, found the key to the inner office, and hurried to open the door as Carl stood unnecessarily close behind.

"What about you, Earl? Planning to get out, too?"

"Maybe someday," the PI wheezed as he thrust the door open and scurried across the room to get behind his desk. "Not yet though. I got a good, steady client base in the city. Most of my cases are still in Manhattan. I live here too, you know. Not so easy to pull up stakes in this business." He landed heavily in his cracked leather chair, sending the seat cushion and his clogged lungs into competition to expel the greatest volume of air with the most noise. "What can I do for you, Colonel?"

Carl settled himself in the matching wing chair directly in front of the sweating detective's desk.

"Warm for this time of year, isn't it, Earl?" Carl was cool and comfortable, even in the all-weather topcoat he wore.

"Yeah. Summer's probably going to be a bitch," Earl huffed, blotting his brow with a stained handkerchief and then rubbing his entire face.

Carl had the impression he had just watched the man perform his daily ablutions, but he kept his disgust in check. "How do you manage without a secretary?" He grinned, eyeing the stacks of yellowed paper strewn around the room. The place looked like it hadn't been dusted since VE Day.

Earl caught the sarcasm. "I got a system, Colonel. This may look a little unorganized, but I can put my fingers on anything in the room in seconds."

Carl knew Wannamaker was wondering why he was here. Their business was concluded. Earl had located every name on his list and been paid in cash—well paid—nearly twice the going rate for finding people, especially people not in hiding. "I'm glad to hear that, Earl. You see I've mislaid your report. Can't find it anywhere. I was hoping you might have a copy. I'm terribly sorry to bother you."

"No problem." Earl's relief was apparent. "Let me just fire up the ol' computer here and I'll dig it out for you." He flipped the machine on and swiveled his chair to face the monitor on the side-boy perpendicular to his desk. Earl lit the stub of a cheap cigar as he waited for the machine to boot up. Carl's nose wrinkled with distaste.

"A concession to the modern world, Earl?" Carl indicated the computer with a nod.

“Couldn’t do without it now that I’ve gotten used to it. This little baby has saved me a bundle, if you know what I mean. Who needs a secretary’s salary when Bill Gates’s little brainchild can handle all that clerical shit?”

“You don’t worry about computer viruses or hackers tapping into your files? I’m sure you must have sensitive information in there.”

“No sweat, Colonel. I leave the modem disconnected when I’m not accessing DMV or some such bank.” Earl reddened as he let that slip.

“Do you back up your files on disk?” Carl asked. “I have heard these things can be temperamental. A power surge can erase everything.”

“Yeah.” Earl looked sheepish. “I haven’t gotten around to yours yet, though. I’ve been busier than a one-legged man at an ass-kicking.”

“No doubt.” Carl glanced around the unkempt office. The sagging, adjustable shelves crammed with phone books and assorted periodicals looked as tired and worn as Wannamaker’s threadbare suit. Brown stains on the walls—where pictures or plaques had been removed and not replaced—looked like geometric ghosts. Nicotine coated every surface of the ancient room like lacquer.

“You do have access codes and passwords to keep prying eyes from reading people’s secrets, don’t you?” Carl asked.

“Uh—certainly.” The hesitation told Carl that Earl had not mastered the machine to that extent.

“Printed copies?”

“Nah. Print is dead. Takes up too much room. Here it is now.” He smiled after a few taps on the keyboard. “Only time I use this,” Earl pointed to an old dot matrix printer on the other side of the battered cherry desk, “is when a client needs a hard copy of something. Let me run you one.”

Earl turned to face his client. His plastic smile disappeared. His mouth fell open. The cigar dangled from his lower lip stuck there as if glued. He was staring at the razor-sharp tip of a mini-crossbow bolt. The one-handed weapon was leveled at his face.

“No need to be embarrassed by your DMV slip, Earl. I know how you tracked my people down. Everybody drives on Long Island. You traced them through the department of motor vehicles to their insurance companies, which leads to everything—address, telephone, employer—the works. All you needed was an unscrupulous broker with access to the data banks, right? I could have done it myself, but why leave electronic tracks? This way, if the fuzz get that far, you—”

He emphasized it with a short thrust of the weapon. "—are where they wind up—a complete dead end."

The bolt leaped from the bow with a twang, flew the four feet between them, and struck Earl's doughy throat with a thunk. Carl jumped back, toppling his chair as blood spurted from Wannamaker's neck, splashing the top of the cluttered desk. The dying man clawed at the shaft with both hands and tried to stand, but he couldn't lift his own bulk from the seat.

Earl's struggling hurried his death. The bladed steel point sawed through his windpipe as he twisted the shaft. His overtaxed heart simply quit. He collapsed in his chair, eyes staring for eternity at the cobweb-draped ceiling, his death mask a study in disbelief.

Stepping carefully to avoid the blood pooling on the unraveling carpet, Carl slipped on surgical gloves before he yanked the computer's power cord from the wall outlet. A shrill beeping sound began instantly.

"Not so inept after all, were you Earl?" he said to the dead PI.

He traced the power cord to a shoe-box-sized unit under the desk. A green LED flashed beside the letters AC on the machine's face.

"You had enough sense to back yourself up with a UPS." He looked closely at the machine. "Cheap one, but adequate I suppose." He punched the button labeled POWER and the alarm stopped.

Next, Carl slipped a Leatherman multi-tool from a case on his belt, opened it to a screwdriver blade, and removed the computer cover. He disconnected the hard-drive, dropped it into an inside pocket in his coat, and then replaced the panel.

"Did you lie to me about the disks, you tub of shit?" Wannamaker's dead eyes mocked him. "If you think being dead will protect you from me, you are wrong."

Carl searched the office, methodically checking every drawer, cabinet, and closet. He found no computer disks and no paper files more recent than 1995.

"Lazy bastard," he said to the lifeless PI.

He tucked his weapon back into his coat, checked to be sure he had left no trace of himself in the office, and left, locking the door behind him. He sauntered down the steps, through the deserted lobby, and strolled out the front door, removing his gloves once outside. With any luck at all, it would be several days before anyone found the dead PI. He felt certain that no one would have any recollection of the man in the raincoat by then.

He took the subway to Grand Central Station and changed trains for Jamaica where the Long Island Railroad could take him back to Nassau County. He was probably being overly cautious, but he had plenty of time and saw no reason to let anyone see his face twice in the same morning by retracing his steps. Little things like that could jar the memory of some citizen being questioned by the police. He had no doubt the police would soon be hunting him twenty-four hours a day. They would be asking lots of people lots of questions. Before he was through, he would have them talking to themselves and crying in their sleep. The image brought a smile to his face.

At Jamaica Station, he went down into the street where he walked to a construction site near the busy railroad interchange. There, he watched laborers pour the concrete foundation for a new apartment tower. Carl slipped a paper bag from his coat, reached in, and produced an apple from the sack, leaving the crossbow, gloves, and hard-drive in the bottom. Munching the fruit, he waited for the workmen's attention to be diverted by a passing pretty girl in tight pants. He too watched the rhythmic twitch of her buttocks.

No one noticed the deft flick of the wrist that sent the brown bag arcing into the concrete form, to be buried moments later by several tons of wet cement. He waited a few more minutes before taking a different route back to the railway station. Once on the train to Wantagh, he relaxed, closing his eyes to savor his success.

An electronic bell rang, shrill and insistent. The conductor babbled something unintelligible on the intercom and the doors closed. The train jerked, slowly began to move, and then accelerated as it left the station. Carl watched a westbound train across the platform disgorge its load of commuters, scurrying like rodents to begin their day.

What lackluster lives civilized men lead, he thought. He would put an edge on their dull days. He settled back in the vinyl upholstery to let the clicking of the rails lull his mind. Like a dozing wolf, his eyelids drooped, and he rested his body while his mind danced.

Dotty had deserved to be first. She had seduced him, fried his brain with LSD, and laughed when they had left him in the drainage ditch beside the Thruway. The memory of her terror the previous evening was delicious. When he was finished with her, she had nothing left. No more haughty pride, no more sexy wiles, nothing. The rest would be stripped of their individuality, humiliated, and slaughtered one at a time until the last of the traitorous scum was eradicated. All of it was so necessary. Had the six not set this in motion by their own hands?

Had they not ruined what would have been his glorious military career? It was karma personified. Action and reaction. Fluid seeking its own level. The way of the universe.

As he reviewed his steps, he considered the electronically altered phone message to the police last night. It had been an irresistible act of arrogance—breast beating—a gauntlet thrown.

He promised himself not to repeat such challenges. Vanity was weakness, an inability to understand the cosmic order. The lion does not taunt the antelope, he accepts it for what it is: sustenance.

Anyway, to flaunt his superiority he merely had to proceed. The opposition was way out of its depth. The plan was flawless. Every angry moment he had endured for the past thirty years had been worthwhile. He had thought of everything, including the ironic twist that any wounded survivors of last night's booby trap would wind up under the care, indirectly at least, of one of his targets.

Laughing softly, he vowed to follow the plan. It felt so good to be doing what he did best.

Killers should kill.

Chapter 5

The detectives sat at a long table, sipping coffee in the Homicide Squad conference room at police headquarters in Garden City. Despite its actual address, the cops still referred to their headquarters as Mineola, a holdover from the original building just blocks away in that closely bordering town, and what some saw as proof of the intransigence of the enforcement arm of the law.

Four tired investigators and their equally exhausted commanding officer sat, either slumped forward against the elongated conference table, or leaning back in swivel chairs. They had spent the remainder of the previous night walking the streets surrounding the murder scene, searching for evidence of the killer's passing. With the dawn, they began to knock on doors to question those neighbors remaining at home in a two-block radius from the Kohler residence. Once they had spoken to every available citizen, they had each returned to the shattered house. A quick look at the wrecked home of Dorothy and Jason Kohler surrounded by a horde of reporters hovering at the sawhorse barriers had caused them to beat a hasty retreat. Leaving the technical types to sift through the rubble they had withdrawn to HQ for a skull session. Someone would have to go back to the neighborhood tonight to interview those citizens who had dashed off to work ahead of their canvass, but a pause to examine what had thus far been learned was deemed apropos.

Lieutenant Schiff, silhouetted at the head of the table by the morning sun's harsh rays through the window behind him, was right in his prediction. It would be weeks before Forensics—better known as "The Lab"—got anything from the bomb blasted house, if at all. Even with The Bureau of Alcohol, Tobacco, Firearms & Explosives (ATF) lending a hand, as they must, since exploded bombs automatically brought them into the picture, the prospects for swift discovery were slim.

Flipping through notebooks, the detectives exchanged opinions and reactions. Tony let out a slow wolf whistle as he thumbed through his notes, and said, "Dotty Kohler must have been a pretty wild broad."

"I'd be inclined to agree," Doc said, glad to have his attention brought back to the matter at hand.

Concentration was becoming difficult. His tired mind kept wandering. His head throbbed like a teenager's boom box. He smelled things that were not there—mud, cordite fumes, mildew, and blood—especially blood. Even the room was getting on his nerves. It looked like every government space he had known since the army. Everything in it was plain, utilitarian, and dull. Why, he wondered, do they always hang portraits of the current administration in these places? As if we might forget who our leaders were if we didn't have their homely mugs smiling down on us from the walls.

"If one old biddy tells tales of sex and drunken revelry," Tony continued with his train of thought, "I tend to chalk it up to imagination and a smattering of envy."

"But when everybody on the block tells the same stories," Doc concluded, massaging his temples, "you do have to admit the lady must have been a piece of work."

"Makes sense," Jack Kobrigian agreed. "You think we should work that angle? Crazed boyfriend? Jealous lover?"

"Hard to ignore, isn't it?" Doc leaned back in his chair and avoided the governor's gaze from the chrome frame opposite his seat.

"Like horns on a priest." Tony tapped a pencil on the table.

Schiff directed, "Let's put some time into digging around in her extra-marital affairs. See where she hung out and who with. Maybe get a line on her lovers.

"What about the husband? He seems too squeaky clean, practically the invisible man." Doc made a note on the yellow legal pad before him and looked questioningly at the assembled detectives.

"Yeah," Tony said, gingerly rubbing his swollen eyes. "It's weird the way everybody's got lots of hot dirt about dear old Dotty, but nobody can even remember what Saint Jason looked like."

"Hard to picture what sounds like a bona fide pansy with a swinger like Dotty," Ray Beckwith thought aloud. "Anything on their financial status yet?" He looked with distaste at his own illegible notes.

“Should have something today,” Schiff answered. “They found one of those cheap safes in the back of a closet in the den.” Doc’s questioning frown prompted Schiff to explain. “Court Order came through in record time. It looks pretty straightforward so far. Bankbooks, savings bonds, jewelry, stock certificates, and deeds—the usual shit. Nothing to raise any eyebrows so far, but everything will be scrutinized to the nth degree.”

Doc said, “Hopefully their records will all be in there. No doubt the media will speculate that it was a—” He made quotation marks in the air with his fingers. “—drug related killing. It will be interesting to see what sort of wealth they had squirreled away. Maybe they ripped off the mob.”

“Wouldn’t it be nice if it turned out to be that easy?” Beckwith verbalized everyone’s hope.

“Let’s get back to the husband, Doc,” Schiff said. “From what you and Tony tell me, he really didn’t want to go into that room.”

“You mean like he knew it was about to go bang,” Doc said.

“That’s exactly what I mean.”

Doc pondered for a moment, and then said, “I’d say, no.” He looked to Tony for corroboration.

“Doc’s right.” Tony shook his head. “Kohler was a mess, but I’d say it was from seeing his old lady all sliced up. Remember what he said, Doc? ‘I told her never to bring them home.’ Like he wasn’t so upset with her screwing around, just that it had gotten her killed.”

“That’s my impression, too, Charlie,” Doc said. “The guy was crying like a baby when it went off. He wasn’t trying to get out of the way. I’d say he had no idea. Poor bastard loved her, no matter what.”

“Not the first guy to get the shaft when the missus blew up,” Jack Kobrigian mumbled.

Beckwith grinned. “The voice of experience.”

The sharp looks from everyone in the room sent Ray back to deciphering his notes.

Schiff tried to focus the discussion. His detectives were tired and rambling. “Don’t get your hopes up on the financial stuff. There doesn’t seem to be any felonious trail, cold or otherwise. We’ll run the money angle down anyway, but I want to concentrate on the neighborhood the rest of today. Somebody must have seen something last night.”

“Lucky for us, people are nosy.” Beckwith grinned with a sidelong glance at Kobrigian’s oversized beak.

"Let's just hope the nosy ones were peeking through the curtains last night." Kobrigian stared icicles at Beckwith.

"Amen." Beckwith nodded, now totally absorbed in his notes.

"Doc and Tony," Schiff ordered, "knock off for a couple hours. Get some shuteye. Both of you look like shit." To the others, he said, "They can handle the evening canvass and we'll compare notes tomorrow morning. Let's check with The Lab on anything they've turned up.

"Jack, you and Ray get back up to Oyster Bay. Take another run at the neighbors and see if ATF and the Bomb Squad've found anything interesting." As an afterthought, he stopped Doc as the detective rose to leave. "If the people you talk to this evening are singing the same old song about Mrs. Kohler's immoral escapades, work that angle. Start on the local watering holes. Most likely she did her thing close to the nest or fewer folks would know about it. You can hit some of the local joints, see if Dotty did her cruising close to home. Maybe it's as simple as a whacked-out boyfriend."

"Right. The old whacked-out-boyfriend-who-makes-bombs-and-uses-a-garrote gambit."

Doc could see the smirk on his face annoyed Schiff, but the lieutenant let it go. They were all tired. Schiff probably didn't have the energy to reprimand anyone at the moment. Instead, he stated the obvious. "How many perps try to burn the body, even the whole building to cover the crime?"

Doc knew he could not explain the instincts that told him they were dealing with something beyond Schiff's capacity to comprehend. Charlie Schiff was a smart cookie, but Doc had this sensation in his gut that the perp was much more than vicious. His methods were not only bizarre, they were multi-dimensional. This guy played on several levels at once. Torture murders were rare but nothing new, and attempts to destroy evidence were common. Lose the body and you lose the crime. Everything from incineration to dismemberment had been tried more times than he cared to recall, but the idea was to hide the evidence from the cops. This turkey had set them up. Doc could not help thinking of the Viet Cong. How many times had he seen them bait a trap with the dead? If Jason had been the intended victim, why create a scene so macabre? If the killer knew anything about the husband, his panicky reaction should have been predictable.

No, he had meant the bomb for them. A guy who went to all the trouble this guy had—to murder a middle-aged bimbo and set the cops up to go with her—wasn't going to be a one-timer. He would try this again. It had worked too well not to.

Doc kept his feelings to himself, unwilling to share what was essentially a hunch. Besides, the thought processes that led him to his conclusions troubled him. Long ago, he had fought against and beside some extremely dedicated killers, men who broke new ground in the craft. Although he had carried the aid bag, he carried weapons too, and he had used them well.

ග෧ග෧

Doc entered his four-room garden apartment. Without breaking stride, he shed his suit jacket, and dropped it on a chair. His mind was racing when he reached the kitchen, with thoughts tripping over each other as he pulled his pistol from its holster, ejected the magazine onto the table, and drew back the slide. A bullet leaped from the chamber and he caught it with a deft swipe of his hand. Thumbing the hammer down, he set the Sig Sauer on the table, reloaded the lone round into the clip, and placed it beside the weapon. Reaching for the refrigerator handle, he shrugged off the holster and let it slide down his arm to land hanging astride the back of one of his two kitchen chairs. With a twist of his head to ease the stiffness in his neck, he bent down to peer into his nearly empty fridge. His hand went to one of the three cans of beer on the top shelf but stopped.

"Stay alert; stay alive," he said to the box and wrapped his fingers around a bottle of Poland Spring Water instead. After a long pull on the frosty bottle, he replaced it, looked longingly at the beer, swept the door shut with the back of his hand, and dropped into a chair.

"God, I'm bushed."

The thought of sleep brought another—the dream. He wasn't ready for that. He groaned as he pushed himself erect.

The blinking red eye of the answering machine on the end table beside the sofa caught his attention.

"Now what?"

Resigned, he crossed to the machine and poked the PLAY button.

"You have three new messages," the machine's tinny female voice told him.

He made a rolling motion with one hand, an entreaty to the techno-woman to get on with it.

"Message one," the voice complied.

"Doc, I heard about the booby trap on TV. Are you okay? I'll try again later."

His ex-wife's voice brought on mixed feelings of remorse and anger. The next two messages were variations of the first, spaced at hourly intervals. He hit the erase button, saying, "You're so damned worried, why don't you leave a number for me to call back?"

He thought about calling the phone company. His badge number would get him a printout of his incoming call lugs. From those they could place the point of origin. Barbara was smart enough to use a pay phone, but he would know what state she was in.

"Fuck it," he said and marched to a windowless inner room with a dusty plastic sheet draped across the doorway. Brushing the film aside, he entered his studio—one fourth of his living space now totally devoted to his art. Ikea's modular wood-plank shelves covered three of the four walls, all of which, plus the ceiling, were blanketed in sound deadening fiberglass insulation. Two shelved walls were crammed with sculpture in varying degrees of completion; the third was devoted entirely to power tool storage. A large, gray desk and swivel chair—rescued from the Nassau County PD scrap heap—dominated the center of the room. Vices and clamps of every sort covered the desktop. A power strip was screwed to one corner, connected to the wall outlet by a yellow extension cord. Adjustable-arm fluorescent light fixtures stood guard, ready to cast shadow-free illumination on the dust-cloaked surface on demand.

Rolling up his sleeves, Doc selected a piece from the far wall. He blew a puff of air at it as he picked it up, turned it over in his hand, and examined his work thus far.

Power tool plaster sculpture was an art form he thought all his own. He had become enamored with the beauty of sculpture while visiting the Metropolitan Museum of Art with a date—a divorcee from Roslyn...Marilyn or Mary Lynn, he could not remember. She had been as enraptured with things artistic as she had been with kinky sex and while her identity had escaped him, the world she had introduced him to had not.

A two-foot tall lump of red marble stood on its shipping crate in a corner of the room with a short-handled sledge and a dulled cold chisel leaning against it. The misshapen hunk of rock served as his monument to perseverance. It had taught him that: not only are artistic skills difficult to acquire, a determined will can surmount any obstacle. After several weeks of frustration, bruised thumbs, and calluses, he had abandoned traditional sculpture as something beyond his ken. But the need to create nibbled at his nerve endings.

By chance, a case solved his problem. An estranged lover beat his erstwhile girlfriend to death in her Massapequa ceramics shop and then hung himself in the back room. The investigation took all of ten minutes since a class had been in progress at the time of the assault. Five distraught women had been eyewitnesses to the attack. One had called the police on her cell phone as she ran screaming from the store. The perpetrator was still twitching when the patrolmen arrived, but he had done a good job of it. He was dead when they cut him down.

While Doc made notes for his report, he eyed the green ware stacked on the shelves. Once the bodies had been removed, and the breathless witnesses' statements taken, Doc used his charm to get one of the ladies talking about ceramics. The figurines, he learned, were made from a material known as slip, a beige substance made from powdered clay mixed with water and poured into molds and allowed to dry. "Just like plaster," the woman said. Doc had stopped listening by the time the woman got into the fine points of painting, glazing, and firing.

That night, he cornered one of the sales people at the Pearl Art Supply store in East Meadow, got a quick education on the ins and outs of plaster casting, and went home with a shopping bag full of books and supplies.

After weeks of trial and error, Doc found that half-gallon milk cartons worked best to cast the blocks of plaster he needed to start his work. Next, he took every opportunity to enlist the aid of his neighbors with young children. Each was asked to save their empty milk cartons for their friendly neighborhood cop. Soon, he had a steady supply of molds and one single mom circling his nest like a hungry gull. He kept her at arm's length by dropping hints that he was gay.

His initial idea had been to solve his chiseling dilemma by working in a softer medium, but he soon found that the plaster castings were even less forgiving than marble. After several shattered blocks, he was almost ready to quit.

Once again, fate intervened. On his day off, browsing the tool crib at Home Depot for want of something better to do, Doc watched a demonstration of a Dremel Rotary Power Tool. When the demonstrator cut a neat hole in a slab of plasterboard, Doc beamed. The tool and a host of attachments were in one hand and his credit card in the other before the kid in the orange apron finished saying, "Can I help you?"

The hand-held electric gimmick proved to be his salvation. For months, Doc spent every spare moment converting the room, refining his skills with the tool, and buying additional hardware. Now, an eclectic assortment of electric drills, rotary and reciprocating saws, sanders, and polishers covered the shelves.

The piece in his hand was still rough, but the image of a kneeling soldier huddled over his radio was beginning to take shape. He sat at his workbench, fitted a dust mask over his nose and mouth, stretched the elastic band on a pair of goggles over his head, turned on the Shop-Vac with its hose poking through a hole in the work surface, and reached for the Dremel.

As the tool whined its joyful song, he gently cut, shaped, and altered, changing bits as required. Time stood still. The plaster soldier's face took on the look of determination and fright that Doc remembered so well. Stopping to hold the hunk of white over the vacuum hose to suck off the excess dust, he thought about a title for the piece. The soldier's expression said it all—In Contact.

He decided to paint this one, seeing with the artist's eye that color would add reality that the stark white figure would lack.

When his eyes would no longer stay open without conscious effort, he set the sculpture down and turned everything off. Just before he hit the light switch, he thought about trying to sculpt something new, something other than soldiers. Dozens of tiny faces stared back at him from the shelves.

"How about a round-eyed beauty for a change? Maybe a nurse?" he said. A picture of Madeline Maclear in fatigues came to mind. "Be a nice break from you dog-faces," he murmured, and stumbled off to bed.

Exhaustion sometimes held the dream at bay. Sometimes it made it worse.

ꕤꕤ

Stale tobacco smoke and alcohol were akin to the bouquet of a rare wine for Gregory Collins. On Monday mornings, Greg enjoyed his special time, the only private hours he had with the only mistress he had ever loved—his club. Chez Laughs was not The Improv or The Comedy Shop, but it was his—his and the bank's—but Collins suppressed the thought that his darling was mortgaged to the rafters. When he closed his eyes, he could see his name on the lighted awning above the door. Greg Collins' Chez Laughs the words proclaimed in flowing white script on burgundy canvas. The lights were out now with the club closed until tomorrow night, but in Collins's mind they always burned bright.

An imitation Tiffany swag lamp with ruby cherries set in asymmetrical fragments of pebbled amber hung inches above his graying hair. He shuffled bills and receipts in an umbrella of light, his private oasis in the back corner of the dark club. While Greg labored at what he called "creative accounting," his cordless phone rang. He scowled at the beige hunk of plastic on the table for a moment and then snatched it up.

"Chez Laughs." He smiled for all he was worth. "Mr. Collins? Hold the line, please. I'll see if he's in."

The bellowing reply made him pull the phone from his ear. His smile dissolved.

"Calm the hell down, Sid. I'm a busy man. You could have been a telemarketer for all I knew. Now, what can I do for you?" He listened with a sour expression spreading across his face.

"Keep your voice down, Sid. There's nothing wrong with my ears." Greg's head bobbed impatiently as he listened again. "What open invoice? We're all paid up." Another tirade ensued in response. He put the phone down and rubbed his temples. He could hear his angry supplier clearly, even with the handset away from his ear. He lit a cigarette, counted to five, and grabbed the phone again. "Sid! Shut up already. The check went out Friday."

The invective on the other end resumed. Greg flipped the phone in the air and caught it. He looked with ferocious eyes at the instrument, held it at arm's length, and roared, "Shut the fuck up, Sid. I don't need this shit. You'll get your money. Every fucking cent. Just stop breaking my balls. Goodbye!"

He threw the phone against the wall and was pleased to see it fly apart.

"Goddamn prick. How am I supposed to pay for his shitty booze when these cheap cocksuckers don't drink enough to give my dead mother a buzz?" he yelled into the darkness where the broken phone laid, "Asshole!"

He went to the bar, poured himself a neat, double scotch, gulped it down, poured another, and took it back to the table.

"Prick," he growled. The liquor warmed his middle and he dreamed. The dream was all he had left.

The hopes of the young man died hard in middle age. Collins could still see the stars flocking to his table, begging to go on. Johnny was gone, but there was still a chance for Jay's or Dave's gig. One break, that's all he had ever needed. One sky rocketing young comic to make his debut at Chez Laughs and he'd be on his way. It could still happen, maybe tomorrow night. That kid from out east. He had potential.

Those hated practical shreds of intellect kept intruding on his dreams. Those insistent, lucid synapses whispered to him, nagging like his ex-wife: It's not going to happen. Sell it. Torch it. Walk away. Quit!

Taxes and regulations, cops and their crusade against drunks—the mainstay of his business—the lack of comic talent in this most humorless of generations and the pitiful seriousness of Joe Average Citizen he was certain, were the things making it so difficult for him to get his club off the ground. It had nothing to do with his ability. Maybe tomorrow night…

Harsh daylight silhouetted a figure in the opening doorway. Collins blinked. The door slammed. A man picked his way past the little, round cocktail tables, marching inexorably to Collins's back booth enclave. The briefcase and suit and tie said: salesmen or bill collector. Neither was welcome at any time, especially not on a Monday morning.

"We're closed," Collins growled, loud enough to be firm without being offensive. Not smart, he thought, to be too abrasive before one knows to whom one is speaking.

"I know. That's why I'm here." The stranger grinned as he entered Greg's sanctuary of light. He slid into the half-moon booth without being invited, laid his case on the table, sprang the latches, and opened it halfway. He peered over the lid and held it so that Greg could not see the contents.

"Perfect time to talk to you, Greg," the stranger said, and leered in a way that Collins imagined a wolf might as he happened upon a lamb alone in the forest.

"Just what I need," Greg said, "a slick salesman. No doubt you're going to pull something out of your little bag of tricks that I simply cannot live a moment longer without."

Collins had a wary yet admiring light in his eyes. He had a soft spot for hucksters. They were brothers under the skin, but that didn't make him anybody's sucker. He would turn this guy down politely, but in such a way as to let him know he had met his match. This might be fun.

What came out of the case changed his mind.

"Jethro, you don't look at all well." The stranger's grin was a death mask. "I'm amazed at your psychic ability. You should have a nine-hundred number." The man screwed up his face and added, "But it's something you can't live another moment with, you see." He turned a short, fat-barreled pistol over in his hand and examined it, never letting his aim stray from Greg's forehead. "What is holding your undivided attention is a modified marine flare pistol. There's a shotgun slug nestled in the breach. At this range it will blow your brains all over that tacky wallpaper."

"I don't have much cash here," Greg said. "It goes in the night drop as soon as we close on Sunday. You're welcome to what I've got. You don't have to hurt me."

Collins was amazed at the steadiness of his voice. He didn't feel steady at all.

"Jethro, I'm hurt. You don't remember your old buddy?"

There was something about the face, something vaguely familiar from a long time ago. Jethro? Nobody had called him Jethro since high school when he had become fond of bib overalls. The man leveling the gun at his nose did not fit the context. Greg shrugged, hoping it wasn't a fatal mistake.

"Flower power? Skinny dipping? 'Love the one you're with?'" The man paused for a beat after each phrase, eyebrows raised above saucer eyes.

Collins looked so completely lost that the man with the gun began to giggle.

"Nothing, right? A total blank." He shook his head, smiled and then grimaced in rage as he slammed the case closed. "Woodstock, you dumb fuck."

Collins jumped back in his seat and the man's gun hand shot forward, the maw of the cylinder inches below Greg's chin.

"This is better than that bitch Dotty trying to apologize with her ass," the gunman said. "Okay," he snickered, "three guesses." He pulled the gun back and rested the butt on the table.

"I—I—" Collins smelled the stench of his own fear.

"That's two." The man sneered. His face twisted into a snarl. He shoved the flare gun across the table again, pushing the stack of invoices sliding into Collins' lap. "I'll give you one more hint." The muzzle of the stubby pistol was directly beneath Collins' nose. "You left me in a ditch on the interstate at the end of the festival."

"Oh, Jesus." Collins moaned.

"Ooh, not even close. Forget the nine-hundred number, Jethro," the man whispered. His finger tightened on the trigger.

"Carl," Greg rasped.

The weapon inched back.

"One too many, but maybe I'll give it to you for old time's sake."

Collins exhaled audibly.

"No, I won't."

The orange blossom of hot light that exploded from the muzzle startled him so, it was a moment before Greg realized he had been shot. In another moment the pain hit him. His left shoulder was on fire. He looked at it, horrified to see blood oozing from the shreds of his shirt, but amazed at the minimal damage to his body.

"Rock salt," Carl said. "Not much tissue damage, but it burns like a son-of-a-bitch, doesn't it?"

Tears flooded Collins eyes. The wound felt as if a blowtorch was being held to his skin. He leaned forward, setting his feet for flight, but Carl slammed the table into his middle, pinning him.

Carl cracked the pistol and plucked the spent casing from the breach. He put it in his jacket pocket and retrieved a fresh one.

"This one's double-ought buck," he said, chambering the round and leveling the gun once again on Collins' face. "That one was to get your attention. Do I have your attention, Jethro? We've got lots of time now, don't we? Won't be a soul around until late tomorrow morning."

Greg Collins clutched his shoulder and moaned.

"I'm confident," Carl said, "that shot will be ignored as a backfire in this busy commercial section."

Outside, the traffic on Merrick Road was moderate but steady, normal for this time of day. It was probable that the flat report had not been heard at all outside the walls of the club. Greg Collins felt panic rising like the crest of a monstrous wave as Carl held the gun on him with one hand and, with the other, removed items from his briefcase, recounting, in a matter-of-fact tone, the events of his life in chronological order, starting with his abandonment on a busy upstate roadway in 1969.

Chapter 6

On the stage above Chez Laughs' dance floor, Carl, in shirtsleeves, toiled. A workman's utility belt festooned with leather pouches encircled his middle. Electrical tools with colorful, rubber coated handles jutted from the openings. As he worked, he hummed an indistinct tune an octave below the whine of his battery-operated screwdriver. The Masonite back of the floor speaker fell out as the last screw disengaged and he caught it. Carl's wiry arms, marred by jagged scars, bore mute testimony to the tale of a violent life he was beginning to relate.

"Perfect," he smiled as he peered inside the speaker box. "Where was I, Jethro, old buddy?" He looked expectantly at Collins, who was bound hand and foot with plastic zip ties in the circle of light at the back of the room beyond the parquet dance floor. Duct tape over Greg's mouth made an effective gag.

"You're such a good audience." Carl's eyes crinkled with glee. This was the perfect place to deliver his speech—center-stage, two feet above the room.

"A couple of State Troopers found me in the ditch where you and your friends abandoned me. They found my military ID and my West Point pass. 'You're a disgrace to the uniform,' one of them said. They took me to their barracks, called my commandant, and held me until the MPs came to fetch me. My military career was over. I knew I'd be tested for drugs and drummed out of the corps post haste."

He paused to do something with his wire cutters in the guts of the speaker.

"I had no choice," he resumed when he had completed the cut. "I didn't wait for the charges to be brought. The MPs brought me back to my dorm where the CQ placed me on restriction until my court martial could be convened. I packed a bag, left my mom a note, and ran away. I couldn't face my parents. How could I explain that their All-American boy had his brain fried? My father was a war hero, you know. Got the Silver Star at Anzio. I was going to be a son he could be proud of until you and your friends blind-sided me. That's why I'm doing this, you see. You people destroyed my last chance to make my dad love me.

"Why did you do that? I did nothing to you. I was curious, that's all. I wanted to see what made you longhaired freaks tick. What made you turn your backs on your responsibility to the republic? Didn't your fathers pound a sense of duty into you?" He sneered. "Probably not."

"Anyway, I hitch-hiked all the way across the country after that. When my money ran out, I joined a commune in the California desert. Stayed for a year or so with the weirdest bunch of burned out freaks you can imagine. Worst part was that I fit right in." He shrugged and returned to his task. "Eventually, I got bored and drifted east. Wound up in a little town in Colorado. Prettiest country I've ever seen. I'd learned a few things about living underground from my friends in California. There was always somebody hiding out with us in the commune. Draft dodgers, deserters, radicals—a veritable plethora of misguided youth."

Struck by a thought, again he looked up from his work to stare into space. "Do you know, my dear Jethro, just how easy it is to disappear in this wide land of ours? More importantly, how easy it is to establish a new identity? There are books you can get in any library that tell you how to do it. Frederick Forsythe's Day of the Jackal is one of my favorites. That's how I became Carl Esterbrook, my latest alter ego. I've had several, you know. The real Carl Esterbrook died when he was two days old. It was so easy to get his birth certificate and apply for a social security card. Once you've got that, you can get anything—driver's license, passport, even credit cards.

"I'd changed more than my identity by then. You see I'd begun to realize I was truly exceptional. That's how I choose to think of myself. Exceptional. Slow witted people such as yourself might call me insane, but what's in a word?" His head whipped around to stare with maddened eyes at Greg Collins. "Does that surprise you, Jethro old buddy? That it doesn't bother me? Maybe it was from all of the drugs I did in California. Who knows? You see, in this marvelous age of acceptance, when alternate life styles are to be tolerated, even praised as courageous, who would deny me mine? Ah, what a wonderful country we live in.

"Anyway, with my new identity—I thought it nice that my first name could once again be Carl. I've always liked that name. Suits me, don't you think? Forgive me, I'm rambling. Where was I? Oh, yes. Colorado. I got a job as assistant to a nice old guy, a retired master sergeant, in that little town I mentioned. The name is unimportant. Loose lips sink ships, as they used to say and I've gotten into the habit of being closed mouthed in most things."

Squatting flatfooted, his chest resting on his thighs in what was an extremely uncomfortable posture to westerners, Carl resumed his work, chatting as he labored. "Strange how things work out. I stopped to help an old guy load some freight on his pickup truck just outside the Greyhound depot and bam! My life turned on a dime. We hit it off right away, old Sarge and I. Of course, I never mentioned West Point, but he used to say I'd have made a helluva soldier. He had to know there was something I wasn't telling him, but he never questioned anything about my past. Not that there wasn't ample opportunity. We burned the midnight oil on many occasions, gabbing about everything and anything. He told me all about his days in the army, how he missed it, and how much he regretted retiring.

"Sarge bought and sold antiques. He got to dabbling in it when he moved to Colorado and found out he had 'a gift.' It wasn't a gift. It was the absolute determination of a man who didn't know the meaning of quitting. He could have done anything he wanted to but the antique business fascinated him. Sometimes he'd buy entire estates on speculation and parcel them off. The theory is that the sum of the parts is often greater than the whole. If you know your onions, it's a certainty. He did and I learn fast. Once I learned the ropes, my job was to travel to the more distant prospective sellers, evaluate the property, and offer a bid."

Shaking his head, smiling at sentimental memories, Carl continued, "We cleaned up. Oh, what a team we made. The best part was I had so much free time to pursue my hobbies. Electronics—" he gestured with both hands at the speaker. "—has always been a passion. And, of course, weapons, as you know." He winked and patted the flare pistol on the floor beside him. "The skill to modify this into a lethal weapon is not really all that precise, but if you don't know enough about pressure—expanding gas dynamics and such—you can blow your hand off. To further my pursuit of practical knowledge, I took correspondence courses—always under an assumed name. I virtually lived in libraries.

"Forgive my lack of modesty, but I became rather expert in both fields, especially where they relate. There was one rather intense young man I met at the commune. He was with one of the more radical groups." He pursed his lips in thought. "Was it SDS or the Weathermen? It's not important." He waved it away. "What is important is that he made bombs. Crude devices for the most part, but effective. He left a lasting impression on me.

"I studied guerrilla warfare, insurgency, covert action, and to top it all off, martial arts. The last, naturally, had to be done in person. You can't study karate without physical contact, but martial arts schools don't do background checks as long as the one with which you pay them doesn't bounce. The man you see today is probably the most well-rounded killing machine you will ever meet. Not that you'll have much chance to meet others after today."

Collins' eyes went wide.

"Did you think you were going to get out of this, Jethro?"

Carl heard Greg Collins sob.

"Be a man, Jethro. Make believe you're on death row condemned for your crimes. Today is execution day. Maybe the governor will call."

Carl set his tools down, walked across the room to the broken portable phone, picked up the pieces and took them to Collins. He placed the pile of parts on the table.

"That's a problem, Jethro." He laughed all the way back to the bandstand.

While he worked, Carl told Collins of his experiences in the Rocky Mountains: hunting, trapping, and fishing, living off the land. He bragged of his proficiency with gun, bow, and knife. As proof, he offered a detailed account of two hunters he had killed on one of his excursions in the wild, just to find out what it was like to do humans.

Finished with his task, Carl returned to the table to extract three sticks of dynamite, a blasting cap, and a glass jar of one-inch roofing nails from his case. He turned, and walking across the dance floor to the bandstand, said over his shoulder, "I knew then that my destiny was to be a soldier, no matter what, and that I wouldn't be content until I realized my dream. I got on a bus and went to Texas, got tinted contact lenses, another new identity, and joined the army.

"I did almost three tours in Vietnam. I started out as an enlisted infantryman thanks to you and your friends. I knew I couldn't become an officer. If I went to Officer's Candidate School I'd shine, but sooner or later someone would look closely at my background and that I couldn't have. I made sergeant on my first tour, became a squad leader, and bagged lots of dinks, which got me noticed. My CO offered me a job running a Lurp Team if I'd extend for another tour. That's L-R-R-P, Long Range Recon Patrol for you civilian types. I jumped at it. They tried to get me to accept a commission many times, but I always refused." He glared at Collins. "I should have been an officer, Jethro. I would have made general. I'm that good. But, again, thanks to you, I never went higher than staff sergeant before the chickenshit politicians started to pull us out. That pissed me off. I didn't want to quit. I was killing like there was no tomorrow. It was glorious." Shaking his head, Carl sighed. "But all good things end. My team was ambushed one night near the Parrot's Beak. They cut us to pieces. One of my guys was all fucked up. His head was smashed. No face. I saw my chance. I put my dog-tags on him, hacked off his hands—finger prints, you know—and slipped away."

While inserting a blasting cap in the dynamite, stripping insulation from lamp wire, and making splice connections, he explained how he'd worked his way to Cambodia dodging NVA, ARVN, and American units, stealing food and ammunition. He laughed about a family of farmers he had killed in their sleep one night for a sack of rice.

"I spent the next few years as an independent contractor working for whoever would pay for my talents. Cambodia was tailor made for an individual with my…shall we say…unusual abilities. There were drug lords, rebels, disenfranchised royalty, zealot patriots—fanatics of every sort—and all in the market for talented killers. It was perfect.

"The Khmer Rouge eventually screwed things up. They had this irritating nationalist-racist philosophy. An American didn't stand a chance. I had to pass myself off as a Russian or an East German to keep them out of my hair. That wasn't as difficult as you might think. No one I met could speak or understand any European language except French and I'd picked up enough of that at The Point to get by. My Vietnamese is better, but they are less fond of their next-door neighbors than anyone."

Carl rubbed his jaw, pondering. "Living by your wits," he resumed, "is exhilarating. I made sure to eliminate all threats at an early stage, of course. With the tide of war turning on a dime, as it did almost daily for quite some time, and the various factions littering the landscape with bodies, who'd notice a few more?" He grinned.

"Eventually, I had to leave. There were so many amateurs with automatic weapons running around the countryside it was only a matter of time before my luck ran out. Even highly skilled operatives, such as I, cannot thwart stray bullets. With no place better to go, Colorado beckoned. A thousand American dollars bought anonymous passage on a tramp steamer bound for the Philippines. In Manila, I stowed away on a freighter to Hawaii. American citizens don't need a passport to travel within their own country. I was home. By the time I left Honolulu, I was an American businessman, flying first class I might add, returning to the mainland from a well-earned vacation.

"The old man took me back without question. His only concern was that I was all right. Never once asked where I'd been. He was like a father to me. Until he died four years ago. I miss him."

Carl cleared his throat and resumed his soliloquy. "Sarge left me everything in his will. When I began to catalog the contents of the house, I found it." Placing the explosives and the jar of nails inside the rectangular box and connecting some wires, Carl went on to relate his accidental discovery of a small armory in the basement of the old house. In a hidden room behind the coal bin, he had found a storehouse of weapons, explosive ordnance, and military gear.

"I saw it as a sign from a higher power. Well, maybe not higher, but definitely greater. With no ties, the old itch came back. A change of scene seemed appropriate. The northeast looked ripe."

He replaced the speaker's backboard, screwed it shut, and began unrolling light gauge wire, tacking it with staples along the floor.

"I packed the whole kit and caboodle, bought a truck, and headed east. I had found an untraceable cache of weaponry. I myself am untraceable. This was too good an opportunity to pass up. I could resume my former hobby. All I needed was a target.

"A newspaper provided that. One of you has become rather famous. The article was the catalyst. It all came back like a red wave. The six of you had to pay for what you did to me. You're a blot on my record. No one since has wronged me and survived."

Carl saw no point in mentioning the money. At the bottom of a pile of moldy rucksacks he had found a footlocker stuffed with stacks of cash, mostly American long green. The smallest denominations were ten-dollar bills and they were the least common notes. Twenties, fifties, and hundreds were more abundant. There were also

Deutschmarks, Lira, Pesos, Yen, even Rubles, the last all but worthless. Happily, for Carl, the foreign currency was the smallest portion of the treasure. He remembered the day fondly. With a liter of a fine old cognac at his side, which he sipped from an antique snifter, Carl had spent several ecstatic hours counting and arranging his windfall by denomination. There were over one and three quarter million dollars, in non-sequential serial numbers, in American bills alone. He had rolled in his newfound lucre and laughed until his sides ached. The knowledge that Sarge had been some sort of covert arms dealer struck him as riotously funny.

The foreign stuff he didn't even bother to count, but he occasionally dropped large amounts of it to bolster his other identity, that of the mysterious colonel. There was no reason to tell Jethro about that part, either.

"Finding the bunch of you turned out to be the easiest part," he said. "Remember that discussion you were all so immersed in at Woodstock? Matt brought it up, as I recall. You were all engrossed in your roots, tracing your lineage, your ethnic derivation. So pitifully bourgeois. Each of you announced your family names, pondered the mysteries that had brought you to your hometowns and finally together at Woodstock, that magical place in the Age of Aquarius. Well, not for all of us."

He fastened something to the club's front door below the bottom hinge and clipped the wire to it. Then he touched the probe of a continuity tester to the metal and was rewarded with a light. He smiled his satisfaction and then turned angry eyes on Greg Collins.

"Those names came back to me as if etched on my soul. Both of the girls got married, but the detective that I hired said that hardly slowed him down. You were all kind enough to stay on Long Island. That helped. Thank you."

Finished, Carl padded back to the table. The stench of sweat and urine hung in the air.

"Jethro, you've pissed your pants," he said, hefting the flare pistol. He cocked it.

Collins whined an unmistakable plea through the tape.

"What's that, suh? You day-uh to insult mah honor? Ah demand satisfaction."

Carl bent his right arm double so that the flare pistol pointed to the ceiling from beside his ear. He turned his back on his groaning prisoner, counted off three paces, turned, bringing the weapon down as he did so until his arm was fully extended, and fired.

Greg Collins' face opened up as if it had been a melon. The back of his head bounced off the wall behind him. His lifeless body fell forward and his ruined face splattered on the table.

Carl lifted the muzzle of the gun to his lips and blew smoke from the barrel. He then twirled the gun on his finger and dropped it into his pocket. He cocked his head to one side.

"Jethro, do you hear that?"

He snatched up the broken phone and put it to his ear.

"Oh, hello, Governor." He paused, nodding. "Hang on, sir, I'll see if he's in." With one hand covering the mouthpiece, he looked down at the bloody mess on the table. Replacing the phone to his ear, he said, "No, sir. Nobody here resembling him. Thank you, sir. Goodbye."

To Collins's body, he said, "Wrong number."

Next, he pulled a dark blue coverall from the briefcase. He immediately stripped to his underwear and proceeded to slip into the jumpsuit. After inspecting his shoes and finding no trace of blood, he stepped into them and turned once again to the dead man at the table.

"Nice touch, eh?" he grinned, pointing to the Long Island Power Authority patch above the breast pocket. "Makes me invisible." With that, he snapped the empty case closed, carried it across the room, and stood it behind the speaker that he had rigged to explode. The bloody clothes he burned in a large kettle on the commercial gas stove in the kitchen, being careful to start the exhaust fan in the hood above the range, first.

The smoke would not last long enough to attract attention. While the flames consumed the garments, he held the circular head of an iron rod with a wooden handle in the blue teeth of the gas jet until the metal glowed orange-red. Snapping the knob to the off position, he hurried back out into the club proper.

"Almost forgot," he smiled, abashed, and then pressed the glowing iron to the exposed neck of the late Gregory Collins. The stench of burning flesh wrinkled Carl's nose.

"There," he crooned with pride, "the maker's mark."

He stood in the middle of the dance floor to survey his work and double-checked his moves in his mind. Satisfied, he nodded and made for the back door and the alley behind the club.

On the way out, he said, "Good to see you again, old buddy. Thanks for hearing me out. Explain it to the last four when you meet them on the other side. I won't have time to go through it with the rest. Sorry I didn't stop to gab during my previous visits, but I was casing the joint, as they say." He took a long last look around and said, "Nice place you had here, Jethro, but I have to tell you, that wallpaper really sucks."

ꕥꕥ

Carl's eyes darted from the road, to the speedometer, to the rearview mirror. He was doing sixty—five miles over the limit on the Meadowbrook Parkway—and cars still passed him as if he was in reverse. Long Island drivers seemed to have decided that all speed limit laws had been repealed. He was tempted to keep pace with the pack, but he had to be cautious. It would not do to be stopped by a trooper. A search would reveal some things that would be hard to explain.

If he could do Madeline this afternoon, he thought, he should be able to get to good ol' Matt this evening. By then, things would probably get sticky. The cops were not stupid. When they tallied the body count tonight—with more than a few of their own among the score—they would start putting things together.

The booby traps were a nice touch. They set him apart, gave his work an identity. Plus, they worked well as misleading trails. The man-hours the cops would waste trying to establish his profile with that sizable red herring stinking up the landscape could only delay them. He wondered what they would make of the heat in Dotty's home. That had been a last-minute whim, the beauty of which was: it meant nothing. They would be looking for connections. How long would they take to sort out that all of the victims had known each other in their formative years? Unknown, but they would eventually dope it out. He'd make adjustments on the fly.

The last two would be the toughest. That had been known from the beginning. It might delay the outcome, but it would not change it. He was just too good for them to compete with. His biggest problem was what to do for an encore. Never before had his work been so satisfying. The mission gave him something he had longed for: a sense of purpose. When the six were all gone, he would be famous. Unknown, but famous. It tickled him. He might become as notorious as London's Ripper, and as mysterious, the stuff of folklore and nightmares, a legend. What to do to afterward was the problem.

Still pondering this weighty dilemma, he flipped his directional signal on and moved to the right-hand lane. The Stewart Avenue exit was just ahead, the road to Garden City.

Chapter 7

Evenin', gents." Jack Kobrigian flipped his cigarette butt into the bright, green buds banked against the curb in a quiet suburban lane in Oyster Bay. "Nice day for field work."

It was classic Kobrigian understatement. The waning sun still warmed the clear spring air, redolent with new growth. It had been a beautiful day, marred only by the deeds of one perverse individual. Everywhere Doc looked, the promise of regeneration bloomed. He noted several lawn sprinklers showering front yards and one man, still dressed for the office, vigorously tidying up his property, digging stray leaves from beneath his azaleas with a plastic rake.

Doc smiled at his colleague's rumpled appearance. Kobrigian always looked like he had slept in his suit. Among the detectives, Jack was known as Columbo, but no one said it to his face. Possessed of a cynical, wry wit, Jack Kobrigian took his work, if nothing else, seriously. His unkempt appearance was born of disdain for things conventional. To Jack, clothes were merely to be suffered. Style was beneath his notice. Custom, such as departmental dress code, was endured. If they told him to come to work in a loincloth and high tops, that was how he would show up, but the loincloth would not be pressed.

Kobrigian was interested in the job first and last, but this was not to say he had no curiosity beyond police work. He was a veritable gold mine of insignificant information. He read incessantly and could hold his own on a remarkable number of topics. No one played Trivial Pursuit with Jack Kobrigian twice. Alex Trebek was purported to have Jack's phone number on his Rolodex. The depth of the man's knowledge of the most obscure subjects had often flabbergasted Doc. One night in a cop's bar, after the county had lost its case against a kiddy porn producer, the dicks on the case had met to drown their sorrows. They were angry and railing against the cracked system that let child molesting creeps walk on trivial technicalities. They were more furious with themselves for letting it happen. Disgusted and guilty that a minute gap in their chain of evidence had released the bastard to do it again, they wallowed in self-pity steeped in alcohol. Lashing out at everything and anything, Doc made a crack about Kobrigian's grimy neckwear.

"For God's sake, Jack," he slurred, "couldn't you at least have taken the stand with a clean tie? It's an embarrassment to the whole department. I mean, look at that thing. When's the last time it had an oil change?"

The smoky saloon fell abruptly silent as the assembled cops overheard Doc's drunken insult. The room braced for the inevitable confrontation. Kobrigian turned to the then-young detective with such pained astonishment that Doc felt like Brutus must have felt when Caesar spied the bloody knife in his protégé's fist. Slowly, deliberately, Jack set his drink on the bar and faced his accuser. Shoe leather scuffed as feet shifted. Chair legs screeched. The jukebox stopped. Every man in the crowded bar fully expected to have to pull the two detectives apart. The very air crackled. Doc was in no position to recant without losing face. He stared back, holding his breath.

"Did you know," Jack said, in his usual gregarious way, "that neckties originated as Croatian battle amulets in ancient Europe?"

Doc waited.

Kobrigian nodded as if confirming unspoken affirmation. "That's precisely correct," he continued, the respected professor imparting wisdom to the ignoble student. "Western European cultures admired them and adopted them as a decoration rather than a talisman of war. Eventually, the necktie became a standard accouterment of gentlemen's apparel throughout the Christian world, even until today." He scissored his fingers around his cravat and held it up to examination. "My own replica of a Croatian battle amulet looks a bit ragged. Maybe tomorrow I'll go buy a new one. Whaddya think, Doc?"

Doc wagged his head, astounded by Kobrigian's poise, and said, "Fuck it, Jack. That one looks fine to me."

Doc smiled at the memory and said, "Spring has definitely sprung, Jack. How goes it?"

"Fair to middlin'. You?"

“About the same. You don’t look any the worse for wear. Any after-effects from last night?”

“Naw. That little surprise did all its damage upstairs. Me and the uniforms got nothing worse than some ringing ears.” He rummaged in his pockets for something. “Beckwith and I have been poking around at the crime scene. Place is a zoo. Media types coming out of the cracks. Found this an hour ago.” He proffered a battered address book bound in darkened red leather. “Thought it might help so I came looking for you. Found your car and figured you’d be back to it eventually. Been admiring the new greenery the past half-hour. Anything new from the evening canvass?”

Doc shook his head and thumbed through the book, grinning tight-lipped at Kobrigian’s stoicism. If Jack ever came unglued, there would be no one who could keep his head.

“Lots of names and numbers, mostly males,” Doc thought aloud. “The shady lady’s little black book?” The initials, DK, embossed on the cover, confirmed it.

“Little red book, Doc,” Kobrigian said patiently.

“I stand corrected.” Doc smiled.

One dog-eared page stood out, heavily used. “The Pig and Pistol,” Doc frowned at the solitary entry. “Didn’t we pass that on the way up here, Tony?”

“Yeah,” Cordova nodded, “on One-o-six. Little pub across from the shopping center.”

“We’ve gone about as far as we can go here.” Doc checked his watch. “Almost happy hour. Let’s go see if anybody knew the lady.”

Kobrigian declined to accompany them, claiming Beckwith would be lonely with no one to talk to but forensic wizards and reporters. He said he’d check with them later in the squad room.

The Pig and Pistol was an out of the way leftover from the early seventies when English pub-style watering holes dotted Long Island’s landscape. It had survived solely on its merits as an anonymous, low class gin mill whose appeal rested in its lack of appeal to the upper crust. Ideally situated on the outskirts of town in a dark hollow beneath towering cliffs, it was the perfect cheater’s joint. Weathered, clapboard sides beneath a sharply gabled slate roof gave the place an authentic, historic aura. The building’s massive beams rested on a solid foundation of mortared fieldstone. A faded and split wooden sign hanging from an iron rod above the door barely depicted the name. Two low wattage spotlights, poorly aimed on opposite sides of the shingle, lit half each of the tarnished gilt letters at night. Most of the clientele shunned daylight and knew the place as the Pig and something, or the something Pistol, depending on their usual direction of approach.

The tavern reeked of nostalgia. The bartender radiated animosity at the cops' intrusion into his domain.

Two male customers stood beside a pool table. They were brightly lit from the torso down by the fluorescent fixture hanging above the table, while their faces remained in shadow. Both abruptly departed, their half-filled drinks abandoned as if each had suddenly remembered a pressing engagement. The only remaining patron, an old man with flinty eyes, lifted his newspaper and became absorbed in it.

"What'll it be, Officers?" the bartender asked flatly, dealing two paper napkins on a polyurethane bar top scratched to a haze from years of service. The expression on his face wasn't a sneer, but it was close.

"Two Buds?" Doc raised an eyebrow at Tony.

Tony shrugged. "Can't dance."

The tattooed dragons on the barman's hairy forearms rippled as he popped the caps on two longnecks and slid the bottles across the counter.

"Anything else?" he growled, narrowing nasty eyes.

Doc pointed to the Newsday shielding the fellow seated in front of elongated white ceramic and brass taps at the center of the bar. The front page screamed, OYSTER BAY BOMBED. The picture below it showed the black-bagged body of Dorothy Kohler being loaded into the Coroner's wagon.

"You know this lady?"

"Dotty? Sure."

"So?" Doc prompted, with just the right amount of impatience. "And I'll need your name, pal."

The detectives waited while the barman looked from Doc to Tony and back again, as if weighing his options. He took a breath, exhaled through his nose, and said, "Max—Max Schroeder."

Tony produced his notebook and a pen and wrote something.

Doc said, "Dotty?"

Max cleared his throat. "Right. Dotty's a regular. Used to be, anyway," he corrected himself with a gold-toothed grin. The detectives' deadpan stares convinced him to dispense with the sarcasm. "Dotty's been coming in here for years, on and off. Used to sit right down there." He pointed to an end stool at the back with his chin as he grabbed a filthy rag and wiped the counter to keep his nervous hands busy.

"Tell me about her," Doc said.

Max looked from one detective to the other again and thought for a moment before saying, "Why not?" He flipped the rag into the sink and leaned his elbows on the back bar. "Dotty liked men. Seldom left early. Seldom left alone. Didn't talk much, except to whatever stud she latched onto."

"Ever latch on to you, friend?" Tony asked.

"Me?" Max laughed without humor. "Not a chance. Horny old hippy broads aren't my style. No, Dotty liked 'em young—mid-twenties or so—good looking dudes mostly—wild ones—bikers—truckers—crazy motherfuckers. You know what I'm saying? The kind of characters that everybody watches and nobody turns their back on."

"Where'd you get the tattoos?" Doc asked.

The bartender rubbed his scraggly black beard, looking down at his arms as if he had never noticed them before. He showed the gold tooth again as he said, "I see where you're going. You're wrong, man. That ain't me." He rolled his tee shirt sleeve up to his shoulder, revealing a fouled anchor. "Navy. Vietnam. Brown water sailor. PBRs. Got drunk on R and R in Bangkok in sixty-seven. Got hepatitis from these fuckers. I can walk the walk and talk the talk, but I'm strictly a business man."

"Did the lady have a main squeeze?" Doc asked. "Somebody who might get pissed off if she was banging somebody else?"

"Naw. Strictly one-night stands. She picked on drifters."

"You get many of those in here?"

"You'd be surprised."

"What about her old man?" Tony asked.

"Jason?"

Doc nodded. Max looked with curiosity at Tony's blackened eyes, and opened his mouth to say something, but Doc's intense gaze seemed to change his mind.

"Jason didn't have a thing to say about it," Max resumed. "Dotty did her own thing. Hell, she brought him here one night. Introduced him around. Showed him the place and bought him a drink—champagne cocktail." He winked. "Then she kissed him on the cheek and waved bye-bye. He left. Didn't look happy, but he didn't bitch, either. It was none of my business so I didn't ask, but I got the feeling she was saying: This is where I screw around. Now you've seen it, so don't ask me again—and don't come here no more.

"That was the only time I ever met him. Never came back. Wimpy little shit. But, like I say, none of my business."

"Dotty do drugs?"

"I threw her out of here twice for lighting up a joint at the bar. Other than that…" He raised both hands, palms up, and shrugged.

"You the owner?" Tony asked.

"Sole proprietor." Max twisted his head to show his pride.

"Where do we call you? If we have to." Doc bared his teeth, devoid of humor.

"Right here." He reached into a small basket beside the cash register and handed each of the detectives a business card. "I live behind the joint."

Doc slid three dollars across the bar for the untouched beers. "Happy hour, Max. Have a nice day."

In the car, Doc said to Tony, "Vietnam vet. Knowledge of explosives?"

"Probably. Then again, he said he was navy. Would a navy guy know how to rig booby traps?"

"I take it you never met any SEALS." Doc jabbed his chin toward the gravel driveway. "Let's get out of here. Max has pissed me off."

Tony put the car in gear and pressed the accelerator. As the wheels crunched on blue stone, raising a smoky haze behind them, he said to Doc, "You think Max is telling us all he knows?"

"I think Max would lie to a cop just for practice," Doc said. He sat silently for several minutes, staring through the windshield, and then he sighed and said, "Shit."

"What?" Tony said.

"Nothing."

"Damnit, Doc. What?"

As they headed south, Doc said, "Do you remember the feeling you used to get in Nam when you knew something wasn't right? That crawly feeling in your spine when the peasants wouldn't look you in the eye, when the baby-sans stopped trying to sell you pussy, when you just knew the shit was about to hit the fan and your ass was hanging out a mile."

"Hell, yes." Tony glanced sideways at Doc before his eyes darted to his rearview mirror, back to Doc, to the road ahead, and then to the darkened verges. His whole body shook with the shiver that ran through him. “And I wish to God you hadn’t said that.”

Chapter 8

Behind a stack of broken wooden shipping pallets on the rear lot of a defunct tool and dye factory in an industrial section of Garden City, Carl hummed the tune to Paint It Black. He affixed the last of a set of numerals and logos fashioned from self-adhesive labels to the doors and bumpers of a stolen automobile. The end product was an authentic looking Long Island Power Authority vehicle.

His PC, a good graphics program, and an ink-jet printer, manufactured forgeries of a quality that would make the counterfeiters of yesteryear weep from envy.

The car, a compact Chevrolet Cavalier stolen from a shopping mall in Richmond, Virginia, was painted the same shade of blue used by the utility. He could have stolen the car from the company and saved himself some work, but the police tended to look for missing high-ticket items, particularly those of rich, influential corporations. It was smarter to do it this way. An extra company car was less conspicuous than one on the negative side of the balance sheet.

The license plates came from his stock of discarded tags. Carl had spent weeks finding the right, single, female, department of motor vehicles employee to furnish his supply of sterile plates and still more weeks courting her. From their serendipitous—as far as Mona knew—first meeting in a singles bar in Long Beach to their steamy first date, the ensnarement had taken skillful planning and research. Shadowing her every move and establishing beyond doubt that she fit his criteria had been an all-consuming campaign. Once he was convinced that she was alone, lonely, and approachable, her seduction and corruption had been choreographed like a Bolshoi production.

Mona Freedman, recent expatriate out of Gary, Indiana, never had a chance once Carl had selected her as his accomplice. He had brought a plain, forgotten woman from a life of resigned drudgery to the brink of glorious hope. In Mona's girlish romanticism, Carl was a man of sensuous strength and vision. He was bold, daring, brilliant, and he loved her as she had prayed to be loved since she had escaped her foster home at seventeen.

So what if he was larcenous in his ambitions? Great men made their own rules, or so he had convinced her. He had concocted the most ingenious scheme to rip off the insurance industry the world would ever know. In one stroke they would be multi-millionaires and retire to a life of sensual bliss in the Bahamas. All he needed were some old license plates—the ones people turned in when they junked their cars—the ones she was entrusted to destroy each day.

The specifics of the plan were never made clear. It was a "need to know" situation. That made sense. A robbery this big had to be a big secret. Mona wasn't really interested in the details, only the results. Her initial trepidation evaporated in a sea of passion and longing. She was amazed how easy it was to purloin the plates, and she was thunderstruck one night in her rumpled bed when her daring lover snapped her neck like a dry twig.

Carl had even convinced Mona to write her letter of resignation so that no one would suspect her when she disappeared into the Caribbean with her partner.

Jamaica Bay, within sight of JFK Airport, was as close as Mona ever got to the jet-set life he had promised her.

The meter reader's uniform he now wore had been easy. He had swiped it from a laundromat when the owner's wife had left it in the dryer to grab a slice of pizza in the take-out place next door.

Carl took pride in his ability to act swiftly on opportunity when it presented itself. The LIPA disguise, indeed the whole scenario, had come to him in an instant.

The new electronic pad that was now used to record customer's usage had not been so easy. Try as he might, Carl had been unable to steal one. He had nearly been caught in one attempt when he followed a worker into a locker room at the Northport Power Plant. In the end, he had simply copied it. An oversized digital calculator case was sufficiently similar to pass casual scrutiny. Some doctoring of the face, and he had a passable replica. It didn't have to work. It was window dressing like the yellow plastic bubble light attached by a suction cup to the roof of the Cavalier.

With the car suitably disguised, he drove to within a block of his target's house and parked on a tree-shrouded street. The carpet of new buds gave the pavement a picturesque look he found pleasing. Curbside parking was forbidden in this pristine neighborhood, but the gendarmes ignored the working stiffs who serviced the community so long as they didn't take advantage.

Inna Godda Da Vida pounded in Carl's brain as he strolled down the street, his carefree countenance showing none of the roaring in his mind as he advanced for the kill.

A meter reader making selected stops would be as noticeable as the normal driveway-by-driveway route of the legitimate article was transparent. He wove in and out of four backyards as he approached the object of his mission.

Mrs. Gebhardt stared accusingly through the screen door as he checked the meter at the rear of the house next door to the one he wanted.

"Afternoon, ma'am," Carl smiled, beguiling the suspicious, old woman.

"Young man," she rasped, "why are you here?"

"Meter reader, ma'am."

"They read the meters last month," Mrs. Gebhardt hissed. "What are you doing back? Residential customers pay every two months."

Carl never wavered. He proffered his electronic clipboard. "Technology, ma'am. We're still getting the bugs out." He stepped under the green and white striped canvas awning and cast a surreptitious glance around the yard. There were plenty of high, thick evergreens to give privacy to the homeowner. He stopped in front of the white crossbuck door and peered through the black nylon screen. "We wouldn't want to overcharge nice people like you, would we?"

Mollified and inclined to believe that these new-fangled gadgets were not all they were cracked up to be, but still intent on establishing her credentials as ruler of the roost, Mrs. Gebhardt snapped, "May I see some identification, young man?"

"Of course," Carl said. He fished in his shirt pocket and pressed a laminated, pink library card to the screen.

Mrs. Gebhardt squinted to discern the printed information. She leaned forward and gasped as the door flew open. The man's free hand clamped on her throat. In a blur, he was inside, kicking the inner door shut behind him. Her feet were off the floor. She hung in mid-air like a hooked carp, stunned by the speed of the attack, powerless to resist, strangling as Carl's talon-like grip crushed the life from her puny body.

He lifted her effortlessly and placed her in a kitchen chair. Clucking his tongue, he quipped, "Now you know why they call us the power company. Thank you for your business."

Carl strolled back to the street the way he had come, to amble down Madeline Maclear's driveway. He did his cursory inspection of the electric meter and pretended to be storing the information in his bogus recorder. A glance confirmed he was unobserved. Mounting the back steps in a leap, he tried the back door. It opened without a sound. Inside, he stood stock still, sniffing the air like a wolf examining a hen house, salivating at the scent of his prey.

Bare hooks lined white wainscoted walls. A bronze shoe scraper was bolted to the floor just inside the door beside a washer and dryer. He was in a combination mudroom and laundry. He heard humming within the house. His mouth fell open as he twisted his head from side to side to enhance his auditory perception. The voice was female but did not fit his expectations. There was a resonance to the tone that didn't match his memories of the delicate pitch of Madeline Maclear. But, he thought, she was seventeen then. She had aged, of course. That was about to cease.

Eyes darting, Carl moved silently into a mauve and white kitchen, taking a moment to admire the decor.

The melody was coming from upstairs. He prowled the length of the center hallway and climbed thickly carpeted steps. A maze of unpacked and half packed boxes, cardboard drums, and mover's blankets told him he was just in time. His quarry was preparing to flee.

On the landing at the top, he paused. The tune sounded like church music. He followed it to the back bedroom where he crept to the open door.

The image of a statuesque African-American woman unfolding bedding startled him. An involuntary gasp betrayed him. Marjorie Green whirled, but Carl recovered instantly. He was on her before she could scream. She fell backward across the bed beneath him with Carl clawing at her mouth. She fought to escape his grip. With his left hand on her mouth and his knee in her stomach, he flicked a thin, sharp blade from his sleeve. The point pricked her throat and a trickle of blood sprang from the wound. She moaned. Terror filled her bulging eyes.

"Not a sound," he whispered.

The incredible strength of his grip and the razor edge of the knife secured Marjorie's tearful cooperation. She nodded, frantic.

With the point an inch from her eye, he relaxed his hold on her mouth and then removed it when he felt sure she would not cry out. Tears streamed down her smooth, chocolate-brown cheeks.

"Now, who in the hell are you?" Carl asked patiently, a mildly annoyed expression on his face.

"I'm Marjorie Green," she whispered, shaking.

"How nice," he crooned. "Now, what are you doing here?"

"I—I live here."

"And where is the mistress of the house?"

Marjorie's baffled expression angered Carl. "Madeline, you dumb bitch. Where's Madeline?" The knife shook in his hand and Marjorie whimpered. "Answer the question or I'll pluck your eye out like a peach pit."

"I don't know," Marjorie wailed. Carl's hand clapped onto her mouth and squeezed. Marjorie squirmed with pain and fright. He sliced her ear. Blood ran into her hair. The blade was sharp enough to be a surgical instrument. She wept, her body quaking.

"Stop it," he snapped. "I'm going to give you one more chance. When I take my hand away, start talking. Scream and I'll carve you like a pumpkin." Malevolence bored into her eyes. She nodded agreement.

"She moved," she said. "She sold us this house."

"Us?"

"My husband, Doctor Green, and I. He works with Madeline at the hospital. Please don't hurt me. Take anything you want."

"Don't insult me," he hissed. "I'm not a burglar." He smiled. "Not today, anyway."

Marjorie looked sick to her stomach, but Carl saw the wheels turning behind her eyes. She was going to try something. He hoped she would.

Carl couldn't imagine how this could have happened. He'd tracked them all so carefully. How could she have gotten away from him? Especially her: the snooty one—Miss Toogoodforyou. He saw Madeline in his mind. The cute kid with the sexy eyes, turning her nose up at the LSD tablet Dotty held in her palm and the look of contempt when he had taken it instead.

"Where did she go?"

"I don't know," Marjorie sobbed. The knife nicked her cheek. "I don't." She gasped. "My husband said she rented an apartment near the hospital. That's all I know. I swear it."

Carl looked crestfallen. His grip slackened.

With a sudden twist of her hips, Marjorie toppled him sideways and yanked him by the hair to add to his momentum, clawing for purchase with her free hand on the mohair mattress ticking. She rolled free of him. As she struggled to a sitting position and hauled her legs around to spring from the bed, his fingers clamped on her arm and her body rocked with the force of a blow to her ribs.

Time seemed to slow nearly to a stop. Marjorie looked down to see blood welling from her side, onto the powerful hand holding the knife. The blade was buried in her to the hilt. Her jaw hung slack as she stared dully into those maddened eyes. But they weren't mad anymore. They were happy, almost warm.

"Nice try, but you lose." Carl smirked. The blade came out smoothly. She stared dumbly at her deep red blood dripping from its point.

"Pity. We could have had fun," he said, with a nonchalance Marjorie could only observe in a detached, unreal fashion through her shock. He stepped in front of her. The knifepoint thrust deftly forward and pierced her heart.

Carl pulled the blade back and watched the woman's body keel over. He then crossed to the closet to paw lazily through Doctor Green's clothes, wiping the blade on a gray flannel suit.

"The guy could be a Sumo wrestler," he giggled, holding a pair of worsted slacks to his waist in front of a full-length mirror. He tossed them on the bed where they covered Marjorie's staring, dead eyes and then stripped off the coverall.

"Madeline's old man was more my size," he told the corpse. "This is making it difficult."

He settled on a sweatshirt and jogging pants, hitching the drawstring as tight as it would go. A faded Baltimore Colts ball cap with the bill pulled low over his eyes completed his ensemble.

Dressed in Ben Green's running clothes, he bent to pull the slacks from Marjorie's face and said, "Don't take it personally, Marjorie. You'll have a place in my speed bump file, an inconvenience on the road to glory." He patted her head and strode from the room.

Downstairs, he folded the bloody coveralls before placing them on the kitchen counter beside a half-consumed bottle of iced tea. He sipped from the bottle, paused, said, “Refreshing. Thanks, Marjorie,” and replaced it. With a shrug, he flipped a switch in the back of the makeshift meter-reading gizmo and set it carefully atop the garment, pressing it down as he gently withdrew his finger.

“What the hell. Why waste it?” He laughed as he jogged out the front door and trotted back to the car.

Chapter 9

Good God, what a pig sty!" the police sergeant wheezed, fanning the space in front of his nose with his hand to dispel the dust motes tickling his nostrils. Earl Wannamaker's midtown apartment smelled the way the he imagined the tomb of King Tut must have smelled when archeologists reopened it after four millennia. He would be willing to give odds that the boy king's place had not been as dusty. Stepping gingerly over a cobweb cloaked crate of empty beer bottles, the sergeant mumbled to his junior partner, "You sure this guy's name wasn't Collier?" He poked his baton into a kitchen cupboard. A swarm of cockroaches scrambled for cover. He recoiled.

"Naw," the young patrolman replied, distracted by the remains of a moldy tee shirt hanging from a rust speckled wall sconce, "Wannamaker, Earl C. Who's Collier?"

"Never mind. Ancient history." He sighed. "Forget it."

The two New York City uniformed police officers looked with twin grimaces of disgust at the filthy, rubbish strewn railroad apartment of the late private investigator. From the kitchen, where they stood, they could see the room and the adjacent living room separated only by a waist-high partition.

Stacks of brittle newspapers, magazines, files, and racetrack betting sheets covered every stick of furniture and square inch of floor space. Three-foot aisles, barely wide enough to accommodate the deceased detective's girth, staggered drunkenly through the mess. Half eaten snacks were stashed in forgotten crevices amidst the debris. Dozens of empty liquor bottles, and an even greater number of crumpled beer cans were scattered virtually anywhere not covered by musty paper. The only uncluttered area was in the living room: a clearing in front of the twenty-five-inch console TV leading five feet back from it to a soiled, overstuffed easy chair facing the set. It was Earl's favorite resting place, lumpy and ripped, like his life. A standing glass ashtray on a fluted brass pedestal stood beside the chair, mounded over with crushed out butts. Cigarette burns in the matted shag carpet made the cops wonder how Earl had not burned himself to death. Dishes, encrusted with enough green fuzz to suggest Earl had been starting a Penicillin factory, jammed the greasy sink in the kitchen to overflowing. Crumpled Pizza Hut cartons, Chinese food containers and Burger King wrappers overflowed from a wire wastebasket beside the door. The sergeant wondered when Earl had decided to forsake home cooking for take-out. Probably, he guessed, right around the time he ran out of unsoiled crockery.

"A real gourmet, our man Earl, eh?" the young cop wrinkled his nose at his own observation. "I'd start looking for the perp at the Board of Health," he quipped.

The gray-haired sergeant nodded. "Or the EPA. This guy was a one-man pollution plague,"

"Whoever whacked him struck a blow for a cleaner New York, that's for sure. What a frigging slob. I haven't seen this much dust since Saudi." The younger cop took every opportunity to bring up his role in Desert Storm.

Weary of debating the perils of a hundred-hour war versus his brother's thirteen-month stint in Vietnam, the sergeant said nothing. He stooped to pick up an envelope from the floor beside the easy chair, being careful to grasp only the corner between thumb and forefinger.

"Better set this aside for the homicide dicks," he said. "Might be something."

"Whatcha got?" The younger man stepped gingerly to his partner's side. "Looks like a list."

"Numbers. Six rows of nine digits, some smeared. Looks like he used it for a coaster. See the rings?

"Yeah. And what's that at the top? A name? Geez, this guy writes like a Chinaman."

"The colonel," the sergeant read.

"What's that? A horse? Maybe he had a hot tip."

"Then what are the numbers?" the sergeant thought aloud. "Too many digits for phone numbers."

"Local numbers anyway." The young cop smiled, gratified at the chance to outwit his senior partner. "You're forgetting area codes."

“You’d need ten digits for area code, exchange, and number, asshole, not nine.”

The junior man was stung by the offhand dismissal of his deductive reasoning. “Some kinda code, probably. Or, do you know what kind of number’s got nine digits?”

“Social security numbers?”

You would think of that, the young cop didn’t say, but the sergeant saw it in his eyes.

“We’ll let the gold shields chew on this,” the sergeant breathed. “Most of them can’t find their ass with both hands and a map, but that isn’t our worry. Where the hell are they, anyway?” He glared at the door as if that would hurry them along. “Goddamn detectives, and goddamn cross-town traffic.”

The body of Earl Wannamaker had been discovered much sooner than Carl had anticipated. An angry landlord had chosen to confront his past due tenant in his place of business. He had been more deeply moved by the irretrievable loss of two months back rent than by the sight of Earl’s bloody corpse. No stranger to carnage, the slumlord had seen enough mayhem in Beirut, before permanently immigrating to the Land of the Free, to harden his heart to violent death.

While a thorough, yet fruitless investigation of the crime scene took place in Earl’s office, the NYPD had dispatched a radio car to enter and secure the victim’s dwelling with orders to await the detectives. The hapless patrolman had no way of knowing that the first clue in an ongoing string of brutal murders had just been unearthed.

Chapter 10

Doc sat with his head between his knees atop the red brick steps leading to the black lacquered front door of the Green's colonial home.

Tony leaned down and squeezed Doc's shoulder, saying, "Take deep breaths. Sit for a minute. You'll be okay."

Doc could not get the smell of blood out of his nostrils. His stomach churned, and for a moment he thought he would lose his lunch.

"Watch yer back," he heard from behind him, and quickly averted his eyes as two ambulance attendants carried out a heavily bandaged, moaning policeman on a stretcher. Another patrolman trotted alongside, murmuring words of assurance. The group moved down the walk in perfect step, loaded their cargo into the back of their waiting vehicle, slammed the doors, and sped away.

Doc had seen things gristlier than most people could imagine in his years in homicide, and before that in the war. He was not without compassion, but he had learned to compartmentalize his feelings, to adopt the attitude of professional detachment necessary to his work. Now, the killer's booby traps brought back a feeling of impotence he had thought he would never have to suffer again. The mere words, booby trap, recalled terror and frustration beyond description. The cloying, coppery scent of blood that filled his nostrils was more reawakened memory of past horrors than of present ones.

He felt the color returning to his face and sat up straight. "Sorry, Tony. I'm okay now," he lied, as he inhaled through his nose and let it out in a rush.

Tony shook two cigarettes from a pack, lit them, and passed one to Doc, saying, "Here. All this fresh air is a shock to the lungs." Doc nodded his gratitude, put the cigarette between his lips and sat staring at the ground, unable to summon the will to inhale.

"Here's what we got." Tony forged ahead, sitting opposite his friend with his back against the wrought iron railing, knowing that dwelling on Doc's near breakdown would only add to his embarrassment. "Mrs. Marjorie Green—that's the lady upstairs—apparently died of stab wounds. Looks like two. Left lung," he indicated his side with a pointing finger, "and straight through the heart. Kids came home from school and found their momma dead. Came running out here screaming. Neighbors came out to see what the commotion was about. One of them went upstairs and found the body. She called nine-one-one and took the kids home to her house—there." He pointed to a large, English Tudor home across the street. "Sector car arrives, followed immediately by a back-up unit and the two uniforms do a quick once over. They call for detectives. This time, thank God, they used the neighbor's phone instead of the radio, hence the lack of media as yet. While they're waiting, one cop decides to do a little detecting on his own. From what his buddy tells me, there was a dark blue uniform folded neatly on the kitchen counter. Says it looked like a jumpsuit, full of blood, and there was something on top of it, some kind of electronic gear. Maybe a laptop computer or something. There isn't enough of it left to be sure. The Lab guys might be able to tell us what it used to be.

"Anyway, the sector car guy says the other cop was eyeing this thing. Seems he's a bug on the latest hardware. The PO says he warned him not to touch anything and left him in the kitchen while he came out here to watch for us. Not ten seconds later, he hears a big bang and a scream. When he runs back in, the guy's on the floor with both hands gone and his face all burned and torn up. He calls for an ambulance, which, of course, was already on the way for the lady upstairs. They're taking him to Nassau County Med Center. Medics think he'll probably be blind as well as handless, if he lives. That's why we got pulled in on this."

"Our Oyster Bay bomber," Doc stated flatly.

"Bingo." Tony made a motion with his hand resembling firing a gun. "Leave a body, leave a bomb. How many guys do you think are working that MO?"

"Not many, I hope." Doc closed his eyes and saw Viet Cong in black pajamas scurrying like ants. He immediately opened them.

Cars with flashing lights were filling the street. An army of cops poured from the vehicles. Several ran past them into the house. The medical examiner and the technicians were arriving. Detectives and patrolman were fanning out, interviewing the neighbors.

"Better get back to work," Doc said as he hauled himself erect, knuckles white on the black railing.

"Hey! Over here!" came a shrill voice from next door. "We got another one."

"Get out of the house!" Doc bellowed. "Cordon off the block," he barked to a uniform. "Evacuate every house within a hundred yards," he ordered another. "Tony, call the Bomb Squad. Move!"

ꕥꕥ

Carl was infuriated. The thrill of the kill was wearing off. His anger at the disruption of his plan was coming to the fore. How could Madeline have eluded him? He had spent months studying his targets, establishing their habits and schedules. There had been no clue to Madeline's decision to sell her house and move. Why would she leave such a perfect home? To forget, why else? The everyday reminders of her dead husband in that big house had probably become more than she could bear. But, so fast? It took months to sell the average home on Long Island with the glut on the market. What was that the black lady had said? Her husband worked with Madeline at the hospital. Of course! She had a ready-made buyer. Maybe the black broad's old man had seen an opportunity to take advantage of the grieving widow. It didn't matter. What did matter was that he would have to find her again. That shouldn't be too difficult. After all, he knew where she worked. He knew her schedule. That was part of the operational logistics. Today was her day off. She was home. She was supposed to be in that house. Damn!

He could follow her, but that would be dangerous. The cops would be piecing things together. If they added it all up before he was finished, they would be watching her. They would have them all staked out, his entire hit list, as soon as they figured it out. He'd have to move quickly on the rest. Saving Madeline for last might be fun. It was a deviation from the plan, but flexibility was the key to good planning. After all, as some famous general had said: No plan survives contact with the enemy.

He parked the blue car, stripped off the LIPA markings behind K-Mart on Old Country Road in Westbury, and grabbed a suitcase from the trunk before he walked across the street to the Holiday Inn.

Waving politely at the desk clerk, who hardly noticed him, he strode purposefully down the hall until he came to an open room. There was no one in sight in the corridor. The room was devoid of luggage and personal articles, left for the maids to make up by the departed guest. The key was on the dresser, probably left by a hurried businessman who had checked out electronically.

Carl slipped the Do-Not-Disturb sign on the doorknob and hurriedly changed into the jeans, maroon polo shirt, and loafers in his bag. A tan, Ralph Lauren casual jacket completed his attire. He stuffed Doctor Green's running clothes into the bag. On the way out, he tossed the suitcase into the hotel's trash bin.

A public bus took him to Route 107 in Hicksville, where he got off and walked at a brisk pace until he was behind Sears' sprawling department store where he fished in his pocket for a set of keys.

A silver-gray, BMW 325i sedan chirped hello as he disarmed the alarm and unlocked the car with the push of a button on his key fob. The soft, black leather seat felt cool and Carl enjoyed the new car aroma as he adjusted the mirrors and settled into the seat. He was proud of his purchase. The Pennsylvania dealer had given only a cursory glance at his customer's credentials, his greedy eyes much more interested in the pile of cash Carl had plopped on his desk. The MD plates Carl had slipped into the chrome frames affixed to the bumpers was his idea of whimsy.

"Sit tight Matt," he chuckled, "Doctor Carl is coming to make a house call." A model of respectability, he carefully slid into northbound traffic, driving sedately, a man of medicine on a mission of mercy.

A frazzled young mother pulled alongside and stared with unabashed envy at the well-groomed man in the opulent import while they waited for a traffic light to change. Four hyperactive young boys bounced around in the back of her dented Plymouth Voyager like Ping-Pong balls in a wind tunnel. Carl cast a benevolent, knowing smile at the harried woman. She returned it as an embarrassed grin, a wordless what-can-you-do?

Carl had an urge to follow her home. He preferred killing women. He could do it with so much more intimacy. The touch of a woman in those delicious final moments was exhilarating. Most of the women he had murdered had been done bare handed or with contact weapons. The thought of such intimacy with men was repugnant. He had almost always shot men, at close range if possible. He liked to see every aspect of his work—the frustration and hopelessness in the last seconds when they knew they were going to die—the shock when the gun blasted a hole in their future—the pain—especially the pain. And the blood, that was the best. Carl loved the scent, the color, and the taste of fresh blood. His eyes glazed over remembering the blood. He'd left it splashed across fifteen states since he had set out on his mission.

Training. That was how he thought of the wanton rampage he had begun after finding the old man's stash in Colorado. Traveling aimlessly, he had picked targets of opportunity whenever and wherever they presented themselves until he'd lost count. What were there? Three dozen unsolved homicides? Maybe a few more or less. It didn't matter. He would check his files when he got a chance.

He wondered, not for the first time since he had resumed killing, how he had abstained during the years in Colorado. Was it the serenity of the setting? The climate? He thought it probably had more to do with the old man. Why, he couldn't imagine. But the need to kill had abated for a time. The old man's death had reawakened it. He thought of that stage in his life as his cocoon phase, awaiting final metamorphosis. Now he was in the adult stage—the consummate predator.

There was still that other thing he had to address. What to do next? Everything before had been preparation for this. The thrill of purpose added so much more to the hunt. Focus: that was the key to meaning. Hate: that was fuel for the flames. It made the toil and attention to detail so much more pleasurable. Who could he hate with such passion when the six were dead? Cops? No. Cops were merely an amusing sideline. Taunting them with his clever traps simply added flavor to the six, to make them memorable, apart from the rest. To hunt them alone would belittle the six. Whatever came after must be different. But this would be hard to top.

Impatient honking from a taxicab behind him brought him out of his reverie. Carl started. The light had changed. The woman in the Voyager was half a block away, fading in a cloud of blue exhaust.

"Concentrate," he commanded himself. Instantly back in character, he waved an apology at the cab driver and received a single digit salute in return. He ignored the insult and reminded himself there would be time enough to worry about the future when the mission was done. There would have to be another mission. He pressed the accelerator pedal. This was too good to end.

ↄↄ

Madeline Maclear gulped the last of her steaming mug of coffee while she put the finishing touches to the hint of makeup she allowed herself for work. The one-bedroom apartment she had rented, just five blocks from the hospital and upstairs from a sweet elderly couple, was still a mess. Her drive and fervor to start anew had waned in the two weeks since she had moved out of her home in Garden City. It had been impulsive, she had to admit, but necessary. Paul's memories lived in that house like persistent ghosts. There were too many little things to set her off. The sticking front door lock that he had never gotten around to replacing. The kitchen table, scratched where he carved his sandwiches. Oil stains in the garage from that tired old mower he refused to throw out. The place vibrated with his life force, both good memories and bad. Regret lurked in every corner.

He was gone. That was that. Nothing could bring him back. She would love him forever, but she was still here and he was not.

"You've got to be practical," he would have said. "Face facts. Go from here." If only he had followed his own advice.

The ache in her middle caused her hands to shake. Through tear filled eyes, she blinked at her ruined lipstick, snatched a tissue from the box, dabbed her eyes and wiped her mouth clean.

"Now look what you made me do." She sighed, exasperated, and laughed through her pain. "Same old me, Paul, blaming you. Did you know how I loved you? Even when I hated you?"

She shook her head, picked up the brush and paused with her hand poised to reapply the ruined lip liner.

"Oh, to hell with it." She tossed the brush onto the vanity. "It's been more than a year, dammit. Little Maddy's got to grow up." She pressed her long fingers together in a prayerful pose and placed them to her lips. Squeezing a tear from her eyelids, she inhaled sharply, stood, snatched her purse from atop the dresser, and headed for the door.

She locked the apartment, trotted down the steps, knocked on her landlord's door as she passed it at the bottom, and sang out, "Going to work, Mister and Misses D."

The two old dears worried like a second set of parents. At first their meddling had dismayed her until she realized that it was genuine concern. They watched her every move out of caring. Their protective hovering seemed sweet, once she had gotten used to it. It was nice not to be all alone, and she didn't mind letting them know of her comings and goings. She wondered if they would approve of her bringing a man home.

She stopped as she locked the outside door. What made me think of that? Detective Wiley's smile came to mind. Smooth bastard. God, I'm horny.

Looking at the sky, she was thankful the daylight hours were getting longer. The nights were long enough.

ぐつぐつ

Carl hummed merrily as he unloaded the trunk of the Beamer. He tossed his loafers and socks into the carpeted cavity and stepped into comfortable deck shoes, making little smoke-like puffs swirl around his feet in the powdery soil.

The marina was one of his favorite places. Fresh air, tinged with the smells of the sea, the bell chime of halyards on aluminum masts and the sensation of being on the brink of adventure always engulfed him here.

"Goin' out, Doctor Bauer?" The weathered wrinkles in the dock master's face looked like folded leather when he smiled.

"Righto, Cliff. I thought I'd try my luck with the snappers." Carl flashed even teeth at the nosy old salt.

"Keep an eye on the weather, sir. Wind picks up suddenly this time of year."

"I will. Wish me luck."

"Luck." Cliff waved over his shoulder as he shambled back to his tiny office on the sea wall.

With a large, heavy nylon sports bag on his shoulder, two assembled fishing poles in his hand, and a tackle box held by two fingers, Carl walked, sure-footed, down the steep incline of the rolling gangway. He strode along the floating wooden finger to his boat, which was neatly tied two slips from the end, and tossed his gear aboard.

The twenty-foot Shamrock was built for speed and maneuverability. Its cuddy cabin and canvas covered pilot station took up coveted space that serious sport fishermen would have shunned. For Carl's purpose, they provided needed privacy.

He had bought the boat from a real doctor who was leaving the country for a dream job in a Swiss clinic. He had had no trouble convincing the naive and eager young medico to leave the paperwork to him. Cash in hand, the impatient MD had handed over the registration and immediately forgotten the sleek little vessel, his mind on his bright future. Carl had simply closed out the former owner's account at the south shore haven where the young doctor had moored his craft and sailed out Jones Inlet into the Atlantic. The long trip around the West End, up the East River, and into Long Island Sound, had been good experience and fun. Like most things he put his mind to, Carl had mastered handling the speedy craft in no time. Papers in hand, along with hard cash, he had no trouble securing a slip in the marina of his choice. It was well sheltered, set back in a quiet cove and predominantly populated by large cabin cruisers and sailing yachts. Berthed among the giants, Carl's modest twenty-footer went practically unnoticed by the snooty yacht owners. It was a truism that the bigger the boat, the less frequent the voyage, and Carl was gratified to see that his fellow yachtsman tended to ignore him and his puny craft. They left him out of their floating cocktail parties and that suited him.

With his gear stowed, Carl flushed the bilge and started the engine. The powerful inboard roared to life. He slipped the lines from the cleats on the dock and backed her out into the canal. Keeping his speed down to five miles per hour to prevent any damaging wake in the confines of the marina, he pointed the prow toward open water. When far enough into the channel, he pushed the throttle forward until the bow rose out of the water and the stern settled in, the prop pushing the boat at a steady twelve knots. He was in no hurry. The sun was low on the horizon, but it was still a few hours from darkness. With his right hand resting on the wheel, he dug into a brown paper bag with his left and pulled out a thick, ham and cheese sandwich on a Kaiser roll with plenty of mustard. Balancing the white paper wrapped sandwich in his lap, he popped the tab of a Diet Pepsi and settled in for a relaxing cruise to his destination.

Until sundown, he had to maintain the appearance of a recreational boater so there was nothing to do until then. After dark, he'd continue the mission. Munching his dinner, he enjoyed the salt breeze on his face and tossed crumbs to hungry gulls.

This was living.

Chapter 11

What kind of friggin' maniac have we got running around out there?" the chief of detectives' bellowing roar could be clearly heard in the executive suite hallway when Doc and Tony stepped from the elevator.

"Welcome to headquarters," Tony said, standing aside, "this should be fun."

With a backhand wave and a shallow bow, he politely suggested that Doc precede him. A fluorescent light blinked in a recessed fixture above them. To Doc, the intermittent flashing was an SOS.

"Chicken," Doc said, pushing the glass doors to the chief's reception area open and reaching into his jacket for his badge. Flipping the case open, he smiled at the pretty receptionist. "Detectives Wiley and Cordova to see the chief."

The hint of circles under her eyes and the few hairs out of place in her usually impeccable coiffure were signposts declaring the abnormality of the situation this evening. Overtime for the chief's secretary was a rare and unwelcome occurrence. The cool light of unassailable power that greeted those misfortunates summoned to the ivory tower was lacking this evening in her tired eyes.

"Go right in," was the best she could do.

Lieutenant Schiff sprang from his seat, welcoming the detectives in a manner resembling a man about to be rescued from a slow, painful death.

"Hello, Doc. Hello, Tony. Thanks for coming so quickly," he said, pumping their hands. His palm was clammy.

"We were in the neighborhood," Tony mumbled.

"Sit, gentlemen," Chief Needleman ordered, attempting a smile of greeting but failing miserably.

It was said that the chief had been born without the facial muscles to create a genuine smile. Doc didn't believe it, but he could see how the myth had come to be. The chief made no attempt to offer his hand or any hospitality beyond a place to sit. His florid complexion was a few shades darker than Doc remembered from previous encounters, attributable, no doubt, to the pressure being exerted on his already overtaxed blood vessels.

"Do we have anything concrete on this wacko yet?" the chief was saying even before they landed in their respective chairs.

Doc realized, with no small degree of discomfort, that the question had been directed at him. Tony and the lieutenant looked expectant, leaning forward in their seats. The chief, still standing, awaited a positive response.

"No, sir," Doc said.

The hopeful looks became frowns, which degenerated into woeful stares of disapproval. Wagging heads surrounded Doc. Even Tony adopted the air of an aggrieved parent, mimicking his superiors. Doc was appalled by the overt blame intrinsic in the looks from his bosses. He felt betrayed by his friend's siding with the brass until the glint in Tony's eye became apparent.

The smartass little bastard was laughing at him and the other two were so embroiled in their panic they didn't see it.

"It's too early in our investigation to report any solid leads," Doc fudged. "The connection between the murders is obvious," he continued, but realized he had nowhere to go. His mind galloped but could not find a way out of the blind alley he was headed down so he let his mouth run, hoping his own words would prompt his brain to inspiration. "By this, I mean the methods employed. We have nothing to suggest a connection between the victims other than their gender." He toyed with and discarded the an-arrest-is-imminent cliché. They would ask what led him to that conclusion and he didn't have anywhere to go with it. The brick wall at the end of the imagined alley was about to smack him in the kisser.

"The explosive devices lead you to this conclusion," the chief said, profoundly stating the obvious.

Doc took comfort in that. "Of course," he said. "The modus operandi is too…uh…unusual to be coincidental."

"Of course," Chief Needleman said.

"Of course," Tony echoed.

Doc shot Tony an unmistakable I'll-get-you-for-this glare that Needleman missed as his mind raced to frame his next question. Tony's eyebrows shot up, innocence itself.

"We have some new information from the ME's office," Lieutenant Schiff said. All eyes shifted to him. He cleared his throat. "They found fragments of a mouse trap in the rib cage of the Kohler woman in Oyster Bay, along with bits of wire and what appears to be the remains of a blasting cap. ATF reports residue from the explosive is consistent with plastique. The Bomb Squad thinks the thing went off when her body was moved."

"A mouse trap?" Doc was incredulous. "You're saying this guy made a pressure release mine out of a mousetrap?"

"That's what they think," Schiff nodded, his lips compressed in a thin line.

"The one in Garden City sounds like the same kind of deal," Doc thought aloud. "It was spring loaded, a variation on the same mechanism."

"More evidence that the two were connected," the chief deduced.

"But why?" Schiff asked. "What's the connection?"

"When we know why, we'll be closer to who," Doc said.

The rest of the meeting involved logistical planning: areas of responsibility, manpower, scope of the investigation, and the urgency to catch the killer, or killers. Everyone went back to breathing in and out without conscious effort, now that the chief's initial demands for substantive responses relaxed.

Terrorism was considered as a motive and ruled out, for the moment. No one had claimed responsibility. No demands had been made. The victims were not prominent or politically active. The possibility of a non-political motive was discussed. They all looked with horror at Doc when he suggested that the murdered women might be bait and the officials who would be inevitably summoned to the scene could be the killer's actual targets. He also pointed out that the murderer's reasons might have no basis in logic at all. Doc verbalized the worst-case scenario. A nut was slaughtering innocent people for the hell of it and taking as many cops with them as he could. Random killers, he reminded them, are the toughest to catch.

Speculation was made on whether to enlist the aid of the FBI and any and all agencies and organizations with serial killer profile information. No firm decision was made in that regard. Inter-agency cooperation is always a last resort in law enforcement. No self-respecting government agency likes to ask for help from outside its jurisdiction. The implied inadequacy can shake the foundations of power, and when the foundation jiggles, the uppermost parts of the structure tend to topple.

No one was willing to utter what all of them knew was the sad truth, like a childish superstition which, once spoken, might summon the evil it foretold. The killer would probably strike again before any kind of pattern emerged, assuming he had not already completed his unknown agenda.

A stenographer was called. Memoranda were drafted and sent for distribution to all law enforcement agencies in the county. No one was to disturb anything found at the scene of any homicide or suspected homicide until further notice. The Bomb Squad was to be called immediately upon discovery of any corpse.

It was half-past midnight when the meeting broke up. The detectives walked across the street to get a burger and a beer at a restaurant they avoided during the day because of its popularity among lawyers. The kitchen was closed so they settled for the beer and a few mouthfuls of bar snacks before going home. Exhausted, Doc collapsed into his bed at two a.m. without bothering to undress and without so much as a glance at his sculpture studio. Before dropping off, he looked around his apartment in the glow filtering through the blinds from a street lamp too close to his window. The net gain of his lonely life consisted of some cheap furniture, a nineteen-inch color TV, a few sports trophies, photographs, and memorabilia. Piled against one bare wall were dozens of twice read books he kept promising himself to arrange on shelves he had bought, but never installed. So many plans made, but never carried out. So many missed opportunities. So much junk.

He wondered briefly what Madeline Maclear was doing just then. He pictured her curling up with a handsome boyfriend and sighed.

He set his alarm for seven a.m. The other dicks working the case would inform him and Tony of further developments in the morning or—he hoped not—as they broke.

Sleep came quickly, but his beleaguered mind refused to rest. He was in the jungle again. Berryhill was bleeding again. They were in the stream. The VC girl was coming. He knew it, but he could not change the outcome. The dream always ended the same way, with Berryhill dead but still accusing him, the VC's bayonet stuck deep in his own back and death preventing him from answering his friend's condemnation.

It wasn't my fault. Was it?

Chapter 12

Carl cruised past the object of his voyage but barely glanced at the mini-mansion atop the cliff. A half-mile further on, he tossed out the anchor and went through the motions of rigging lures and casting his line before he settled down on the engine hatch cover to assume the role of the patient angler. When darkness engulfed him, he switched on his anchor light to avoid any chance encounter with patrolling Coast Guard vessels and resumed fishing. He wanted to avoid even a cursory safety inspection.

After two hours of this charade, he reeled in his line then dislodged and hauled in the anchor. With the engine running at dead slow, he came about and motored back to the vicinity of the house on the precipice. A quarter of a mile short of his target he doused his running lights, turned ninety degrees to port, and throttled back until the trim craft barely made way against the current.

When the shapes of trees blacker than the sky alerted him to his proximity to the shoreline, he cut the engine and drifted into a tiny, dogleg cove that offered concealment. Carl let the gentle breeze push the boat into the narrow passage formed between the wooded finger jutting into Long Island Sound and the main island. The action of the tide slowed his momentum to a stop and then threatened to counteract his drift. He used a boat hook on an eight-foot pole to push along the bottom until he was nearly to the crotch of the little cove where he set the anchor flukes without so much as a splash.

Carl's pupils strained to gather light. The night was black as a tomb. He congratulated himself on his careful timing of every phase of his plan. This night had been selected for his assault on Matt because of the absence of any moon. Darkness was an old friend and trusted ally.

With the boat secure, he crawled into the cabin, curled up on the cushions of a narrow bunk, set his wind-up travel alarm next to his ear, and pulled a down-filled sleeping bag up to his neck. He was asleep in minutes, rocked in the arms of gentle waves lapping at the hull.

The alarm buzzed at two a.m. Carl, instantly awake, snapped it off. He stretched, yawned, unzipped the bag, and undressed. With the cabin door closed, the forward hatch dogged, and the portholes duct-taped, he lit a portable battery-operated lantern. By its light, he unpacked his gear from the sports bag and wriggled into a black neoprene wetsuit and hood.

While he changed, Carl mused about the little frustrations one encountered when purchasing gear for an operation. The diving enthusiasts of the day were enamored of bright colors as fashionable trim on their scuba togs, so gaily-trimmed wetsuits were all that the stores stocked. Solid black was essential to his night camouflage, and he had spent an inordinate amount of time shopping for that one item. Dogged determination had eventually paid off and he had found what he needed in a shop in Bay Shore. The solid black high-top sneakers had been easier to procure. These, and a pair of woolen socks, also black, he placed in a zip-lock plastic bag, which he hung around his neck with a cord. A diver's knife, with a striking resemblance to the famous K-bar combat knife, went into a sheath strapped to his calf. Next, he wrapped an Army surplus pistol belt around his waist and adjusted the keeper to a snug fit. The belt had been olive green from the factory but Carl had died it black. To the belt he fastened a rubber ring to hold a waterproof flashlight, a watertight tool pouch and another zip-lock bag containing a silenced Beretta .22 semi-automatic and spare clip of ammunition. The weapon was a favorite of the navy SEALs and Carl had been thrilled to find it among the weapons in the old man's arsenal. He extracted the last item from the big nylon carryall, a small backpack of the same black nylon, similar to the type children use to carry their books to school. The contents of Carl's pack were far more sinister than any grade school child's innocuous load.

He smeared black grease paint in streaks on his exposed face. He could have rubbed it in evenly to hide every trace of flesh but he wanted to look like a commando, not the straight man in a minstrel show. Finally, he stretched tight rubber diving gloves over his fingers. Mentally inventorying his gear, he gave himself a thumbs-up and clicked off the light. In total darkness, Carl waited a full five minutes for his night vision to return. The smell of mildew, bilge fumes, grease paint, and sweat were intoxicating in the confined space. He felt completely alive; a sensation reminiscent of jungle combat. The only thing missing was the sickly-sweet odor of blood. That would come soon.

The cool night air heightened his exhilaration when he emerged from the cabin. The time in the pitch-black interior had produced its desired effect. In comparison, the dark night was only slightly hindering to his darting eyes. With feline grace, Carl walked the gunwale to the bow where he slipped into the water while holding fast to a half-inch line secured to the guardrail. The water was up to his armpits when his bare feet touched bottom. It was icy cold and took his breath away. The shallow draft of the Shamrock was another plus in the boat's design. The keel rode well off the bottom, even in this shallow cove. He let out the coil of rope as he plodded to the shore, slipping on algae slick rocks. He had to hurry before his feet cramped in the freezing water but he took pains to set them firmly with each step. It would not do to turn an ankle.

Wading ashore, he selected a stout pine tree near the water's edge, looped the rope around the trunk, and fashioned a sturdy knot. He would be humiliated should he return to find his escape foiled for lack of his boat.

One last look around assured him that the Shamrock was invisible to the casual observer. He slipped into the socks, grateful for their warmth, pulled on the sneakers and began his trek along the rock-strewn shoreline to his objective.

ᏣᏣ

Matt Bradley yawned and rubbed his eyes. The image on the thirty-two-inch television screen blurred and he blinked several times to regain focus.

"Falling asleep," he mumbled, squinting at his watch. "Better go to bed."

He decided to finish his snifter of brandy before turning in. In minutes, he was absorbed once again in the movie playing on his TV. It was a favorite of his: True Believer, starring James Woods as a jaded, middle-aged shyster complete with graying ponytail, forced into a reawakening of his principles and defending for once, a truly innocent man.

Matt could not help but reminisce on his own idealistic passion as a young man. He had set out to save the world. Exactly when he had forsaken the holy quest, he could not be certain.

The front page of today's paper had stirred memories of lost youth. Dotty was dead, strangled by some unknown assailant. Funny, he hadn't given her a thought in…what? Twenty years?

That was one crazy broad. She must have balled half the male population of Long Island in her day, including him. What a way to end up—choked to death and then blown to bits. Who could do such a thing? The cops would find out eventually. He wondered if his indifference to her passing could be a symptom of his decline from the lofty attitude of righteous indignation he had attained as a teenager. More like the erosion of time on the rough edges of innocence, he decided. Shit happens. Where he had gotten the idea that he could make a difference, in the larger sense anyway, he didn't know. He didn't regret his life's choices but he was aware of a peripheral guilt, like some forgotten important detail.

A swig from the balloon glass warmed his innards, melting the chill of remorse. The laughing faces of long forgotten high school and college acquaintances swam before his mind's eye.

"Those were the days," he told James Woods.

But what did he have to moon about? He had done pretty well for himself and his family. His bleary gaze took in rich surroundings. The high ceilinged, Victorian home that his wife loved so much was really something to be proud of. And Linda. What more could a man want in a mate? Beautiful, charming, smart, a tigress in bed even after all these years and most of all, his best friend. Matt glanced at the graceful archway framed in massive bent oak leading from the den into the hall and at the balustrade of the broad staircase. He mentally climbed the steps and pictured his wife snuggled under the covers, sleeping peacefully above him. Maybe he should awaken her. Show her that he still had it in him.

Matt sipped the fiery, amber liquid, pulled his silk robe tighter around him, and drifted back to years gone by.

He came out of college full of piss and vinegar, ready to take on the world. Unsure where to start he soon climbed back into the scholastic womb as a graduate student. He opted for the law as the foundation of his crusade. If the system stank, those who were best suited to change it should do so. He had dreams of pounding a desk in the halls of Congress, making them see the light. Mr. Deeds, a.k.a. Bradley, goes to Washington. Hah!

The impatience of youth and a hunger for the finer material rewards soon had him wavering in his battle to save the masses. A job as a law clerk exposed a gift for digging into hidden details in complicated litigation and a wealthy client wooed him away from his chosen path. Impressed with young Matt's talents, he groomed him as an insurance investigator to guard against fraudulent claims by larcenous policyholders. Once he had proven his abilities, Matt requested and was granted compensation based on a percentage of recovered assets.

Ten years ago, he had gone freelance, made a modest fortune in a very short time, and bought this house, repaying Linda's confident patience.

They had also raised a lovely daughter along the way. Beatrice would be coming home from college for spring break before long. He missed his little girl, although it was becoming harder to think of the ravishing young beauty as a baby.

Yes, he had done all right. Life was good.

He heard a thump. Was that upstairs, or outside? He listened, holding his breath. Probably nothing. James Woods had the jury's rapt attention on the TV screen. It was almost over. He glanced again at his watch and decided to stay up for the finale. He'd sleep in tomorrow, and work from home in the afternoon. What the hell, he'd earned a break.

ꕥ

The climb up the nearly vertical, sandy cliff had been taxing. Carl lay panting in the weeds at the top. The white, split rail fence—more a reminder to the careless of the sharp drop beyond than any kind of barrier to intrusion—was within arm's reach. When his respiration slowed to a near normal rate, he checked his gear to insure he had lost nothing in the ascent and crawled under the lower rail. His pulse pounded in his ears. He stopped to scrutinize the target.

Everything was as expected. The house was dark except for a shimmering light in the den. It changed color and intensity with sudden pulses of energy.

TV set, he concluded. Someone was watching late night cable. Playboy channel? One could only hope. How nice it would be to find the esteemed Mr. and Mrs. Bradley enjoying a carnal interlude.

Sticking to the plan, Carl slithered across the broad lawn and around the side of the house in a smooth, relentless alligator crawl. The back porch was inviting but Carl knew the easy ways would be electronically monitored. When he reached a point midway along the north wall, he rolled into the mulch beneath the landscaped bushes to shuck his pack.

Listening for any sound foreign to the rhythm of the night, he extracted a rubber-coated grappling hook and a coil of rope from the backpack before he slipped the straps back onto his shoulders. Walking crablike to a spot several feet from the wall, he twirled the hook like a lasso and flung it to the roof. It caught the ornate iron fencing that graced the edge of the cornice on the first toss. Carl tested the purchase of its hold with a firm tug on the rope. Satisfied, he climbed the clapboard wall, lifting his weight with his powerful arms, walking perpendicular to the vertical face and silently setting his feet as he rose. He reached the second-floor bathroom window easily, looped the rope around his left wrist, and checked the window with his free hand. It opened with ease, barely making a sound. He was inside in seconds. "She Came In Through The Bathroom Window" played as background music in his mind.

Carl crossed the marble checkerboard floor in one fluid motion and paused to listen at the partially opened door. He grinned a devilish grin in the dark. It had been child's play to breach the Bradleys' expensive security system. Even with all his money, Matt had not been able to resist the temptation to save a few bucks. A second story window above a sheer wall had not only been neglected when they wired the house, it wasn't even locked. How predictable were these hypocritical bastions of the community.

Hearing nothing but indistinct dialogue from the television, Carl advanced into the hall.

"I'm in," he mouthed to an imaginary radio mic, "proceeding to primary objective."

This was by far the best scenario he had planned. All of the elements of a covert assault were in play. He hadn't had this much fun since Cambodia. He was showing them all what they had done to themselves by not allowing him to attain his destiny. If he could not fight for them, he would fight against them. He was a killing machine. These six, self-centered, oblivious morons had sidetracked him. They had done it without so much as a second thought, careless of the consequences of their actions. Now they were learning the price of their folly. He was back and collecting the debt.

Carl found the master bedroom at the head of the stairs exactly where the plans in the archives had shown it to be. Matt had made it easy for him when he bought a house with public access to its historical origins. He tried the knob. The door glided open on oiled hinges.

There was one sleeping form in the huge four-poster bed. The spray of long, curly, strawberry blonde hair on the pillow, shining dully in the trapezoid of light escaping the slightly ajar door of the master's bath, established the identity of the lone sleeper. Mrs. B. The insomniac video watcher had to be Matt. Carl wiggled gloved fingers at the sleeping woman and mouthed, "I'll be right back, darling," and eased the door shut.

Carl crept to the stairs and descended, gliding like mist down a mountain. He saw the back of his quarry's head nestled against the headrest of a big, leather recliner as soon as his field of view cleared the ceiling. He paused to stifle a laugh. Male pattern baldness made Matt a ridiculous caricature of his youthful good looks, ala Peter Fonda. He recalled with vivid clarity a pompous, young Matthew Bradley pontificating for his doting compatriots on the destiny of the children of Aquarius. He also remembered the nasty grin as Matt left him lying in a muddy ditch when the acid trip turned bad. He left Carl pissing in his pants, frightened out of his mind of conjured beasts that clutched at him from every angle.

He walked the rest of the way with his eyes locked on his prey, the gun held loosely in his fist, leveled at his target.

"That you, honey?" Matt said, as Carl entered the room. Some sixth sense, its acuity dulled by evolution and a false aura of civilization, was warning him of another human presence.

Cold steel pressed against Matt's ear.

"Not a peep or I'll blow your old lady's tits off," Carl said.

Matt gasped then clamped his mouth tightly shut as the implications of the threat registered. He froze.

Carl circled the tufted red leather recliner until he stood in front of Matt, whose eyes grew wide at the sight of the black clad figure, and wider still at the sight of the gun.

"Surprised to see me, old friend?" Carl grinned, teeth bared, wolf-like.

“Do I know you?” Matt’s eyes danced, flitting from the intruder’s face, to the gun, to the knife hilt on Carl’s leg, and then taking in the entire image, starting at the toes and rising to stare aghast at the black streaked face.

“Remember Woodstock?” The eyebrows above the shining eyes arched. “You left me for dead.”

The lost expression on Matt’s face enraged Carl.

“Was I so insignificant that you really don’t remember? Were you so stoned that you don’t recall your arrogance?”

Matt’s mouth dropped open. His jaw hung slack.

“Honey, who are you talking to? Is someone here?” They heard Matt’s wife; her voice drugged by sleep.

Carl raised the gun to point it at Matt’s face, the threat plain in the silent snarl on his lips. He saw bare feet beneath a flowing powder blue dressing gown descending the stairs. A graceful, manicured hand slid along the polished banister rail.

Linda stooped to peer below the ceiling, trying to see whom her husband was having a conversation with at this late hour. The sight of Carl in his commando garb startled her. Her hand went to her mouth.

Carl raised the pistol and fired. Matt saw a flash from the muzzle and started, shocked by the coughing sound the silenced weapon made as it jumped in Carl’s hand. There was a noise like a hammer hitting bone, a grunt, and then the unmistakable rumble of a body tumbling down steps.

“Nooo!” Matt shrieked and leaped from his chair.

Instantly, Carl dropped his sights and fired again, his blazing eyes following the track of the muzzle. The bullet slammed into Matt’s abdomen. He slowed, but staggered forward, the force of his momentum carrying him toward his wife’s murderer.

Momentarily regretting having chosen a weapon with so little stopping power, Carl lowered his aim further and squeezed off another shot. The round shattered Matt’s left kneecap and toppled him to the floor. Writhing on the Persian carpet, Matt could see the foot of the stairs and the body of his beloved crumpled in a heap on the hardwood floor. Tears streamed from his eyes as he turned to Carl, the silent question burning in them as plain as a scream.

“Because you’re a prick,” Carl said. Almost casually, he stood astride the broken shell of a man on the floor. The slim automatic bucked in his hand again as it spat another projectile. Matt’s head bounced once as the bullet punched through his temple and the energy caused his skull to recoil.

Carl held the imaginary radio handset to his mouth and whispered, "Subject terminated with extreme prejudice. Out."

He dropped one shoulder. The backpack fell to the floor. Quickly, he dumped its contents on the rug and selecting one item from the pile of materials that tumbled out, moved to the gas fireplace. A remote-control wand left on the mantelpiece ignited the flames beneath the carved lava logs. Carl thrust the branding iron into the heat and sang, "Burn baby burn," until the metal glowed red. When the tool was sufficiently hot, he danced to Matt's body, still singing, and applied the glowing end to the dead man's cheek, chuckling as the skin hissed and smoked.

Setting the rod in an ashtray to cool, he scooped up the remaining articles from the floor, being careful to retrieve the shell casings from the Beretta, and dashed into the hall, to the body of Linda Bradley. He hauled her lifeless form onto the stairs and arranged it on its back on the steps. The neat round hole in her forehead paid tribute to his hours of practice with the pistol in the marshes of Staten Island. After spreading her thighs, he stood a Claymore mine on its flat metal legs on the stairs, in front of her crotch. To the back of the plastic mine he taped a hand grenade using strips from a roll of electrical tape. Warily, he eased the pin from the grenade, stopping just short of releasing the spoon. He had replaced the four-second fuse with the instantaneous primer from a smoke grenade—a little trick from the jungle.

Next, he tied a length of monofilament to the ring and ran it to the knob on the front door, leaving some slack. He flipped off the porch lights outside at the foyer switch and, with a swing of the gun barrel, smashed the etched-glass swag lantern hanging by a brass chain from the cathedral ceiling in the foyer. When he had double checked to be sure he had thought of everything, he opened the front door a few inches, checked the line of sight from the opening, took up the slack in his trip wire and wound it around the door knob.

The silent alarm showed the unauthorized breach of its net by a flashing red indicator light in the control panel near the door. Carl had tripped the house alarm twice in the past. Once with a stone from a slingshot fired through the kitchen window, and again, a few weeks later, by fraying the telephone line. Each time, the local private police had taken twenty minutes to respond.

Skipping merrily into the den, he snatched the branding iron from its resting-place, tapped it with his fingers to be certain it had cooled, and jammed it in his belt.

He ran to the steps, vaulted over Linda's corpse, and stopped. Looking down, he bent over the body. Holding fast to the banister with one gloved hand, he deftly draped the hems of the dead woman's nightgown over the deadly mine with the other.

"Voila." He giggled and raced to the same window he had used to gain entry.

He rappelled down the rope, bounced on the balls of his feet at the bottom, snapped the line once, caught the grappling hook one handed as it fell, then ran across the yard to the fence. There, he anchored the rope to a post and repeated the method he had used to exit the house. He was long gone when the security patrol arrived, blue light spinning atop their white compact car.

Seeing the front door open and the sprawled figure of the lady of the house on the stairs beyond as they played flashlight beams over the scene, the officers charged through the door, guns drawn.

They never heard the deafening roar that signaled the end of their lives as the seven hundred steel balls in the Claymore shredded their young bodies and the attached grenade nearly obliterated the mistress of the manor, whom they had meant to save.

ഗഗ

Doc pounded on his alarm clock until it fell from the nightstand. The nerve-jangling ringing persisted. It was intermittent and louder than the familiar buzz he was accustomed to arousing him. He wondered if he had dealt the clock a disabling blow. Half asleep, he sincerely hoped so, but he would have been far more pleased to immobilize the clanging monster entirely.

That rude interruption of peace known as consciousness nagged at him until it won out and his mind cleared enough to allow logical thought to resume.

The dream had rendered even his sub-conscious mind too winded to hang on, having weakened his grasp on guilt an hour before. The phone was the merciless disturber of his blissful respite. Barbara? She hadn't called back since she had left the messages after the Kohler murder.

Doc's eyelids fluttered and he squinted to see the illuminated hands of the clock. It wasn't there of course. He had just put it down for the count. His hand slapped the receiver of the bedside telephone and his clumsy fingers dragged it from the cradle. Jerking the handset to the pillow beside his head, he tucked it into his ear and coughed into the mouthpiece.

"Wiley. What?"

"Reveille, good buddy. Up and at 'em."

"What the—Tony?" Doc rolled over and fished around on the floor until he found the capsized alarm clock. "It's barely five in the goddamn morning. What the hell do you want?"

"My, my. Aren't we testy before we have our coffee?"

Doc could see the grin on his friend's face. "This better be good."

"Anything but. Splash some cold water on your face and drag your ugly ass up to Glen Cove. We got another one."

Alert as if a switch had been thrown, Doc sat bolt upright in bed. "Give me the address," he ordered, snapping on the light and scrabbling for a pencil on the night table.

Tony read it to him from his own note, hastily scribbled from the message he had just received from an excited desk sergeant at his precinct. Doc repeated it back to him.

"You got it. See you there. Oh, and Doc…"

"Yeah?"

"Do yourself a favor, don't eat breakfast."

The line went dead before Wiley could comment.

Chapter 13

Madeline had no desire to go home. She had spent the night in her office to be close to Doctor Green and his children, gotten only a total of forty-five minutes of sleep in short naps on her office sofa and now wandered the halls, debating with herself whether or not her stomach would tolerate solid food if she braved the cafeteria for breakfast.

A payphone across from the elevators triggered a thought. She should call the Dietrich's and let them know she was all right, but she didn't have the strength to field the barrage of questions Mrs. D would surely have. She leaned wearily against the wall beside the public phone to gaze at the new coat of semi-gloss, pastel paint.

Lilac. Ugh! They finally get around to painting this dump and they hire the decorator from Hell.

Her train of thought made a connection. She recalled the giddy delirium she and Paul had enjoyed while decorating their home in Garden City. The silliness of matching swatches, paint chips, and scraps of wallpaper seemed so childish now. At the time, she and Paul had been almost desperate to get it right, to make a statement all their own. She knew now that their love had been the most important thing in their lives, not the house, or the stuff to fill it up. She regretted their decision to wait to have children. If they had tried to start a family sooner, they might have been able to do something about it. Paul had reacted badly to the news when the doctors told him his sperm count was to blame. That was when his issues about Vietnam first manifested. From that point on, he was almost bi-polar. He was either angry and withdrawn or more loving than she deserved. It was as if he could compensate for his mood swings and inability to make babies by making money. They were probably the only couple to ever fight about having too much money.

Why did you have to lose what was important before you recognized it for what it was? Why did Marjorie Green have to die so horribly just when she had begun to live? Why should that poor woman's loving husband and those sweet little girls have to suffer so? Why wasn't she the one lying in the morgue? It was her house. If she had not succumbed to self-pity, she would still be living there.

No, she wouldn't. She would be with Paul and Marjorie would still be with Ben.

Madeline stared at the ceiling as if trying to see through the plaster, concrete, and steel. She wanted to look into the face of the callous God who had let this happen, to demand an explanation. Tears burned her eyes. With a moan, she pushed herself from the wall and stood shaking with rage.

"Damn You," she spat. She dug in her lab coat pocket for a tissue, dabbed at her eyes, and wiped her nose. "Not now, Maddy," she whispered to the empty hallway. "Doctor Green and the kids need you. You can fall apart later."

The doctor and his daughters had been sedated. Benjamin Green, after learning of his wife's murder, had managed to hold himself together just long enough to be driven home, where he attempted to comfort his distraught children. The police had, at his insistence, shown him his wife's remains. He stumbled, trancelike through their questions, answering in monosyllabic grunts. There was no one to care for the girls. They were new in the neighborhood. He had no relatives within driving distance.

The concerned administration staff of Oyster Bay Hospital had sent an ambulance and a team of volunteer physicians and nurses to bring the shattered family back to the hospital where they could be cared for and watched over in their grief.

The kids were in Pediatrics. Doctor Green was just down the hall in a private room. All were mercifully asleep through chemically induced means. Madeline wanted to be there for them when they awoke; to comfort; to console; to share in their grief; and to apologize.

Chapter 14

Sean O'Hara popped the disk from the CD player built into the dashboard of his brand new, fully loaded, candy-apple red, Chevy Camaro.

Buy American—that had been Sean's motto ever since he had adopted this rich land. The payments were a stretch on his salary, but the satisfaction of flaunting his first taste of luxury in front of his brother-in-law made the sacrifice sweet. His sister's spouse would eat his words one day. The gall of that pompous ass, calling him—Sean Thomas O'Hara—shanty Irish. Someday, when he owned his own little pub, he vowed to publicly belittle his brother-in-law. It would do his heart good to see the Polack bastard eat his words.

Sean was still savoring his future triumph when he unlocked the door of Greg Collins' Chez Laughs. A long way from his intended aspirations, his job as manager of the sluggish club was the first step toward what he envisioned as a stellar career. Mister Collins was not the easiest man to work for but, to be fair, he had given Sean a job when jobs were scarce, especially for an unskilled immigrant. Sean's fictional tale of his prowess as the maitre'd of one of Dublin's busiest nightspots had been sufficient background for Collins. Mutual need and Collins' frugal distaste for international phone bills precluded Greg from delving too deeply into Sean's resume. The extent of Collins's pre-employment background check had been a blunt, "You wouldn't bullshit me, would you?"

Chez Laughs' potential as an emerging in spot was questionable. In fact, Collins had no hope of hiring anyone with the level of experience and credentials he deceived himself that the young Irishman had. However, the arrangement did provide an imaginative, ambitious young waiter employment and in the bargain the deluded restaurateur found a willing workhorse. A marriage of convenience for all concerned, it had worked surprisingly well. Sean was bright and determined and soon held a respectable grasp of his duties, which Collins continued to expand.

The smell hit him as soon as he opened the door.

"Sweet Jesus! The bloody shitter's stopped up again," he growled as he automatically punched the code on the keypad to cancel the alarm. The stench distracted him so, he failed to notice it had not gone off. Pushing the door wide to allow fresh air to circulate, Sean unwittingly activated Carl's contact switch. The sound system blared to life at full volume. "Sunshine Of Your Love" bounced off the walls and rattled the windows.

"What the bloody hell—"

The mess on the back table caught Sean's eye and he stood stock-still. Gathering his nerve, he walked slowly, warily, to the booth, terrified of what his eyes were showing him, but unable to resist the magnetism of the macabre image. He was drawn to it, fascinated by its sheer barbarity. Fragments of white light whirled around him and across his frightened features as tiny pin spots, wired to the sound system, sent reflected shards of light scattering from the spinning, mirrored ball on the ceiling.

His boss's splattered skull, caked with congealed blood, lay in the center of the table. Greg's arms, extending forward as if clutching for life, framed the gristly tableau. Flies swarmed in his hair and ears.

Clutching his chest, gasping for breath, Sean staggered backwards and tripped over his own feet. He spun in the direction of his fall to slam face first onto the hardwood dance floor and barely felt the smash he took on the chin. Fighting to regain his feet, he crawled, and then ran to the phone behind the bar.

Sean punched 9-1-1 and rasped into the mouthpiece as soon as he heard a human voice, "I need help! My boss has been murdered."

"I'm sorry," a woman's voice replied in a conversational fashion, "I cannot understand you. Please remain calm. Can you turn down your radio? I cannot hear you clearly."

"What?" Sean's building panic was not being eased by the casual voice on the other end of the line.

"Your radio, sir. Can you turn it down?" the woman asked, firmness bordering on impatience stiffening her tone.

Sean stared at the receiver for a moment, struggling to comprehend the woman's request. The beat pounding in his ears helped him to fathom the distorted entreaty. The noise sparked comprehension. He yelled, "Right! The music! I'll be right back. Hold the line."

He ran to the switch secreted behind the stage curtain, placed there so that performers could start or stop the music as they began or ended their acts. He was standing in front of the speaker as he flipped the toggle. The dim club lit up like a thousand-watt strobe. A giant hand swatted him from behind, lifted him from his feet, and propelled him across the room. His last thought on earth, just before he jack-knifed into the barstools, was: There goes a bloody good career.

Chapter 15

Doc and Tony were doing their best to sort things out at the Bradley residence. The exclusive neighborhood's private police force had sent the remnants of its entire staff—five officers—to assist with the investigation. The fact that the four men and one woman were essentially security guards and ill-prepared for this sort of work was having a detrimental effect on the initial stage. Sickened by the hideous fate that had befallen two of their own, but well aware that the people of this tiny community put bread on their families' tables, the rent-a-cops were firmly in the way. Their chief, a handsome young Hispanic, was making a great show of bluster, demanding his people be given a preeminent role in the investigation. That he had not the faintest idea where to begin was left unsaid.

An off-duty Nassau County Police sergeant, who had monitored the call on his bedroom scanner and responded dressed in sweat suit and slippers, was less than diplomatic in his evaluation.

"No way, Jose," he proclaimed, standing firmly in the private chief's path.

Three City of Glen Cove patrol cars had swept into the oak shrouded lane on the heels of the private cops. Nassau County's Bomb Squad, backed up by a dozen very anxious looking patrolman in full riot gear, were also doing their best to affirm their place at the top of the pecking order. ATF was on the way. The situation was approaching confrontational proportions.

Tony met Doc at the curb, muttered, "Maybe we should lock all these local yokels up and be done with it," as they edged past the knot of yelling uniforms.

"Tempting, but I think not." Doc flashed his gold shield. No one took any notice. He led Tony up the meandering, pebbled path to the front door. As they walked, Tony gave him a run down on everything that had happened so far, ending with the turf battle that had begun just prior to Doc's arrival.

"Let the brass wrangle over it," Doc said. "We have jurisdiction and we know it. I'm not going to waste time arguing over who does what."

The remnants of the double doors, which had once served as main entrance to a magnificent old manse, hung precariously by single hinges. Just inside, the real devastation began.

The lieutenant in charge of the Bomb Squad caught up to them as they were entering the house.

"Better wait for us to clear the area, guys," he said.

Tony said, "A little late for that." He pointed down the path to the red-faced private cop captain who was squaring off with the NCPD sergeant. "Those fellas have already cleared the area. They did it the hard way. They've all been in and out of here at least twice from what they told me when I got here."

"Shit," the lieutenant said.

"That about sums it up," Tony said.

Doc and Tony sidestepped into the vestibule with the chagrined lieutenant close behind.

"There's not much we can learn from this mess," Doc said.

His stomach roiled and he swallowed to stop the bile rising in his throat when he passed through the blood-spattered foyer. Tony had prepared him for what he was now seeing, but carnage on this scale was always worse in actuality than one imagined. It looked like a direct hit from a howitzer. The highly polished hardwood floor was pockmarked, charred, and cracked. Blood smeared everything. Doc's eyes were drawn to the gaping hole in the center of the staircase where he could just make out what was left of a corresponding flight of cellar steps beneath. It looked like the shattered entrance to a catacomb.

"Let The Lab guys sort it out with their tweezers and whisk brooms," he said. "We'll concentrate on the guy in the den. At least there's a whole body to examine in there. They may never figure out what part goes with what corpse in here." He indicated the shattered foyer with a wave of his hand, never allowing his gaze to linger on the torn bodies.

Tony followed Doc into the den, careful to avoid the bits of gore on the splintered floor. The Bomb Squad lieutenant followed; his face chalk-white beneath his Kevlar helmet.

Doc's concentration was being taxed on two levels. Outwardly, he was maintaining his professional aplomb, gathering evidence, studying the scene with a detached and businesslike attitude. He was almost thankful there were no surviving family members to interrogate or restrain. The scene at Doctor Green's house—was that only yesterday?—had been heart rending.

Inwardly, Doc fought the urge to run screaming from the house. This twisted individual—something told him it was one man—was a specter from Hell. He was something more terrible than anything Doc had faced in the war. This one killed with efficiency, as violently as possible, with a variety of weapons, and so far, it seemed, at random. There was no apparent connection between the victims. The killer had a hunger for butchery on a monstrous scale, and he had it in for cops. Not as primary targets, not like a sniper or an ambush freak. No. This one liked to blow them up. He was an egotist bent on a final, irrevocable insult to those who tracked him. It was like chasing Charlie Cong. You began to wonder if you might be better off leaving him alone. Every time you got close, he'd kill some of your men. Sooner or later, it would be your turn. Letting him go wasn't an option then, or now. It was his job to put this maniac away. The guilt of the terror he had felt as a nineteen-year-old slogging through the swamps and thrashing through the jungles of South Vietnam—the guilt he'd learned to live with—had come back to haunt him.

Tony was a vet, but he obviously did not feel the fear as strongly as Doc. Or, did he? If he did, he had it under control. Then again, Tony had not been a Ranger. He had been a straight-leg grunt stomping the paddies with an infantry company to protect his ass.

Doc felt a mixture of shame and pride—shame at belittling his friend's contribution and pride at having served with the elite.

It was all coming back. Doc hoped it didn't show in his face, but he wondered how long he could mask his burgeoning panic with so many eyes on him. This wasn't police work. This was war, and he had had all the war he could handle.

His hand slid into his jacket, an instinctive action. His fingertips brushed the butt of his nine-millimeter Sig Sauer riding snug in his shoulder rig. The temptation to walk around with the gun in hand, locked and cocked, ready to rock and roll, was making his skin crawl.

He cleared his throat and wished for a glass of cool water.

"Three shots," Doc mumbled. "Small caliber. Close range. Like an execution," he observed as he knelt on one knee beside Matt Bradley's supine corpse. A thought struck him. He froze and asked in a whisper, "You sure they checked the body for booby traps?"

"Positive." Tony shook his head. "You'd think what happened to the poor bastards who answered the alarm would have made them a wee bit cautious, but nope. Our friends, the square badges, rolled Mister Bradley on his back and tried CPR."

"He's got a bullet in his brain for Chrisakes."

"I didn't say it worked."

"He left his mark on this one. Look." Doc pointed with a shaking forefinger at the brand on the victim's neck. The GI's derogatory description of the nostalgic symbol came to mind, and he said, without thinking, "Footprint of the American chicken."

The Bomb Squad Lieutenant was visibly relieved to see the CSU team, Lieutenant Schiff, and a few more detectives arrive, ending his peering over Doc's shoulder at the dead. The new arrivals spread throughout the house to begin the painstaking gathering of evidence. As the sun rose higher in the sky, the media arrived in force. The private cops, grateful for something to do within their capabilities, did a reasonable job of crowd control. The uniforms fanned out to do the neighbor interviews while the suits combed the property for clues.

Schiff reported almost constantly to Mineola via cellular phone. His conversations seemed to become louder with each call. Handing an officer the phone with orders to say he was tied up if he was summoned, he grabbed Doc and Tony and led them out to the back patio.

"Some crazy son of a bitch is waging war on my turf," Schiff snarled, "and I want his ass."

Doc and Tony exchanged glances before looking down, seeming to study the craftsmanship of the slate beneath their feet. The morning chill left tiny dewdrops on the gray stone that glistened in the rosy light.

"Well?" Schiff growled.

"C'mon, Lieutenant," Tony groaned. "We're working on it."

Doc silenced him with his right hand coming up, palm vertical. "Let's not waste time playing: I-want and we're-trying. We've got a real bad one loose in the streets." He heard his voice rising but knew he couldn't reign in. "There are going to be lots of shit-ass accusations coming down before this is over. Let's clear the air right now. If you've got people who can handle this job better than Tony and I,

Charlie, now's the time to bring them in. If not, get behind us and let us go to work."

Schiff glared at Doc, seething. With obvious restraint, he gritted his teeth until his anger abated. Thrusting his hands into his pants pockets, Schiff finally spoke. His demeanor was almost avuncular when he said, "You know the heat I'm getting already. It's gonna get worse. You know that, too. Get this fucking maniac, soonest."

"Let's start checking for released or escaped crazies," Doc said, as if the previous conversation had never taken place, "anybody that might fit the bill."

"Right," Schiff agreed, "and known wackos with military backgrounds."

"Special forces types in particular," Doc nodded. "This guy's a pro."

"What about spooks and terrorists?" Tony suggested.

"You'll have a hell of a time getting anything on either one," Schiff said. "We've been on the phone with Washington." He drew a breath and let it out in a rush. "Since we have no evidence of terrorism, they're reluctant to commit resources. If we insist they look into it, they insist on complete control."

"Fuck it," Doc said. "If we have to give the feds all the credit, let's do it. We need their data banks."

"Whatever it takes," Schiff offered.

Doc smiled. "That's what I like to hear."

Schiff was about to add, within reason, when a uniform came bustling through the French doors, cellular phone in hand.

"I said I'm not available for the moment," the lieutenant barked.

"Thought you ought to know, sir. There's been another one," the patrolman said, "in Wantagh."

"Who the fuck is this guy?" Tony asked the clear, blue sky. "The Terminator?"

Adrienne Boyd, perched with her camera crew on the high deck of a nearby house, picked up this last scrap of conversation as her soundman switched on a directional microphone. They filmed the breakup of the meeting as cops jogged to their cars. After dispatching one of the technicians to follow the departing policemen, she set up her piece.

"This is Adrienne Boyd reporting from a private village in the City of Glen Cove, Long Island." She narrowed her eyes to use her this-is-serious voice. "Police here are frantically searching for clues as to the identity of a bloodthirsty killer, a killer who has struck three times in the past two days."

She went on in grim tones to describe the scene at the most recent crime. For the wrap up, Adrienne beckoned the cameraman to zoom in for a close-up, her fingers wiggling beneath the lens frame.

"This frightened community," she said, staring hard into the camera's cyclopean eye, "waits in fear of the killer's next attack. A man the police are calling…" She breathed the last two words as if afraid to say them aloud, "…The Terminator."

Her producer loved it.

Chapter 16

Adrienne Boyd's news broadcast had the desired effect, at least from the network's point of view. They had purchased rights to the piece and aired it on their six o'clock show. It riveted the attention of viewers throughout the tristate area. By the time the show aired, footage of the bomb blasted club in Wantagh had been added to the Glen Cove piece along with a dramatic voice-over description of the murders in both places. A promise of immediate updates and a complete report at eleven insured a jump in ratings, which guaranteed happy sponsors until the crisis was resolved. In an effort to keep public interest high, the station manager called an emergency staff meeting to plan bulletins to interrupt shows that enjoyed large audiences. No one at the meeting was so openly heartless as to express hope that the spectacular murders would continue, but no one said anything to the contrary, either.

ᏟᏍᏟᏍ

In an artfully disguised room in the basement of Carl's home, the killer gobbled pepperoni pizza and guzzled imported beer while he watched his status grow in the annals of famed serial killers.

Everything in the ten-by-ten room was white. The soundproofed walls; the Celotex ceiling; the plastic molding; the steel door; the countertop workstation; the wheeled leather command chair; even the tiled floor was snowy white. The only color in the room came from Carl's clothing and the computer monitor's screen.

Carl wore starched tiger fatigues and spit shined paratrooper boots when he worked in this room. Colonel's eagles gleamed on the collar of his uniform. A red beret hung from a white peg next to the door with a black shield flash sewn to its front. Polished brass, infantry crossed rifles decorated the patch.

This room was his headquarters and he saw it as a place of purity. His seventeen-inch, flat screen, color monitor was the only link to the outside world in this, his operations center. When the newscast ended, he entered a command on his computer keyboard and the broadcast disappeared, replaced by a split screen surveillance image of the front and rear doors of his home.

No one could surprise him in his hideaway. The best security equipment money could buy protected him from unwanted intrusion. The good people of Rockville Centre would be traumatized to learn of the beast in their midst. The quiet, unassuming dealer in estate jewelry and fine old furnishings would never be suspected of jaywalking, let alone murder.

The news was the most entertaining he had ever seen. He, Carl The Terminator Esterbrook, was the star. The moniker delighted him.

"I'll be bock," he laughed as the picture changed, threw his feet up on the countertop, and took a huge bite out of a wedge of steaming pizza.

The fact that his identity was wholly unknown added to, rather than detracted from, his ego trip. Not one sliver of evidence had been left behind. Clueless, as the kids would say, that's what the cops were.

He finished his meal and wiped his hands on a paper napkin. After tidying up the refuse from his hurried dinner, Carl laced his fingers behind his head, closed his eyes, and reviewed the events of his most recent operation. "Time for a break," he told himself, "a brief respite to marshal one's forces and regroup."

Standing, he painstakingly disarmed the thermite grenade in a decorative porcelain pitcher atop the file cabinet. A hole, drilled through the bottom of the vessel, was mated to a similar opening in the cabinet. Fine steel wire ran from the inside of the locking mechanism to the arming ring of the incendiary. Anyone opening the lock without first disconnecting the wire would set off the grenade. The heat would shatter the pitcher, which would, in all probability, blind the intruder before burning through the cabinet top and incinerating the contents within seconds. The entire room would be engulfed in flames in two minutes. Carl knew well the risks imposed by this, his most damning breach of evidentiary security. The drawers contained a record of every one of his kills. Newspaper clippings, videotapes, and editorials written by outraged tabloid chiefs told the story of his unsolved crimes. Vanity prevented him from destroying the lot.

"What the hell," he snickered. The thought that his fetish might someday be his undoing jousted with his meticulously careful nature. "I am exceptional, am I not? I am, therefore, entitled to do exceptional things."

He yanked the handle on the top drawer of the steel filing cabinet. From the drawer, Carl pulled six red file folders. Each was labeled, SECRET * EYES-ONLY * FOX ONE. He stacked them neatly on the counter in front of him. One by one, he opened the folders and read the contents. When he had finished all of them, he separated them into two piles. Next, he selected a rubber stamp from a tray beneath his work surface and an inked pad. Ceremoniously, he stamped first the cover pages and then each folder with, MISSION ACCOMPLISHED * SUBJECT TERMINATED, in bold black letters. With a flourish, he returned these files to the drawer.

He drummed his fingers on the remaining folders with the air of a man on the verge of a momentous decision, then abruptly scooped up one and pushed the others aside. Once again, he dropped into his chair, propped his feet on the counter and leaned back to peruse the contents of the file.

NESTOR, PHILIP E., the heading stated in block letters, followed by, BIKER BUM in parenthesis. The text was a complete dossier on the subject. Carl pictured his next victim and imagined the projected scenario of his coming demise. He tapped his teeth with a gold pen he pulled from his uniform blouse breast pocket. Studying the page, he stopped to make a note next to the box marked: WEAPONS ALLOCATION.

Chapter 17

The FBI will not be called in and that's final," Lieutenant Schiff announced to the assembled men in the briefing room at police headquarters. "The subject is closed."

"This morning you said..." Doc let the sentence hang, incomplete.

He knew it was a lost cause. Schiff had that pit-bull look about him. When he got that way, the Four Horsemen could not drag him to the other side of an argument. Schiff did not make idle statements. He meant it when he had agreed it was time to get help from the Feds, but someone disagreed, someone higher up. Lieutenant Charles Schiff had new marching orders.

"That was before the commissioner vetoed the idea," Schiff said.

There it is, thought Doc, countermanded by the brass.

"We have no evidence of a federal crime," Schiff explained, "no state lines have been crossed and the obscurity of the victims doesn't jell with terrorism."

"That we know of," Tony interjected.

"Correct, and until we do, no feds. Period." Schiff's steely gaze left no doubt as to the futility of further dispute as it settled on the man from whom he expected a vociferous riposte.

Doc avoided eye contact and moved to the window. It was the only way he could keep from losing his temper. Now was not the time to go toe to toe with his boss. Schiff didn't like having his knuckles rapped, as he most certainly had, and Doc knew better than to corner him. Still, he was furious with the armchair quarterbacks, the meddlesome bureaucrats with their expedient political agendas. Again, he felt that dismal similarity to Vietnam. Don't use the heavystuff. We don't want to piss anybody off.

He ground his teeth and looked down at the street. Normally, the wide avenues surrounding headquarters would be all but empty by this time of night but the sidewalks looked like Radio City during Christmas week. Clamoring reporters, incensed by the seemingly dumbstruck police spokesman, had turned the neighborhood that was home to the county seat into something resembling bedlam. The news hounds had settled down to watchful waiting now, but it was apparent they were here to stay. No one but the commissioner himself was authorized to speak with the media under pain of dire consequences. The six o'clock news was just another bad memory by the time the investigation had reached a stage where the detectives could extricate themselves from the two most recent crime scenes.

Doc turned from the window to weigh the possibilities. Tony met his gaze with a barely perceptible shake of his head. Jack Kobrigian and Ray Beckwith stayed mum on the subject of federal aid. Doc wasn't sure if it was from exhaustion or out of self-preservation.

"So," he said, with an irresistible pinch of condescension, "we use the county's limited resources to wade through the reams of possible perps?"

"You've got it." Schiff nodded, meeting Doc's challenging stare.

"Round up the usual suspects," Tony sighed.

"Knock off the bullshit, Cordova." Schiff's blowtorch stare switched from Doc to Tony without losing one degree of heat. "Did you guys think this was going to be a piece of cake?"

"No, sir, we didn't," Doc answered for them both. "But this is like nothing we've ever seen before. There is no precedent for this. Every instinct tells me this nut is not of the homegrown variety. Serial killers are not exactly commonplace around here."

"They're not commonplace anywhere, thank God, but they aren't unheard of either," Schiff parried. "Here or anyplace else. We've had our share."

"Not like this guy, we haven't."

"Look." Schiff's tone became patient. "I'll get some people working on the military angle. For once, manpower is not a problem. After that press conference, the legislature will bankrupt the budget for the next five years to bag this bastard."

"Was that a press conference?" Tony's lips curled in a mock smile. "I thought it was media feeding time and politicians were the main course."

"That's just how our duly elected officials perceived the event," Schiff said. "Don't kid yourselves. They want blood. Ours will suffice if we can't provide an alternate appetizer. If they ever find out where that Terminator label originated, you will be the first live target at the academy range, Cordova."

Tony's eyes widened; the whites accented by the blue-black bruises. "You can't pin that on me. I didn't repeat that anywhere."

"Well, somebody goddamn did," Schiff snarled. "Learn from it. Be very careful what you say and where you say it—all of you. Now get back out in the field and dig into the victims' backgrounds. Interview every friend and relative they had. Talk to the neighbors. This crackpot doesn't live in a vacuum."

"Fine," Doc relented. "Would you mind terribly if we order out for some food, first? My stomach thinks my throat's been cut."

The other detectives looked to Schiff and nodded agreement.

Ray Beckwith said, "I get light-headed when I don't eat."

"How can you tell?" Kobrigian murmured.

"We can go over what we know in the meantime," Doc said, "and maybe come up with something."

"Go ahead," Schiff sighed. "Maybe some chow will get the brain cells working." With that, he left the room.

While the desk sergeant placed an order for sandwiches from a local deli, the four remaining men rehashed the crimes.

To focus his thoughts, Doc sketched a chart on the blackboard at the head of the table. Stepping back from his artwork, he rubbed his thumb on the tip of the chalk protruding from his fist.

"That's our boy's hit list so far," he said. "The Kohler woman, then Collins, then Mrs. Green, and her next-door neighbor, and then the Bradleys."

"Shouldn't Collins be last?" Beckwith suggested. He looked quickly to the door to be sure that Schiff had not returned. The lieutenant was in no mood for inaccuracies and Beckwith was visibly confused.

"Medical examiner estimates Collins's time of death sometime Monday morning," Tony advised. "His manager bought it this morning, but Collins was dead already. The nine-one-one tape is distorted. There was a lot of background noise, but you can make out the guy saying someone's been murdered." He added, "Relax, Ray. We're all a little discombobulated."

"Let's start with the similarities." Doc gave Tony a quick nod of thanks and stepped back to the board. "These four were rigged with booby traps." He jotted asterisks next to the names. "That's significant. He had the time to wire them up and that shows planning. Now, there's no way he could have known who'd trip them, so we'll assume he's rigging certain ones for a reason."

"Why did he skip the old lady?" Kobrigian wondered aloud. "He would have had time."

"I got the impression she wasn't his primary target." Doc put down the chalk. "Remember where she was found."

The detectives watched Doc as closely as an audience watches prestidigitation.

"Just inside her back door," Tony thought aloud.

Doc tapped his nose and said, "And, she's the only one done by hand. Snapped her neck like a match stick and propped her up in a chair, almost like he didn't want anyone to notice her for a while. Mrs. Kohler and Mrs. Green were killed in their bedrooms and the Bradley guy was whacked in his den. We don't know where his wife got it yet, but I'd say right there on the stairs." Doc looked to each man in turn.

Beckwith said, "They saw him."

"That's what I think," Doc said. "I get the feeling that Bradley's wife and the Gebhardt woman got in the way. He was stalking the others." Nods of acceptance around the room cemented his opinion.

"He strangled the lady in Oyster Bay too, Doc," Beckwith pointed out.

Tony defended Doc's reasoning, "But he tortured the shit out of her first and he used a garrote while he was screwing her, and that's an assumption since there was nothing left to check out with a rape kit. The old lady was a quick snuff. He didn't strangle her. He broke her neck. Remember, he took the trouble to rig that bomb under the Kohler woman, but not the old lady."

"He put one with the Bradley woman, too," Ray said.

"Again, he didn't rig the old lady," Doc reminded them. "He left the thing in Mrs. Green's place downstairs, but it was in her house, not the old lady's. It seems to me that if he had meant to get them both, there would have been a booby trap with each of them." He tapped the chalk against each of the names he had annotated, once each for emphasis. "These people were selected." He looked to each of them for comment and was rewarded with nods of agreement. "What else do we know?"

Intensity shone from Doc's eyes like a cold light. He was totally absorbed in the hunt. Doc took a personal interest in certain types of killers. He hated the ones who preyed on helpless people. Cop killers, of course, were a passion for all who wore a badge. It became a family matter. This one had hit a nerve. He was more than a bloodthirsty monster. He frightened them, and frightened men were dangerous, especially men like Doc.

"What about the mark?" Kobrigian piped up. "You know, the thing he burns into them."

"That's right." Doc riffled through the preliminary coroner's reports. "They didn't all have it. Mrs. Kohler, Collins, and Mr. Bradley all had that…thing branded into them." He looked at the board. "Why not the rest? The cops and civilians he got with the explosives were secondary. These three," he waved the reports, "had special significance. He's trademarked them."

"Silver hatchets?" Tony said.

"I've been thinking along those lines myself," Doc said.

"Jesus." Tony shivered.

"Creepy, isn't it?"

"What the fuck are you guys talking about?" Kobrigian asked.

Doc leaned forward, placing both palms on the table. "There's a legend from Vietnam. I don't know how much of it is true. The way I heard it; some airborne unit got the idea to play with the enemy's heads—a little psychological warfare. They all carried silver hatchets on their packs—stainless steel tomahawks, actually, that some tool manufacturer in the States fabricated for them, special order. They used to cut off ears and even heads from the bodies of their kills. Mutilation is particularly frightening to some cultures. Once word got around, people would shit when this unit walked into a village."

"It was a variation on a theme," Tony said. "Another outfit dropped the ace of spades on their kills. That got so popular playing card manufacturers started selling decks of nothing but the ace of spades by mail order."

"And there were plenty of units who left patches and unit crests on bodies. The idea was always the same. Let the bastards know who did it. Sign your work."

"The doctor's wife wasn't burned," Tony pointed out. "How come?"

Doc shrugged.

“The booby traps may be some sort of trademark too,” Jack interjected. “There was one at the Green’s place, even though she wasn’t branded.”

“I think the booby traps are window dressing,” Doc said. “The burns are like staking a claim. The brand is his signature; the booby traps are a warning. There’s some special significance to the ones he marks. I’d bet on it.”

“Why a peace symbol?” Tony asked.

“Is it?” Doc pondered. “That’s what it looks like to us, but is that what it is? Can we have somebody research that? Maybe there’s some other meaning, some Satanist cult sign or who knows what.”

Kobrigian volunteered. “I’ll see if any of the local colleges have anybody on staff that can help with obscure symbols.”

“You mean you don’t know all about them?” Ray feigned shock.

“No one knows all,” Jack answered with exaggerated disdain, “but knowing whom to ask is the mark of the intelligent man.”

Beckwith flushed and the others broke into laughter.

“Touché,” Tony winked. “You’re over matched, Ray. Give up.”

Beckwith smiled and bowed to Kobrigian, who bowed back with smug acceptance of due homage.

The food arrived, but the formerly ravenous detectives picked at it, forgetting their hunger as they fed on the scraps of leads, energized now that they had made some sense of the horror. No one was certain that the speculations had any validity but it felt good to intellectualize after all the mopping up. They were doing what they were paid to do, trying to solve the crimes.

While his colleagues debated, Tony called Oyster Bay Hospital, only to learn that Dr. Green and his children were asleep and unavailable for questioning. The investigators agreed that the doctor’s family was their best bet for fresh information as the only surviving next of kin available. The investigation had revealed that the Bradleys had a child, a young woman away at university in Europe. Overseas phone calls had determined she was not at school but on holiday somewhere in France. Her roommate said she was traveling with friends prior to returning home. Interpol was making inquiries, but the movements of nomadic teenagers with no definable itinerary would not be easy to ascertain. The odds were that the newly orphaned girl would learn of the deaths of her parents in the tabloids. Doc and Tony said they would speak to the Greens first thing in the morning.

They brainstormed the snatches of evidence until yawning was the most common feedback in the room. Notes to check out traffic tickets issued in the vicinity of the murders and all connecting routes were jotted down. More than one killer had been bagged by an alert highway patrolman. The coast guard and harbor patrol would be called. There was a fair chance that the killer had escaped the Bradley scene by boat. Tracks had been found along the shore and on the cliff face. The Lab was scouring the site, but an exterior scene on a windswept stretch of coastline was the worst type of ground to cover.

It was after midnight when the meeting broke up. The tired policemen went home, trusting to others to track down some of their leads and praying the energetic madman would have the decency to take the night off.

Chapter 18

The day was still new when Carl lay down on his stomach on the third floor of an unfinished condominium complex across the channel from his marina. The damp chill of the concrete caused him discomfort, but he refused to yield to the temptation to shift his position. A by-law of sniping was to be motionless as a rock once secreted in a hide. A heavy, canvas drop-cloth, splattered with mud and cement, covered him almost entirely. It was perfect camouflage. From the windows of nearby homes, he would appear to be a discarded pile of rags, unremarkable in the skeletal structure.

Construction of the waterfront apartments had been halted when a local environmental group had complained long and loud to the mayor's office. The debate had raged in the courts for months, a political hot potato that threatened to burn many hands. The machinations of local politicians mattered little to Carl, but the good fortune of finding such a ready-made shooting platform did. The city's responsibility to guard the bare bones of a building ended with having passing police motor patrols eyeball the lock on the gate. The budget-conscious builder saw no reason to sink precious dollars into security of a project suspended in embryonic stages of erection. There was nothing to steal. Fencing provided adequate protection from attractive nuisance lawsuits.

Carl had found the chain link less than formidable. He hurtled the barrier and secreted himself in the hour before dawn, blessing Adrienne Boyd for her dogged coverage of the case.

An insomniac when he was wired—as he was now in the midst of an operation—Carl habitually scanned TV news programs in the quiet of his home until the small hours of the morning. He had caught the bulletin on Channel 30 by accident as he flipped past it with the remote.

"Channel Thirty," Adrienne had announced, "has just learned that the police are investigating the possibility that the infamous Terminator—the homicidal maniac who has terrorized Long Island—is believed to have escaped by boat from the Bradley murder scene."

She prattled on about footprints investigators had discovered and a length of rope tied to a tree in a nearby cove. Carl hit the mute button at the end of the bulletin. His analytical mind checked off the likely steps the police would follow.

"A—" he said aloud, "—check the logs of coast guard and harbor patrol boats on duty. Nothing will be ignored. Everything and anything will be checked out. Dammit."

He had neglected to put on his running lights after he had dumped the gear he had used at the Bradleys' place. At the entrance to the channel leading to his marina, a police launch had hailed him, given him a warning, and let him go.

"So, B, they never got a good look at my face, but did those cops get my registration number? Assuming they did, they'll check the maritime reggies to see who owns the boat and where it is kept.

"C, question the owner. Whoops! Can't find him." He chuckled. "He's out of town. Okay, D, check out the boat. Nothing there. Just a boat. E, now what?" Carl sat up straight. "Question the marina management. Shit! A weak link." Carl pursed his lips and nodded in the darkness of his living room. "Sorry, Cliffy, early retirement for you my friend."

Cliff couldn't tell the cops anything beyond what he knew—the bogus name and address of a doctor who didn't exist—an owner who would not match the boat's registration. But he could give them a pretty fair description. He had been in close contact with Carl several times. Carl had taken great pains over the years to avoid, disguise, or expunge any record of his physical appearance, even to the extreme act of changing the photograph in his military personnel records. That little escapade was a story in itself.

With high-powered binoculars, Carl now watched the entrance to the marina. The sun was just over the horizon and promising a beautiful clear spring day when Cliff's Pathfinder rolled through the gate.

Without taking his eyes from his target, Carl lowered the glasses and raised the sniper rifle—a match-grade M-14. Pressing the scope to his eye, he pulled the stock in tight, getting a good cheek weld on the polished wood. He wondered if the hairs on Cliff's neck were rising as he tracked him.

Oblivious, Cliff sauntered toward his office. Carl waited until the marina manager stood motionless in front of the door with the key in the lock. Exhaling half of the deep breath he was holding, Carl gently squeezed the trigger. A hair's breadth before the rifle barked its roar of death, Cliff stepped aside.

Jerking his index finger from the trigger as if burned, Carl looked to the left to see what had distracted his victim's attention. A dark blue sedan kicked gravel behind it as it skidded into the lot. Two men in suits occupied the front seat.

Cops!

Ray Beckwith whipped open the driver's door and emerged, hailing the marina owner. Jack Kobrigian alighted on the far side with dignity, exuding authority, despite his wrinkled suit. Cliff obligingly walked to greet them.

Carl watched the three men introduce themselves and exchange pleasantries. While they talked, he sighted in on his prey, who had obligingly halted with his back to him. It was an easy shot, barely a hundred and fifty yards. No wind. The crosshairs settled on the seam in the center of Cliff's Navy P-coat.

Kobrigian looked startled when the friendly mariner's chest exploded. He looked down, incredulous to find a neat hole in his own necktie and what looked like blood. He turned to say something about it to Beckwith, but Ray's features were twisted in shock. Kobrigian was about to berate him for standing there with his mouth flapping like a carp when the pain enveloped him. Like someone had clapped two bricks together on his heart, Kobrigian's arms came up to clutch at his chest, but the man they had come to question dropped into them. They fell together, embraced in agony.

Beckwith was too astonished to react. He stared, open mouthed, at his stricken partner.

Carl was halfway to the condo fence, laughing like a grade school prankster. "Two for a nickel. Give the man a kewpie doll," he cackled.

Several moments passed before Beckwith recovered sufficiently to duck behind the car door and fumble the radio mike from its cradle.

ꕤꕤ

Doc trotted up the three granite steps to the main entrance of Oyster Bay Hospital.

"I'm not looking forward to this," he said over his shoulder to Tony.

"I don't feature questioning the bereaved doctor and his children either, but it has to be done. Look at the bright side. Maybe you'll get to see that pretty Nursing Director."

"Don't start."

"Hey, it would be nice for you to find somebody to keep you out of trouble."

"Fuck you."

"Wrong gender. Besides, I'm a T."

Doc whirled on him.

"Take it easy, Doc. I'm just breaking your shoes."

"Zip it. I'm in no mood for your jokes."

As Doc reached for the door handle, Tony said, "Seriously, Doc, you need someone to share your hopes and dreams with, or at least to give you some. You can't keep this Lothario shit up forever."

"You're starting to sound like an old lady, Cordova. Mind your own business."

They crossed the lobby in silence. The volunteer at the reception desk lost her perky smile when they announced themselves. Both cops were acutely aware of the suspicious glances they received from the staff as they waited in the lobby. Why, Doc wondered, do people act like it's our fault when bad things happen? It's as if they think it will all go away if only we will.

Mister Strechman, the hospital's director, shook their hands and invited them to follow him. The three men strode down corridors lined with cells of misery. Most of the patient rooms were occupied by elderly wraiths, hollow eyed people with skin like crumpled parchment, their hopeless stares both accusation and a promise of retribution. The hallways stank of disinfectant. Both detectives were relieved to finally reach the door to Ben Green's room. Their relief was short-lived.

Benjamin Green, wrapped in a frayed blue terry-cloth robe, sat in a high-backed pale blue vinyl visitor's chair, staring vacantly at the bed when they entered his room. He acknowledged their presence with a barely perceptible nod.

Tony took up station in the corner while Doc sat on the edge of the bed, facing the distraught doctor. The hospital director stood by.

“I’m very sorry about your loss, Doctor Green,” Doc offered. The misery in the doctor’s face said volumes. He would be of little help. Ben Green was functioning on marginal awareness, as close to catatonic as Doc had ever seen. “Can you help us at all, Doctor? Do you have any idea who would want to do this?”

The big man looked lost. Tears rolled down his deflated cheeks, the luster gone from his once bright eyes. His skin was more gray than black. Doc thought, this must be what’s left when a man’s soul is gone. Grief was such a constant companion to the detective he had almost grown accustomed to it. Almost, but not quite.

Tony tried to ask a question, but Doc cut him off with a shake of his head.

“He’s in bad shape, isn’t he, Doctor?” he asked of Strechman when they were back in the hall.

“Yes, he is, but I’m not a doctor, Detective.”

“Oh? Sorry. I thought—”

“A logical assumption, but today’s complicated houses of healing are often run by people with degrees in business administration rather than medicine.” He sighed. “Doctor Green will need care and time to recuperate from his tragic loss. Such a shame. So senseless. Would you like to see the children now?”

“No,” Doc said abruptly, “thank you. Maybe at some future time.” He couldn’t bear to look into the kids’ faces after seeing their father’s empty visage.

Tony, having seen the devastation in the doctor’s eyes, had to agree. They would get nothing from the family.

“Would you care to speak to Mrs. Maclear?” Mr. Strechman suggested.

Doc covered his shock with a cough. Was it written on his forehead? Did everybody know?

“She sold the house to the Greens, you know. The one Mrs. Green was, er…”

“Murdered in?” Tony finished for him.

“Yes. That’s right. She’s here. She stayed on to see to the family. She feels responsible somehow. I told her that was ridiculous but she hasn’t left their bedsides. She’s with the children now. I can get her for you.”

The detectives were momentarily at a loss. They knew that the Greens had recently moved into the house in Garden City but the investigation had not revealed its previous owner, at least not to them.

The killer had kept them hopping from one crime scene to the next. Doc made a mental note to dig into the reports with more attention to detail. What else had they missed?

Mr. Strechman led them to the doctor's lounge. He shooed out two interns, who seemed more than happy to vacate their place of rest and left with them. Tony wondered aloud if interns were so inured to following commands that their response was Pavlovian or if their swift disappearing act was a symptom of cop-itis. His rumination was cut short by the appearance of Madeline Maclear.

Her suffering showed on her exhausted face. Those seductive eyes were swollen and bloodshot with dark circles beneath them, bereft. Several stray hairs hung limp over her ears. She had lines in her face that they hadn't noticed before. Maybe it was the down turned corners of her mouth, as if the humor had been sucked right out of her, but Madeline Maclear had aged before their eyes.

Doc stood there, feeling like a kid who had just seen his hero beaten to a pulp.

Tony loudly cleared his throat, and said, "Thank you for seeing us, Mrs. Maclear," while striding deliberately across the room to take her hand. "Perhaps you remember Detective Wiley and me. We were patients just the other night."

She forced a smile and nodded. When her gaze shifted to Doc, he thought he saw a spark, maybe just a glimmer.

"How's your head, Detective Wiley?" She seemed intent on his answer. "And yours, too, Detective Cordova," she added.

"Fine. Good as new," they answered in unison. They looked at each other and laughed quietly. Tony's wife always said that the two of them could complete each other's sentences.

"How are you, Mrs. Maclear?" The way Doc said it a blind man could see the deeper meaning behind the phrase.

"I'll be okay. Do you mind if I sit down? I'm dead on my feet." Madeline seemed upset by her choice of words, but quickly recovered as the detectives made room for her to pass. Sitting on the leather sofa, she seemed tiny, fragile. She appeared out of place, like so many things in the utilitarian room that its inhabitants had tried unsuccessfully to humanize. A vase of wilted flowers sat on a small, Formica topped table. Gaily personalized mugs hung on hooks above an institutional looking coffee maker. Doc suppressed the urge to hold her hand.

Tony got right to the point. "We've just learned that you sold the Greens their house."

"That's right, Mrs. Maclear," Doc chimed in, aware of the need to get down to business.

"Yes. I did. It's something I'll regret for the rest of my life," Madeline said.

"Why is that?" Tony forged ahead in spite of the you're-kidding look he got from Doc.

"Because Marjorie Green would be alive today if I hadn't."

"Mrs. Maclear, you mustn't think that." Doc's admonition was kind, yet firm. "You had no way of knowing this nut was going to do what he did. It could have happened anywhere—to anyone. It's sad, yes, but no one's to blame except the vicious animal that killed that poor woman."

"Except, I think he was after me."

Doc and Tony sat on opposite sides of the stricken woman, on the edge of their seats.

"Why?" Doc said, as steadily as he could manage. "Mrs. Maclear, do you know who did this?" Inwardly he was quaking with excitement and fear.

"No." Madeline shook her head violently. A hot tear landed on the back of Doc's hand. He pressed it to his mouth, attempting to look thoughtful as he framed his next question.

"What makes you think he was after you?" he said.

"A little while ago, I came in here for a cup of tea. I don't normally do that. It's the doctor's lounge, but every time I go into my office the damned phone rings and someone wants some trivial detail looked into." She paused, frowning. "That has absolutely nothing to do with your question. I'm sorry."

Doc said, "Go on."

"It was early this morning. The girls—Doctor Green's girls?" They nodded their understanding. "They were asleep, so I took a break. The TV was on." She indicated the set, mounted on a bracket high up in a corner. "It was tuned to CNN. They were doing a story on the murders. I've been hearing snatches of conversation around the halls. Everyone's talking about this maniac. I hadn't heard any details until the newscast, though."

Doc fought the urge to pull it from her.

"I almost shut it off," she went on. "It was too horrible. But a doctor was watching and I had no right."

They sensed that she was dragging it out, as if she subconsciously dreaded the words.

"I started paying attention when they mentioned Matt Bradley."

"You knew Mr. Bradley?" Doc prodded.

"And Greg Collins," she poured out in a rush. "We were friends in high school. Well, not really friends. I was two years behind them. I had a crush on Matt for the longest time. I hung out with them whenever I could. They put up with me, I suppose. They were seniors, the coolest kids in school. I was trying to be mature." She nearly smiled. "You know."

"What about the others?" Doc asked. "Mrs. Gebhardt?"

"Of course. She was my neighbor."

"Why didn't you call us?" Doc said.

"I did. Isn't that why you're here?"

Tony said, "What about the Kohlers, Dorothy and Jason?"

"No. I didn't know them."

Tony said, "There were no pictures found of Dorothy Kohler, not even a wedding album. The lady must have been exceptionally camera shy." He yanked his notebook from his pocket and riffled through it, saying, "Hang on a sec." He raised a finger when he found the page. "Here it is. Dorothy Kohler's maiden name was Conway, Dorothy Conway."

Madeline's color drained away like sand from a broken hourglass.

Chapter 19

Philip Nestor gave a spark plug a last quarter turn with a torque wrench and felt the steel threads find their seat. He dropped the wrench into his toolbox and smiled his satisfaction. His fingertips stroked the teardrop gas tank of the Harley-Davidson Electra-Glide. By the weekend he would be ready to put her on the road. Two years of hard work had gone into restoring the old bike, but Philip never thought of anything related to Harleys as work. He had owned and ridden nearly every collectible motorcycle ever built—Hondas, Indians, BMWs, Triumphs—but he had always had a special love for Harleys.

This metallic-green vision of chrome and tan leather was both a gift to himself and his idea of personal therapy. When Helen got sick, he had sold his collection, one by one, to pay the medical bills. When she began to recover, he had bought the Electra-Glide, paying a hundred bucks for the rusty hulk. Every spare moment since had been spent in restoring the classic machine to its original beauty. The parts he could salvage, he refurbished. The rest he bought at garage sales, auctions, swap meets, and junk dealers. The finished product cost him sixteen-hundred out of pocket. It was worth several times that now, but selling it was out of the question. Helen would be thrilled to see what he had created. She loved to ride almost as much as he. By summer, she should be well enough to go cruising.

Philip envisioned winding Adirondack Mountain roads dappled with sunlight beneath the trees. Helen loved the mountains. Maybe they could take an extended camping trip and live out of a haversack as they had when they were young.

"Just me and my ladies," he said to himself and stooped to rub the gleaming leg pipes with a soft cloth.

Phil Nestor had known happy times in his life and some not-so-happy times. As a wild-eyed youth, he had rebelled at every turn. When his parents shipped him off to State University of New York at Cobleskill in the fall of 1969, they were thinking in clichés. The Nestors had "high hopes" for their son and were optimistic he would "straighten out" in college, "get his head out of the clouds" and "his feet on the ground." Young Philip was out to prove only that he was "Born To Be Wild," like the Steppenwolf song emblazoned in a flashy tattoo on his left bicep, and in so doing, disappointed his parents completely. Conspicuous only by his absence in class, Philip didn't last a semester in the halls of higher learning. When he wasn't hustling a buck in some less-than-legal fashion, he was drinking, smoking, or snorting his tainted income. The quest for the perfect high lead to some absolute lows. When the young hellion was apprehended with a stolen Pontiac GTO in Harrison, New York, a judge gave him an ultimatum.

"Join up, or lock-up," the crusty jurist had rasped. "What's it gonna be, hotshot?"

Phil chose the apparent lesser evil, but the US Army wasn't thrilled with his persona either, and he soon found that a stockade was merely military jargon for jail. He volunteered for Vietnam to get out from under his predicament, only to discover what was meant by the frying pan into the fire.

An old war-horse sergeant major saw something of himself in the tempestuous youth and took a hand in Phil's rehabilitation. He put him to work in the Da Nang motor pool where Phil's gift for things that ran on fossil fuels came to light. He was a natural mechanic, seeming to know what was wrong with an engine by intuition. Under the careful tutelage of his mentor, he learned a marketable trade and stayed out of harm's way in the sprawling complex.

When his tour was up, he signed on for a six-month extension and bought himself an early out to finish his military career in two years, a year shy of his enlistment. The GI Bill paid for Phil's further education as a master mechanic and got him a low interest loan to start his business.

With no guru to channel his hyperactive hormones, the old temptation to run with the pack nearly put him back where he started. The road warriors that his shop—Wheelies-R-Us—attracted, were all too willing to lead him astray, and Phil soon slipped back into anti-establishment mode.

Helen saved his life.

He met her on a road trip while he traveled with the Nomads one summer. She was managing a convenience store they stopped to terrorize in Vermont. As his companions trashed the shelves and stared down the horrified patrons, Phil boldly ogled the pretty brunette behind the counter. Instead of quivering with fear, or better yet, with anticipation, Helen stared into his freckled face, and said, "You're too nice a guy to hang around with these jerks."

Stunned, he had left without reply, telling the rest of the pack that, "This scene is lame," and he was, "outta here." They followed him as they always did. He was the one with the bread.

He left them that night, twenty miles up the road in a dive roadhouse that deserved them, and he rode back to the store. Helen showed no surprise at his return. She acted as if it was expected when he pitched in to clean up the mess.

He put a lot of miles on his bike that summer, shuttling back and forth between Long Island and Vermont. They were married in the fall and moved to Oceanside on the south shore.

His oldest boy was married now and Phil was looking forward to being a grandpa. The other two were in school, a year apart, but as close as brothers can be, short of being joined at the hip. Both were bound for Cancun for spring break. Mexico would probably never recover. Helen had misgivings, but Phil didn't have the heart to say no. Hypocritical was too mild a word for the way he would feel if he repressed his boys' lust for adventure.

He missed them all, but he had always known one day they would be men on their own. That was what he had raised them to be. All things considered, he hadn't done a bad job.

The shop was not the gold mine it had been in days gone by. The price of gas had become an accepted fact of life for the complacent citizens of the USA. Airbags, seat belts, steel passenger safety cages, crumple zones—these were what young consumers considered when contemplating personal transportation. To Phil, it was a generation of pussies. The few free spirits that yearned for the wind in their teeth and the throb of hot metal between their legs were enough to provide an adequate living for Phil and Helen, but the days of the money rolling in were a thing of the past. One by one, he had let his help go. There just wasn't enough work to keep employees.

Maybe Helen was right. Sell the place and move back to Vermont. It was cheaper to live in the Green Mountain State and the boys could visit there as well as here. If Helen stayed in remission for a few more months, he'd do it.

"You sell motorcycles, or just fix 'em?" The stranger jolted Phil out of his reverie.

"Both," he answered, smiling. "You looking for something in particular?"

"Triumph Seven-Fifty. You wouldn't know of one for sale, would you?"

"Not off hand." The tall, lean customer looked familiar. Phil would have sworn he remembered that crooked smile. "Do I know you?" There was a tantalizing gleam in the stranger's eye, as if he was laughing at some private joke. "I never forget a face. It's getting harder to connect the names to the mugs, though. I'm not getting any younger."

"You're okay until you're not getting any older."

"True, true," Phil snickered.

"I'm surprised you remember. It was a long time ago."

"I haven't got it yet," Phil waggled a finger at the man. "Don't tell me, it'll come to me."

"No doubt in my mind. About that Triumph—"

"I can take your name and number, do some checking around, and call you." Phil pulled a pen from his shirt pocket and held it poised over the back of his hand.

"Give up already?"

"What? Oh. No, no. Give me another minute. How about some coffee?" He turned toward the Mister Coffee on the workbench at the back of the shop. "I've almost got it."

Phil was enjoying this. He loved to be reacquainted with old friends.

"Coffee sounds good," the tall stranger said. "Black, please."

"Coming up." Phil poured two Styrofoam cups of steaming brew. Laughing softly, he said over his shoulder, "I'll get it. I never forget a face. Just need another minute to place you."

He heard the man murmur, "Times up."

Stars exploded before his eyes as Carl bashed him behind the ear with a two-foot long, open-end wrench. Phil heard running footsteps and the garage door clattering closed as the workbench tilted crazily before rushing up to meet his nose.

 cscs

The cellular phone warbled its electronic song as Doc and Tony climbed into their car. Scooping it from the seat, Doc breathed, "Wiley," into the mouthpiece.

"Where the hell have you been?" Lieutenant Schiff's irate growl made Doc flinch.

"Oyster Bay Hospital. Why? What's up?"

"Why didn't you answer your damn phone?"

Doc took a breath, rolled his eyes heavenward, glanced at Tony, and said, "The phone was in the car. We were in the building. You know—the hospital—where cell phones are banned. I picked it up when I heard it ringing. What's the problem, sir?"

"The problem is—" Schiff paused. In a gentler voice, he continued, "Jack Kobrigian's been shot. He's alive, but it's bad." Doc heard the blood roaring through the arteries in his head. He gulped for air as Schiff said, "A sniper got him and the witness he and Ray went to interview. I'm sorry, Doc."

Doc felt like he had the wind knocked out of him.

Tony was saying, "What?" over and over again. He shushed him with a curt wave.

"Where?"

"A marina in Glen Cove. We got a lead on a boat from the harbor patrol."

"Where is it?" Doc twisted the key in the ignition and gunned the engine.

"Never mind. It's covered. There are cops crawling all over the area as we speak. Bomb squad's checking the boat. Latents is standing by. We'll know everything there is to know about that bucket by nightfall. The weapon was found where the guy dropped it. The Lab and ATF will do their thing on that. There's nothing you can do."

"It's him, isn't it? The fucking Terminator."

"It seems likely. There was a news bulletin on Channel Thirty late last night. They broadcast the lead on the boat. He could have seen it and been waiting for them."

"So, the first order of business is to shoot the son of a bitch who broke the story."

"Your first order of business, Detective Wiley, is to get your ass to Mineola. Leave the leak to me. The media is doing its job, that's all. The culprit we want is the guy feeding them the info. One of our own did this."

"What the hell am I supposed to do in Mineola?"

"Make yourself available for a conference with the commissioner."

"For what? I've got a fucking maniac running rampant out here and you're telling me to come play footsie with the brass."

Schiff's silence told Doc he had gone too far. He didn't care. This was spinning so far out of control it didn't look like it was ever going to come back.

"I'm going to bear in mind," Schiff said deliberately, "that you're upset, Detective Wiley, and disregard your remarks. Now get your smart-ass carcass in here and report to my office. Do you read me?"

Doc slumped behind the wheel, deflated. Déjà vu was becoming a constant companion. Ambushed. Jack was ambushed. He had a new, enigmatic enemy, and this one was kicking his ass, too.

"Wiley!" Schiff barked.

"Yessir, loud and clear." His mind raced. He had to forestall this summons. Something was screaming from his subconscious. There was one more thing to do. "There is something you should be aware of, sir." Doc marveled at the matter-of-fact way his own voice sounded. He might have been commenting on the weather. "The director of nursing here at the hospital may have given us some kind of connection. She grew up with three of the victims—the ones with the brands. The old lady in Garden City was her next-door neighbor before she sold her house to Doctor and Mrs. Green. Her name is Madeline Maclear."

"There's a message here for you to call her back," Schiff said. "I thought she was your latest conquest. Jesus! Bring her in."

"And show our friend where she is? I don't think so." Not the most tactful way to put it, but he was past caring.

"You think she might be next?" Schiff seemed to take no notice of Doc's refusal to obey.

"From what's happened to Jack," Doc said, "I'd say bringing her in is the best way to make sure. If someone on the inside is feeding this asshole information, we can almost guarantee it."

"Point taken. I'll get a couple of dicks up there to baby-sit. We'll figure out where she fits later. Right now, you get over here."

"I'll wait for the baby-sitters."

"Now, damnit."

"Yes, sir, Lieutenant, sir."

Doc mashed the END button with his thumb to break the connection. He turned to Tony, trying to find words to tell him the awful news.

“Well,” Tony urged, “what the hell was that all about?”

“Jack’s been shot. This maniac fuck shot him.”

“Oh, Christ. How? Is it bad?”

“Sniped him—and a witness they went to see. The witness is dead. Jack’s not good.”

“Did they get him?”

Doc wagged his head as if it weighed too much to bear.

“Ray all right?”

“Yeah. I guess so. Schiff didn’t say.”

“No news is good news.”

The references to news made Doc think of Adrienne Boyd. He just knew that Adrienne had been the one to break the story. She had a gift for using other peoples’ misery to further her own ends. Doc pounded the steering wheel in frustration.

“Take a breath, Doc,” Tony said. “Maybe I should drive. Where is Jack?”

“We’re not going there. Schiff’s sending some people to guard Mrs. Maclear,” he said. “We have orders to report to the commissioner ASAP.”

“Happy fucking birthday.”

“You said it, brother.” Doc sighed as he switched off the engine.

“What are you doing?”

“Fuck ’em. The commissioner can wait. Let’s go inside and talk to the lady some more.”

Chapter 20

Philip Nestor felt his pulse throb in his brain. Pain radiated from a spot behind his right ear. He tried to rub it but found he could not move. The attempt resulted in a bout with vertigo. He opened his eyes. Everything was upside down. The shop spun, blurred and inverted.

Slowly, his vision cleared and he could see that he actually was upside down, hanging in mid-air with a length of thick steel chain wrapped tightly around his ankles and body, securing his arms to his sides. The monorail crane he used to move engines and heavy equipment held him suspended with its hook holding the links between his feet. The top of his head was three feet off the floor. His long, red hair hung in sweaty ringlets, the right side matted with drying blood from the wound behind his ear. Duct tape was wound around his jaw and neck, covering his mouth, muffling any cry. His tormentor held the control box for the crane. He depressed the lift button with his thumb and Phil was jerked an inch higher.

"Welcome back, Phillie. I thought I might have tapped you a little too hard." The stranger's kindly tone belied the animosity in his eyes.

Phil struggled, but only caused himself further discomfort. A wave of dizziness swept over him and he retched. Vomit shot out of his nose and he wriggled like live bait on a fishhook, terrified that he would choke to death.

"Easy, big fella." The grinning villain laughed. "We wouldn't want you to strangle in your own puke, would we?"

Carl tilted his head from side to side. "Still can't place my face? Bet you've figured out I wasn't your best friend by now, hey, Phillie?"

Phil's mind reeled. He could not believe this was happening. Who in his life had he pissed off badly enough to warrant this? His face burned with outrage. He cursed and swore but the only sound that escaped the sticky gag was a collection of squeals and grunts. He let his body go limp and puffed air rapidly into and out of his nostrils. The stink of his own vomit nearly caused him to retch again. Forcing self-composure, he looked around the shop, frantic, searching for any means of escape or rescue.

The rollup door was closed. The shade was drawn over the glass in the front entrance. He could see the silhouette of the Gone Riding sign he hung in the window when the shop was closed. Every window in the building was glazed with smoked, wired glass to prevent thieves from entering or seeing what the room contained. But for the bright light through the translucent panes, he would not be able to tell whether it was day or night.

From the slant of the sun's rays, he decided it was late morning. Helen wouldn't be here for hours.

Suddenly, he was afraid, more that this bastard would still be here when she arrived to pick him up than that he, himself, would not.

"Hopeless, isn't it?" the sadistic creep was saying. "I wanted you to feel some semblance of the despair I felt when you and your rotten friends abandoned me. You still don't know me, do you? Haven't you been following the papers? The TV news?"

Phil's blank look told Carl that he had no idea what had been going on.

"Where do you live? On the moon? Dotty? Jethro? Matt? Don't you know what's happened to them?"

Phil wished he had kept up on current events. He never read anything that was not about motors. His television was used only to play videotapes. He hated commercials. His own little world gave him all the headaches he could handle. Other people's problems were just that.

"You really don't know, do you?" Carl was incredulous. "I've been busting my hump killing off the lot of you for the past three days. I spent years in preparation, months in actual planning, and you, you ignorant slob, weren't even paying attention. You deserve it doubly, you stupid shit.

"But I can see I now have your undivided attention by the white showing all around those baby-blue irises. Good. I'm Carl, you insufferable slug. You dumped me on the side of a road at Woodstock more than thirty years ago. You know the world still marvels at the brotherhood all those kids displayed on that miserable weekend. Half-a-million kids and no trouble. But, that's not true, is it? There was one altercation, wasn't there?" Carl nodded slowly. "Well, it's payback time, asshole."

Phil struggled to loosen the gag. He had to talk to this guy, calm him down. What was he making such a fuss about? His own buddies had stripped him naked one summer and loaded him on a southbound freight, drunk as a skunk. He hadn't come to until the car got shunted to a siding in Baltimore. He survived it. Sure, there had been some anger and embarrassment but it was funny after. They had all gotten drunk when he got back, he and his friends, and pissed themselves laughing about it. What was this guy's problem? They were just kids then.

He remembered now. They picked up a hitchhiker in Matt's VW bus on the way upstate. The guy was as square as patio block. He had a crew cut, for Pete's sake. He hung out with them throughout the concert, fucked the ass off of Dotty, and freaked in the van on the trip home. Bad acid or some shit.

So what if they booted him out? The cops were everywhere. Nobody felt like getting busted for some lamebrain. What was the big friggin' deal? It was one of those things you weren't proud of, but he had never lost any sleep over it, either.

Phil's eyeballs nearly popped from their sockets when Carl slid the knives from his waistband at the small of his back.

"Beautiful, aren't they?" Carl said, displaying the weapons. "Perfectly balanced throwing knives. The handles are flattened so that you can carry them on your person without a bulge in your clothing. Quick, silent killing tools—the mark of a craftsman."

Carl tapped his forehead with the knives held in a fan by the blades. Phil could see there were four of them.

"Speaking of tools," Carl said, distracted by something, "don't go away." He placed the weapons on a worktable and withdrew a rod from his sleeve. There was a wooden, tubular handle at one end. From his pocket he produced a blackened hunk of metal and screwed it onto the threaded end of the shaft.

With a flourish, like some clown entertaining children, he held the completed tool up for Phil to inspect and then walked to a corner of the shop behind Phil's field of vision.

Phil found him to be more frightening when he was out of sight than when he was in view. He heard the familiar scritch, scritch, pop as the flint cup ignited the acetylene torch. The hiss of the flame made him sweat. After an eternity, that was in fact only minutes, Carl came back. The glowing brand in his hand was enough to make Phil whimper.

Carl flicked his eyebrows up and down several times, grinning horribly, staring into Phil's frightened eyes.

"Yup," he nodded. "Good guess."

Phil's tears flowed freely, running into his bushy brows and dripping onto the dirty cement floor. With a jerk, Carl ripped his captive's shirt open, exposing the dangling man's hairy belly. He pressed the iron to the flesh, just above the navel. Phil nearly swallowed his tongue in his effort to scream. He hung panting and whimpering, his eyes closed so as not to look at his smoking flesh.

Carl waited until the groans subsided, then wiped Phil's eyes with the remnants of his torn shirt. "This will all be over soon, Phillie." He patted him on the head. "I'm afraid it's going to hurt like hell before we're done, though."

Chapter 21

Doc was flabbergasted to be sharing the spotlight with the brass at a full-blown press conference that began within minutes of his arrival at police headquarters. Strobes flashed and Mini-Cams whirred while Commissioner Shaw whipped up a snow job for the fourth estate that would bring a White House press aide to tears. Doc could not believe they were swallowing any of it. The usual bull was shoveled and, incredibly to Doc, hungrily devoured by the assembled media. Shaw used the whole bag of buzzwords and catch phrases. Doc heard, "several solid leads" and "imminent apprehension" toward the end, and for the first time, he knew just how panicky his superiors were.

The detective's preparation for the conference had been as direct as it was brief. "Just stand there and look solemn. Nod if the commissioner says something positive. And for God's sake, look confident."

No problem. Doc was confident—confident that these people were at least as crazy as the guy they were trying to catch. He and Tony managed not to show their amazement when they learned, along with the reporters lined up wall to wall in folding chairs, that a task force had been set up with Lieutenant Charles Schiff appointed its principal investigator. Doc and Tony, sharing the podium with their bosses, heard that they would figure prominently in the fieldwork. Tony looked ridiculous in the black frame dark sunglasses he had been handed before stepping up on the platform. The brass didn't want his twin shiners causing speculation. No one seemed to care that he looked like a stand-in for a sequel to Men in Black.

Doc was thankful to learn, during Schiff's segment of the farce, that he would not be personally available for questions as the pressures of the case precluded his spending more of his precious time here at headquarters. Doc, Tony, and Schiff were ushered from the stage surrounded by a phalanx of uniforms as the inquisition began.

The brass hats were taking no chances. The detectives never had the chance to utter word one to the media. They were escorted from the conference hall to Commissioner Shaw's office and told to wait. As soon as the door closed behind the minders, Doc unleashed his pent-up fury on his boss.

"It pleases me no end," he snarled through clenched teeth, "to know that my 'valuable time' will be spent in the field, investigating this 'horrendous affair,' where I goddamn was before you dragged me in here to pose for the commissioner's photo op."

Tony grabbed his buddy's arm to pull him back from climbing the lieutenant's shirt. Doc was ready and willing to wipe the righteous indignation from Charlie Schiff's expression, and Tony knew that look.

"This is not a good idea, old buddy," he hissed.

"Sit down, both of you," the lieutenant snapped. He waited several moments while the detectives reluctantly settled themselves in two of three richly upholstered matching wing chairs arranged in a semicircle before the commissioner's massive desk. Then, he let Doc have it. "Wiley, I'm sick of having to explain myself to you," he said, with his arms folded and his buttocks braced against the desk. "The chief and the commissioner will be here shortly, as soon as they can extricate themselves from that circus out there." Schiff indicated the room they had just left with a sharp snap of his head. "Cool down and be prepared to brief them on where we are."

"What for?" Doc still glared at his bullet shaped boss. "They seem to have their own idea of where we are. I'd say Never Never Land from what I just saw at their dog and pony show."

"Enough!" Schiff pulled his chin in and glowered at Doc. "Detective, you better start acting like the ace crime fighter I have purported you to be by the time those two heavyweights step in here, or you will be suspended for insubordination. Don't push me, Doc. I'm not in the mood."

Doc opened his mouth, but Tony's look said: Bite your tongue. He did, but he was still chewing on it when the brass arrived.

"Gentlemen," Shaw gushed, "forgive me for subjecting you to that ludicrous side show." The commissioner took the wind out of Doc's sails with his first remark as he breezed into the room. "It was necessary. I'm sorry you weren't completely briefed beforehand, but time did not allow it."

Mollified but confused, Doc shook his head as if to clear away the cobwebs. "Sir, what the hell is going on?" he said.

"That's what you're here to tell us, Detective Wiley," Chief Needleman said from his position a half step behind the commissioner.

"Would you mind filling me in on this task force I just learned I'm a member of first, sir?"

Shaw frowned at his lieutenant.

Schiff explained, "My men haven't been given the details as yet, Commissioner. We, uh, were discussing other aspects of the case before you came in."

"I see," Shaw said, although it was plain that he did not. He glanced at Chief Needleman, checked his manicure, stole a glance at his Rolex, and said, "I see," once again while he walked with a measured gait to the high-backed chair behind his desk.

Shaw shot his cuffs and took his seat, the picture of intense thought as he looked from one man to the other until he had made the rounds of the room.

Chief Needleman leaned against the wall behind and to the left of his superior, mimicking Shaw's man-by-man study of the occupants and looking very much a part of the framed awards and testimonials decorating the grass-cloth covered wall.

Nodding slowly, like a man who has come to a momentous decision, Shaw said, "To put it in a nutshell, we're trying to regain some control over the investigation. As I'm sure you gentlemen are aware, this thing is escalating at a phenomenal rate. The perpetrator or perpetrators are killing citizens and police officers faster than we can organize our efforts to stop him or them. That media event which you just participated in was designed to allay the fears of the population and restore confidence in this department. Such productions are regrettable but unavoidable in times of crisis."

Doc had no doubts that this was such a time. He had never seen the brass react in such a precipitous fashion. Press conferences were invariably held when the big wheels felt confident of what information they had to disseminate. A rush job, like the one he had just witnessed, and the second one in as many days, was unprecedented.

"Detective Wiley, you are now the point man in this effort," Shaw went on. "All evidence and information from your field investigations will be funneled through Lieutenant Schiff. You will extend every effort to give your supervisors what support they need."

The explanations were over; the commissioner was laying down the law.

"May I offer my condolences with regards to your friend, Detective Kobrigian." The abrupt shift in tone caught Doc by surprise. "That vicious attack is a blow to the entire force, as have been the deaths of the other officers killed by this madman."

Doc compressed his lips, nodded, and examined his feet. He had to admire the guy. Shaw had not gotten where he was by being slow on the uptake. He had homed in on Doc as the root of any disharmony on the investigation team from the vibes in the room and, Doc was certain, from his personnel file. His reputation as a maverick had preceded him.

In fairness, Doc knew there was some truth to the commissioner's speech. He had not forgotten his own little tap dance when he had been put on the hot seat just a few short days ago. What could you do? This was how the game was played.

"Thank you, sir. I appreciate your kind words," he said, to be diplomatic. Schiff watched him closely.

"Let me fill you in on the overall picture, gentlemen," Chief Needleman was at the peak of his didactic form as he explained, "so that you can fully appreciate the magnitude of the situation beyond the obvious dilemma of the crimes." The tone was now set for the meeting. This was not going to be a debate.

Shaw watched their reactions, making eye contact with each of his subordinates individually as the chief spoke. The message was clear. Listen well. Your careers hang in the balance.

"The mood out there," Needleman continued, encompassing the rest of the world with a sweeping hand, "is bordering on panic. Gun dealers, legal and otherwise, are doing a land office business as citizens arm themselves at an alarming rate. Accidental shootings are bound to increase with all that hardware floating around in the hands of untrained civilians. Home and personal security equipment is disappearing from the shelves in retail establishments as fast as it can be restocked. Locksmiths and burglar alarm installers are working round the clock to keep up with the demand. Private security firms and bodyguards—amateurs as well as professionals—have more work than anyone can remember.

"The tension is palpable. This wacko has scared the bejesus out of everyone. Our own personnel are affected. A series of surprise inspections this morning, held at precincts around the county, unearthed a record number of personal weapons in the hands of our patrolmen. They're bringing in everything from semi-automatic shotguns to meat cleavers. A search of one officer's locker produced a machete and three Chinese throwing stars. Naturally, we put the word out that anyone playing Rambo will face the full weight of prosecution. We know, of course, that most of our officers will adhere to policy. The few who do not, the borderline nuts—and let's not kid ourselves, every police force has them—may escalate matters by blowing away some innocent citizen. Even comparatively mild problems, such as the enterprising individual who called the procurement office early this morning to offer to sell us a truckload of ten-foot bamboo poles—" Needleman's face twisted into what passed as a smile at the quizzical looks from the detectives "—to poke dead bodies with before approaching them," he explained. He waited for the expected titter of nervous laughter. He was not disappointed. "Even silly incidents like that fuel the embers of hysteria that threaten to burst into flames at any moment. The situation is volatile. We have to get a handle on this thing, and quickly. Have I left anything out, Commissioner?"

"No, Dave, you've summed it up admirably."

Good doggie. Sit.

Tony placed his hand over his mouth in a prayerful pose to hide the curling corners of his spreading grin. Doc knew Tony had little respect for the well-tailored and well-groomed prima donnas that occupied Mount Olympus, as headquarters was irreverently referred to by the troops. He had to admit, however, to a smattering of jealousy regarding their polish and aura of command. At the same time, he knew in his heart that guys like he and Tony would never rise to such lofty posts. They were too direct, too honest. These two honchos were setting him and his buddy up. If they performed as advertised and nabbed the bastard, they'd be second-string heroes. The brass would take the major credit. If they failed, they'd be buried by the shit storm.

"The only thing I'd care to add," Shaw tactfully contradicted himself, "is that we want to guard against overzealous police action. As is always the case when a cop killer is loose in the streets, we have an abundance of manpower to draw upon. Officers are postponing vacations and deferring time off to work on this. That precludes the unhappy need to cancel leaves and bring in people that would otherwise be off duty." The commissioner paused before he let his voice darken. "The downside is that the temptation to shoot first and ask questions later becomes prevalent in this sort of charged atmosphere. If humanly possible, we want this man alive. I want no speculation that this nut has accomplices waiting in the wings to continue the crusade. I want proof that it's over when we catch him."

Shaw took a moment to weigh his words before pressing on. "The other matter concerns the funerals of the fallen officers. We feel it would be wise to postpone the burials and the services until this fellow is apprehended." He held both hands up as if to ward off a blow at the shocked reaction on the faces of the detectives. "We can't afford to have thousands of cops off the job and lined up in ranks like a shooting gallery while this guy is on the loose."

Doc opened his mouth, but Shaw silenced him with raised eyebrows and index fingers. "The PBA will not hear of it, however. Still, the last thing we need is to have him pick off one of our people while his head is bowed in prayer. We need you to bring this animal to justice so that the proper ceremonies can be observed in the appropriate atmosphere of decorum."

"He wouldn't have the gall," Doc finally had to say.

"Our psychologists fear that he would," Needleman put in. "We're not dealing with a rational individual."

"No shit," Tony said without thinking.

"You seem to be convinced we're dealing with one man, sir." Doc deflected the brass's attention from his verbose partner.

"Aren't you, Detective Wiley?" Shaw asked.

"Yes, sir, I am. The fact that informants and street people know nothing about him, coupled with the personal touches—like the brand and the booby traps—suggest a twisted single personality. If this were some underground demonic gang or something, somebody would talk. Something would slip. The lack of information leads me to suspect a lone wolf."

"Precisely the observations of the head shrinkers." Shaw smiled. "It seems your confidence in Detective Wiley is well placed, Lieutenant." Shaw did a slight bow to Schiff's judgment.

"Thank you, sir," Schiff said, relief on his face.

Doc felt shame for his lieutenant. Welcome to the mutual adoration society, Charlie.

“Now, what have you got for us, gentleman?” Shaw folded his hands in front of him on his desktop and looked expectantly at the detectives.

“A couple of additional questions if you don’t mind, sir,” Doc answered.

Tony nodded as if he knew where his friend was going and imitated the commissioner’s air of expectation.

Shaw knitted his brow. He had expected these men to brief him on the latest developments in the case, not interrogate him. He was uncomfortable in any situation where he didn’t know the questions and their answers beforehand. He hesitated, glancing at Needleman, who shrugged almost imperceptibly, before nodding acquiescence.

“Do we know that Detective Kobrigian’s shooting is related to the other murders?” Doc asked.

“Not with any degree of certainty,” Schiff fielded the question to the delight of his superiors. “It is a logical assumption, however. Jack and Ray were following up on a lead with a probable connection to the case. As you know, we agreed to check with the maritime agencies responsible in connection with the killer’s possible egress by boat from the Glen Cove crime scene.” Schiff paused and the others nodded. He nodded as well and went on. “We noted an encounter with a small motor boat at a period that would coincide with the crime, assuming some elapsed time for the killer to get back to his boat and make his escape. It seems the marine patrol stopped some guy running with his lights off, coming from that direction. Unaware of the crime as they were at the time, they let him off with a warning. They noted his bow registration number in their log. “Jack and Ray ran the number and got the owner’s address. The super in the building says the guy, a Doctor Weiss, left the country several months ago. He did not know where the doctor was headed for. We’re checking with Emigration. Nothing yet.

“Kobrigian decided to do the next best thing and check out the boat. The berthing was listed as that marina. The coincidence of its being in the vicinity of the murders seemed too good to be true.

“They were about to interview the owner of the place when the sniper opened up. He fired one shot. It took out the witness and passed through his body and hit Jack. Maybe a fluke, maybe not. It doesn’t matter. The result is the same.

“The fact that the marina owner was a possible witness leads us to believe there is a strong connection. The dicks that caught the case are running a separate, but parallel investigation with orders to report their findings to me."

"What about the gun and the boat?" Doc asked.

"Nothing so far. The rifle was US military, stolen from an armory in California back in the 'seventies, according to the serial number. Not much we can get on that. The theft was never solved.

"Bomb Squad went in first to check the boat. No surprises this time, thank God. It was clean. Latent Prints has found nothing they can use yet. The corrosive actions of salt and moisture do not lend themselves to clear fingerprints, I'm told. No evidence of any kind suggesting a possible link to anyone. The odds and ends found aboard were all common boat owner articles that can be bought in any marine hardware shop. We'll know more when we locate the owner of the vessel. In the meantime, we've got people questioning every boat owner and employee in the basin. Unless he's the invisible man, whoever has been using that boat had to be seen by someone."

"Okay. Thank you." Doc took a breath and nodded vigorously, his concerns assuaged for the moment. "Tony and I have uncovered a possible lead in Oyster Bay. Has Lieutenant Schiff advised you of Mrs. Maclear's information?" he asked of the two senior men.

"There wasn't time, Doc," Schiff advised. "Brief the commissioner and the chief now, if you would."

Ain't we all so nice and polite now that the hatchets are put away, Doc thought. He sketched the details of Madeline Maclear's revelation.

"Where is this woman now?" Needleman asked.

"Still at the hospital with two men watching her like hawks. I gave them specific instructions not to let her out of their sight."

Doc couldn't resist the chance to let Schiff know he had disregarded his orders to leave immediately. He was serving notice that he had his priorities straight and that the brass's sensitivity to media pressures in no way affected him. Schiff said nothing but his icy stare told Doc he had gotten the message.

"We have to bring her in," Needleman said.

"With the press circling the building like vultures, we thought that unwise." Tony put in his two cents for the first time.

Doc stated his total agreement with his friend. The brass hats had given them a certain amount of clout. Doc knew Tony would enjoy dueling with them on a more level plain.

"You might be right," Shaw pondered the ramifications of having another witness slaughtered under their noses. It could cost him his job. "Still, she has to be questioned at length. This could be the break we've been praying for."

"May I make a suggestion, sir?" Tony said.

"Certainly, Detective Cordova."

Tony outlined his plan.

"Lieutenant Schiff—" Shaw's face split in a toothy grin. "—any doubts I may have had are fading rapidly. With brilliant men such as these on the job, The Terminator's days are numbered. Get it done." He rubbed his palms together, obviously pleased with the way things were shaping up. "How about lunch, Dave?"

ଔଔ

By two o'clock that afternoon, they were loading Madeline Maclear into the rear of a Nassau County Police ambulance. Strapped to a stretcher with her head swathed in bandages and her face hidden by a pressure dressing, Madeline was unrecognizable. They had even left her bare feet exposed to add a touch of realism.

Doc and Tony, clad in green Nassau County Emergency Medical uniforms, slammed the rear doors and ran to the front to climb into the cab.

"Lights and sirens?" Tony asked.

"Let's not get carried away," Doc replied. "The idea is to be covert, remember?"

"Gotcha, but you're the one who wanted to play this thing to the hilt."

They didn't relax until they were barreling south on Route 106 at fifty-five miles per hour.

"Do you think we're overdoing this?" Doc cast a sidelong glance at Tony before flicking his eyes back to the road. He was unaccustomed to handling the big van and he was nervous about his driving.

"If this guy turns out to sleep hanging upside down in a closet and can read minds, I won't be surprised. The one thing we can be sure of is: there's no such thing as being too careful."

"I'm glad you said it. I was afraid I was the only one who thought this guy might be supernatural."

“I don’t know about supernatural but this asshole is definitely super-bad.”

“Mrs. Maclear?” Doc said over his shoulder.

“Can I sit up now?” she asked. Her voice sounded so childlike that Doc wanted to hug her.

“Yes, ma’am. There’s a crossing guard’s uniform back there. It’s hanging from the curtain over the window. Would you please put it on?”

They had explained the hastily laid, but carefully thought out plan to Madeline when they had returned to the hospital in the borrowed ambulance. Being forthright about the necessity for secrecy, while downplaying the chances of any real danger, they convinced the reluctant witness to cooperate. Doc felt bad about heightening the woman’s anxiety but he thought it essential to protect her anonymity for the present. Once she was safe in their custody behind the walls of HQ, she would settle down. When her initial apprehension with the cloak and dagger bit had subsided, she assumed her role with enthusiasm. The bandages and the bare feet had been her idea. Under her direction, Mr. Strechman and a team of trusted nurses had thrown themselves into the deception. She was a gutsy lady, this angel of mercy.

Doc glanced in the rearview mirror and caught a glimpse of her freckled back above the clasp of her bra. She was slipping into the white blouse of the uniform and asking, “Would it be possible to get something to eat where we’re going? I just realized I’m famished. I haven’t eaten since yesterday.”

“Certainly Mrs. Maclear. We’ll get you anything you want.” Doc snapped his head to the front as she turned her head to speak. He thought she caught his eye as his reflected gaze lingered a fraction of a second too long. It irked him. He’d thought he was way beyond embarrassment by so trivial a thing as male voyeurism. Something about this woman brought out the gentlemen in him.

“The blouse is a little tight,” she said, “but the jacket will cover that. Can I change back into my own clothes once we get there?”

“You can change into anyone’s clothes you like,” Tony quipped, “once we have you safely tucked away, Mrs. Maclear.”

Doc’s glare made Tony cringe. He shrugged his, What-can-I-tell-you? I’m-a-jerk, shrug.

“Well, who says cops aren’t fun people?” Madeline said.

Tony laughed, lit a cigarette, and said, just loud enough for Doc's ears, "Sharp and cute. A man could do worse."

Doc drove on in silence, trying to ignore Tony, doing his best to quiet the nagging doubts in his head.

Chapter 22

The late morning sun was warm on his face when Carl slipped out the back door of the late Philip Nestor's repair shop. He moved deliberately, like a man who belonged exactly where he was. He even stopped to wave goodbye to give the impression there was someone alive inside the shop. Not a crate, rusted bike part, bald tire or bit of junk escaped his scrutiny as he examined his surroundings in detail, but no observer would have seen anything but the passing of a disinterested man without a care. The cluttered yard was silent. Not even the call of birds broke the stillness. To Carl, it seemed that even Mother Nature walked softly in his presence.

After glancing left and right, he walked quickly to a gaping hole in the rusted chain link fence and stepped through it to emerge alongside a railroad right-of-way. His long strides carried him swiftly along until he came to another opening in the dilapidated barrier that opened onto a railway station parking lot.

With the air of a man with nothing on his mind beyond a brisk stroll in the spring sunshine, he zigzagged his way between the cars and emerged on the street. He passed no one until he was several blocks from Wheelies-R-Us, and then only one fellow pedestrian who ignored him, intent on his own destination.

In his olive-green, Jeep Grand Cherokee—a vehicle Carl thought of as his command car—he started the motor and pulled into the street. Switching the radio to a news station, he headed north on Long Beach Road. As he drove, he stretched a wavy blonde wig over his straight brown hair and covered it with a white Panama hat sporting a wide black band. He stripped off his Windbreaker at the red light at the intersection of Sunrise Highway and pulled on a mustard-colored, fringed suede jacket over his flowered Hawaiian shirt. Tortoise-shell mirrored sunglasses completed his disguise. The car was sporting vanity plates today—2 COOL.

His outfit was outlandish, but he had learned that garish dress distracted the eye. Witnesses remembered almost nothing about the features of a person they had encountered whose clothing consumed all of their attention.

Just before he pulled into the parking lot behind the Seventh Street shopping district in Garden City, he popped open the glove compartment and palmed a .25 caliber automatic, which he slipped into his pants pocket as he exited the car.

Around the corner, in the post office, Carl waited patiently in line. When his turn came, he flashed his most beguiling smile at the bored counter clerk.

"Could you give me the forwarding address of Ms. Madeline Maclear?" he said. "I understand she's moved, and I don't know where to send the balance of her order." He gave the clerk Madeline's previous address.

He had a brief moment of anxiety when the woman fixed her stare on his hidden eyes as if she could discern the thoughts behind the glasses. Had the police alerted the postmaster to have his minions be on guard for just such an inquiry? Did the woman remember the address from a news account of the killings?

His hand gripped the tiny pistol in his pocket. The woman turned without a word and stepped to a desk in the sorting area. Carl, although outwardly nonchalant, watched her closely. If she raised any alarm he would shoot her and the woman directly behind him to clear his escape route. He calculated his odds of getting away in the ensuing confusion and judged them to be acceptable.

The clerk returned momentarily and in her practiced monotone said, "That'll be a dollar, and I need to see some ID." She held a slip of paper face down on the counter with her fingertips securing it. Her omnipotent smile told the world she was not going to release any information until this weirdo coughed up a buck and identified himself.

Carl pulled a single from his wallet and a stolen driver's license. He slid both items across the counter. The picture bore no resemblance to his present self beyond the blonde hair. The height and weight depicted on the laminated card were not even close.

The clerk, a civil service worker of some twelve years, gave him her best you-are-insignificant-in-the-eyes-of-the-Federal-Government look and copied the license number onto a form. She said,

"Sign here," and pushed the slip of paper across the worn Formica. Carl scratched Francis Sinatra in an illegible scrawl and shoved the form and a dollar bill back across the counter. Without looking at it, the clerk dropped the slip it into a drawer and the money into her till before handing Carl the address.

"Have a nice day," she said, dripping insincerity, but she was already talking to his back. "Next!"

Humming merrily, with the scrap of paper folded neatly in his wallet, Carl shucked the hat, wig, and jacket as he sped along Stewart Avenue. He stuffed these items into a plastic garbage bag before throwing it on the floor. Ripping the purloined license into tiny pieces, he sprinkled the scraps out the window as he drove.

Ten minutes later, in the relative darkness of the ground floor parking spaces of Roosevelt Field Mall, he changed his shirt to a pale yellow, button-down Oxford and jammed the sports shirt into the bag before tying the black plastic into a knot. After retrieving his own license plates from the glove compartment, he slipped into his Windbreaker and stepped from the car. He used his battery-operated screwdriver to remove the vanity tags and refasten his own. After slipping the unwanted plates into a gap behind a drainpipe, he tossed the bag into a handy trash receptacle and entered the busy mall.

It had been a highly successful day and it was barely late afternoon. He decided he would enjoy lunch upstairs in the food court. He could sit beneath the silvery mockup of the dirigible and imagine it was the Hindenburg on her final trans-oceanic run. Mexican would be nice—tacos, or maybe a burrito. And why not take in a movie? He deserved a little R&R.

∽∽

The cellular phone bleeped insistently. Doc glared at it but kept both hands on the wheel. Tony reluctantly plucked it from the ambulance's front seat.

"Detective Cordova," he said, listened, and then said, "Yessir, we're on the way in. He's right here. Hang on." With his palm over the mic, Tony swung the phone to Doc, saying, "Your master's voice."

Grumbling, "Now what?" Doc snatched the instrument from Tony's outstretched hand. "Yessir?" He listened for a moment before saying, "Can't it wait 'til we get there?" Doc nodded. "Okay. Tony, write this down." Doc repeated a telephone number as Schiff dictated.

He listened for a few seconds, nodding impatiently. "Right, I'll call him and get back to you." He broke the connection.

"What's up?" Tony inquired.

"Old buddy of mine on the NYPD called Schiff. Says he's got something for us that might help—big time."

"Why didn't he just give it to the desk?" Tony asked, annoyed. "If it's hot, they'd put it on a lead sheet and get it to you post haste."

"I know that and so does he. I also know Mitch. He wants something. He always does." Doc tried to brace the wheel with his knees and depress the buttons on the keypad.

"Let me do that before you get us all killed," Tony snorted.

"Be my guest," Doc scowled, flipping Tony the phone.

When he heard a ring, Tony passed the plastic set back.

"NYPD Anti-Terrorist Unit, Sergeant Numkeenaestwa speaking."

Doc's eyebrow shot up when he heard the unit that his old friend was now assigned to. Could the Terminator be connected to some terrorist cell? It didn't feel right.

Mitch was in Homicide, like himself, the last time Doc had seen him. They met while working a border crossing case. The suspect lived in Queens Village—New York City turf. His victim, however, had been a housewife in Valley Stream, a community astride county lines. Her home, the place of her death, was on the Nassau side, so Doc investigated the crime and the city cops assisted. The case went well, largely due to Mitch.

Numkeenaestwa, a full-blooded Navajo, was a crack detective and an insatiable womanizer who could also drink with the best of them. Doc couldn't help but smile at his fond memories of the irreverent Native American. He had liked the guy instantly, a rare occurrence for Doc.

Mitch's only irritating trait was his driving ambition. He had told Doc outright, their first night carousing the hot spots of Queens Boulevard, that he was destined to rise to the top.

"What else can I do?" Mitch had said, with what Doc remembered as abject resignation. "I'm the great grandson of a great chief. I'm honor bound to assume my place as head of the tribe, but the tribe's scattered to hell and gone. Only place to be chief is right fuckin' here. Shit! You white-eyes pricks ripped us off to get this burg. 'Bout time one of us took it back."

"I thought you shortened it to Numkeena?" Doc said into the phone, surprised by Mitch's use of his ancestral surname.

"I did, but I can't say it on the phone. Can't have the damn microwaves carrying the Americanized version to my ancestors. They'd go buffalo shit."

"You're as crazy as ever." Doc laughed. "What's so important? And where the hell are you working now?"

"I'm in Anti-Terrorist. It's a blast. Get it?"

"Very funny. What does it have to do with me and what do you want for it?"

"I'm hurt, Doc. What makes you think I want anything?"

"I haven't seen anything on the news yet about New York City honoring its first chief of detectives to wear a war bonnet to work so I figure you're still taking scalps on your way to the big, brick wigwam at One Police Plaza. Give, Mitch, then we'll circle the wagons."

Mitch laughed so hard, Doc had to pull the phone from his ear.

"I gotta get you to quit that Boy Scout outfit and come to work for a real police force," Mitch said, still laughing. "We could use a guy like you to liven up this joint. You never seen such grim looking palefaces as we got here."

"Mitch…"

"Okay, Doc, here we go." Mitch took an audible breath and began to explain. "Couple or three days back, we got a PI name of Wannamaker whacked in his office over near Eighth Avenue. Dude had a crossbow bolt through the jugular. Sitting Bull himself couldn't have put that arrow any closer to the mark. They tossed the premises and the guy's pad. He's got enough paper in both places to start a recycling company. Homicide's been sifting through the shit ever since."

"So?"

"We got involved when a PO who entered the deceased's apartment on day one found an envelope that he stuck in his pocket but forgot to turn it in until the following day. There's a bunch of numbers on the envelope and a name—The Colonel. Now there's this character known as "The Colonel" been popping up in all sorts of nefarious shit for the last year and a half. Strictly background, mind you, never directly involved in anything where the action happens, but on the fringes of all sorts of nasty crap. This clown's connected to everything from bomb factories to illegal aliens and just about everything in between. Us, Homicide, Narcotics, Vice, the feds, everybody's got a file on this turkey and nobody's got anything solid.

The guy's a ghost and I mean that literally. We got some decent partials from Latents in one bomb factory we believe he set up. Fibbees matched 'em to a GI name of John Campbell. Long range patrol specialist, Vietnam type. You know, the kind of shit you did. Ever meet up with him?"

"It was a big, small-country, Mitch." The hair on the back of Doc's hands was standing up. He felt the blood draining from his cheeks. Speaking deliberately to keep the quiver out of his voice, he said, "Drop the other moccasin, Mitch."

"Good instincts, white eyes." Mitch paused. "That's what I meant about the ghost part. He's dead. Blown away on the Ho Chi Minh Trail near Cambodia in 1973."

"Remains unviewable." Doc breathed the dreaded words Graves Registration tagged the coffins of those bodies too ghastly to expose to the sheltered citizens back home.

"Bullseye."

"But he's not dead," Doc said.

"So it would seem. Faked it, I'd guess. Leastways, that's what I'd choose to believe. I like my spirits eighty proof, as you know. Looks like one very mean mother is still practicing old, bad habits. This boy learned well. No one that we've turned up has ever laid eyes on him. Handles everything he gets into through dead drops and cutouts. I mean a total mystery man. The guy makes Carlos look like a klutz."

"How can you be sure the prints were his?"

"We were tipped to this bomb making place over on Third Avenue. The broad who dropped the dime specifically mentioned The Colonel. We busted the joint. It was vacant but there was mucho evidence. Explosives up the yingyang—mostly homemade—and enough forensics to make The Lab boys cream in their drawers. Prints galore. But the only prints we couldn't connect to a known creep were Campbell's. They came up when we got access to the feds' computer files. Army records say the whole unit was wiped out. No survivors."

"But all of the bodies weren't recovered," Doc probed.

"Right again. One missing. I knew you would see the silver lining. If you weren't so damned Caucasian, I'd swear you were Navajo, bro."

"What happened to the tipster—the lady who blew the whistle?"

Mitch sighed. "Unknown. Never called back. If he rolled to it, she's probably one of the Jane Doe floaters we pull from the Hudson now and then."

"What's the connection to The Terminator?"

"Patience, paleface. I'm coming to that. By the way, who dreamed up the catchy nickname? Even the press ain't that clever."

"I'll introduce you some day. You'll like him. He's a smartass, too. Now can the suspense shit. The connection?"

"Okay, okay. Dig this. The numbers on the envelope turn out to be social security numbers. Six sets. It took a while for The Lab boys to bring them up. Some of them were smeared, but they finally got all of them. We ran the whole batch through the computer and guess what."

"What? Dammit."

"Three of them are the names of three of your Terminator's score."

"Holy shit."

"My exact words."

"What about the other three?" Doc had to force his eyes to watch the road.

"Hang on. I've got them right here."

Doc heard paper rustling. A moment later, Mitch was back. "Here ya go. Nestor, Philip E, Barbarosa, Ron…"

"The Ron Barbarosa, the Mets batting coach?" Doc interrupted, aghast.

"The same. Maybe he should reconsider that offer from Detroit."

"That's five, Mitch. One more."

"Maclear, Madeline P., RN."

Doc's knuckles went white. His countenance matched.

"Doc?" Mitch said. "You still with me, buddy?"

"Yeah, Mitch. I'm here," Doc answered when he could catch his breath. "You got last knowns on these?"

"Does Mister Rogers like kids?"

"Good. I'm going to put Tony Cordova on the phone. I've got my hands full at the moment. Give him the addresses and phone numbers if you've got them. Can you fax me all the stuff you've got on this colonel character? And please say you've got a photo ID to go with the prints on this Campbell guy."

"No prob, Kemosabe. Living black and white, military ID card and 201 file. All these folks live out your way and we've got a shitload of other stuff to work on so I'll gladly leave them in your capable hands. If the fax don't come through clear, call. I'll bring it all out pony express. You buy lunch."

"A bargain. Thanks pal. I owe you."

"Funny you should say that."

"Go on." Here it comes.

"I'd like to call in the marker now. Do me a favor?"

"If I can, Cochise. What?"

"Feed me anything you find that connects to The Colonel. If he's not your boy, he's his public relations man. There'd be a lot of faces around here redder than mine if I were the guy to fit a jacket on this dude. One more step up the old totem pole, you dig?"

"Count on it, Mitch. You'll be the first."

"That's what she said."

"Here's Tony. You take care, Mitch."

"You betcha, Doc. And hey, let's get together sometime soon and chase some more of that paleface tail. If I can't take scalps, I'll settle for beaver."

"Sure, Mitch," Doc said absently, "thanks." He handed Tony the phone and pantomimed writing in the air. Tony nodded and produced his notebook. Doc concentrated on his driving while Tony took notes. He tried not to think that the lady in the back was into something vile right up to her pretty little nose. When his partner hung up and handed him the pad, Doc stared hard at the last name, the one with the Garden City address.

"Is this what I think it is?" Tony wanted to know.

"It ain't Santa's Christmas list." Doc quietly filled him in on the rest, careful not to let Madeline overhear.

"Mrs. Maclear?" Tony called, leaning sideways and craning his neck to face Madeline. "Do you know Philip Nestor or Ron Barbarosa?"

There was fear in her eyes as she bobbed her head to indicate the affirmative. "From high school," she said, "Why?"

Doc stole a glance in the rearview mirror. Tony looked to him, unsure how much to let on.

"She's got to know," Doc said quietly. Raising his voice to what he hoped was a conversational tone, he said, "Mrs. Maclear, that phone call was to a friend of mine in the New York City Police. They found a list at the home of a murdered private investigator. Those names were on the list, along with Mrs. Kohler, Mr. Bradley, and Mr. Collins." Doc paused. How did he tell her?

"Was my name on the list?" Madeline asked.

"Yes, ma'am."

"Then he's after me, too." She said it quietly, devoid of emotion, a simple statement of fact.

"We have no proof that this is related to the killings out here, Mrs. Maclear," Doc tried to reassure her.

"Detective Wiley," she said, "I'm not a fool. What else could it be? And I'm not some hysterical female that you can keep in the dark. My life may be at stake here. It almost certainly is. I have to be sure that I can trust you to level with me, to tell me everything that's going on. Can I depend on that?"

"Absolutely." Doc said it as if it were a vow.

"Mrs. Maclear." Tony chose his words carefully. "After hearing the names of everyone on that list, can you make any connection among you and your high school friends that might lead us to the killer? Can you think of any event, any conversation, any shared experience or ideology that would make someone track you all down and murder you one by one?"

"Detective," she said. "I've been wracking my brain to remember just the kind of thing you're suggesting ever since I saw that story on CNN. But you have to understand: we were friends in a loose definition of the word. Acquaintances might be a more accurate description. We were not members of any radical group. With the exception of Ron, we didn't even go out for athletic teams. I haven't seen any of them since they graduated. I cannot imagine who would want any of us dead, or why. You have to believe me."

"We do, Mrs. Maclear," Tony said. "But right now, you're the best hope we have of figuring out who we're after. Once we know who he is, we get up to bat. Until then, it's his ball game and we don't even know the rules."

"I'm sorry. I just can't remember anything that might help."

"Just relax for now," Doc said. It sounded stupid. He heard the fear in her voice and it bothered him. "We can go over it piece by piece in Mineola. We'll figure it out. You can take that to the bank." He wished he felt as confident as he was trying to sound. "Tony, call Schiff. Give him the run down on the list. Have him get some cops to the other two people's homes. We'll figure out what to do with them after we've got them under guard and can get around to talking to them. Maybe between the three of them, they can dope this out." His own words made Doc shudder. Was this related to drugs? The level of violence had the smell of the cartels. It would break his heart to find out that the uncannily attractive lady in the back was mixed up in anything as sordid as cocaine.

"Barbarosa's in Florida, Doc," Tony advised him.

"Huh? Oh yeah, spring training. Tell Schiff to have someone call him down there. He's gotta be warned. See if Jack and Ray can go to this guy Nestor's house."

"You mean just Ray, don't you?"

"No, I—Oh, Christ," he choked.

"Yeah, I know. I can't believe it either."

When Tony got the lieutenant on the phone, Doc added, "Tell him about that fax that's coming in for me and how this colonel guy fits in. Have him get somebody to look it over and run the picture and prints through the computer. See if this Campbell's got a sheet." To Madeline he added, "We'll want you to look at the picture. Maybe you'll know him." He hoped it would be that simple, but something told him it was false hope.

The tension in the ambulance was palpable. Even Tony was quiet. For once, his whit had forsaken him.

Chapter 23

This is Bellwood. I'm at the Nestor house," Detective Gene Bellwood reported to his sergeant via his cellular phone.

Bellwood and Sam Ogus waited in their car outside the modest frame dwelling. Gene Bellwood, behind the wheel, was apprehensive. Ogus, beside him, leaned against the passenger door with his vacant eyes trained on the house. A bunch of kids played street hockey half a block in front of them.

In-line skates had replaced the noisy, clamp-on metal wheels of Bellwood's youth. The boys glided over the blacktop, their plastic rollerblades whirring a carefree song.

When I was a kid, Gene thought, we'd have the balls and bats out by now. Times had changed. Kids today played hockey all year round. He thought it sad.

Sam Ogus disliked kids. For that matter, Sam Ogus disliked almost everybody. He wore an expression of perpetual disdain that Bellwood thought might have been painted on by some jaded artist forever soured on life. Ogus was as inanimate as Bellwood was animated. He could, and often did, sit for hours without moving a muscle, as he was doing now. Once, when they had just begun working together, Bellwood had asked Ogus how he could stay motionless as a rock for such extended periods of time. Ogus turned his head, and only his head, very slowly, until his eyes settled on his partner. He blinked once, his lip curled into a sneer, and the head swiveled back to where it had been before Bellwood had broken whatever rule he had broken. Bellwood never brought it up again.

Ogus had so many weird foibles that for the first two months they worked together, Gene Bellwood went home every day and complained to his wife about the certifiable cretin the department had saddled him with. At first, she sympathized with his plight, offered moral support and sensible advice. Gradually, her patience wore as thin as the gold on a ten-dollar watch.

"Gene, dear," she said, one night after she had listened to him whine, "tomorrow I want you to put in for a transfer, quit the force, or shoot that crazy bastard Ogus right in the head."

He never complained about Sam again and, although he would never be fond of his colleague, he had grown used to having him around.

Now, Bellwood looked at Ogus for some sign that he was alive and wondered if his very odd co-worker had ever been young. Bellwood could not recall ever having heard Ogus speak of his youth. Actually, he had never heard him speak a complete sentence. Ogus's lexicon of short phrases served as his entire repertoire of speech. Bellwood, on the other hand, liked to talk, especially when he was worried, as he was now.

The sergeant interrupted his ruminations by telling him to proceed as instructed.

"Before we go in there," Bellwood hedged, "I want to be sure of who this guy Nestor is, Sarge. Can we expect this dude to be friendly or is he gonna start shooting?"

"And who am I? The Great Kreskin? Schiff says this guy's a possible target but seeing as how we don't know who the bad guys are just yet, it would seem prudent to watch your butts. Just see if he's home. Ask him if he knew any of the victims and play it by ear. Call back after you talk to the guy. I'll see what's shakin' then."

Bellwood broke the connection, feeling no less apprehensive than when he had initiated the call. He climbed out of the car and motioned for Ogus to follow.

The kids stopped their game to watch the show, either leaning on their sticks or gesticulating with excited hands. Two suits in an unmarked Ford sporting black-wall tires and cheap hubcaps meant only one thing. Somebody was going to get busted. At least, they hoped, in their little boy's fantasies, that this would be the outcome. With any luck at all, there would be a blazing gun battle to boot.

"Mrs. Nestor?" Bellwood said to the frail woman who answered his knock, "I'm Detective Bellwood. This is Detective Ogus."

Her head was wrapped in a purple bandanna and it was obvious that the lady was not well. Helen Nestor hid her body behind the door and her fingers absently rubbed the alligatored white paint at its edge.

She seemed embarrassed, possibly by her appearance. She was visibly upset, but that is not an unusual reaction when two cops come banging on your door uninvited.

"Is it my husband? Is he hurt?" Her eyes bounced from one man to the other.

"Not that we know of, ma'am. We just want to talk to him."

"But he's not here." The woman looked back into her home as if to confirm her husband's absence. "I was supposed to pick him up at the shop, but the car won't start. Isn't that always the way? My husband's a mechanic and my car won't start."

It was easy to see she had been very pretty once. There was a light in her eyes that her apparent pain could not dull. Though visibly distressed, she kept her sense of humor. A strong, proud woman, Bellwood observed with admiration.

"Do you know where he is, ma'am?"

"Yes. That's what I'm saying. He's at his shop. I've been calling and calling but there's no answer. The machine would be on if he went out. I'm getting worried. What do you want to see him about?"

"We have some questions in relation to a crime we're investigating."

"What sort of crime? Phil hasn't done anything wrong."

"Not that we know of, ma'am. His name came up. We just need to speak to him."

"Phil's not involved in anything illegal. Is it one of his old friends? He used to know some pretty strange people, but that was a long time ago." She rubbed her forehead and raised a shaking hand. "I'm sorry. I'm babbling. My husband is a hardworking, good man. Some of his former friends are a little screwy, but he hasn't hung out with them in years. Could you go over there? To the shop? It's not far. It's over near Oil City. You know, the street that runs back past the tanks? Have him call me, please. I'm really getting worried."

She gave them the address. Bellwood called in on the way to advise his sergeant of the result of the contact. He was told to proceed with caution.

"No shit," he said to the dial tone.

At the shop, which they located after one wrong turn, they tried the front door, found it locked and started to walk back to the car to report that the place was closed. The worry he had seen in the brave wife's eyes made Bellwood want to look for another way in. He stopped halfway to the curb and launched into a lengthy rhetoric as to why they should try again that was equally divided between altruism and pleas to Sam's humanity.

Ogus waited until Bellwood ran out of steam and said, "Back door."

Bellwood circled the building with Ogus in tow. They found a narrow alley that led to the rear of the shop and, after negotiating a mud puddle closely resembling a lake, located a steel fire door. It opened easily, but noisily, on hinges that had never tasted oil. The gloomy interior of the garage had an air of menace. The sour smell of vomit hit them as soon as they set foot inside. Bellwood backed out and bumped into Ogus.

"Something stinks in there. Let's call in," he told him.

"Lieutenant Schiff," he heard before the phone had completed one ring. He raised an eyebrow, wondering why the lieutenant was taking a personal interest.

"Yes, sir. This is Detective Bellwood. Are you apprised of my situation?"

"Are you at the witness's place of business?"

"Yes, sir." Bellwood nodded as if Schiff could see the gesture. "Something's wrong. The front door's locked and something smells bad in there."

"Detective Bellwood," Schiff commanded, "you are not, I repeat, not to enter that building. Do you understand?"

"Completely." Sweat broke out on Bellwood's shiny black forehead. "Is it him? The Term—er, uh. I mean…"

"It's a possibility, Bellwood. We are not taking chances with this bastard anymore. The Bomb Squad is on the way. The sector car will arrive any minute. Seal the street at both ends, at least a block from the building. You will have all the help you can ask for, shortly. Just don't go in there."

"Uh, sir, I already did."

"Say what?"

"The lady, Mrs. Nestor, she was awfully worried about her husband. The front door is locked but I found one in back that's open. I only went in a coupla steps. It smells like puke in there. The guy may be sick. Maybe he got hurt or something."

"Bellwood, your concern for these people is admirable, but we don't know what to expect next from this asshole. You follow orders and let me worry about it. Okay?"

The patrol car was nosing into the street as Bellwood emerged from the alley. "Yes, sir. I understand. Backup has arrived."

By the time the Bomb Squad rolled up with their containment truck, which resembled a Quonset hut on wheels, the street was a beehive of blue. All occupants of adjacent businesses were gathered at either end of the block behind police barricades. The people leaned on the crossbars or milled about behind the sawhorses, speculating or just watching the drama unfold. The Bomb Squad, in their flak suits and Kevlar helmets, conferred with their colleagues on the scene and elected to enter the same way Bellwood had. What they found in the shop sent two of them trotting back outside to lose their lunch.

Philip Nestor had bled white. A sticky crimson pool spread outward from beneath his inverted, gently swaying body. Droplets of blood dripped into the stain, sending sluggish red ripples radiating from their impact points. Four, razor sharp throwing knives were embedded in his lifeless shell, resembling the quarter hours on a clock and encircling the brand burned into his middle. His eyes bulged from their sockets. You could almost hear his silent scream beneath the silvery tape.

The explosives experts meticulously checked every feasible corner, toolbox, vehicle, cabinet, and point of entry. They paid particular attention to the corpse and its method of suspension. The monorail crane lay in many small pieces on the floor when they were finished. Dogs sniffed the corpse for hidden explosives. After three hours, they declared the building, "Clean."

"Dry hole," the officer in charge told the detectives as he peeled off his body armor. "Maybe he's out of ordnance."

"You wish," the detective sergeant snorted.

"Don't we all? Anyway, it's all yours."

The coroner loaded a black, zippered body bag into a black station wagon and the Crime Scene Unit took over. Darkness overtook the investigation and the lights in the shop were lit. One hour later, they suddenly went out. Everyone froze. Hands groped for guns as the three remaining detectives swiveled their heads in the blackness.

"It's a timer," Bill Fredericks called out. "The lights are on a timer. I heard it click. No big deal. Stand still. I know where it is. Over by the breaker panel. Don't nobody get trigger-happy. I'm going to reset it." He lit a penlight flash and aimed it at the box. The dim glow cast eerie shadows outside the halo of light.

"No way," Sergeant James O'Toole stated flatly. "We're outta here. This asshole is too tricky. We beat feet and call the Bomb Squad back in. Bill, shine your light on the back door. Mike, you first. Move easy. Don't bump nuthin'. Bill, you follow. I'll be right behind you."

They might have seen the faint glow from the little red indicator light on the motion detector that guarded the back door had Bill's flash not destroyed their night vision. The Bomb Squad had understandably missed the explosive charge secreted in the ballast compartment of one of the overhead strip lights. The block of Semtex fit snugly in the empty transformer casing. Unless you opened it up, something no one was likely to do, it looked like any other fluorescent ballast. Carl had used a squeeze bulb full of dust swept from the floor to mask the grime he had disturbed. The wiring was original, but subtly rerouted. The timer was common equipment for energy conscious businesses. The motion detector was activated when the timer shut the lights off. It was all very normal and obviously very old. Carl had rigged an ingenious trap from existing equipment. The explosive ballast was the only addition, and it replaced one he had removed and discarded. It did not light the lamps, of course, but there were other burned out bulbs in the system so these did not stand out. The technicians were looking for something recently installed or disturbed. Even the dogs had not picked up the scent of the charge, encapsulated as it was in its steel casing.

Mike's body broke the infrared beam, which activated the alarm switch that had been wired to the charge. He alone survived the blast that hurled him through the open door.

Chapter 24

Madeline Maclear had a headache—not your ordinary take-two-aspirin-and-sit-quietly-for-half-an-hour headache. This, she believed, must have been the kind Quasimodo must have suffered before the bells of Notre Dame hammered his eardrums into jelly.

She wondered how her life could have gone from bad to worse so swiftly. What would have happened if she had not seen that CNN newscast?

Doc and Tony briefed her on the plan to smuggle her into police headquarters. "Plan-A," Cordova related, as much to distract Doc from punching the siren to part the sea of automobiles known as rush hour traffic as to explain, "goes like this. Doc takes this bus to the parking lot. You and I walk from there to HQ. We stroll in through the rear entrance, cool as can be, just two more cops going into Cop Central. Just follow my lead and act natural. We don't expect to attract any attention. Our nosy friends in the media will be looking for bigger fish. Inside, we go to the conference room and we're home free."

"What about Detective Wiley?" Madeline tried to keep the anxiety out of her question, but the detectives were too well attuned to the subtle inflections in human speech patterns not to notice.

"I'll follow along as soon as I return this chariot to its stall," Doc promised.

"We figure it's safer that way." Tony needled Doc with a leer. "My friend here is a bit of a celebrity in his own right as of this morning."

"I—" Doc said, "—was dragged into the limelight at a press conference, I'm sorry to say."

"Really? I'm impressed."

"Not that we think anyone's going to ask for his autograph or rip his clothes off." Tony was obviously enjoying Doc's discomfort with his Warholian fifteen minutes. "It's just that some of these reporters have near photographic memories and we don't want to take chances."

"Uh huh," Madeline said. "So that's Plan-A. What is Plan-B?"

"Plan-B," Tony said with a sigh, "is whatever we do in the event something goes wrong with Plan-A."

Plan-B proved to be unnecessary as Plan-A went off without a hitch. Once safely ensconced in the conference room, Tony's comment about the media, "salivating like a pack of hyenas at a pig roast," went over like a mesh parachute with Chief Needleman. Tony winked at Madeline. She swept her hand swiftly across the top of her head. Tony's nodding smile behind the chief's back said he agreed. The jokes were definitely over Needleman's head.

Madeline decided she liked the flippant detective's personality.

Hours later, sitting in a comfortably upholstered swivel chair with black plastic arms, Madeline kneaded the bridge of her nose. Her headache was reaching legendary proportions. The long conference table was littered with refuse from fast food meals. Brown glass ashtrays, overflowing with cigarette butts, dotted its length. The ban on smoking in workspaces seemed to have been rescinded.

Gone was the light humor of the early stages of the discussion. Mitch Numkeena's faxed documents had done little to help zero in on a suspect. The blown up, grainy photo bore more resemblance to Howdy Doody than anyone else in Madeline's memory. The shaved head and the big ears on the kid in the picture lost their comic aura when she remembered that this boy was either dead or very much alive and murdering people she had once called friends. The file made it clear that finding anyone with any information on John Campbell was going to be nearly impossible. His entire unit had been wiped out. The bodies were badly decayed when recovered, and Campbell, or what the army had assumed to be Campbell, was mutilated. He had no family. In fact, his entire background was fictitious.

The missing member of the team, one Eric York, had lived in Nebraska, had no living relatives, nor any friends or acquaintances that could be located who might shed some light on his past. Orders had been given to begin a search for anyone with whom either man had served while in the military, nearly twenty-five years ago. The prospects were bleak.

The horde of detectives that had, by turns, catered to Madeline's human needs and then bombarded her with interminable questions, had, for the moment, vacated the room.

Having steadfastly denied any knowledge of the motives or the identity of her supposed nemesis with innocence, vehemence, and finally, exasperation, she had reached an impasse. She was ready to chuck it, to take her chances, and go home. The round robin interrogation, with detectives throwing questions at her from every angle, was wearing her down. How could she ever remember what she needed to remember if they would not give her time to think?

Doc came back into the room alone. She looked at him and turned away. She wanted to trust him, but he had been as relentless as his counterparts in her cross-examination. He set a mug of steaming tea on the table in front of her and sat in the adjacent chair. His face was ashen. She thought he might be much older than her original estimate.

"He got Philip Nestor," Doc whispered.

"Oh, God."

He reached over and held her trembling hand. Tears dribbled down her cheeks. Her eyes and mouth were clamped tightly shut as she shook with silent sobs.

"He won't get you. I swear it."

When she looked up, Madeline was almost as frightened by the ferocity in Doc's eyes as she was of the beast that stalked her.

Chapter 25

Carl left the movie theater disappointed in the motion picture industry. He felt cheated. The film had lacked the true flavor of violence a connoisseur such as he required. In his estimation, Hollywood's version of blood pudding paled in comparison to the richness of the actual event. They should hire me as a consultant, he thought. The police, he was sure, would be happy to foot the bill. It would be cheaper by far, no matter what he charged, than to have him practicing his craft freelance. Toying with the notion of sending a proposal to the legislature, he synopsized the draft of the text—Pay me a million a year and I'll stay home. He laughed aloud and then winked at passersby, who gave him a wide berth.

As he rode the escalator down, he looked through the oblong, domed skylight and noticed that the sky had a purplish hue. It was nearly time to get back to work. Glancing at his watch, he wondered if anyone had found Phillie-baby yet. He smiled.

A pretty woman going up on the opposite side self-consciously grinned back. Carl looked right through her, conjuring images of tearing flesh as he envisioned the charge in the light fixture detonating in slow motion, spraying those beneath it with white hot metal shards and bits of glass. He hoped the shop was packed with cops when it went off.

He bought a Hagstrom Street Atlas of Nassau County and a Newsday in a Hallmark store on the first level and took them to Orange Julius. There, he sipped a creamsicle drink and found the street noted on the scrap of paper in his wallet. While he sucked on the straw, he memorized the roads in the surrounding vicinity. After dinner, he would do a reconnaissance of the target's new home and formulate a plan.

He took his time walking the length of the bustling mall, pausing to browse in several shop windows. In Houlihan's Bar and Gathering Place, he requested a table for one and ordered a rare shell steak with a baked potato. He read the page one account of his exploits to date while he tasted a stein of Killian's Red. When his food arrived, he dropped the paper on the chair nearest him and attacked his meal with gusto.

Over desert—cheesecake with strawberry topping—Carl returned to his reading. He went directly to the sports section and perused the articles until he found the one he wanted.

BAD BACK BENCHES BARBAROSA, the small headline read. The body of the article stated that: Sources close to Mr. Barbarosa said that the hapless Met had wrenched his spine while playing golf. It speculated on the infamous batting coach's questionable future with the home team. Finally, it confirmed that the ballplayer had uncharacteristically failed to arrive in sunny Florida for spring training, citing personal business as his excuse. Barbarosa had categorically denied the injured-back story in a telephone interview. The famed former star's future, if one took his checkered past into account, was in serious doubt, according to the reporter.

"An astute prediction," Carl murmured, folding the paper before tucking it and the maps under his arm. The article made no mention of the injured player's current whereabouts but Carl did not care. He knew exactly where to find him.

ઙઙ

Word of the delayed-action bomb in Oceanside and its victims deepened the gloom at police headquarters.

"I better get down there," Doc heaved himself from his chair and reached for his coat. He failed to see the look of panic on Madeline's face as he prepared to leave.

Tony rose to accompany him, watching his friend closely.

"What the hell for?" Schiff snapped, bringing them up short.

Doc froze, halfway into his jacket. Dumbfounded, he looked to Tony. His eyes pleaded. Tony could only shrug and shake his head. Collapsing back into his seat, he said, "He's right, Doc. What would we do?"

The look on Tony's face was one Doc had thought he would never have to see again. The thousand-meter-stare they called it in Vietnam.

He had once worn it himself. Shell shock or combat fatigue was how veterans of earlier wars referred to it. It was a way of putting into words the vacant, lost soul expression of men who had seen more horror than their minds could bear.

Unable to bear the pain in Tony's eyes, Doc looked away, only to meet his own reflected image in an office window. The darkness outside turned the glass into a mirror. The cold fluorescent lights above him heightened the effect of abject futility he saw in his own visage.

"Everything possible is being done as we speak." Schiff's insistent tones grated on Doc's nerve endings. "The personnel on scene know their jobs. Anything of significance will be reported to us immediately. From what we know so far, there's not a lot left to investigate. It'll be up to The Lab boys from here. Mrs. Nestor will be questioned at length, as soon as she has recovered enough from the shock of her husband's death. If the previous killings are any indication, there'll be damned little she can tell us."

"So, what do we do now, Lieutenant?" Doc pounded the table with his fist. "Carve another notch for this sick son of a bitch?"

"We do what we're paid to do, Detective. We analyze the facts, formulate hypotheses, and solve the crimes. If you feel that you are not emotionally equipped to continue—" Schiff stared unblinking into Doc's wild-eyed, red face, his voice cold, his meaning clear. "—perhaps you should go home."

With an embarrassed glance at Madeline, Doc took his seat, shaking his head, unable to meet Schiff's withering gaze. There was an uncomfortable silence.

"Mrs. Maclear." Tony cleared his throat, "all of the victims have been acquaintances from your high school days, correct?"

"That's right," Madeline tore her gaze from Doc's back, "but I lost touch with all of them."

"Which tends to suggest that the key to this thing is somewhere back there," Tony said. He turned to Doc, nodded once, and tapped his fist on the table with the thumb raised.

"Detective Cordova," Madeline said, "we've been over that. I've told you. I've told all of you." She swept the occupants of the room with her eyes. "I can't remember a thing that might have any bearing on this…this…"

"Madness?" Doc gave her the word she sought. With his back to Schiff, he mouthed to Tony, "Okay."

“Exactly,” Madeline said. “I’m at a complete loss.”

“Tony’s got a valid point.” Doc picked up the thread. He needed focus to fight this nameless dread. If Tony could work through it, so could he. “Why don’t we get your high school…” He shot Madeline a questioning look.

“Bellmore High.”

“Right,” Doc said. “Why don’t we get a copy of your yearbook from Bellmore High. Maybe a stroll down memory lane with pictures of the kids you knew in front of you will jog your memory.”

“Let’s get all the books from four years prior, to four years after Mrs. Maclear graduated,” Tony jumped back in. “Who says the guy we’re after was in the same class? He could have been in another grade and still had a hard—er, uh—an ax to grind against you and your friends.”

Madeline ignored Tony’s near profane slip.

“That makes sense. The others were two years ahead of me.” She shook her head and sighed in frustration. “I have no idea where my high school yearbook is. I just moved into an apartment a few weeks ago. I’m still not completely unpacked. I threw a lot of things away and I put more in storage. I wouldn’t know where to begin.”

“No problem,” Tony promised. “First thing tomorrow morning—”

“Tomorrow morning, my eye,” Schiff cut him off. “Get on the horn right now, Cordova. Get the duty sergeant in central records to find out who the superintendent of schools is in that district. Call him at home. Tell him we will have a car pick him up and take him down to the school. I want all those yearbooks on this table ASAP. If you cannot reach him, find someone who can get us in there. If anybody gives you static, threaten him with obstructing governmental administration. If that doesn’t work, explain how difficult life can be if we decide they are uncooperative. If you haven’t located someone who can help us within the hour, break into the damn school and get them yourself.”

“We don’t even know if they keep yearbooks on hand that far back,” Doc reminded them all. “We may have to settle for records of the students attending classes for those years. They should at least have that, maybe on microfilm.”

“If that’s the case, we may have to locate them one by one.” Schiff’s pained expression bespoke the enormity of the task.

“And ask them nicely if we can have a look at their high school yearbooks,” Doc’s sarcasm underlined the monumental job they faced.

No one was in the mood for sifting through mountains of detail, but each man knew that most cases were solved in just that way.

"Doc's right," Schiff breathed. "Pray they have them in the library."

Tony was on the telephone before the lieutenant finished, mumbling, "Please don't let this be a wild goose chase," as he dialed.

"Lieutenant Schiff?" Madeline got his attention by raising her hand like a schoolgirl. "The Dietrichs? They're the people whose house I live in. Well, I'm sure they'll be worried about me by now. They are a couple of old dears, and they watch out for me like mother hens. Would it be all right if I call them and let them know I'm safe?"

"Of course, Mrs. Maclear. You can use the phone in my office. Just don't tell them where you are. A precaution, you understand." Even Schiff seemed to melt when he spoke to Madeline. Tony hid his grin with the phone.

"Shouldn't we put Mrs. Maclear's place under surveillance?" Doc suggested.

"Not a bad idea. You're thinking like a cop again, Doc." Schiff clapped his hands softly in mock applause.

The faint praise was enough to remind Doc to guard against letting his feelings for this woman interfere with his work. He would need all of his faculties at peak performance to stop this butchering juggernaut.

"Any luck reaching Barbarosa in Florida yet?" Doc asked Schiff as the lieutenant helped Madeline from her chair.

"You mean Ron Barbarosa, the Mets batting coach?" a young detective asked.

"Yeah, why?" Doc turned to the cop.

"Don't you read the sports pages, Doc?"

"I've been a little busy." Doc scowled.

"What I mean is," the detective clarified, "he ain't in Florida. Hurt his back at a golf outing. He's right here on The Island."

"Shit!" Schiff took the word out of Doc's mouth. To the young detective, he snapped, "Get a car over to his house. Now! Doc, get him on the phone. Tell him not to open his door for anyone but a cop."

Doc was already flipping rapidly through Tony's notebook before Schiff gave the order. When he found Barbarosa's address and phone number, he punched the number. On the seventh ring he cursed and slammed the receiver into its cradle. "Get that car going," he demanded of the youthful detective while scribbling on a pad, "and keep trying this number. Charlie, get someone to take over the school thing for Tony. Let's go," he barked to Cordova.

They left the room at a dead run and sprinted down the hall to the fire stairs.

"Like the man said," Tony yelled over the clatter of their feet pounding down the steps, "Shit!"

Chapter 26

Ray Beckwith was coming down the wooden steps of the Dietrich's converted summer cottage in Oyster Bay when Carl drove slowly past. Beckwith's features were clearly illuminated by the coach lantern pole light beside the front walk.

"The other cop from the marina," Carl hissed. "Well, the pigs have finally put it together." He scanned the street for the others that he knew would be nearby.

The neighborhood was quiet. Not a soul, save the detective, walked the night-shrouded sidewalks. Nothing moved on the short front lawns or in the doorways and windows of the turn-of-the-century dwellings lining the street, but he knew they had to be there.

His eyes scrutinized every inch of the area as he rolled past the address he had gotten from the postal clerk. Where? Movement attracted his eye. There!

Two plainclothesmen sat in a darkened vehicle directly across from the house. Beckwith stepped into the street and climbed into another unmarked car. The engine started immediately and the headlights winked on as the vehicle pulled away. Carl turned right at the corner, watching in his rearview mirror as Beckwith proceeded through the intersection and disappeared.

He assumed that the detective had been there to question Madeline, and that a stakeout team sat in the remaining car. It was safe to assume as well that there would be another car stationed in the back. Barbarosa would be getting similar attention. He drove slowly along the tree shrouded street, thinking.

"You knew this would happen," he whispered. "You accurately assessed the time frame for them to wake up. The only thing you did not envision was the shift in target rotation. No problem. The operation is on schedule. You just need to adjust your priorities. Both subjects are now under guard." His eyes narrowed; his expression radiated hate as his brain—a perfect engine of evil—weighed options. "Road trip," he concluded, chuckling. Without a backward glance, he drove south.

ↀↀ

Tony was grateful when the harrowing ride to Great Neck ended. He had spent the time alternating between talking by radio with the dispatched sector car and begging Doc to slow down. Doc, oblivious to his friend's pleas, careened around corners on two wheels and pushed the straining six-cylinder to its limit on the straightaways.

They screeched to a halt in a cloud of smoking rubber in front of the baseball coach's massive, white brick home. A lone uniformed officer was ambling down the walk when they leaped from the car.

"Nobody home, gents." He slowed their forward momentum with vertical palms.

"You're sure?" Doc asked, puffing as if he had run all the way.

"Affirmative. Place is locked up tight. There are drop cloths on everything I can see through the windows. Scaffolds and ladders everywhere. I'd say, our friend Ronny is having the joint painted. Looks like he's moved out for the duration."

The cop went to his car to report in, wagging his head as the detectives confirmed his assessment for themselves.

"Told you," he smirked when they met him at the curb.

"Someone's got to know where he is." Doc kicked a stone from the sidewalk, exasperated. "This fucking nut could be carving him like a turkey while we're trying to figure out where. Try the neighbors."

The equally impressive edifice to the left of Barbarosa's home was also empty. At the house on the right, the man who opened the door in answer to Doc's pounding was decidedly miffed by the intrusion. Staccato introductions and gold shields flashed by impatient gendarmes did little to allay his suspicions. If his friend Ron was in trouble, he did not want to contribute to his problems.

"We are not looking to hassle Mr. Barbarosa, sir," Tony said. "He's in trouble, but not with us. We are trying to protect him. He'll thank you for it if you can tell us where he is."

"If you're sure—" The man still hesitated.

“He could,” Doc snapped, “be very dead by this time tomorrow if you don’t tell us where to find him.”

The neighbor looked from one cop to the other and shrugged. “Sands Point. He’s staying at his girlfriend’s place. You know, the singer, Natalie Graille. I have the address somewhere if you’ll wait a minute.”

The man closed the door while he went to find the information, leaving the detectives to wait on the front steps.

“What does a guy, slightly more than half our age, do to amass the amount of bread it takes to own this kind of joint?” Tony grinned at Doc while they waited. “Probably got coke and cash piled up all over the place. Ever wonder where we went wrong?”

“No, but I often wonder why we didn’t.”

When he returned, the man told them, “Ron doesn’t want any paparazzi bugging him while he’s recuperating,” while Doc copied the address. “You know how it is.”

“Sure we do.” Tony smiled. “Did he leave a number?” He pantomimed a telephone with his fist beside his jaw.

“No. It’s unlisted of course.”

“You’re telling me he gave you the address, but not the phone number.” Doc’s caustic tone ruffled the neighbor.

“That’s exactly what I’m telling you.” The man’s obtuse pleasure at Wiley’s annoyance tempted Doc to lean on him.

“Of course.” Tony flashed a plastic smile. “Let’s go, Doc.”

“Another private community, no doubt,” Doc grumbled as he started the engine and swung the car around in the narrow street, bouncing over the curb. “Call the phone company.” He handed Tony the cellular. “Have them ring Mister Baseball so we can warn his ass. Then get Schiff to call the local silver-spoon cops to clear the decks. Maybe we can get to him before this clown douses his lights. If that won’t disturb his beauty sleep, of course.”

Doc found his way back to Middle Neck Road and stomped on the accelerator until he hit Northern Boulevard. With the teardrop winking red in the center of the windshield and the dual headlights flashing, he hung a left that brought northbound traffic to a screeching halt. Tony would later swear that they never had all four wheels on the ground at any time during the race to Sands Point.

He focused on his telephoning and tried not to notice the repeated close calls.

"Yes, operator, this is a police emergency," Tony said as he waited for the connection.

"Natalie Graille, huh?" Doc raised an eyebrow.

"She has a place on the North Shore. At least that's what I read somewhere. Ol' Ron has good taste."

They were rocketing north along Port Washington Boulevard when the operator told the male voice answering the phone that this was a police emergency.

"Detective Cordova calling for Mr. Ronald Barbarosa," she announced.

"Mr. Barbarosa isn't taking calls at this time," the voice replied.

"He'll take this one or he might never take another," Tony cut in.

"Are you threatening Mr. Barbarosa?" The tone of the man's voice implied menace. "I assure you, as his attorney, I will not have my client harassed."

"This is Detective Anthony Cordova, Nassau County PD. Who am I talking to?"

"Mr. Barbarosa's attorney, Mark Kornberg."

"Listen, Counselor. Your client doesn't need a lawyer right now. He needs a bodyguard, probably several. His life is in danger and we're trying to protect him."

"Mr. Barbarosa has adequate security protection, Detective Cordova. He—"

"The local cops are not prepared to deal with what's coming after your boy, Kornberg." Tony's patience was ending. "He'll need a lot more than they can manage if this joker pays a call."

"Which is precisely why we have employed additional security personnel. Trust me, Detective, we are well prepared for any eventuality." The lawyer's pompous dismissal of his emphatic alarm annoyed Tony, but the dial tone that followed the highhanded barrister's parting shot infuriated him no end.

"We'll see about that." He dropped the instrument on the seat. "Seems Barbarosa is expecting trouble," he said to Doc.

At Doc's request, Tony got through to Schiff. Doc took the phone and sketched the situation as they knew it, ignoring Tony's pleas to use both hands on the wheel. "Naturally, we're going to talk to this character anyway," he said. "I wanted to see if you had reached him," he explained when he had summed up the events since they had left Mineola.

"No," Schiff said, "we tried, but we couldn't find anyone who knew where he was. How could he know he's in danger? And how long has he known? You say his lawyer says he has hired extra security? Something stinks, Doc."

"My sentiments exactly."

The house was easy to find. It was the only one on the dark country road with fifty thousand watts of electric light illuminating the grounds.

"Our boy planning a night game?" Doc mused aloud as they stopped in front of high wrought iron gates.

The armed guard on duty was, at first, adamant about his instructions to bar visitors from entry. "Mr. Kornberg said—"

"Mr. Kornberg is going to have his nuts in a wringer, along with his client, if I don't get in there right now," Doc promised. "Look, pal—" He paused for emphasis. "—if I have to arrest Mr. Barbarosa and everybody involved for withholding evidence, I will. Do you doubt my sincerity?"

The guard spluttered, "Who the hell do you—"

"Detective Wiley heads up the Terminator Task Force." Tony leaned across the seat, smiling. "Don't fuck with him. Some friendly advice."

"But we were told—"

"Kornberg is putting you and your people in jeopardy. Now open the fucking gate—please."

The flustered watchman made a hasty call on his walkie-talkie.

"I didn't know I had such extraordinary powers," Doc said, as they proceeded through the opened gate.

"Me neither," Tony murmured. "Jesus, will you look at this place."

The meandering driveway was a quarter of a mile long. They were greeted at the entrance to a sprawling ranch house nestled among tall pines by a man in a very expensive hand-tailored suit. Two others, whose right hands stayed inside their jackets, flanked him. The trio stood just outside a pair of massive, carved teak doors.

"Mr. Kornberg, I presume." Doc introduced himself and Tony.

"What is the meaning of this intrusion, Detective? I told you on the phone—"

"You hung up on me, Counselor," Tony cut him off. "Your client is in deep shit and we need to talk to him."

"Mr. Barbarosa is aware of the threat. We don't need your help."

"Which is one of the things we'd like to discuss with him," Tony said. "May we see him now?"

"I have advised my client to make no statements at this time. We will be happy to discuss the matter with you in my office tomorrow morning."

"Counselor—" Doc stepped closer and lowered his voice so that only the lawyer could hear. "—if you make me get a warrant, I will storm this joint with enough cops and hardware to make you think you're at the presidential palace in downtown Baghdad. Don't be an asshole. Let us speak to your client."

"Mr. Barbarosa is innocent of any wrong doing. A hypothetical discussion does not constitute a crime."

"But slaughtering a dozen people does, Mr. Kornberg."

The shock on the attorney's face told Doc they were talking about separate issues. "I think we can clear all this up if you'll be reasonable and let us see Ron," he said.

"Come in," the shaken lawyer acquiesced.

The attorney marched ahead of them, erect and purposeful, trying to salvage what he could of his ego. His perfectly sculptured white hair shone in the glow from the recessed floodlights. His thousand-dollar suit bolstered his superior air.

The house was not what Doc expected. The sweeping roof and stacked fieldstone walls gave the exterior a decidedly masculine feel. Inside it was all rosewood and pink marble, rounded corners and floral print wallpaper, crystal and modest touches of brass—feminine, yet hard. Doc got the feeling that its owner was a tough cookie. Natalie Graille's summer home said what her songs did—I am woman, and I will bash your brains in if you forget it.

Ron Barbarosa sat at the far end of a peach-colored, sectional sofa near a huge terrazzo fireplace in the sunken living room. He looked small in the immense space. His puffy eyes and pasty complexion told of sleepless nights and hard drinking. The half-filled glass and freshly opened bottle of twenty-five-year-old scotch on the glass-topped table before him said he intended to continue his self-abuse.

Kornberg made the introductions and explained to his client that he did not have to answer any questions. Barbarosa waved him away and fixed Doc with a bleary-eyed stare. "If I tell you what I know, do I get immunity?" the disheveled ballplayer asked.

"Ron, I don't think—" Kornberg tried to say, but Barbarosa halted him with another wave.

Doc and Tony studied the man in the wrinkled, sky-blue silk shirt and black chino slacks. He wore kidskin Gucci loafers without socks. His gaze, though lackluster, was steady and determined.

"The DA makes deals, Mr. Barbarosa," Doc replied, "but I can assure you that cooperation is rewarded whenever possible. You seem to be entrenched here. Between the muscle and the legal representation, I'd say you have something to tell us. It may or may not have any bearing on the reason for our visit." Doc looked into Barbarosa's eyes. "You asked about immunity. Your attorney understands that term far better than you do. I will say this, that cooperation that I spoke of carries a lot more weight when it is freely given, rather than bargained for—if you follow me."

The lawyer bristled but Ron again shushed him with an offhand gesture. The detectives were wondering what they had stumbled into. They had no wish to jeopardize the case by playing fast and loose with the rules. Barbarosa had given them no grounds to suspect him of a crime beyond some rather elaborate security precautions. If they questioned him without Mirandizing him first and he implicated himself in anything, there might be repercussions. If they read him his rights, his lawyer would insist he shut up until charged and advised of his legal situation. They needed him to tell them what he knew immediately.

"I'm not stupid, guys," he said, "although at the moment I feel like the world champion chump."

"We just want to be sure you understand the gravity of the situation," Doc finished.

"Fine," Barbarosa nodded his thanks. "My illustrious mouthpiece here is scared shitless I'll slam the cell door on my fingers." He grinned without humor, like a man who's tasted something foul but hates to admit the tasting.

"Why don't you start at the beginning, Mr. Barbarosa?" Doc suggested.

"Fair enough. And why don't you call me Ron? Everybody does."

Doc nodded.

Barbarosa sipped his drink and set it down on the table. "I twisted my back playing a little pre-season golf a few weeks ago. No big deal unless you're one of the oldest batting coaches in the major leagues. I didn't want to go to the team doctors." He let out a short, derisive laugh. "They'd love an excuse to bench me. You see there's a paragraph in my contract, thanks to my astute attorney—" He nodded to Kornberg. "—that says they have to pay me a fat bonus if I'm on the job for more than a certain number of games. A little game within the game that players play. The other side of the coin is: they can put me on the block if I fail to show for those games. If the team docs examine me, I'll be cultivating splinters for the first couple of months of the season and my attempt at hiding my injury could be construed as breach of contract.

"Get hurt giving your all for the team and you're a hero. Get hurt on your own time and you're a screw-up. Player screw-ups get traded. Coach screw-ups get the axe. At my stage of the game, I could kiss my career goodbye."

"But it's public knowledge now," Tony interjected.

"Things change." Ron sighed deeply and reached for another pull on his drink. "A couple of weeks before the golf thing, my alma mater had its twenty-five-year reunion. I refer to my high school, dear old Bellmore. I went, in the interest of public relations and, surprisingly enough, had a pretty good time. It was fun to see my old school chums." The sardonic tone belied his words. "In the course of renewing old acquaintances, I ran into several people I haven't seen in more years than I care to admit," he continued. "Dotty Conway was one. That's the late Dotty Kohler to you. Dotty was the class round heels. If the sexual revolution started anywhere, it was in Dotty's bed. We had a thing going for a while. It didn't last long, but I didn't mind. Nobody kept Dotty interested for long. As it turned out, Dotty hadn't changed in some respects. She came to the party stag, as did I. We got it on together in a little motel afterward." He paused. "You're wondering why I'd jump on a broken-down old slut like Dotty with a babe like Natalie on my string."

Neither detective acknowledged the statement, although both had been wondering exactly that.

"Dotty had a rare talent for sex. I won't elaborate out of respect for the dead." He lifted his glass to his lips, but continued, replacing it precisely on the wet ring on the table without drinking. "Afterward, Dotty tried to rope me into this wild scheme to buy a load of cocaine from some whacked-out biker she'd been screwing. I laughed in her face. She got pissed off. Told me I'd be sorry for making a joke out of it. Said these were badass dudes with Colombian connections. Said she'd show me and all the jerks at the reunion. She swore all she had to do was sic these bastards on all of us and we'd be sorry. She really went batshit." He looked at his drink as if he had suddenly remembered its importance and gulped half of it. “Anyway, I got the hell out of there and forgot about it until people started dying.

“Natalie’s on tour. My house needed a paint job. I told the front office that I had picked up a stomach virus and I’d be late reporting in. I didn’t tell them where I’d be. I figured they might send someone to check on me. I was hoping I’d be well enough to get the hell out of here and down to Florida before they got too suspicious.”

He was rambling. Doc wanted to get him back to the point. “Ron,” he said, “what’s this got to do with all the guards? What are you getting at?”

“Don’t you see?” Barbarosa snorted and looked to his attorney for confirmation. “Those drug pushers killed Dotty. I don’t know what she told them but they are systematically killing all my old friends. I decided the best thing to do was to come clean about my back. Maybe they’ll figure I’m no threat to them. These are bad people. Don’t you see?”

What they saw was a man driven to irrational conclusions by fear. Doc and Tony exchanged glances and an unspoken agreement.

“Would you come with us to police headquarters, Ron? Mr. Kornberg is welcome to accompany you,” Doc added.

“Am I in trouble?”

“Not the kind you might expect.”

As they rose to go, Doc asked, “Was Madeline Maclear at the reunion, Ron?”

“Who?’

“You knew her as Madeline O’Keefe,” Tony said.

Barbarosa looked puzzled for a moment, and then smiled. “Maddy? No. She wasn’t in our class. Younger kid. I’d almost forgotten her. Now there was a cute piece of ass. Great tits. Why?”

“Never mind,” Tony said, stepping in front of Doc, blocking Barbarosa’s view of the anger in Doc’s face.

Chapter 27

Lake Hopatcong, New Jersey, was the rural community Carl had chosen to house the bulk of his weapons and cash. After spending the night in a small motel on Route 80 to avoid arriving in Hopatcong in the middle of the night, Carl's Jeep rolled into the graveled driveway behind his warehouse at nine a.m. The bulky padlock on the barn-style garage doors opened easily and he drove into the building.

Carl's storage facility had been carefully selected. When he had decided what to do with what he had found in Sarge's basement room, he realized he would have to move the cache. Once the operation began, he would need free access to the gear and the cash and commuting to Colorado was out of the question. He had made up his mind to sell the house quickly and placed the property with several real estate brokers. Knowing that potential buyers would soon be poking their noses into every corner of the antique home, Carl was too cautious to trust to luck that none of them would tumble to his horde. He had found the stash. Others could do likewise. Removal of his booty—once it was boxed, crated and labeled: Fragile ~ Antiques—was an expected outcome by the time he carted it away. Everyone in town knew Sarge and what he did for a living—at least they thought they did.

Once he had relocated to the East Coast, setting himself up in an out of the way haven was the next logical step. He needed a place on the mainland. It was too easy to be cornered and cut off on Long Island. Manhattan and Staten Island had the same logistical pitfall. Lake Hopatcong, New Jersey was ideal. It was far enough away from the action for the populace to be unconcerned, yet close enough to major arteries to be convenient should he have to move through hastily with the cops on his tail.

The basement level garage of an art and antique shop on an out of the way street in the tourist-oriented town was perfectly suited to his needs. The main entrance to the store was at street level while his means of ingress and egress was below grade, accessible only from the parking lot carved from the hilltop upon which the commercial strip center was built. Flanked by a restaurant and a seasonal clothing store, The Critical Eye was the perfect cover for his storage facility. It was the only business of the three that stayed open year-round. Carl's timetable would have him gone by summer, before the tourists flooded the vicinity.

The shop's owner, Marvin DeKalb, although technically Carl's landlord, was everything he could ask for in a caretaker—greedy, larcenous, and cowardly. Marvin's mother, the founder of the business had, to Marvin's chagrin, taken the sum total of the family business acumen to the grave. The surviving DeKalb had been left with a gold mine of a business that petered out once deprived of the old girl's keen nose for opportunity. Lacking his mother's eye for quality and the sense to market it profitably, Marvin had watched the vital generator of his fortune wither. A thriving concern built on know-how and charisma that catered to the tasteful wealthy of the region had degenerated to a backwater peddler's stand dealing with a few transient suckers—until Carl arrived on the scene.

Carl befriended Marvin over drinks in a lakeside pub, bragged of his successful career as an antique dealer, and mentioned that all he needed was somewhere convenient to store his merchandise. A mutual phobia for taxes came to light. Rent was negotiated, mutually agreed upon, and paid in cash for months in advance. Unable to distinguish between an entrepreneurial genius and a master charlatan, as well as being too desperate to care, Marvin had leaped at Carl's scheme of mutual profit.

Valuable antiques and art began to flow into Marvin's inventory on consignment. Carl really did have a knack for the business. Marvin's sagging bottom line soon sprang back. In the black again, without knowing what gods of good fortune to thank, Marvin troubled himself not a whit with trivial legal niceties. Mister Fleming, as he knew Carl, was the answer to his prayers. They dealt in cash. Mister Fleming trusted Marvin to give an honest accounting of what he sold and to divide the net gain fairly. Marvin always seemed to sell Carl's pieces at about ten percent below value, but apparently, his trusting vendor never noticed. The extra skimmed commission Marvin figured as his due, for enabling his benefactor to beat the taxman. In exchange for the surplus profit, which Marvin also failed to report on his highly inventive Form 1040, he kept his promise of privacy, resisting the temptation to peek at his tenant's private collection stored in the basement. Marvin would never admit that he was just a tad frightened by his strange and secretive silent partner.

Carl often wondered what the sticky-fingered proprietor would do if he knew of the fortune in cash stashed in his cellar. He deemed it an acceptable risk, owing to Marvin's spineless nature. Marvin was smart enough to realize the folly of jeopardizing his newfound windfall with excess curiosity. A series of diabolical traps set to mortally discourage prying eyes served as Carl's insurance policy. The need for a place where he could be certain he was not followed when he made pick up runs for weapons and gear outweighed his aversion to accomplices.

The day would come when Carl needed to move on. Marvin would serve his purpose until then. Whether or not he would leave him alive when he finally moved out would depend upon circumstance and his mood at the time.

After locking the doors from inside, Carl selected a portrait in an ornate gilded frame from a stockpile of antiques. He climbed the dusty wooden steps and unlocked the door to the shop from his side. At Carl's insistence, access to the basement was impossible from the shop. Although a flagrant code violation, Marvin deemed the risk of a summons from the volunteer fire inspector on his semi-annual perusal a risk well worth taking.

After spending a few moments observing the customs of reunited partners, Carl abruptly put platitudes aside. With the avaricious appetites of his guard dog assuaged, he left Marvin to ponder the extra percentage he could filch from this latest rare find to return to his stockpile.

Along with the bulk of his arsenal, he kept a well-equipped workbench. The house in Rockville Centre held only the essentials for day-to-day operations. A small assortment of combat knives, guns, and explosives were stored in the white room, as well as some load bearing web gear and military clothing. The house was also rented; Carl had no desire to establish a record of ownership. His lease, which he had recently renewed, contained a clause granting him privacy and the right to demand notice before visits from his absentee landlord. Said landlord was happy to grant his tenant his idiosyncrasies in return for prompt payment of rent, which was usually made in advance of the date due by postal money order. Carl was opposed to bank accounts and their inherent paper trail. He also varied the post offices in which he purchased the money orders.

Now, comfortable in his secret warehouse, he set to work collecting the gear he would need for his next sortie. Owing to the fact that he did not know exactly what equipment he might need in the coming days, he opted to be heavy handed in his armament. A Heckler & Koch MP-5K machine pistol was his first selection, followed by an M-79 grenade launcher, two 9mm semi-automatic pistols—a Browning Hi-Power and a Glock—a .45 caliber M-2 "Greasegun" sub-machinegun and an SKS bolt-action assault rifle.

He piled the guns, along with assorted ammunition and magazines, on one end of his worktable. Next, he pried open a crate and removed several pounds of plastic explosive in cellophane wrapped blocks of one pound each.

He added a cardboard carton of blasting caps, half a dozen fragmentation grenades, fuses, detonators, and a variety of timers to the pile.

Humming like any man happy in his work, he began to assemble a bomb.

In a six-inch-square-by-two-inch-deep Tupperware food storage container, he placed a pound of the plastique, molding it like a sculptor working in clay, fitting it to the case. Next, he carefully inserted the blasting cap in the center and crimped the end to wires, which he soldered to a battery and a digital timer that he similarly pressed into the soft charge with his thumbs.

Finished, he applied the lid to the tub and applied pressure along the rim until the last corner burped it tightly shut. He wrapped the charge in brown craft paper from a roll under the bench and neatly folded one end, securing it with cellophane tape like gift-wrap, leaving the other end unfastened. Laughing, he addressed it with a black, felt-tip marker to: Mr. Will Gobang at a fictitious destination in Wisconsin.

The package, with the rest of his weaponry, he stuffed into a duffel bag, which he loaded into the back of his car. He then locked the vehicle and went back upstairs to exchange small talk with Marvin before he walked downhill to a picturesque restaurant at the water's edge.

Carl was in no hurry. The operation could not proceed until nightfall. With his friendliest smile spread wide on his face, he ordered the catch of the day and a bottle of Pinot Grigio from a pretty young waitress and sat back to enjoy the pleasant afternoon.

After a satisfying meal, Carl took the remainder of the wine out to the dock built to allow easy access for the boating clientele and settled himself in one of the canvas director chairs provided by the restaurant. He sipped wine and watched the afternoon light wane until the sky turned to plum. With a sigh of pure contentment, he lifted himself from his seat and turned to go. As he passed her on his way through the dining room, the waitress gave him a friendly wink.

"Going so soon?" she asked.

He winked. "Things to see and people to do."

She laughed. "No rest for the wicked."

"Words to live by," he shot back.

"You're a funny guy," she said.

"Yeah, I kill 'em where I come from."

She was still laughing as she sang, "Don't be a stranger," to his back.

"Be careful what you wish for," he said under his breath.

Chapter 28

Doc tried to ward off the angst hospitals caused him as a dour faced surgeon explained Jack Kobrigian's condition to him in the hall outside his friend's private room at Nassau University Medical Center.

"The bullet fragmented when it struck the breastbone of the other victim, Detective Wiley. Your friend is a lucky man. Only a small piece of the projectile pierced his body. It nicked his heart and the shock sent him into cardiac arrest. We removed the shrapnel and repaired the damage surgically. Detective Kobrigian is responding nicely to the procedure. Barring infection and unforeseen complications, he should recover. His future on the force depends on the findings of your department doctors, but I would venture to say that lighter duties would be recommended."

How Jack would react to that, only time would tell. The job had been his whole life since Connie had left him.

"Can I see him?" Doc felt silly asking this kid for permission to do anything. He was experiencing an irritating awareness of late. Too many people in positions of responsibility were younger than he deemed wise.

"I suppose so, but only for a few minutes, and don't do anything to excite him."

Doc had to smile at that. The doctor obviously did not know Jack Kobrigian.

"Wait a minute." Doc grabbed the surgeon's arm as he began to step aside. "I thought he was in a coma."

"That's something your people asked us to put out to keep the media at bay." The doctor smiled, obviously tickled by the police department's discomfort with the press. "He's awake, although still a little woozy."

Doc had stopped by to see Kobrigian on his way home for a few hours rest. The escorting of Ron Barbarosa to Mineola had gone smoothly. They brought the half-soused coach into the building through the delivery entrance, disguised as a detective garbed in a sports jacket with a borrowed cap pulled low over his eyes. The reporters staking out that part of the building were not allowed close enough to the doors to get a clear view. The small stir that the unusual entrance made was quickly forgotten as the tired news hawks settled back into hovering.

Barbarosa had perked up considerably when he was introduced to Madeline and had been far more interested in renewing old acquaintances than in answering questions related to the case. He seemed convinced that his scenario of rampaging Colombians was fact.

The investigators decided to pursue the drug deal link as a remote possibility, regardless of its bazaar aspects, but to concentrate primarily on the high school connection. When Madeline dozed off in mid-sentence, all agreed that the witnesses, as well as the detectives, were running on empty and that sleep was the best thing for the moment. Both witnesses were eventually bedded down for the night on couches in separate offices, although Doc got the distinct impression that coed accommodations would have been more to the batting coach's tastes. Doc was surprised more by his jealousy than by his immediate dislike of Barbarosa. Happily, Madeline seemed revolted by Ron's attempts at close contact.

After a terse conversation with Schiff, who complained of the unorthodox housing of witnesses in the offices of the inner sanctum, Doc promised to make more appropriate arrangements in the morning and left for some badly needed sack time. The visit to Kobrigian's bedside had been a spur of the moment decision. Sleep, although unavoidable, was not something he looked forward to. The dream would begin as soon as he closed his eyes.

As he stood at the foot of Jack's hospital bed, looking at a frail old man with an oxygen tube taped to his nose and IVs punched into his veins, he thought for a second that he was in the wrong room. Kobrigian's gray stubble and waxy complexion reminded him of his father's last days. He wondered if his daughter would one day be as distraught when his time came. He shrugged mentally, wondering, too, if she would even know of it. Barbara might never allow him to see her again, and the longer she kept Jen hidden from him, the more poisoned his daughter's mind might become. Was it already too late?

"Thank God you didn't bring flowers," Kobrigian rasped.

Jack's voice startled Doc. Kobrigian's deep baritone had deteriorated to a rattling whisper that reminded Doc of wind-blown leaves skittering across concrete.

The fingers of the hand resting on the sheet beckoned urgently. Doc moved closer without conscious motor function.

"Gimme a sip of that water, Doc." Kobrigian's eyes shifted to a white plastic pitcher on his nightstand. Mechanically, Doc inserted the flexible straw protruding from the cover between Jack's lips. His friend closed his eyes and sucked hard until his thirst was quenched. When he paused, Doc replaced the pitcher and waited.

"That's better," Jack said. "Thanks. So, how's the boy? Nail this prick yet?"

"No. Not yet, but we'll get him."

"No worries, mate." It was an Aussie expression, one of many from Kobrigian's repertoire of phrases. He used many such colloquialisms from around the world but to the best of Doc's recollection Kobrigian had never been outside of the continental United States. He had certainly never set foot in Australia, but he collected phraseology that struck him as fitting to circumstance, using his favorites like gems to add sparkle to his speech.

"Easy for you to say." Doc grinned and was pleased to see the laughter in Kobrigian's eyes, although it did not venture beyond.

"Watch yourself with this guy," Jack warned. The mirth was replaced by concern. He seized Doc's sleeve and shook it feebly. "Bad one. Real bad. Dangerous son of a bitch."

"I know, Jack, I know. We'll be careful. You just take it easy and get well. You'll be back before you know it."

"Bullshit. I'm done."

Doc's features went rigid. He rocked back on his heels as if struck.

Jack shook his head. "Not what I meant. This—" Kobrigian's eyelids drooped, his head sagged to punctuate his sad predicament. "—temporary setback. I'll be fine. Just take a while. No. I meant the job. No more. Gonna pull the pin. Get out. Go fishing. No fun anymore." He thought about what he had just said for a moment and added, "Cripes. That one should go in the Guinness Book—Most Outlandish Understatement." He laughed until a spasm of coughing shook the bed and he clutched his chest with both hands.

"I'll get the doctor," Doc started to turn for the door.

"No."

Doc half-turned, one foot still poised for flight.

Kobrigian rubbed his chest. "Jesus, that hurt."

"Let me get the doctor."

"Not necessary. Don't go calling that knife happy quack. He's done enough carving for one day."

"You're sure?"

"Yeah, yeah. As I was saying, the rat race is over. I concede the contest to the rats."

"Just get well, Jack. We'll talk about it when you're better."

"Sure, we will. Do me a favor, Doc?"

"Anything."

"Stop by my summer place. You know where it is." Doc dipped his head, an affirmative nod. He had been to Jack's bungalow on Oak Island on three occasions. The first had been when Jack had inherited the place from his parents, who had died within weeks of each other. Doc had helped him pack their belongings and drink most of their liquor stores. The second time had been for a party celebrating Jack's only son's wedding. The son announced plans to move to California with his bride, never to return. There was a scene. Kobrigian never mentioned him again.

The last time had been after the divorce. Connie never forgave Jack for, "driving her only son away," to put it her way. Kobrigian had not invited anyone to the place since.

"The key is in the big flower pot on the porch. Just see that everything's all right. I'm going to move in when I get out of here. Recuperate. Reflect. Maybe write my memoirs." The gleam was in his eyes again. He squeezed Doc's hand and Doc was surprised by the strength in his grip. "I'm okay Doc. Really. Kobrigian knows when to make an exit."

"Anything you say, Jack."

"Damn right. Now go get some sleep. You look awful."

In the elevator, Doc burst out laughing as he reflected on the parting words of the indomitable old detective. He pounded his fist against the elevator wall, tears streaming down his cheeks as he guffawed. His fellow passengers all found sudden compelling reasons to exit the lift at its next stop before the hysterical rider with the unbridled solitary good humor went totally berserk. By the time he reached the ground floor, he had the once crowded car completely to himself.

For the first time since this nightmare began, Doc found he had hope. The Terminator was one bad-ass-son-of-a-bitch, but he was just a man and no mere man could beat the likes of Jack Kobrigian—or for that matter, Doc Wiley.

Chapter 29

A poorly lighted garden apartment complex, not far from the Oyster Bay business district, provided the necessary transportation Carl needed to complete the night's mission. He parked his car on a darkened side street a block from the development and walked to the parking lot. He picked an older model Mercury station wagon, slipped a Slim-Jim into the window track, and popped the lock. The car was not alarmed, as he felt certain the late model imports that dotted the tarmac would be. With a slap hammer, he sprang the ignition and hot-wired the vehicle, which purred to life. He eased the wagon from its space and swung into the street before switching on the headlights.

Carl was confident that the owner would not miss his wheels until the next morning when he arose to go to work. By then, Carl would be long gone.

He parked the stolen wagon behind his own car and quickly transferred the gear he would need for his night's work. He then drove cautiously through the deserted streets until he found a vacant parking space two blocks from Madeline Maclear's home. With the motor off and the lights out, he slipped the Tupperware bomb from its wrapper, set the timer for three a.m., replaced the lid, and watched the red LED display count backward through the translucent plastic cover. Satisfied, he slid the charge back into its brown paper wrapper and neatly folded the open end before sealing it with cellophane tape. He walked the four blocks to the hospital quick but casual. In the blaze of light at the front entrance, he thrust the package into the maw of the mailbox at the curb, pausing to read the pickup schedule out of habit. The sticker warning him to: STOP! nearly broke him up. The federal government reminded him in red print on a field of white, that it was now illegal to mail packages weighing more than sixteen ounces, etcetera, etcetera.

Grinning, he said, “That should stop people from mailing bombs. Well, most people anyway.”

He eased the counter-weighted door up, thrust his hands in his pockets, and ambled back the way he had come, just a forgetful citizen hurrying out in the middle of the night to do some urgent mailing. The uncomfortable stakeout guards parked outside the Dietrich house noted his passing both times. Neither man saw his face and each dismissed it from his mind.

Back in the station wagon, Carl climbed into the rear cargo compartment, set his wristwatch alarm, pulled a blanket over himself, and dozed. The glare from a sodium street lamp bothered him only marginally as its harsh orange rays pierced the budding canopy of trees lining the curb. The comfort of the large station wagon offset the minor annoyance. He liked big cars. The faint memory of his dad’s Chevrolet Impala, the first car he had ever driven, crept into his mind. Then he remembered the beating his father had given him when he found the scratch in the driver’s door. Carl was sure he had not been responsible for the tiny nick in the paint, but his father called him a liar. The imaginary chain of events his dad recited as proof that the blemish had been caused by his son was all the old man required to justify the punishment. Dad was prosecutor, judge, jury, and executioner, and there was no room for defense once he had made up his mind about anything. Carl wondered if his parents were still alive. Maybe he would look them up when this was over. Just pop in to his boyhood home, and say, “Hi, how has life been treating you? I’m doing fine. Gotta run. The cops are trying to kill me. Have a nice day. See you in Hell.”

Carl looked forward to Hell. He was sure he would be a favorite son.

At twenty minutes to three, the alarm buzzed. Carl was instantly alert. He depressed the tiny button to silence the tone and peered over the seat back. The hospital entrance was not visible from his hiding place, since the streets did not run in straight lines. He was two blocks from his target and three from the hospital. How convenient a place Madeline had found.

At five minutes to three, he slid over the seat and eased the rear curbside door open. No light betrayed his movements. He had had the foresight to smash all the cabin lights before parking the car. Pressing the door closed to avoid noise, he huddled in the shadow of the vehicle close beside the right rear tire and watched the minutes tick by as the radium hands of his watch jerked to the hour.

At exactly three o'clock, the street lit up in a bright orange flash, followed a split second later by a thunderous blast. Every light in view winked out a second later.

"Blackout. A bonus."

The mailbox was launched like a missile from a silo when the explosive blew its bottom out. The curved dome acted like a baffle, sending the energy released by the blast back down, ripping the legs from their bolts, propelling the heavy gauge steel box high into the air. It snagged on the overhead power lines, which stretched and then snapped under the load of the speeding projectile, shorting out the entire grid. The whole neighborhood went black with the exception of the front of the hospital where the branches of a tree had caught fire. Burning letters and scraps of mail floated to the ground in flaming pirouettes. The smoking mailbox rang like a bell when it landed in the middle of the street.

Carl trotted up the sidewalk, running in a crouch, staying close to the nearly unbroken line of parked cars. He stopped within earshot of the stakeout vehicle. Both cops were out on the street.

"What the fuck was that?" the one nearest to him was yelling to his partner, five feet away.

The radio under the dash interrupted any reply. The cop in the street snatched the mic from its cradle. He spoke excitedly to someone and then threw the instrument on the seat.

"The cocksucker hit the hospital. Blew the shit out of the front door. Let's haul ass down there."

"I don't know, Lenny. Maybe we oughta stay put."

"And be the only guys left out of the collar? Not me, man. This is the kind of shit that gets you noticed."

Unconvinced, the hesitant cop looked at the sparks flitting above the trees like crazed fireflies. His partner stood poised, one foot in the car. "You comin'?"

They jumped into the vehicle and sped from the curb in a cloud of exhaust smoke, their headlights, and flashing red emergency beacon the only bright spots in the inky blackness below the canopy. Another car, lights flashing, narrowly missed their speeding vehicle as it slued around the corner half a block further on.

"Lenny, that's Andy and Vic," the skittish one said to his buddy. "That leaves nobody watching the house."

"See what I mean? They know a good thing when they see it."

Carl pulled a black knit ski mask from the pouch pocket of his hooded sweatshirt. The shirt, his sweat pants, and sneakers were also black. He ran across the street to the Dietrich home, whispering, "Guards diverted. Execute phase two, now." His heart pounded. With a broad bladed combat knife held in a death grip in his right hand he vaulted the three steps and landed, catlike, on the front porch. As he reached for the doorknob, he heard voices from within.

"Don't go out there, Fanny. Something's wrong."

"I know something's wrong you old fool. The lights are out. I think I heard an explosion."

Fanny Dietrich opened the door before Carl had time to think. The sound of two people in the house, old people from their voices, was not in keeping with his expectations. Could he have the wrong house? Again?

He had barely enough time to sidestep the opening door. The old woman in a pink quilted bathrobe nearly collided with him as she stepped out onto the porch. In the dim glow of the fire two blocks away she had time to gasp as she discerned the black silhouette of a tall man directly in front of her. Carl reacted instantly, throwing a hard jab at her jaw. The brass knuckled hand guard of the heavy knife split her cheek and sent her slight body toppling backwards. Mrs. Dietrich crashed into her husband's arms as he hurried to follow her. Both septuagenarians toppled to the floor at the foot of the staircase leading to the second floor.

Yanking the door shut behind him with his free hand, Carl fell on them. Mrs. Dietrich moaned as his weight pressed her down. John Dietrich tried to cry out but Carl flailed at his head until the butt of the knife found his temple. Dietrich's skull struck the first step. Carl hammered at the two of them with the knife guard and his gloved fists until the couple lay senseless.

Without hesitation, he bounded up the steps and burst into Madeline's apartment, correctly assuming she had rented the upstairs rooms. A quick, angry search, crashing around in the darkened flat, confirmed she had eluded him again. Furious, Carl raced back down the steps and straddled the unconscious pair.

"Where is she?" he snarled, slapping both of the elderly couple repeatedly in the face, his blows sure, now that his vision had adjusted to the darkness.

Mr. Dietrich came to and cringed when he saw the wild eyes of their tormentor in the flickering light through the lace-curtained glass in the top of the door. He begged for mercy for his wife.

"Please don't hurt my Fanny," he whimpered.

Carl spat, "I'll kick your fanny all over town, you sniveling shit. And hers, too," he added with a chuckle, jiggling one of the old woman's breasts with the point of the knife. "Tell me where Madeline is. Maybe I won't cut your old lady's throat if you tell me now." He pressed the point of the blade to Mrs. Dietrich's neck.

"I don't know where she is. I swear," John groaned as Carl pressed the point deeper into his wife's flesh. "She called. Said she was all right. That's all I know. She didn't tell us where she is."

"Ah well," Carl sighed, "if you don't know, you don't know." He saw a flicker of hope in the old man's eyes. "Tough," he breathed, and plunged the blade into John's eye. He clapped his free hand over the man's gasping mouth and put his weight behind it until he felt the blade break through to pierce the brain. Before John Dietrich's death throes had ended, Carl pulled back and slashed Fanny's throat from ear to ear.

When he stepped onto the front porch the street was filling with panicked homeowners. The blast and the ensuing blackout had aroused the citizenry. Shadows moved warily along the sidewalks amid the calls of frightened neighbors seeking knowledge of the sudden disaster. A man with a flashlight was running toward Carl, whipping the beam about like a sword.

Carl yanked the Glock from his waistband and cracked off three rapid shots, one at the flashlight wielder and two more at random. The flashlight went black as it shattered on the pavement.

"Jesus! Get inside!" a woman shrieked.

"Good thinking," Carl agreed.

He was back in the car before he remembered the hand grenade in his pocket, the one he had brought along for the booby trap. He started the wagon and pulled into the street. He was at the corner when he saw the lights of an approaching vehicle and the telltale red teardrop on the roof. The cops had decided to get back to their post when no sign of him had been found at the hospital. The shots had convinced them to hurry.

“Heads up,” he sneered, pulling the pin and lofting the football shaped bomb in a hook shot over the car’s roof as he leaned into a left turn.

The grenade bounced once on the pavement and rolled under a parked Mazda Miata. It exploded directly under the gas tank, twenty feet ahead of the onrushing Crown Victoria, flinging the tiny yellow sports car over to land inverted in its path. The driver stood on the brakes and covered his face with his forearm. He slammed into the spinning wreck, powerless to prevent the sideways slide that wedged both cars between two parked autos like a cork in a bottle in the narrow street. The two cops sat dazed and bleeding from flying glass and jagged metal. Both suffered broken limbs and clung to consciousness, powerless to free themselves, unless help arrived before leaking gasoline ignited their prison.

Without a glance behind him, Carl shot up the dark side street, his foot to the floor. He could hear the blare of sirens and fire engine horns bouncing off the surrounding homes. If he did not get out of the area quickly, he would be trapped. Like many towns on Long Island’s irregular north shore, Oyster Bay had limited access. How long the cops would take to set up roadblocks was anybody’s guess. He hoped the blackout and its confusion would buy him time.

After three sharp turns, each changing his direction of travel, he hit the headlights and slowed to a more moderate speed. How he had avoided hitting something in the dark with the car flat out, he would never know. Apparently, luck had not deserted him entirely.

A block from his Jeep, he doused the lights and coasted to a stop beneath a huge old oak beside the curb. Panting, he smelled the coppery scent of fresh blood. He was covered in it. The knife lay on the seat beside him. In blind fury, he snatched it up and rammed the blade into the seat cushion to the hilt.

“Chill out,” he hissed. “Think.” The wagon shook as he pounded the driver’s door with his fist. How could I be so reckless?

The cacophony of emergency vehicles’ varied alarms drifted to him from the calamitous scene below. He was on a lonely hilltop about a mile from the hospital. The cops would get organized quickly and begin the search, widening the pattern emanating from the center. The clatter of a helicopter rotor came faintly to his ears. Scrambling over the seat, he ripped the jogging suit from his body and tossed it onto the floor. His skin felt wet and he was sure the blood had seeped through his clothes.

"Can't be helped," he decided and rolled over the back seat to lie on the floor of the cargo area. He clawed at a brown paper bag and pulled fresh clothes onto his naked body.

Despair nearly overwhelmed him. His lust for the blood of Madeline Maclear had become palpable. During the drive from Lake Hopatcong, he had fantasized the details of her death until the erection he had attained became a painful thing, yearning for release. The image of her ripe body, held tightly in his powerful arms as he plunged the knifepoint into her sternum while pressing his stiff member into her, had been almost unbearably sweet anticipation. The fiasco of the actuality of his night's work made his head swim.

Suppressing the urge to scream, he fought the quaking of his limbs, took a deep breath, and slid out of the station wagon. He tossed the bloody gloves and the gun in some nearby bushes, walked quickly to his car, started it, and drove away.

By the time he reached Northern Boulevard, the pounding of the blood in his temples had subsided to a dull roar. Hanging a right, he saw a police helicopter's blue-white searchlight stab the sky to the north. It swung in swift, rigid, powerful arcs, searching for the station wagon. Carl had no doubt they would find it before long. The forensic specialists would examine everything in it. They would find some hair samples, lint, some traces of various types of earth from his shoes. They would search the surrounding environs and find the gloves and gun.

There was nothing to connect him specifically with the vehicle, the gloves, or the pistol unless they caught him. His hasty evacuation had ensured that would not happen. With more careful planning, he would have brought along another bomb and left one of his special surprises in the car. Too late for self-recrimination, he told himself. Concentrate on escape.

He turned south on Glen Cove Road and felt better about his chances immediately. Even at this late hour, actually early morning, there was enough traffic on the heavily traveled artery to afford him anonymity. At Jericho Turnpike, he turned right and cruised the quiet thoroughfare until he found a twenty-four-hour diner. Checking his appearance in the rearview mirror by the glow of the mercury lamps in the parking lot, he smoothed back his brown hair and marched straight for the restroom with his hands thrust in his pockets. With the door latched, he scrubbed traces of blood from his wrists and a few flecks he found on his face. Only when he was satisfied that there was no outward sign of his activities in the past several hours did he go out into the dining room and order a large breakfast.

Dawdling over refills of weak, but scalding coffee, he stalled until the sky brightened with the first hint of dawn. Leaving a less than noteworthy tip, Carl paid his bill and quietly left the all-night eatery to drive slowly home.

He vowed he would not make another move against Madeline until he had carefully evaluated her whereabouts, once he had discovered them, as he was certain he would. Barbarosa would get his attention in the meantime. He knew where he was. Or did he? The night's disaster was enough to make him double-check his information. There must be no more mistakes.

Chapter 30

Something amorphous and evil waited just outside the pool of ghostly light that bathed Madeline's cowering form. It was cunning and ravenous. She dared not sleep. It wanted that. With the slightest lapse in her watchfulness, it would spring, snapping and slashing. It would rip her to pieces and gorge itself on her blood. Madeline could smell it, as rank as corruption. It was putrid; hungry; eternally patient. It waited in the blackness for her to doze, and she was so tired. Doc promised to keep it at bay. She heard him say it again. Where was he? Behind her? She crouched and spun around, careful not to touch the darkness. Doc was out there somewhere, hunting it. Could she trust the voice? Was it Doc, or the thing shrewdly mimicking him? She needed Doc to stand guard while she slept.

Tired. Slipping away. Someone creeping closer. Please, let it be Doc.

ꕥ

"Mrs. Maclear's been sedated." Lieutenant Schiff watched the bloodshot eyes of his two best detectives. "The shock of her landlords' murders was too much for her."

"Where is she?" Doc asked. He felt as if he had never left this conference room.

After leaving Kobrigian's bedside, he had driven home, where he downed a stiff drink and wandered into his studio with a vague notion to start a new sculpture. His mind refused to focus and he gave it up and fell into bed. The old nightmare had barely begun when his beeper went off. He called Schiff, braced for bad news, but was unprepared for the shock when the lieutenant told him what had befallen the

Dietrichs. He and Tony raced back to Headquarters, arriving within minutes of each other. Tony looked as exhausted as he did.

"She's in the same office as before," Schiff said, "but there's a nurse outside now."

Doc turned toward the door, but Schiff halted him with, "She's resting comfortably, Doc. Let her sleep."

Doc shoved his hands in his pockets and shifted from one foot to the other.

"Have some coffee," Schiff said, "you both look like you could use some."

Tony said, "Can I get mine intravenous?"

Both detectives collapsed into chairs and waited for their boss to brief them. They didn't have to wait long.

"This latest disaster in Oyster Bay changes your role in the investigation," Schiff stated. "From here on out, your main objective is to protect the last two targets on the killer's list. Let the rest of our people run down the leads and conduct the field investigation. I want you on the lady and the ballplayer like stink on shit until we nail this fuck."

Doc sipped cold coffee from a Styrofoam cup. The bruises around Tony's eyes had turned saffron. They added to the bedraggled look Doc knew was a mirror image of himself.

"You think this prick will come after them and our best shot is to wait," he said. It was a statement, not a question.

There was an edge to Schiff's voice when he replied, "The fact that we've got no more idea who we're after than when this shit began tells me we'll get him coming to us, not the other way around."

"Live bait, Lieutenant?" Tony looked disgusted.

"Of course not. This ain't the movies, Cordova. We'll do everything in our power to keep these people safe from this asshole."

"But," Doc added for the lieutenant, "if the bastard happens to get a shot at them, that's our best chance to take him out." The contempt in his face was a challenge.

"Absofuckinglutely wrong!" A vein in Schiff's forehead bulged as he said, "We will take no chances with these people. Their well-being is our primary responsibility. At no time will we place them in jeopardy. Is that one-hundred percent understood?"

"I sincerely hope so," Doc said.

"I'm not enough of a scumbag that I would make points with the dead bodies of innocent people." Schiff's hostility pushed his body toward Doc. The conference table was a flimsy barrier between them.

Tony made a calming gesture with his hands. "Doc didn't mean it that way." He poked a cigarette at the lieutenant. "Let's not get paranoid, gentlemen."

Schiff shook his head at the cigarette but settled back in his chair. Doc used the prop to break eye contact and plucked the butt from Tony's fingers.

"We do have to get them out of here," Schiff continued. "We're not set up for guests you know. How about NUMC?"

Nassau University Medical Center was a favorite place for stashing sensitive witnesses. They could be provided all the comforts of home in a private room.

"Too many eyes." Doc shook his head. "Same with the big hotels. And the little ones are a nightmare to secure. Look who we're up against. Last night was a carefully planned, coordinated attack on Mrs. Maclear's place complete with a diversionary strike. Proof positive that this is one tenacious, smart, and very deadly son of a bitch. He blew up half the fucking town, shot up a suburban street, butchered a harmless old couple, busted up two more cops, and if the gas from that sportscar had ignited, we'd have two more dead cops and God knows how many dead civilians. And the prick got away without a living soul laying eyes on him."

"What do you suggest, Doc? Throw them in a holding cell?"

"No." Doc shifted his weight in the chair, gathering his thoughts. "I think the business-as-usual approach is out the window. We do this by the book, and he's going to shove it up our asses, sideways."

Schiff laced his fingers and rested his forearms on the table. "Tony. Your thoughts."

"Doc's right, Lieutenant. Unorthodox is the only way to fly."

Schiff nodded, pursed his lips and said, "So, assuming for the moment that I concur, what do I tell the chief? Never mind the commissioner."

"Nothing," Doc said flatly. "Mrs. Maclear is sedated and unable to be moved," he recited as if giving a report. "Doctor's orders. The ballplayer is cooperating to the best of his ability. We feel they should be kept together for the time being, until—together—they can make the pieces fit." He leaned back and lit the cigarette. Squinting through the cloud that enveloped his head as he exhaled through his nose, he said, "Stonewall the bastards. That's what they'd do to us. Fuck 'em."

Schiff sighed. "Okay. We'll play it your way for now. But you had better come up with something. They don't like the 'Puzzle Palace' being disrupted. I can't keep them off my back forever. They want to see movement, even if it's just to raise dust. Get Barbarosa back on those yearbooks. We stepped on a lot of toes to get them. Persuade him the Colombian gambit isn't panning out. We know it's bullshit, convince him."

"What about the feds?" Tony kneaded his brow.

Schiff slapped the table with his palm. "We've been down that road. No feds."

"Wanna bet? Tell him, Doc."

Doc grit his teeth and groaned. "He's right, Charlie. The mailbox. That spells feds."

"Shit!" Tony snapped a pencil and threw the pieces on the table. "Why couldn't he blow up something else?"

Schiff's eyes went wide. They were right. The mailbox made it a federal crime.

"And when they get wind that we suspect the guy's a deserter," Doc went on, "they'll be all over the place."

Tony hung his head. "Double shit."

Schiff was incredulous. "What's with you two? It wasn't long ago you were begging for them."

"But not now." Doc sighed. "We've gone up against this guy enough to know how devious the bastard is. The Bureau will waltz in here and take over. They'll tie us up in knots. You ever hear of an unorthodox fed?" Doc stood. "You let those pencil necks in here, Charlie, and we'll never get this guy. He'll butcher the two people down the hall and evaporate while we march to a very predictable drummer. If you think your bosses will pinch you on the cheek and pat you on the ass when that happens, Lieutenant, think again."

ঔঔ

Thud! Whoosh! Clunk!

Thud! Whoosh! Clunk!

The rhythmic pounding was wearing on Carl's nerves. By the time he made it back to his house, he wanted nothing so much as sleep. The department of public works was altogether indifferent to his needs.

Replacement of a faulty sewer pipe in the street outside Carl's home began with the breaking up of the pavement at seven a.m.

In the street, a pointed steel ram on a pneumatic punch was being used to pound a series of holes, as if perforating a sheet of paper to tear on the dotted line. The effect was mind jarring. Carl's entire house shook with each jolt of steel to pavement.

Carl threw off the covers. Barefoot and in his under shorts, he padded downstairs to the kitchen. He started a pot of coffee and, while the Dial-a-Brew dripped, walked to the living room to peek through the blinds at the gang of sweating men in grimy work clothes and reflective vests.

The workmen looked bored. He counted six of them standing around, leaning on shovels and brooms, watching the operator maneuver the pulsating monster along the length of the dotted line he was creating. Two more sat beside an idle backhoe, smoking cigarettes and sipping coffee from cardboard cups as they waited for their turn to join in the fun.

Carl could feel the floor beneath his feet reverberate with the repeated impacts. Impatient, he returned to the kitchen and replaced the carafe of the coffee maker with a large ceramic mug. When the steaming liquid approached the lip, he switched back to the glass pot, inhaling the aroma as the fresh brew that missed the carafe splashed and sizzled on the heating element.

He was about to descend the steps to the basement, to his hidden room, when he spied his bare feet. The damp concrete of the cellar floor was not something he wished to subject his naked soles to. Instead, he returned to the living room and dropped down onto the couch, propping his feet on the coffee table. He sipped the scalding fluid and, with his free hand, groped for the TV remote on the end table. He began channel surfing, looking for news. Most of the networks were beginning the day with the smiling faces of their morning show hosts. Carl had no stomach for their cutesy versions of what was happening in the world. CNN was airing a protracted discussion on the political ramifications of the latest White House edict and its effects on the president's popularity polls. He hit pay dirt on Channel 30. A striking blonde introduced a piece, billed: Breaking News: The Terminator Investigation. And there was the woman he had come to think of as his good friend, Adrienne Boyd, on tape, raising the question of why a famous, middle-aged ex-outfielder turned batting coach and an unknown nurse were being sequestered at police headquarters.

Carl sat straighter in his seat, engrossed, the distraction from the street completely forgotten. There was an inset photograph of Ron Barbarosa, smiling, suited up in his team's pinstripes. It could have been a proof from a baseball card. His name appeared beneath it. Beside his grinning image was a pretty young woman in a nurse's cap. Madeline Maclear, RN, appeared below. Carl realized it was an older photo of Madeline in uniform, probably taken before she had risen through the ranks to her present position of responsibility. The station obviously had been unable to obtain a recent picture. Carl did not need identifying captions. He knew those faces well.

"Why are these people being held by the police?" Adrienne asked. "What connection, if any, do they have to the recent string of brutal murders on Long Island? Is it true that Mrs. Maclear was a tenant in the home of Mr. and Mrs. John Dietrich, the elderly couple savagely slain in their home in Oyster Bay last night?" The camera zoomed in for a closeup of Adrienne's thoughtful countenance. "Why do the police neither confirm nor deny the presence of these people in their custody? Channel Thirty has learned from a reliable source that they are, in fact, being held." The scene switched to a shot of the main entrance to the police headquarters building. The barricades and the dozen uniformed officers guarding the doors took on a sinister air as Adrienne's voice became quietly outraged. "Is there a break in the case? Has some hideous conspiracy been unearthed? Why don't the police, who are sworn to protect and serve, want us to know what they know?

"This is Adrienne Boyd in Garden City, Long Island."

The blonde returned to center stage with a look of contemplative consternation. "In other news…"

Carl depressed the mute button. He had no interest in other news.

So! They were together. The cops had gone on the defensive. This would be a challenge.

The pavement punch in the street outside was still pounding away. Carl's coffee cup, propelled by harmonic vibration, began to walk off the coffee table. He grabbed it in time, but something about it bothered him. What fleeting scrap of thought had just eluded him? He had to get some sleep. Even a mind as sharp as his began to dull without rest.

ଔଔ

"Let's keep our eyes on the ball, huh, Ron," Doc said.

Barbarosa's eyes flashed. Tony set his feet beneath his chair, poised to spring.

Doc recognized Barbarosa's look in response to his belittling remark. It was calculated to push him back, to warn him to give way lest he incur the infamous wrath of the angry ballplayer. It had worked on managers, teammates, and most umpires, but the detective leaned closer, daring Ron to make an issue of it. Coffee and too many cigarettes were making Doc's breath foul. He knew it. He could taste it.

"Come on, Ron," he whispered. "Think about it." The batting coach drew back. Doc grinned. "It doesn't add up. The boys from Medelin aren't going to send their sharks after some—" Doc almost said jerk, but caught himself. "—some guy who pisses off a broad who's so low on the food chain she's microscopic. Dotty Kohler had as much to do with organized cocaine traffic as Barney the Purple Dinosaur. The woman was just a burned-out throwback to the 'sixties. We've checked."

Barbarosa's lips disappeared as he clenched his jaw tight, sitting stock-still, immovable, eyes riveted to the table.

"Ronny, Ronny, Ronny," Doc sighed, and inwardly brightened when he saw Barbarosa grimace in reaction to the hated nickname.

Barbarosa reddened but his legendary temper and reputation for physical violence mattered not one iota to Doc.

"Dorothy Kohler's connection to the drug trade," Doc continued to hammer away, "was strictly one of a customer. We've talked to her supplier. He's a slippery little shit—a lowlife, longhaired barfly who gets off on telling stories of friends in high places to horny old addicts. Believe me. The fucker couldn't put a hit on a cockroach if he had a sledgehammer and an instruction booklet. Even if, by some wild stretch of the imagination he could contact the right people, why in the hell would some Colombian kingpin agree to wipe out everybody on that list? There's nothing in it for them and these people don't do anything that doesn't have a positive effect on their cash flow."

Barbarosa was squirming. Doc poured it on. "Add in the fact that most of the people on that list were not at the class reunion and you've got a big fat zero. It is fantasy with a capital F. So, let's get with the program, Ronny. The only thing that makes any sense at all is the fact that twenty-five to thirty years ago, all of the folks who are on that list had something in common. What was it?"

Barbarosa cracked each of the knuckles on each of his hands, one at a time. Tony cringed and looked away.

"I've looked through those yearbooks until my eyeballs hurt," Ron finally said to the floor, his words a measured monotone, as if avoiding eye contact with his interrogators would allow him free reign. "Okay. What you say makes sense. The drug thing does sound kind of crazy now. I admit I was scared. I guess I let my imagination get out of hand. My lawyer didn't help. It ain't his fault. He's more agent than legal eagle. At the time it made sense. Don't ask me why." He dismissed it with a backhand wave.

His head fell into his hands. After a brief pause, he took a long breath, sat straight in the chair, and rubbed his palms on his thighs. "I can't come up with anything else," he said to Doc. "None of the faces in those books brings to mind anything but harmless memories." To Tony, he said, "Sure, there are a couple of kids I can remember having fights with. Maybe a few girls I might have fucked and dumped. Possibly one or two who might not like me very much to this day. But there is no one who would be carrying the kind of grudge to do something like this after all these years. Especially not to all of us. We weren't that tight. We couldn't have hurt anyone that bad. We didn't even stay in touch after high school. Everybody went their own separate way. Maybe Maddy can find the missing link. I can't."

"Doc." A uniformed officer tapped Wiley on the shoulder. "Chief wants you and Tony in his office right away."

A grim-faced Needleman and an equally dour Lieutenant Schiff ushered them both into chairs as soon as they entered the room.

"This was on the morning news," the chief indicated the television built into the wall in his office as he pushed the play button on a VCR. Adrienne Boyd's recent revelation shone on the screen.

"Can I please shoot that bitch?" Tony begged when the clip ended. The stone-faced stares that met his gaze answered his slip of the tongue. "Just thought I'd ask," he mumbled.

"We have to get them out of the building, gentleman," Needleman said, sotto voice.

"Like, yesterday," Schiff added.

ꕤꕤ

If he could smuggle a bomb into the building Carl thought he might be able to force them out. How long would it take to check the records, list the vendors, and decide whose security was lax enough to allow him to insert a package in the next shipment?

Too long. The information was a matter of public record, easy to obtain. Analysis of the information and formulation of a plan would be the hardest part, the most time-consuming part. Breaching the security net was risky. How careful would the cops be? The odds of actually getting to Madeline and Ron with a bomb delivered to who-knew-where in the building were slim and none. Besides, blowing them to smithereens by remote control would deprive him of what he needed most. The look on their faces—that was what this was all about. Without that, it was pointless. It might even cause an opposite reaction. It might cause the cops to reinforce.

No good.

Carl mentally pigeonholed ideas and discarded them as quickly as they came to him.

Then, he thought, suppose he did nothing?

Media curiosity would force them to own up to their secret or cover it up. What better way to deny than to offer proof of falsehood?

They're not here. We don't know what you're talking about.

That seemed likely. So, then what? Move the witnesses post haste. Yes!

Carl was dressed and, in his car, heading for the building on Franklin Avenue by the time Chief Needleman had devised his plan to remove Maclear and Barbarosa from underfoot. He parked in a medical center's metered garage several blocks from police headquarters and walked to survey the scene.

ꕥ

"This is nuts," Tony whispered to Doc.

The chief's underground parking garage beneath the headquarters building was jammed with uniforms waiting for the signal to rush the terrified witnesses outside. The back parking lot was pandemonium as reporters and curiosity seekers milled about. Word had leaked. The mysterious witnesses were being moved. Overzealous observers were gently, yet firmly pushed back if they leaned too hard on the cordon of uniforms acting as pickets for the departing motorcade. The harried cops anxiously glanced over their shoulders repeatedly, looking for some sign from the brass that their detail would come to an end before the mob got out of hand.

"Why don't we hang out a sign?" Tony groused, his voice rising. "Here they are. Come and get 'em."

The throb of rotor blades stopped Schiff's reprimand before he could utter it. His mouth hung open, poised to deliver the rebuke, his mind distracted by the anxiously awaited sound.

The clatter grew in intensity as the Bell Jet Ranger swooped low over the building.

Doc heard the disembodied voices of long ago as memories of Vietnam replayed in his mind.

'Smoke out, Dustoff One-Five. I-dentify.'

'Uh, Roger, Romeo-Six. See yellow smoke, over.'

'Affirmative, Dustoff One-Five.'

'Uh, Roger, Romeo-Six. Say condition of Lima Zulu, over.'

'Roger, Dustoff. Lima Zulu is cold. Say again, cold.'

'Uh, Roger. I copy. Have your Whiskeys ready to load. Comin' in.'

Doc saw the scene in his mind, smelled the foul stench of mud mixed with blood and sweat. He relived the aching dread of the bullet that would arrive before the bird touched earth. He had lived it so many times. Except that last time. The time they had come back without Berryhill—and him.

Tony's hand on his arm and a friendly nudge at his back brought him abruptly back to the present. They were in the car and driving up the ramp and into the sunshine. Madeline Maclear, light headed and nauseated from the sedative, clung tightly to Doc's arm as they were whisked past the surprised reporters. The motorcade swung into the street and accelerated. Tires squealed as they rounded corners, speeding through intersections closed off to traffic by patrol car roadblocks. The cars braked hard at the Supreme Court Building. Before the vehicles stopped rocking on their suspensions, the doors were yanked open and the occupants pulled from their seats by anxious hands.

Uniformed patrolmen encircled the escaping foursome, acting as human shields, seemingly sprung from the earth as soon as the cars dashed into the lot.

A sloping lawn replaced the image of the sodden rice paddy still clinging to the edges of Doc's memory. The helicopter hovered briefly overhead, and then dropped, bouncing lightly on its skids. The wind kicked up by the hammering blades threw dust and detritus into their squinting eyes. There was a brief moment of confusion as the cops and their passengers, thrust into the waiting arms of their guards, jostled one another as they sorted out the boarding order.

And then they were away.

Doc watched the courthouse shrink to the size of a sheet of paper. He noticed the snipers on the surrounding rooftops for the first time. Needleman had worked fast, setting it all up. The rectangle of people surrounding their makeshift chopper pad seemed to collapse into the center as the blue line broke and the onlookers rushed to fill the vacuum left by the rising helicopter. There would be a lot of angry news hounds firing questions at the bosses.

Would they deny that these people were ever there? Probably not. It was politically incorrect to lie when the truth was so apparent. More than likely some half-truths would be mixed with some concrete facts, shaken vigorously and served a-la-carte. The newsies would draw their own conclusions. But, what the hell, they would do that anyway.

With a reassuring hand on Madeline's arm, Doc leaned his head against the seat back and watched the world in panorama below. The police helicopter was far more comfortable than the Huey Slicks he rode in as a young man in Vietnam. It was quieter, too. The whine of the turbine filled the cabin, but the battering of the wind was missing, and the rhythmic beat of rotor blades chopping air was muted to a dull throb.

His happiest moments in Vietnam had been aloft in those ugly green birds. It was the only time he felt safe, above the canopy, out of the mud—brief moments without fear. He felt that way now. Quickly, he scanned the faces of his fellow passengers, apprehensive that they would know by the relief that must be evident on his face how frightened he had been. No one was paying any attention to him. Tony and Ron were enjoying the view. Madeline's eyes were squeezed tightly shut.

And what had he been afraid of? The Terminator? Hardly. Doc realized that his anxiety had peaked in the car, waiting for the pickup. The dustoff daydream had been so vivid it had reawakened the old fear. He had almost smelled the stink of rice paddy.

How he wished that he were with his old team, young again, loaded for bear, kicking ass. Oh, to drop in on this miserable prick with his M-16 in hand, to kick in his door and stitch him from head to toe on automatic. To watch him dance the dance of death, twitching and writhing as the 5.56s tore him to pieces.

Why? Wasn't he the good guy? The guy who wanted to stop the slaughter?

Revenge? Baddest motherfucker in the valley?

Madeline said, "I hope I'm not going to be sick." She was the color of unbleached flour.

"Take a deep breath," Doc patted her hand and was instantly alarmed at the lack of warmth. "We'll be there in a few minutes."

"I'm sorry. I'm acting like a baby. Flying has never been one of my favorite things."

Her fingernails dug into his palm. It might have hurt had he not been so happy she was holding his hand.

"No need to apologize. You're doing fine. Tony. What's our ETA?"

Tony swiveled in his seat and peered around the headrest. A broad, toothy grin sprang into place as he saw the death grip the nurse had on his buddy's paw.

"About five minutes, I'd say. You can see the water already." He winked. "Unless you would like me to tell the driver, 'Once around the park.'"

Doc glowered at him but made no reply. Madeline seemed oblivious, but Doc noticed she did not let go of his hand, though her grip relaxed. Tony shrugged and faced front, his shoulders quaking with mirth. A sidelong glance caught the remnants of a hastily altered grin on Madeline's lips. Doc had the distinct impression he was missing something. At least it appeared that she was feeling better. Strangely enough, so was he.

ꟹꟹ

Carl arrived on the outskirts of the milieu, gasping for breath, winded from his pell-mell sprint after the motorcade, just in time to see the helicopter rise like a giant dragonfly, hesitate, as if contemplating its transition, then swing up and away. The sounds from the crowd scattered against the building facade, lost in the thrumming of the rotating wings. He stood frozen, artificial wind tugging at his clothing, chin pointing accusingly skyward, chest heaving, arms rigid at his sides, fists balled, eyes blazing. They had eluded him yet again, left him stranded on the earth, watching the receding shape as the machine departed with his kill.

How, he wondered, would he ever find them now?

His answer appeared the moment the question entered his mind. A second whirlybird, tail rotor high, pointed forty-five degrees above the horizontal, charged after the first.

A caustic grin spread across his face as he read the electric blue lettering on the white tail boom: Ch-30 Traffic Copter.

“Thank you, Adrienne Boyd,” he breathed, “you beautiful, opportunistic bitch.”

Chapter 31

The chopper touched down on a broad expanse of lawn that would make any golf course greens-keeper salivate. The passengers alighted and were instantly surrounded by a squad of heavily armed police officers dressed in blue-black fatigues and combat boots. Black flak vests and square-looking Kevlar helmets enhanced the storm-trooper personae of the tactical officers. Doc wondered, as he often had, why the PC entrenched brass allowed this provocative imagery. Was it possible that even the spin-doctors knew that shock troops were more effective if they looked the part? Or was the county's wardrobe guy a closet sturmbahnfeuhrer?

With their M-16s at high port, the black-garbed team rushed their charges across the greensward, up a short flight of wide fieldstone steps and onto a knee-walled patio. The group then quick-marched past an eclectic array of cast concrete cherubs and nymphs, through the center pair of a long row of wood-framed plate glass doors and into the back of the sprawling home overlooking Natalie Graille's estate.

Last minute preparations were under way everywhere the anxious witnesses cared to look. Dozens of uniforms and suits trotted hither and yon, talking into handheld radios as they went. Once inside, the witnesses were told where they were allowed to go and where not, the latter being the longer list. After a brief period of time in which to allow Madeline and Ron to settle in, Doc and Tony left them with their guards and set out to inspect the newly fortified grounds firsthand.

By mid-afternoon, Doc had convinced himself that everything possible was being done to secure the home from anything but the most determined attack. What troubled him was that just such an onslaught was precisely what he expected. If they were up against a rifle company, Doc would have been more confident. He knew from experience how dangerous one highly skilled and motivated assassin can be. Their only chance would be with preparation, vigilance, and luck.

Having completed their tour of the grounds, he and Tony stopped on Ms. Graille's fifty yards of private dock to examine the seaward avenues of approach.

"I still think this is nuts," Tony said.

Doc watched a trim, red-hulled sloop jibe far out in the Sound. The mainsail luffed in the changing breeze and flapped like his mother's wash on her clothesline as the sleek yacht came about. Doc could almost hear the snap as the crisp white triangular sheet caught the wind and puffed like a fat man's vest. He guessed that the skipper knew what he was doing. At least it looked well done.

"Hey, we're not cooped up with the brass breathing down our necks," Doc said. "If I had to stay under the same roof with Schiff much longer, I think I might have belted him."

"That's another thing." Tony paused to cup a match in his hands. He lit his third cigarette since they had walked out onto the pier. "What's with you and all this nose to nose shit with Charlie? He ain't a bad guy for a lieutenant." Shaking the match unnecessarily in the stiff breeze, he tossed it into the water and stood with his head cocked to one side, waiting.

"He pisses me off lately."

"Why? Because he's got us playing body-guard instead of beating the bushes for this animal?"

"I don't know," Doc snapped. He met Tony's gaze and realized how deep his friend's concern was. "Don't do that."

"Do what?"

"Don't mother me. I hate it when you do that."

Tony shook his head in exasperation. "You really are a piece of work, you know. You're about as rational as my youngest." He raised one finger to parry Doc's baleful look. "Listen to me." He paused, waiting for Doc to settle down. When he had his friend's undivided attention, he went on. "I don't know what you're thinking. That worries me. I thought I knew you like my own brother, but you're not acting like the Doc I know."

"Now what the hell does that mean?"

"Shut up a minute. I'm trying to tell you."

Doc rolled his eyes heavenward.

Tony countered with both index fingers raised to accent his peaked eyebrows. Doc tore his eyes away from the fleecy clouds and met Tony's gaze. Tony waited another second, folded his arms, and said, "You're the only guy I've ever known who really improves under pressure. It's like you thrive on it. Your mind works faster, clearer. Your reflexes quicken. You're never more confident, more—invincible, for want of a better word, than when your back's to the wall."

"Gimme a break. I—"

"I mean it, Doc. I don't understand it. Never will. But when the shit's coming down, thick as a brick, that's when ol' Doc Wiley's at his best. It's like someone's tightening the screws on a precision engine and the damn thing goes into overdrive."

"Excuse me while I get my feet off the floor. It's getting too deep for me." Doc grinned.

"Is it?"

"What's that supposed to mean?" The grin was gone. Doc's eyes turned hard.

"Remember that night in Hempstead, when we were rookies?" Doc made a face but Tony stopped him with the finger thing again. "We got that burglary-in-progress squeal and chased that big dude up onto the roof of an apartment building."

"We chased a lot of guys—" Doc frowned his impatience.

"Not like this character. He was a friggin' gorilla. Biggest son-of-a-bitch I ever saw. Don't you remember? Christ! He almost killed both of us."

"Oh, that one."

"Yeah, that one. We lost him and we were searching the roof when the bastard dropped on you like a ton of bricks from on top of the elevator room."

"He was kind of big."

"And strong. He tossed you over the parapet like you were a paper airplane."

Doc whistled softly. "Lady Luck was with us that night."

"No shit. If you hadn't grabbed that fire escape rail, we wouldn't be having this discussion."

"The point of which is?"

Tony went on with the story as if Doc had not said a word. "I damn near shit in my pants. I'm still trying to assimilate what I've just seen, namely you, my best friend, going bye-byes in front of my eyes, and this mountain in street clothes turns on me."

"Why didn't you shoot him?"

Tony's jaw dropped. "Shoot him? I couldn't move. I was terrified. I fell over backward trying to get out of his way. I was flat on my ass and this monster was coming for me. Just when I'm sure it's all over, when all I can see is my mangled body splattered all over the pavement, you come vaulting back onto the roof like an avenging angel. You lit into that guy like a two-gallon bucket of whip-ass. It was beautiful. I sat there, stunned, with gravel cutting into my ass while you took the bastard apart. I can still see your baton flashing in the moonlight like a flaming sword. It could have been choreographed, for godsakes. By the time I could breathe again, the guy was a pile of bruised meat."

"So, what's your point?"

"My point is, this time you're all fucked up. You're like a live flounder on a hot griddle. It's not like you. Ever since I've known you, the harder they come at you, the harder you come back. But this time is different and I can't put my finger on it. What's bugging you, man?"

Doc's mouth opened but he said nothing. He felt like that flounder all right. Not in the pan yet but definitely on the hook. He compressed his lips in a thin line and reached for Tony's cigarette, which he used to light one of his own, taking his time, puffing on the butt, gathering his thoughts.

"I really don't know," he finally said, hating himself for lying to Tony, but unable to put his feelings into words. It was Nam, and Madeline, and frustration. He had this gnawing sensation in his guts that once again he had no control over events, that despite everything he could do, someone he cared for was going to come to harm. Was he taking this one personally because he hadn't eliminated the violence before it again touched someone close to him? Did he really believe he ever would? This one had reawakened his urge to kill. He wanted vengeance. This one was after someone he loved, and that, he had to admit, was tearing him apart. He had thought he had rationalized his youthful anger, that he had left it behind. This Terminator character was pushing old buttons, and for the first time in a very long time, he doubted himself. People who took themselves too seriously annoyed him. Yet, here he was second-guessing himself like a tightrope walker unsure of his shoes.

It shook him. He felt like a man given a second chance. Had he ever had a first? Had he been scrambling to fill a void all these years, panic stricken, desperate to regain something lost? What, he didn't know. He only knew when. It started when the war ended. The dream was his milestone. Everything in him tingled with anticipation. This was a shot at redemption. And he wasn't sure if he was ready. Or worthy. Or totally out of his gourd.

"Maybe I'm having a mid-life crisis," Doc whispered. A tentative grin spread across his face.

"At least that's more like you," Tony punched Doc's arm. "You always could sidestep like a matador. I'll make you a deal. After we bag this prick, we'll both have one. Okay?"

"With a side order of paranoia."

"Hold the onions."

"Let's go see how the troops are making out," Doc suggested. The tension wasn't broken but it had slackened to a point where he could breathe.

"Making out?" Tony said with mock seriousness. "Watch where you say that. My wife would kill me."

"I thought you were too young to remember the 'sixties?"

"Not the best parts."

"You know, if you think about it Tony, this isn't bad." Doc looked around as they walked to the beach, their footsteps on the weathered planks muffled by the lapping of the waves against the pilings. "This place is ideal for holing up. Easy to surveille avenues of approach. Water on one side, high fences on all the others, plenty of floodlights and enough cops to guard the crown jewels. I could almost thank Ron for suggesting it."

"Suggesting it? That's a nice way to put it. I thought you'd blow a gasket when he demanded we come here."

"In all fairness, it wasn't my first choice, but the place kind of grows on you."

"I could get used to living like Jacob Astor, if that's what you mean."

"Let's just hope our friend doesn't turn it into a war zone," Doc said. "Ms. Graille might be a wee bit upset with her jock boyfriend if he gets her picture post card place all shot to shit."

"Just as long as he doesn't get us similarly damaged."

ᴗᴗ

The built-in VCR in Carl's TV whined as the tape came up to speed. REC glowed in emerald green on the display. Carl chuckled as the machine recorded the image of Channel 30's fly-by of his quarry's refuge. Leaning back on the sofa in his den, with his feet propped up on the coffee table, he sipped burgundy from a long-stemmed goblet. Scraps of the burger he had consumed as a late lunch were all that remained on the plate balancing on the padded arm where he leaned his trim frame.

"I've got to remember to send a thank you note to the producers at Channel Thirty. It's so thoughtful of them to provide me with aerial reconnaissance of the grounds."

He peered closely at the screen, noting the many heavily armed police officers interspersed among the trees, along the beach, the fence, and the gates.

"This isn't going to be easy." He steepled his fingers in front of pursed lips. "They're not kidding around."

He thumbed the volume button and listened to the reporter describing the scene as if the viewer were blind.

"The only way The Terminator will be able to get at Mr. Barbarosa and Mrs. Maclear while they are guarded day and night in the fortified estate of Natalie Graille, the famed entertainer," the disembodied voice was saying, "would be if he were a ghost."

The talking head went on to verify that they had indeed confirmed the identities of the sequestered occupants of the house on the hill at the center of the manicured grounds as the aforesaid personalities. Madeline Maclear had been elevated to celebrity status by her involvement.

Carl was far more interested in what the speaker had just said concerning what it would take to gain access to the estate than the fleeting fame his prey had been awarded.

"If that's what the situation calls for…" He had to cover his mouth with his hand to keep from laughing. He hit the STOP button and then rewound the tape, pressed PLAY and reviewed the report three times more.

Happy, now that he had a plan, he punched the off button and the television went black. Staring at the dark eye across the room, he prioritized his steps in his mind.

As he left the house, he absently noted the return of the hole-making machine as the construction crew off-loaded it from a mud-encrusted flatbed. He was glad to be getting away before the infernal racket began anew but the sight of the machine reminded him that there was something in the back of his mind that would not come forward. He had that nagging sensation that it might be important but he could not extract it from the deep recess from which it refused to be dislodged.

ଙଙ

"You wouldn't have a Stinger in your little bag of tricks, would you, Sarge?" Tony asked with wry humor in his eyes.

The blond-haired cop with the bulletproof vest and black baseball cap smiled knowingly at Detective Cordova.

"Sorry, Tony. Not that we don't have access to such toys, but we didn't figure anti-aircraft missiles were called for on this one." He looked through binoculars at the news chopper as it made another pass out over the water. "Besides, I don't think the commissioner would take kindly to our shooting down a civilian helicopter."

"Those ain't civilians. Those are media mopes. Hardly human."

"You have a point. Still, there's that little matter of freedom of the press."

"So I've heard. Can't we get the brass to shoo them off?"

"We're working on it."

"Let me know if they come within rifle range," Tony called over his shoulder as he climbed the steps to the back of the house.

The blond cop laughed and shook his head.

Tony passed a fountain that was a statue of a winged cherub pouring out a vase, with her stone mouth hung open in whimsical surprise. "Fuck you, too," he grumbled.

ଙଙ

"Please, Detective Wiley?" Madeline unveiled liquid eyes. "Whatever your police doctor gave me to relax has left me with a pounding headache," she said. "If I don't get some fresh air, I'm afraid my head will pop off."

Doc was reluctant to let the woman walk around outside, especially in broad daylight with that damned news chopper spying on the grounds from on high. Maybe the killer was a media puke. They certainly were doing everything possible to assist him. He thought of

Adrienne Boyd and anger came with the thought. Adrienne was a spoiled brat who had never grown up. She used her daddy's money to buy whatever she wanted and never gave a second thought to the harm she did. Honesty and loyalty were just words to Adrienne. She would sell her soul for a sensational story. Doc thought she already had. The helicopter buzzing the grounds was getting on his nerves because he knew Adrienne had caused it to be there.

"I'm sorry, Mrs. Maclear. It just isn't safe." He saw a flash of anger in her eyes and for a moment he was sure he was going to have a row with the woman. The thought made him cringe. Going toe to toe with the baseball player did not faze him. He would welcome the chance to physically restrain Barbarosa. There was something about good ol' Ron that made him want to slug him. The mere thought of heated words with Madeline made his insides turn to liquid. That really bothered him. What was it about this woman that screwed him all up?

She seemed to sense his unease and the flare of temper subsided as quickly as it had come. "I know your job is to protect me, Doc." Her voice was silky, seductive. She reddened slightly at the use of his nickname. He had not given any outward sign that he would allow such familiarity. It was something assumed, as if she knew he wanted her to be more than an assigned responsibility. Strangely, in the midst of all the terror, Madeline was behaving like a woman wanting, no, needing to get to know Doc. There was urgency, almost as if she had to take the chance now or lose it forever.

"Mrs. Maclear, I—"

"Madeline, please call me Madeline." Her eyes shone.

They were alone in the sunken living room. Doc's heart pounded in his chest. He felt short of breath. His eyes cast about for his colleagues. Madeline Maclear was the first woman in almost twenty-five years to make his pulse race, his cheeks hot, his knees weak, just by saying his name. If the other cops knew what effect this woman was having on their vaunted swordsman, he'd be laughed off the force. The really funny thing was, he didn't care.

"Please, Doc? Just for a little while?"

"You have to stay close to me."

"Always."

Your mouth to God's ears.

Chapter 32

The sun was a red splash on the underside of loose knit cloud as Carl swung the Jeep into the yard of Islander Oil. The company occupied the dead end of a commercial street nestled between two canals in the North Shore town of Sea Cliff. Limited access made traffic sparse. Consequently, the land was unattractive to most businesses as evidenced by the two adjacent vacant lots. The only other active concern on the quiet back street, an auto junkyard situated at the other end, was already closed for the day.

The concrete pavement was yielding to the onslaught of weeds. Leafy shoots pushed through ever-widening gaps in the cement. A small Cape Cod house with cedar shake shingles weathered to a rusty black-brown sat like a tired old codger beside the hardstand. Peeling white trim and parchment-like window shades behind wavy glass panes set in frames begging for caulk completed the impression of neglect. Behind and to the left of the old house, a barn with double doors leaned precariously, as if attempting to get closer to its forlorn and ancient friend.

In front of the barn sat the object of Carl's visit. A Fruehauf straight bed fuel-tanker truck, in surprisingly good shape for its late 'seventies vintage, stood bathed in the glow of the setting sun. The truck's bright red paint stood out in sharp contrast to the ramshackle look of the buildings. It was not difficult to discern where the owner's priorities lay. Snow white lettering, tinted pink by the failing rays, proclaimed the vehicle to be the pride of Islander Oil. High up on the rear of the blunt ended cylinder, No. 4, limned in the same crisp white, gave the impression that the truck was part of a fleet. In actuality, the inscription described the latest in the frugal owner's list of infrequent replacements of other singular vehicles.

Joe Ludlow, the president and entire staff of Islander Oil, tenaciously hung on to his business in spite of falling profits and a disintegrating customer base. The old man simply did not know what else to do with his time. He had been an oilman all of his adult life and since the passing of his wife, Loretta, for whom he had built the business, he did not have the heart to pack it in.

"Hullo, Joe, whaddya know?" Carl smiled as he strolled past the tanker.

Ludlow peered over the lenses of half-glasses at the source of the greeting, wiping his hands on an oily rag as he unfolded his body from beneath the raised hood of the gleaming vehicle.

"It's Carl Esterbrook, Joe. I hope you haven't forgotten me."

Ludlow squinted at the tall, thin man walking toward him. Recognition dawned and his lined face split into a welcoming smile.

"Mr. Esterbrook, how nice to see you. You'll forgive me if I don't shake your hand." Ludlow proffered his greasy digits as proof of his sensibility.

"Engine trouble, Joe?"

"Naw, not this old girl. She runs like a dream. But you got to perform your preventive maintenance if you want her to keep on goin'. Jist changin' some filters. You gotta keep the grit out of the system or she'll gum up on ya when you need her most." He wiped his hands on an oily rag and continued with his diatribe. "Most folks don't take proper care of their machinery. They piss and moan quick enough when things break down, though. Truth be told, half the mechanical failures on the road today could have been prevented with proper maintenance." He removed the safety bar and let the vented cover slam down with a bang. "Like I used to tell Loretta—"

"Do you have a moment to discuss some business, Joe?" Carl interrupted.

"Heh? Oh, sure, sure. Why don'tcha come inside, Mister Esterbrook? I'm done for the day. Mebbe for the week, if this goddamn weather keeps up."

"It has been unseasonably warm."

"That's the damned truth," Ludlow swore. "Seems like even Mother Nature's against me making an honest dollar these days." The old man continued to complain as they climbed the steps of the back porch. "Have a seat," Ludlow offered as they entered the kitchen, gesturing toward a small kitchen table and four chairs.

He stepped to a chipped, porcelain clad, cast iron sink and proceeded to wash his hands with a bar of brown soap, so smeared with grease that Carl ceased wondering at the permanence of the black grime embedded in the callused skin of the old man's fingers.

"Can I offer you a drink?" Ludlow queried with his brow creased in expectation. "I'm fond of a taste at the end of the working day."

"Sounds good."

"Bourbon all right with you?" He pulled two jelly glasses from a knotty pine cupboard without waiting for a reply and poured three fingers in each. Sitting down across from Carl at the Formica topped table, he slid one drink in front of his guest. "Cheers," he toasted and drank half of the fiery liquid in one gulp.

"Business a little slow, Joe? I mean with the early spring and all."

"Slow would be a welcome improvement. People don't give two shits for real service anymore. Everybody wants cheap. Only accounts I keep nowadays are old duffers like me that don't like change."

The wistful look in Joe Ludlow's eyes told of disappointment tempered by grim resignation to the inevitable.

"Only thing in life that's guaranteed, you know," he said in his customary didactic way. "Nothing's permanent. Things change."

"Wisely put."

"Bullshit, but nice of you to say so." The gleam in his eye said that he truly appreciated the compliment. "Now what brings a young feller like you callin' on old Joe Ludlow? Surely, you don't need a new oil company. The south shore is a little out of my stomping grounds. Or have you moved up here?"

"No, I'm still at the same old stand. Besides, my place is heated with gas." Carl missed the grimace of distaste brought on by his thoughtless remark as he glanced about the disheveled kitchen, outwardly nonchalant as he formed the lie in his mind. "I was wondering if you might have had a change of heart about that beautiful dining room set, the one you wouldn't part with when I sold the contents of your old house. I have a client who will pay serious money for it. It's just what she's been looking for."

"Sorry, Mr. Esterbrook, but no. Loretta loved that set. I still couldn't let it go. It's as if she was still with me when I sit down to dinner every night. It's about all I have left of the good old days. No, I couldn't sell it. You tell your client to be patient. I've left instructions with my lawyer for you to handle the sale of my estate when I kick the bucket." He swirled the whiskey in the glass and Carl felt as if Joe was looking right through him when he said, "Won't be long now. I ain't gettin' any younger."

"I understand. And thanks for the vote of confidence."

"Think nothing of it. You treated me fair when Loretta passed. I'm grateful. I suppose you know there are a lot of unscrupulous folks in your business, present company excluded."

"I guess we're a dying breed, you and I, in today's cut-throat world of business."

"That's a fact. Care for another taste?"

"Thanks, but no. I've got to drive."

"You're a level-headed young man."

"Thank you, but I'm not all that young."

"When you get to be my age, everybody still standing upright is young. Thanks for the visit. You be sure to mention my name to any of your customers might be looking to sign on with a dependable oil company."

"My pleasure."

As the old man rose to escort his guest to the door, he offered Carl his right hand. Ludlow's shock was absolute when Carl seized it with his left and yanked him forward. The karate punch that slammed into Ludlow's temple stunned him. He tried to focus on the face of the previously genteel antique broker from where he suddenly found himself, sitting on the worn linoleum of his kitchen floor.

"Look at it this way, Joe," Carl said, as he reached into his pants pocket, "Loretta's waiting."

The lead-filled leather sap cracked the old man's skull like an egg. Carl admired the efficiency of the weapon. It easily smashed bone without splitting surface skin beyond a superficial abrasion at the contact point. Too bad Joe Ludlow was not a younger man. That would have made the next step in his plan unnecessary. But, if getting away with multiple murder was simple, everybody would be doing it.

Carl carried Ludlow's lifeless body upstairs, passing the dining room set he had inquired about as he went. It was nice to know he would be entrusted with its sale. A shame he did not really have a ready-made buyer, he thought, but it would not be hard to find one. It was a beautiful set.

He placed the body beside the roll top desk in the upstairs bedroom where Ludlow had done his paperwork and kept track of his day-to-day affairs. Pulling on surgical gloves, he rifled the drawers and scattered the contents on the floor. He found a gray metal box at the bottom of the lowermost left-hand drawer. It had a lock but forcing it was unnecessary. Joe Ludlow, trusting soul that he had been, did not lock his cash box. Carl pocketed the two hundred thirty-six dollars and change he found inside and tossed the container on the bed. Stepping back, he examined the scene and decided to smash the green glass shade of the banker's lamp atop the desk to complete the effect. With a backhand blow, he swept it off the desktop to shatter against the wall.

"Robbery/Homicide, no doubt about it," he smirked.

Back downstairs, Carl climbed into a spare gray coverall with white pin striping he found hanging on a peg beside the rear door. The chances of him being seen while moving about in the yard were minute, but the uniform was camouflage in case of an accidental sighting by a passerby. The coveralls were six inches too short but Carl did not think anyone would come close enough to notice. If they did, they would never get the chance to tell anyone anyway.

He drove his car to the barn, but upon opening the rickety doors found the place crammed floor to ceiling with the collected junk of decades. Discarded tires, parts, boxes, cans, and a variety of soiled clothing stuffed the building. Ludlow had been a man who hated to part with anything. Carl reflected for a moment on the turmoil that Joe Ludlow must have experienced when he had decided to sell the bulk of his wife's things. What a battle the practical businessman in the old bastard must have waged with the sentimental slob who had loved his wife. Carl became convinced he had done Ludlow a favor. It was a shame he would never have the chance to meet him in the afterlife. Undoubtedly, they were going in opposite directions.

He parked the car directly in front of the fuel truck, thereby hiding it from the street. Extracting his duffel bag from the trunk, he set to work on the mechanical phase of his plan.

Chapter 33

Doc and Madeline sat on wooden benches in a tiny gazebo where the lawn met the rocky beach behind Natalie Graille's summer home. The structure was perched on a massive boulder, deposited eons ago by the glacial bulldozer that had formed Long Island from the detritus of its push to the sea. The setting sun cast elongated checkerboard patterns of gold and pink through the latticework walls onto Madeline's soft features. Her golden hair glistened like a halo. Their knees touched and Doc could feel her body heat through the fabric of their clothes. He was having trouble maintaining his edge in the intimate setting.

Madeline brushed a stray hair from her forehead, and said, "So, how long have you been a detective, Doc?"

"A hundred years or so." Doc grinned at his own joke, amazed at how tired of the job he had suddenly become. This tantalizing woman with the easy smile and wise sparkling eyes made him feel that everything up to this moment had been a long, drawn-out prologue.

"You don't want to hear about the trials and tribulations of one of Nassau County's least interesting snoops," he said, to avoid saying how beautiful she was. He knew he was going to say something stupid if he didn't get her talking. She made him feel so damned awkward. He had not wanted to come out here. They were vulnerable out here. At least, he was.

"I don't believe that for a minute. You know, I don't even know your first name."

"Let's keep it that way, shall we? There are very few people who know my given name and fewer still with the nerve to use it."

"Oh, come on. How bad can it be? Your parents must have liked it."

How right she was. His mother had loved it. So much so that she had prayed for a baby boy from the day that his sister was born until his birth, two years later. He hadn't forgiven his mom—God rest her—until his teens when he had finally come to understand the honor she had bestowed upon him. Sheila Wiley had named her son after her first love, her hero, a Hollywood star whom she had worshipped as the living example of masculine perfection.

The movement of a guard on the edge of his peripheral vision brought Doc back from the cozy place his mind had wandered into.

That beast was still out there, planning God knew what, and here he was, sitting comfortably in a rich woman's summer retreat, exchanging idle chatter with the most captivating creature he had ever known.

Doc was simultaneously entranced by Madeline's ability to take him away from the fear of the present with no more than casual conversation and distressed that he could be so easily distracted from his work.

"Maybe this wasn't such a good idea," he said. His eyes swept the grounds.

"I'm sorry. I didn't mean to pry. I was curious. Forgive me?"

"No, no. It's not that. It's just that we're so exposed out here. You'd be safer in the house."

"Even I know that Daniel Boone himself couldn't get a good shot at us in here. There are more cops surrounding us than the President of the United States." She took a breath and abruptly stood up. "My headache's easing up. If my prattling has made you uncomfortable, I'm sorry. If you want to go inside, I won't argue."

She was hurt and he was ashamed.

"Wendell," he mumbled.

"Who?"

"Me. My given name is Wendell."

Her mouth fell open, then closed, and then opened again. She tried to speak, but no words would come. She gave up and clapped both hands against her lips. Her shoulders began to quake. Tears sprang from her eyes. Finally, she rocked back in laughter, forsaking all efforts at self-control.

"It's not that funny," he growled.

"Oh, Doc, I'm so sorry, I didn't mean to laugh," she said, giggling.

“Okay, so maybe it is,” he said. Her laughter was infectious and he found himself grinning, partly from relief. For a moment he had thought she was going to cry.

“It’s not the name,” she said, gripping his arm with both of her hands. “It’s the look on your face.”

“What can I tell you? My mom thought Wendell Corey was God’s gift.”

She laughed until she fell helplessly against his shoulder.

“Could have been worse,” he said. “Mom liked Bing Crosby, too.”

She pounded his arm with her fist, begging him to stop. Her laughter gave him so much joy he said any silly thing that came to mind. After several rollicking moments, he remembered where they were and tried to quiet her. His half-hearted entreaties were met with snorts and cackles until she took a deep breath and wiped her eyes.

“Like laughing in church,” she breathed, “hard to stop.”

“It’s the tension. Bound to happen. You okay now?”

She nodded, her head pumping rapidly. When she looked up into his eyes, he was inches away. Her lips parted. His face was drawn to hers like iron to lodestone. He kissed her before he realized he was going to. Her scent was intoxicating. She pressed the length of her body to his. When their lips parted, they stayed close, reluctant to break contact.

“I shouldn’t have done that,” he said.

“I’m glad you did,” she whispered.

Her eyes were glassy. He felt a stirring in his pants. He took a step back, cleared his throat, and said, “We’d better go in.”

She reached for his hand. “Tell me about Wendell Wiley.”

“He’s kind of boring.”

“I disagree.”

“When I was little, the kids on my block played Peter Pan. It got me into a lot of fights.”

She grinned. “I’ll bite. Why?”

“They always said I had to be Wendy.”

She bit her lip and then shrieked in unbridled hilarity, begging him to stop before she wet her pants.

Chapter 34

His work completed on the truck, Carl shed the mechanic's coverall and drove his Jeep out of the lot before pausing to close the gate behind him. There was no padlock. He shrugged it off. Joe Ludlow, he felt certain, would have few nighttime callers. He had left no lights burning in the house to add to the impression that the owner was either out or retired for the evening. With any luck, no one would discover the old man's body until tomorrow, or at least until he was finished with his mission.

John Fogarty and Credence Clearwater Revival sang of a "Bad Moon Rising" on Carl's dashboard radio as he cruised down Forest Avenue into Locust Valley. The commercial section of the small village was the home of several posh bars and restaurants whose nightly clientele were disgorged from the commuter trains at the Long Island Railroad station in the center of town.

After making several evaluating tours of the area, Carl felt he had a feel for the local police patrol routine by the time he parked in a dark corner of a public parking lot opposite the Post Office. He then slipped out of his vehicle, stepped behind it and crouched down, leaning his back against the stacked railroad tie retaining wall at the back of the lot. From here, he could observe the quaint little pub across the street while he remained unobserved.

For more than two hours, Carl watched, motionless. Only his eyes moved. He waited for a particular set of circumstances—a lone male of his approximate size walking past the lot or through it when the street was otherwise deserted. It would happen. He knew it. It was merely a matter of patience and he had that in abundance.

A car drove by with the windows rolled down. Hip-hop blasted from a sound system that probably cost more than the battered Toyota surrounding it. Carl saw a young man behind the wheel bouncing to the beat, baseball cap worn backward. His mind returned to Woodstock as he watched the taillights recede.

A half-million screaming kids danced on a rain swept hillside, soaked, muddy, stoned and deliriously happy—brothers and sisters all, united by the times and the music, especially by the music. For the first time in his young life, Carl had felt part of something. He had finally found friends—people to love, people to love him. His eyes grew misty as he remembered that brief sense of belonging. But they had turned on him in the end, like they always did.

Hatred washed away the brief pang of nostalgia. The lonely boy gave way to the adult predator. The wistful look vanished and the vulpine stare returned.

By half past eight, the pedestrian and motor vehicle traffic had diminished to occasional passersby. The muscles in Carl's belly tightened as a well-groomed fellow in his late thirties, nattily dressed in a Brooks Brothers suit with a slim leather briefcase dangling from relaxed fingers, stepped out of the pub and ambled across the street. He was not staggering but it was plain to see he was far from sober.

Carl checked the street. No one. His car keys were in his hand. He duck-walked to the rear cargo door, inserted the key, and released the lock. As the stranger approached, Carl raised up with the door and beckoned to the man with a friendly wave.

"Hey, buddy," he slurred, "wouldja gimme a hand? I can't figure out this goddamn jack."

Seeing a fellow partier obviously in his cups and thereby deserving of his assistance the commuter complied. Just as he opened his mouth to offer words of empathy, Carl threw a snap kick that rammed into his solar plexus with the force of a pile driver. Gasping, the would-be Samaritan stumbled forward. A vicious flat-handed chop crashed into the back of his neck and the man fell like a sack of rags into the open cargo compartment. His feet were whisked off the pavement by powerful hands and he lay in a ball on the carpeted floor of the storage space, fighting to retain consciousness, panicky, incredulous. His attacker leaned over him, whispered, "Bye-bye, asshole," and hit him between the eyes with a ballpeen hammer.

Carl spread a blanket over the body, tossed the briefcase on top of it, slammed the lid, hopped behind the wheel, and was halfway down the block before any other citizen entered the street. He regretted the risk this kidnapping added to his plan, but it was necessary. Sooner or later the cops would figure some things out and probably come up with a fair description of him. The guy in the back of the Jeep had to bear a resemblance to him for this to work or they might not stop hunting him. To get a shot at Madeline and Ron, he had to get them to back off.

"And now for the good part," he giggled.

ꟹꟹ

"So, Detective Wiley," Ron Barbarosa took another gulp of wine from a crystal goblet, "you and Madeline get to know each other a little better this afternoon?"

The lascivious wink that went along with the remark would have cost Ron some teeth had it not been for two things. One: he was drunk, and two: Doc would rather Madeline was not present when he took him apart.

Doc hoped that the volume of wine the pompous athlete was consuming would hasten the man's descent into oblivion. Already, Ron's lids were heavy, his eyes at half-mast. With any luck, he would fall asleep before it became necessary to help him into the arms of Morpheus. Doc knew it wouldn't help the situation if he was goaded into clobbering the cocky coach, but the thought of it was tempting.

"I'd say that was none of your business." He knew his response should have been more tactful. Fuck him.

"That was an enjoyable meal, Ron," Tony cut in, doing his level best to forestall the inevitable clash between his friend and the ballplayer. A blind man could see the lust in Ron's face whenever he laid eyes on Madeline. Ron, although at least three sheets to the wind, had not failed to notice Doc's romantic interest in the nurse. Since returning from their protracted stay in the garden the two had been almost comically polite toward one another. Their exaggerated attempts at remaining aloof were as opaque as a magnifying glass. Sometime between leaving the house and their return, an hour later, they had become a couple. Tony's wink and Doc's aped bewilderment confirmed it five seconds after they re-entered the living room. Ron had caught on immediately and had visibly bristled. Now, fortified with several glasses of a good red wine that the detectives knew they could never afford—even if they had ever heard of the name on the label—Ron's displeasure was coming to the fore.

If there was something in the witnesses' past, something that could have bearing on the case, Doc's romantic involvement with the female half of the pair was going to make it difficult to delve into the possibility. If Tony let things unfold in their natural order, as he normally would, they might get to the root of this thing more rapidly. With this new wrinkle of budding love between his friend and the director of nursing, things might go awry if he let that happen. His pal's volatile temper when threatened and his propensity for violent defense added up to some hospital time for the aggressive batting coach if Tony let this fester.

A bodyguard, who apparently wore more than one hat, ducked to avoid the massive crystal chandelier hanging like an exploded galaxy above the twelve-foot ebony oval that Natalie Graille called her dining room table. The gun-toting waiter began to clear away the dishes as a tasty supper came to an end.

Tony told Madeline he wished his wife could cook like that, but he could not envision cuddling up to the ham-handed guy in the apron on a cold winter's night. While Madeline laughed, he signaled Doc with a slight nod to Ron and a sidelong shifting of his eyes. Doc tasted the mineral water in his glass, examined the hem of the tablecloth, said something about how he wished he could sample the wine, and waited.

"I think I'll pass on desert," Tony patted his waistline. "If you're finished, Ron, I'd like to talk to you in private. There are some things we should discuss before you hit the sack."

The bodyguard/butler took the hint and reached to remove the wine bottle, but Ron snatched it from his grasp like a line drive going over the fence.

"Whoa, now," Barbarosa said. "That soldier ain't dead yet, Marty. I'll just take him along to keep me company." He turned glassy eyes on Tony. "The living room okay with you, Detective?"

"Peachy."

Madeline dropped her head to hide the smile that threatened to bloom into laughter at Tony's glib shot at the decor. Ron looked knowingly from Doc to Madeline as he struggled to his feet. His smug grin was nearly enough to bring Doc across the finely set, white linen tablecloth, but Madeline's hand on his knee beneath the table calmed him. Tony threw an arm across the ballplayer's shoulders and guided him out of the room, whispering with conspiratorial urgency as they went.

“There’s something about that—” Doc started to say when the pocket doors slid closed behind Ron.

“Son of a bitch?” Madeline asked.

“You might say that.”

“I just did. And it’s safe to say I’m not the first. Even in high school, Ron was an arrogant oaf.” She sighed. “He hasn’t changed much, I’m sorry to say.”

“Were you two…” He let it hang between them, ashamed of the way his mind was working. Was he being a cop, or was he simply jealous?

“If you’re asking if there was anything between us,” she said, examining her water glass, “the answer is no. That’s not to say that Ron didn’t try like hell.” She studied her fingernails for a moment and then met his gaze with a flat stare when she said, “I was never impressed by the possessive type.”

At that moment, Marty returned with Ron’s wine bottle in his fist. Three steps into the room he stopped as if he had seen a bear trap in his path.

“Whoops,” he whispered. Marty diplomatically ignored the apparent tension and said, “Your partner is a silver-tongued devil, Detective.” He stepped to the table and brandished the wine bottle as proof. “The guy talked Ron out of another drink and into the sack as slick as you please.” He set the bottle on the table and stood back.

The seated couple made no reply. Marty stood uncomfortably by for a few seconds more, and then said, “Sorry to intrude, folks. You guys were talking, I can see.” Continued silence from the pair made him hurriedly add, “I’ll finish up later. ‘Scuse me.” He nearly ran from the room.

Doc watched him go and kept his eyes on the closing door as he tried to think his way out of the situation his indelicate question had put him in. He was about to try joking his way out when Madeline said, “What’s Tony’s wife like?”

“Phyllis?” he said, completely thrown by the question.

“Is that her name?”

“Yeah,” he said, turning back to face Madeline with a wary look. “Why?”

“I like your friend. He’s funny and smart.”

“And very happily married. He’s got three kids, you know.”

"Good for him. I hope Phyllis appreciates him. Men like that are rare." She pushed back from the table and stood. "Goodnight, Doc. I'm bushed."

She marched from the room before he could utter a word.

Doc fingered the wine bottle, turning it to read the label. Marty reached over his shoulder to gather soiled crockery, startling him.

"Is my foot still in my mouth?" Doc wondered aloud.

Marty twisted his head to look. "Nope, but that's definitely shoe polish on your teeth." He clapped Doc on the shoulder and said, "It ain't your fault, Detective. We can all thank Adam for making women the way they are."

"Adam who?"

"The Adam, as in, and Eve."

"You Born-Again or something, Marty. Or are you the only guy on the planet that understands women?"

"Think about it," Marty said, as he sat in the chair recently vacated by Madeline. He reached for a water glass, wiped it out with the tablecloth, poured four fingers of the wine into it and set the bottle down. As an afterthought, he pointed to the bottle and raised his brows in a question.

"No, thanks," Doc said. "Go on."

Marty took a taste, smacked his lips, and said, "God gave Adam and Eve Paradise, right? Everything they could want. Then He says, 'Enjoy yourselves, folks, but whatever you do, do not fuck with my apples.' Okay? Fair enough. I mean, they got everything else, right? So, who needs apples?"

Doc shrugged.

"The Bible says Eve couldn't resist. She just had to have a fucking apple." It was Marty's turn to shrug. "Who knows? God didn't write the Bible. Men did. Had to be. Women didn't do shit like writing back then. The way I figure, the guy who wrote the story was married. He's tired of the old lady busting his balls and he sees a chance to fuck with the whole female gender, so he pins the thing on Eve. Who's to argue? This is supposed to be God's word, right?"

Doc smiled, enjoying this. "You stay up late doping all this out, Marty?"

Marty took another sip of his drink, and said, "You sure you don't want to try this stuff? Two hundred a bottle, at least."

Doc wagged his head.

"Suit yourself. Anyway, the way I see it, women realized way back that they got a bad rap and the bunch of 'em have been getting even ever since. It all makes sense if you think about it."

"As much as any other theory on the subject I've heard," Doc agreed, with a wry grin crinkling the corners of his eyes. He sat back and studied Marty with obvious humor. "How did you get into the personal protection racket, Marty?"

"Well, I used to be a minister, but the congregation sort of turned on me."

ଓଓ

Carl parked the Jeep three quarters of a mile from Ludlow's home on a dark street in a factory district. He would not be able to retrieve it later if he left it in the Islander Oil lot and he needed to transfer the body to the truck's cab. This deserted block of silent manufacturing plants and warehouses would be perfect. He checked on his cargo before he left and was surprised to find the hapless businessman still alive. Though unconscious, probably comatose, his heart still beat and his breathing, though shallow, was steady. Carl rolled back one eyelid and checked the pupil. Fixed and dilated. He grabbed the man's chin and twisted his head. Blood trickled from one ear. He wouldn't be going anywhere under his own steam.

"Tough bastard," he remarked, slamming the door. He set out at a brisk pace toward his destination.

When he arrived, sweating from his exertion, he swung himself into the oil truck cab and started the big diesel engine. It rumbled to life at the first turn of the key. Grinding gears until he got the feel of the rig, he made his way back to the Jeep. With the headlights extinguished, he manhandled the inert form of his most recent victim onto the floor of the tanker's cab and ran around the front to climb behind the wheel. Groping in the duffel bag beside him on the seat, he extracted what he would need for the next step, the Hechler & Koch MP-5k and an M-79 40mm grenade launcher. By the time he swung onto Middle Neck Road, he was ready.

Noting the sentries stationed at the gates of the Graille Estate, Carl barreled past at a good clip. He followed the road to its end and did a three-point turn in the cul-de-sac at the head of the lane where he stopped to cock his weapons. Revving the engine, he banged the stick into gear, released the clutch, and started to roll back the way he had come. He drove slowly, pointing a flashlight out the window at address placards and street signposts. By the time he pulled up in front of his target, the cops on guard there had ample time to see a lost fuel delivery driver trying to find his way.

"You guys know where the Palmer place is?" Carl sang out in a friendly, if sheepish voice.

The two cops looked to each other and shook their heads.

The nearest, spread his hands in apology. "Sorry, pal. Can't help ya."

Carl poked the H&K through the open driver's window and cut him down with a three-round burst. He immediately swung the muzzle to engage his second target. The shocked policeman had time to slap his hand over his pistol butt before the next burst sent him spinning into the fence. Carl then flung the machine pistol on top of his unconscious passenger and snatched the grenade launcher from the seat. He snapped off a single forty-millimeter round in the general direction of the house and had the truck rolling again before the high explosive shell impacted on the bole of a stout oak tree twenty feet short of the structure.

The staccato pop-pop-pop of the automatic weapon followed by the flat KARUMP of the grenade burst sent the defenders into frenzied activity. Handheld radios, pressed to lips pulled taught by facial muscles constricted by fear, spread the word of a frontal assault on the main gate. Dark shapes scurried to prearranged positions as the cops sought to defend the perimeter. The truck was a block away and gathering speed before the policemen realized the shooter was running.

Carl watched the side view mirror as he threw gears and built momentum. If they didn't pursue him, this was a wasted effort. He almost missed seeing the patrol car that rocketed from the side street as it screeched to a halt directly in his path. The two policeman it contained threw open the doors and clambered out. With an animal like grunt, Carl jerked the wheel violently to the left and then back again, ramming the accidental roadblock on the left front fender and spinning the car around to be sideswiped by the speeding truck. The rear duels climbed the hood of the police cruiser and pounded down hard on the pavement amid a cacophony of screaming metal and shattering glass. He heard one shot from a policeman's pistol and then nothing but the roar of his engine.

"Hold your fire," the cop's partner yelled to him from the curb where he lay. "That's a fuel truck. You wanna blow up the whole neighborhood?"

Sirens wailed and flashing red and white lights filled Carl's side view mirrors. It looked like a carnival gone berserk had popped out of the ground where he had just been.

"That's the ticket. Chase me," he laughed, turning his attention to the road ahead. He had to time this just right. When he saw the driveway he was waiting for, he depressed the clutch, stood on the brakes and swung the wheel hard over. The big truck groaned and the tires smoked as the tanker slid into the sharp left-hand turn. At the right moment, Carl spun the wheel back, popped the clutch, downshifted, and gunned the engine. The tanker grazed the magnificent black wrought iron gate that stood open at the entrance to the access road.

"He's going into the Sands Point Preserve," Doc heard over the radio as he and Tony raced to catch up to the speeding convoy of police cruisers in hot pursuit. He told himself that Madeline was all right in the hands of the heavily armed cops he had left to guard the witnesses. His place was here. Tonight, they would finish the bastard.

The fuel truck roared along the dark lane leading into the nature preserve, snapping overhanging branches like match sticks, barely clearing one granite wall of a stone bridge as Carl fought the wheel for control. Where the road widened into a tiny parking lot flanked by a brick guard shack, Carl pushed the accelerator to the floorboards. A low, chain link fence on rollers, used to close the museum road after business hours, was flattened under the wheels like aluminum foil, useless against the hurtling mass of steel. The watchmen, with his feet up on the desk, enjoying a smoke and a cup of decaf, spilled his coffee down his shirtfront and pitched backward from his chair as the fuel truck crashed the gate.

Continuing along the wooded road, Carl soon flashed past the brooding shape of Castle Gould, the huge limestone stable and servants' quarters built by Howard Gould in 1902. A glance in the side view mirror confirmed that his pursuers were following at the necessary interval.

Not too close yet. There's time.

He cut the wheel hard right and hung on as the truck's forward momentum threatened to roll it onto the great lawn. Forearms and biceps bulging with the strain, he managed to right the truck and straighten out, quickly downshifting and applying the brakes as the L-shaped far end of the monstrous building rushed to meet him. Wheels locked and skidding in a cloud of burning rubber, he slid the tanker to a halt just beyond the castle, at a right angle to the entrance of the nature trail, effectively blocking it from view.

Carl left the engine ticking over but doused all of the vehicle's lights. He stretched across the seat, slapped the handle on the passenger door and shoved it open. Next, he grabbed a handful of his helpless victim's clothing and, with a Herculean tug, pulled him from the floorboards to occupy the seat beside him.

Working swiftly, he climbed over the battered businessman to shove his duffel out of the cab. It landed with a thud on the gravel below. From beside his unconscious passenger, Carl pushed the limp figure across the seat until he was propped against the driver's door. He then pointed the stubby assault weapon out the window beside the man's head.

The first of the stream of police cars shot into view as it passed the castle wall, lights flashing like fiery jewels. The lead car swerved, lost traction in its attempt to negotiate the turn and slid sideways into the grassy field. The muzzle flash of the H&K lit the side of the truck like a stuttering yellow strobe. The police car driver reacted instinctively, ducking his head, the steering wheel forgotten. The speeding car spun in a series of three-hundred-sixty-degree loops. Brakes squealed as the following drivers pounced on pedals. The file of patrol cars accordioned to a halt. Many skidded directly into the stopped vehicles to their front. Doors sprung open as the cops tumbled to the ground. Weapons ready, they scrambled forward, running crouched, shouting questions and commands.

Doc and Tony, in the last vehicle, narrowly avoided the car in front of them and leaped from their unmarked Crown Victoria as it came to a stop. Hefting his standard issue Sig Sauer 224 automatic, Doc threw Tony a nod and they set off at a loping run for the head of the column.

Carl depressed the trigger of the Heckler & Koch as he saw several cops, spread out in a skirmish line, preparing to rush him. He giggled when he saw them disappear from view, diving behind the corner of the castle in a frantic effort to dodge the hail of lead. The weapon jumped in his hands until the bolt locked back when the magazine was depleted. Without hesitation, he dropped it beside the body in front of him and slid back across the seat to alight on the ground. He scooped up the duffel bag and spun around to jog downhill into the woods. The cops failed to see his retreat. More concerned with not being targets than observation at the moment, they fired blindly over the hoods of their cruisers and around the corner of the museum in an attempt to get the gunman's head down.

Doc pushed himself off the ground, where he had flopped, the instant he heard the crackle of automatic fire. He heard answering shots from the cops at the head of the chain, sounding puny by comparison.

"Tony! You okay?"

"So far."

"Let's go." He led Tony at a dead run along the back of the towering edifice in an effort to get around the shooter's position and take him from behind without exposing themselves to his withering fire.

Carl's sneakers skidded and slid on the wet leaves in the trail until he came to the bottom of the hill. He rolled behind a tree and dug in the bag for what he needed. He heard sporadic fire from the cops. His fingers felt the shape of the flat plastic box he sought. Yanking it from the bag, he pulled an antenna from the top of the device and with his thumb, depressed a button.

The block of Semtex he had taped to the underside of the cargo tank at the front of the blunt ended tube detonated instantly, sympathetically igniting the home heating oil within. The bright red truck erupted in a mammoth ball of flame, arching its back like some huge behemoth in its death throes. The tank and cab separated. Each burning section leaped into the air and fell back to earth to crash against one another with a bone-jarring clang. Flaming debris was flung everywhere. Bits of wreckage, trailing streamers of greasy black smoke, clattered through the branches overhead to fall like bomb fragments in the surrounding woods. Every window in Castle Gould facing the blast disintegrated, sending razor sharp glass splinters ripping through offices and exhibits. The concussion hit Doc and Tony as they rounded the corner and charged through the arched passageway that served as main entrance to the old stable, knocking them on their backsides.

"Oh, shit!" Carl gasped. A river of blazing oil gushed toward him along the sloping trail. He sprang from his hiding place and crashed into the brush.

"Jesus!" was all the only cop who found his voice could say.

"Rest in pieces," Carl snickered as he scurried into the trees.

By the time the astounded policemen had untangled the jumble of vehicles in the narrow lane, the remnants of Islander Oil's sole vehicle were completely involved in the conflagration. The tanker had not been fully loaded. The forward compartment of the segmented cylinder held two thousand gallons of fuel. The other three sections were empty. It was sufficient to fan the flames to white hot intensity in the immediate vicinity of the ruptured shell, but luckily not enough to fire the surrounding woods beyond fifty or so yards. The castle was severely damaged by the blast and waves of radiant heat.

When the Sands Point and Port Washington Volunteer Fire Departments could finally gain access to the area, most of the damage was done. They were forced to establish a perimeter and contain the blaze in the woods while concentrating their efforts on minimizing the destruction to the historic castle.

Doc and Tony were leaning against their car, now parked in the grassy field out of the way of the firefighters, when Lieutenant Schiff arrived on the scene.

"Went out with a bang, eh?" the squat lieutenant quipped.

"One can only hope," Doc said, as he drew on his cigarette and exhaled a long puff of smoke through his nose. "Still too hot to get in there." His gaze slid to the fire, still burning, but rapidly losing momentum as the firefighters knocked it back with a barrage of high-pressure water. "Unless the guy was Houdini, he didn't get out of that."

"Crime Scene, ATF, and The Lab will be all over the wreck as soon as the fire chief gives the nod," Schiff informed them. "I guess this is the end of The Terminator."

"Amen, LT, Amen," Tony said.

Doc raised an eyebrow at Tony's use of the military jargon for a lieutenant. Apparently, he wasn't alone in his reminiscence of war.

"Guess we can call off the troops," Schiff said.

Doc thought Schiff looked like a modern-day warlord with the firelight dancing on that bullet head.

Smug. Self-satisfied.

"To be on the safe side, I'd rather wait until it's confirmed that he's in there." Doc indicated the site of the funeral pyre flickering at the edge of the trees.

"What's the matter, Doc? Afraid he might not be?"

"No sense getting careless, is there?"

"I suppose not," Schiff said, but his tone made his opinion of Doc's paranoia obvious. "Why don't you two head back to the Graille place and fill in our guests on the outcome of the evening's efforts?"

"Tony, you do that," Doc suggested. "I'll stick around. I want to see this for myself."

Tony agreed, saying he had no desire to view the charred remains of whomever they might find in that mess, but he understood Doc's need for closure—to be certain the beast was dead.

As Tony turned to go, Schiff laughed. "FBI's going to be disappointed." He was really enjoying this. Doc and Tony waited. "Special Agent Gilchrist," Schiff went on, "phoned to advise me they'd be taking over the case as of tomorrow. I can't wait to call him back."

ᏋᏋ

Carl needed every bit of his woods craft and stealth to work his way out of the dense forest and back to the road without being seen. The area was alive with police and emergency vehicles. It took him more than an hour to sneak out of the preserve and to walk through the surrounding community. He stashed the duffel bag behind a Dumpster in back of a luncheonette on Port Washington Boulevard before walking back to his car. It took most of the remainder of the night to reach his objective, but he was in superb physical condition and he set himself a modest but steady pace.

Once back in his automobile, he retraced his steps and retrieved the incriminating bag. The sky was lightening and the radio was recounting the events of the previous evening as he turned his car toward home. Three police cars raced past him as he drove south, going in the opposite direction, their lights flashing. He watched in his rearview mirror as they turned onto the road that led to Joe Ludlow's place. By tonight, he surmised, they should be sure that The Terminator was dead. If the missing commuter was reported any time soon, it wasn't likely that the cops would make the connection, busy as they would be with the immediate wrap up exercise that would consume their attention. He would be free to deal with the last of the six.

ᏋᏋ

Doc sidestepped a TV camera operator and his accompanying pesky reporter who thrust a foam-padded microphone in his face.

"No comment," he muttered, turning his back on the crestfallen duo and trotting to escape the mob of media vultures congregating around the scene of The Terminator's demise.

Or was it?

The charred and blackened fragments of skeleton that the medical examiner admitted might never be positively identified had probably belonged to the butchering bastard. Still, it irked Doc to know that it could not be proven. The heat had been such as to melt the fillings in the teeth of the scorched skull. Even dental records would not be conclusive, assuming they had some idea where to look, which they didn't.

The chief and the commissioner were already taking bows, sounding fresh and perky for the drive-time listeners on the morning news radio programs. Doc prayed they had reason. While there was nothing to suggest that the remains in the ashes of the fuel truck were not those of the vicious animal that had terrorized the community for the past week, it didn't feel right.

Doc had a bad feeling that he could not shake. It was not the crafty killer's style to go berserk and slug it out in a last ditch, pitched battle. The guy had been like smoke until last night.

He couldn't help but chuckle at his own pun. Maybe he was being paranoid. He would have liked to drop the hammer on the bastard himself, watch his lights go out and write finis to the entire episode. Maybe that was it. Maybe he was feeling deprived of his vengeance. Maybe it was time to pull the pin and go fishing with Jack.

Maybe.

He cast his eyes about the scene. It was a mess. There were police and fire department vehicles scattered all over the great lawn. Ruts were gouged in the turf that would be evident until next summer at the very least. Uniforms and raincoats scurried in the smoke. Fat water hoses, springing leaks at every connection, had been dumped on the ground like a monstrous can of worms. The fire was reduced to smoke and steam. Doc's eyes settled on the smoldering fuel truck cab.

No. It definitely didn't feel right.

Chapter 35

Carl knew something was wrong when he was still three blocks from home. At first, it was just that strange sensation of premonition you get when you enter familiar surroundings and something is amiss. As he drew closer, he saw fire engines and the neighbors huddled in animated conversation and then the hoses, lying like dirty, fat spaghetti in a tangled mass on the blacktop. He pulled into the curb and stared at the incredible scene a block away.

The smoking ruin at the center of the tableau had been Carl's home. No, that wasn't right. It had been his place to hang his hat, to sleep between forays into the outside world, to grab a quiet bite, and most importantly, to plan.

That was the worst of it. Headquarters was gone. His files and memoranda, his personal computer, his secluded think tank—that was what lay beneath the smoldering embers.

Carl watched the firefighters and officials combing through the rubble of the place where he had lived until today. He did not get out of his car, nor did he succumb to the temptation to take a closer look. The house looked to be a total loss but who could say what they might find in the charred ruins. He was shocked, but he had not survived in his violent world by allowing abrupt alterations of his life to numb him into immobility. This, he felt, was the epitome of inconvenience, but that was all. There were no insurmountable events until one perceived them as such.

"O—kay," he said aloud, "how much of a disaster are we confronted with here?"

He had rented the place in the name of Carl Esterbrook. His landlord would supply the authorities with that information. So what? All that would get them would be more time wasted tracking down a fictitious personality. They would wonder why he failed to return once they were convinced that his body did not lie beneath the ashes. A computer search would reveal what scraps of his identity there were. His driver's license, with his picture on it, would be in the records. He had let his hair grow long, with a full beard and mustache, dyed it all strawberry blond with a water-soluble hair coloring, worn tinted contact lenses, and injected himself with collagen to alter the shape of his face before the picture was taken. Immediately thereafter, he had shaved, cut his hair to its present length, and washed out the dye. He then used his computer scanner to duplicate his license onto which he superimposed a picture with his present features to have a passable facsimile to carry on his person in case he needed identification. The whole idea was to buy himself time in the event that something similar to what had just befallen him, did. Of course, his landlord would say, "That's not the guy," but that would work in his favor. The cops would bring in a sketch artist and he had never seen a likeness drawn from a witness's impressions that bore any resemblance to the fugitive.

"As always, foresight pays off," he said. "Now, is there anything that might have survived the inferno to connect me with my crimes?"

That would depend on the source of the fire. Extensive experience with pyrotechnics made him aware of the characteristics of a structure fire. The point of origin would sustain the most severe damage and the nature of that origin would determine the speed with which the fire had spread. That was the most critical factor. How heavily involved had the house been by the time the volunteers arrived? He tried to remember every detail of his hurried exit, the previous day.

Had he left the stove on? He was certain he had not. An electrical short? Possible, but unlikely. He had personally inspected the wiring before he signed the rental agreement.

The hole-punching machine drew his attention. It sat in the street, blistered and streaked with soot; its huge tires melted to the pavement.

Could that be it? Had the incessant jarring tripped his booby trap? He remembered his coffee cup and how it had nearly walked off the table. That scenario matched the devastation he saw. Even if the fire had not started in the white room, the thermite grenade would have been set off if the firemen had not arrived in time to knock the blaze down. From the utter destruction of his own house and the damage to the adjacent dwellings, it was obvious they had not. His small store of explosives had to have been set off. There would be little left to point to him and his alter ego.

Still, he would have to wrap this up as quickly as possible now. His mind sorted through possible means the authorities might use to trace him. There was only one and he was sitting in it. The Jeep would have to go. He twisted the key, gunned the engine, and pulled a quick U-turn, putting distance between himself and the smoking wreckage. A plan took shape in his mind by the time he reached Merrick Road. The irony of last night's daring farce and the loss of his basecamp to a similar catastrophe were not lost on him. Perhaps it was for the best. No matter what the cops found in his home, there was nothing to prove he was alive. The businessman's body was burned beyond recognition and was assumed to be The Terminator. What harm would it do to have the cops find evidence that he had also lost his lair to the torch? It was almost funny.

ഗഗ

"Why do you look so pissed off?" Tony nudged Doc's arm playfully with his elbow and then cocked his head toward the picture window at their backs. "The sun is shining. The birds are singing. It's going to be a beautiful day. Snap out of it. The miserable fuck is toast. He got a preview to his eternal reward. It is over. O-V- E-R, over. Case closed. Relax, will you?"

"We still don't know who the bastard was, or why he did any of it." Doc grumbled without taking his eyes from the swarm of cops dismantling the makeshift command post they had established in Natalie Graille's den.

The scene at the Graille house was one of exhilaration as the cops packed their stuff and prepared to go home to their families. A bad time was at an end. A cop killer was being swept into evidence bags less than a mile from where they sat, cremated alive, as he had so well deserved. They could all sleep easier tonight. Doc's grudging refusal to take part in the joy of the moment confounded his friend.

"Let The Lab boys sort it out," Tony said. "They'll put a name to the pieces. Bet on it. And Ron and Madeline will say, 'Him? That's the squirrely son of a bitch that tried to kill us. I never would have thought of him.' You wait. It'll happen."

"I hope you're right." Doc wagged his head. "It just doesn't add up. Why would he suddenly come at us like the Charge of the Light Brigade, then put his back to the wall and go down in flames? It doesn't fit the profile."

"The guy was nuts. A certifiable, psychopathic, dyed-in-the-wool fruitcake. Who is to say what made him do any of it? Bottom line is he's history. A crispy critter. A goner. Chill out, Doc. It's Miller time."

Madeline suddenly appeared before them. Doc saw uncertainty in her eyes.

"The two officers at the gate," she said. "Are they going to be all right?"

"We think so," Tony voiced their fervent wishes. "They were lucky. Neither one was hit in any vital spot. Doctors say both did well in surgery and will recover completely."

"That's good to hear," she said with genuine relief. "Weren't they wearing bullet proof vests?"

"Yeah, but that didn't help," Tony said. "Those vests won't stop a hit from an assault rifle. The guy must have just blasted away without aiming. One guy got grazed." Tony pointed to his scalp. "Knocked him cold and permanently changed his hair style but left his skull intact. The other one got it in the legs. Like I said—lucky."

"Will you be needing me for anything else?" Madeline looked lost.

With his brow crinkling above wide eyes, Tony turned his attention to packing some papers into a file, leaving Doc to answer.

"Uh, well, uh, I guess there'll be some further inquiries once we identify the suspect," Doc answered.

"Oh," she said. A brief moment of distress was quickly masked with, "Excuse me, I left my purse in the dining room." She whirled and marched, stiff-backed, from the room.

Tony stepped in front of Doc. "Is that the best you can do?" The look on Tony's face was one of comic horror. "My god, man, what has happened to the inspirational master swordsman we have come to know and love, Detective Wiley?"

"Sometimes you don't know when to shut up, Cordova."

Doc was leaning menacingly close to his friend as Madeline returned. The frightened, childlike sadness in her eyes touched him. He stepped back and leaned against the windowsill, all animosity gone from him.

"I have to find someplace to stay," Madeline said, looking quickly from one man to the other. Her gaze settled on Tony. "Did I miss something? Is everything all right?"

"Fine," Tony said, "we'll give you a lift."

"Uh, thanks, but I don't know where to at the moment. I don't want—" Her words caught in her throat. "I can't go back to the Dietrich's." Her eyes welled up with tears.

"You're welcome to crash here, Madeline." Ron Barbarosa was suddenly standing beside them.

"No," she said. "Thank you, no.

It wasn't her refusal; it was the way she said it. It could not have stung Ron more if she had said she would rather eat cockroaches.

Doc said, "Maybe I can be of help."

Tony's grin completed Barbarosa's mortification as Doc and Madeline walked to the door.

"Ya' win some and ya' lose some, Ron," Tony said over his shoulder as he swaggered after the departed pair. "And some get rained out."

Chapter 36

Carl backed the Jeep up to the open garage door until the bumper was a foot from that of the BMW. He set the parking brake and hopped from the car to jog back to the rear of the vehicle. With the trunk lid of the Beamer and the Jeep's rear cargo hatch open, he quickly transferred everything from the Chrysler four-by-four into the imported sedan. The duffel bag containing his weapons, ammo, detonators, and explosives went first. As he hefted the heavy bag, he came to a decision. He would go to Lake Hopatcong as soon as this was finished and make arrangements to move his entire operation west. Although certain he was still light years ahead of the police, Carl had a premonition. Luck was turning, in infinitesimal proportion, against him. He had not survived for so long by ignoring such delicate warnings from the cosmic aura. He would miss what he had established here. The lucrative diversion The Colonel had provided amongst New York City's abundant depraved would be a shame to abandon, but the vibes were wrong now. It was almost time to get back to big sky country. The dense population centers of the northeast might be target rich environments, but solitary hunters were better suited to the wild. The last thing he wanted was to be sidetracked by something as pedestrian as earning money. The antique business was profitable but boring and while he still had plenty of money in Marvin DeKalb's basement garage, it was finite. Elaborate operations, such as the one he had mounted here, were costly. Stealing was fun but consumed so much time and energy. Investing, while lucrative if you knew the shortcuts, could be thrilling, but success, even in the shadowy world of the black markets, tended to put one in the spotlight. He might have to dip into his Cayman Island numbered accounts if he stayed here too long and that was a taboo he refused to broach. He would see about resurrecting The Colonel and relocating the old boy on the West Coast when this was all over, perhaps in the Pacific Northwest.

He lifted the canvas gym bag from the Jeep as he mused about his finances. Unzipping the top, he reached in and riffled through the banded stacks of currency. About fifty thousand, more than enough for now.

There were three sets of license plates behind the spare tire. One he would use immediately in case the cops had found anyone at the marina who remembered the MD tags on the BMW. The others would come in handy eventually.

An assortment of clothing, several blankets, a first-aid kit, and articles common to motorists completed the transfer. As the sun warmed him, he became aware of the odor of fuel oil clinging to his apparel. He changed into khaki slacks, a navy-blue turtleneck, and a gray herringbone sports jacket. He swapped vehicles next, leaving the Jeep locked inside the windowless garage along with the soiled clothes.

At a pawnshop in Freeport, he made the proprietor's day by dropping over a thousand dollars in cash for two cameras, an assortment of lenses and carry bags for the lot.

By noon, Carl was again speeding north, exhilarated despite his lack of sleep. Emboldened by his spectacularly staged recent death, he intended to inspect the competition at close quarters. The loss of his computer and laser printer meant he would have to rely more heavily on his acting skills since he would not have the added camouflage of forged documents to bolster the role he planned to adopt. He had sufficient confidence to be optimistic.

"When in doubt," he grinned, "brazen it out. Bedazzle 'em with brilliance, or baffle 'em with bullshit. And if all else fails, kill the bastards."

Upon his arrival at Natalie Graille's summer home, any qualms Carl might have harbored evaporated. The road outside the estate was crammed with television news vans and the personal vehicles of the assembled media.

Carl found a space large enough to slip the Beamer between two cars parked on the edge of a neighboring lawn, hung his photographic gear around his neck, and climbed out. He would venture as close to the grounds as he could. If stopped, he would briefly explain that he was a freelance photographer on assignment for People Magazine and hurriedly make his exit citing deadline pressures as his reason for a hasty departure. It should work. If it didn't, he still had the .25 automatic in his pocket. A press pass would have taken much of the worry out of this, but without his printer…

He started snapping frames as he approached the gate, politely dodging his newfound colleagues, smiling and waving to pretended acquaintances that always happened to be standing somewhere behind those who noticed him. It amazed and amused Carl how easily he got inside the grounds. There were still plenty of cops around but they all seemed more concerned with loading their equipment in vans than in guarding the place. The house, he noted, had tighter security. The press was milling around up there in greater numbers than at the gate, but it was plain to see that no one was being permitted to enter. A uniformed police officer with a lot of gold braid was issuing some kind of statement from the steps in front of the closed front doors. Carl drifted off beside a path to have a clear line of sight to the home's entrance. Leaning against a sturdy sugar maple, he screwed a telephoto lens to the Nikon around his neck.

Something was happening. The media was becoming increasingly animated as the officer spoke. The press of bodies packed tighter around the spokesman as the reporters jostled for position, holding microphones and tape recorders aloft like offerings to some god of information, begging to be anointed with the holy oil of enlightenment.

The uniformed cops were forming ranks along the path leading to the front steps, firmly parting the sea of humanity, joining hands, facing one another across the four feet of brick paving.

The huge doors atop the three broad granite steps opened and a handsome man in a charcoal gray suit emerged, blinking in the sunlight and the flash of many photographic strobes and TV lights. A woman followed, hesitated, and then took his hand to be led along the path. She looked bewildered. The reporters barked questions and pushed to get to her but the cops' makeshift chain held.

Carl twisted the telephoto lens to get the image into focus. The expensive lens paid immediate dividends. The face of the woman sprang to clarity. He let out an involuntary gasp.

Madeline!

She seemed close enough to touch and his fist clenched in frustration. He bit hard on his knuckle, his eye never leaving the aperture.

Remembering what he was supposed to be, Carl depressed the shutter lever and the tiny electric motor whined and clicked as the film advanced. The procession wound inexorably toward him until the image blurred and no amount of adjustment could regain it. They were too close and he had no time to change lenses. He dropped the camera to dangle from its strap and hoisted another, hanging similarly around his neck. The entourage passed within ten feet of him. Carl bit his tongue to keep from screaming her name.

Concentrate!

His analytical mind absorbed every nuance of the passing tableau. The guy in the gray suit was a cop. He saw a gold badge affixed to his belt when he reached out to stop an overzealous newshound from accosting Madeline. The shorter man bringing up the rear—the dark, swarthy one—he was a cop, too. Carl saw the man's eyes darting like ferrets, belying the frozen smile on the friendly face. They locked momentarily on Carl, and he knew in that instant that he was being sized up, catalogued, and pigeonholed.

Carl's shoulders relaxed in a subconscious attempt to make himself smaller, to blend with the background, to be harmless, insignificant. The cop's eyes fixed him like a pinned butterfly and then moved on.

A black Lincoln Town Car was driven through the gates. It edged its way through the throng until it met the group as they neared the end of the footpath. The doors flew open and they were inside and backing out without a word being spoken to the frenzied reporters. Behind him, Carl heard a familiar voice.

"That was Mrs. Madeline Maclear, the mysterious nursing director whom the police have been sequestering here at the home of Natalie Graille."

Carl turned to find himself face to face with Adrienne Boyd who then turned her back on him to address her audience by way of the camera recording the event. Adrienne went on to complain that the police were still being less than forthcoming in their explanations as to what part the nurse and the famous ballplayer, still inside, had played in the drama so recently concluded in fiery death. Carl nearly laughed aloud, but his bemused smile vanished as he looked straight into the cyclopean eye of the Steadicam.

He was in the shot.

ꕤꕤ

Ron Barbarosa stood at the window, glowering at the retreating crowd of news mavens as they followed Madeline and that smartass cop to the car.

"Good riddance," he snorted. "She's still a frigid bitch," he snarled, as he turned to face his lawyer. "Get these friggin' cops out of my face and throw the lot of them reporters the hell off the grounds."

"A friendly interview would go far in the eyes of your fans, Ron," Kornberg counseled.

"Fuck 'em. Let 'em read about it in my book." His expression brightened as he crossed to the bar from the window. "Yeah, that's it. Get on the phone to some publishers. See who's got big bucks to spend on an insider's expose about The Terminator investigation. And find me some shithead who can write well enough to not make me look bad." He compressed his lips in a mean-spirited grin as he flung ice cubes into a tumbler, one by one. "Yeah. Why not? Somebody ought to make a buck on this fiasco. And call my house. See if those bonehead painters are done yet. This joint is beginning to get on my nerves."

ೞೞ

Carl sat, strumming his fingers on the steering wheel of the BMW. He had some choices to make. The media was streaming away from the Graille estate. Before long he would become conspicuous by his solitary presence. A bumper sticker on a passing Lexus made up his mind.

Laughing, he read it aloud. "When the going gets tough, the tough go shopping." He put the car in gear and pointed the nose south. At Northern Boulevard he turned right and drove west. Great Neck was only minutes away, but he would need some things before he began the operation. He found a store that sold uniforms and another where he purchased electrical tools. A shop on the Miracle Mile supplied a tight fitting, red, lady's wig, a Styrofoam head to use as a stand, and a pair of scissors.

"For Mom," he winked at the young sales clerk.

He stopped at a drugstore and an optical shop before pulling into a cheap motel. He paid the hourly rate and did some creative barbering in his rented room. When finished, he had enough clippings to fashion a passable Zapata-style mustache that he painstakingly applied to his upper lip strand by strand with Crazy Glue. The fumes made his head swim. Eyebrow pencil in a matching shade put the final touches to his disguise.

Pleased with his new look, he added a pair of tinted contact lenses, rendering his irises a sapphire blue.

He laughed. “Even I wouldn’t recognize me.”

Chapter 37

Doc led Madeline to his couch, saying, "Please forgive the mess. I'll just be a minute."

"Think nothing of it," she said, sitting on the edge of the cushion. She raised an eyebrow at the thin coat of white dust on the end table. "Bachelors' pads are supposed to look this way, aren't they?"

"Is that what this is? All this time I thought it was a train wreck." He ran into his bedroom, saying, "I just need to throw a few things in a bag. Be right with you. Make yourself at home."

She took him literally and rose to wander through the apartment, partly because she was nervous, but mostly to avoid staying on the dusty couch. Everything in the apartment seemed to have that haze of fine white powder on it. The closer she came to the room with the plastic tarp across the door, the thicker the film became.

A photograph in a heavy silver frame sat atop a bookcase crammed with an eclectic assortment of hardcovers caught her eye. She picked it up to look more closely at the teenager in the photo. The frame was the only thing in view that was free of the powdery grit.

"Who's the pretty kid in the photo, Doc?"

"My daughter, Jen," he said from the bedroom.

"Is she the one you told Miss Tuttle about?"

"Who?"

"Your nurse in ICU."

"Ah, yes. I'd forgotten. Yeah, that's her." He came back into the room clutching a battered overnight grip. "God, that seems like a million years ago."

"She lives with her mother?"

He sighed. "Yeah."

She stood waiting for him to say more.

"Hey, did I tell you I sculpt?" he asked, gently taking the frame from her fingers and replacing it on the shelf.

"No, you didn't." She eyed the photograph but let him lead her to the room with the plastic drape.

He was chattering on in a self-deprecating monologue, apologizing for his inadequacy as an artist, when they entered the room. She hardly heard him as she stepped from one piece to the next, examining the finely detailed figurines. While he babbled, she picked one up, turned it over in her hands, and said, "These are amazing."

The piece she held was of a soldier in full combat regalia, clutching an infant to his breast as he huddled against his surroundings. The front of the piece was painted entirely in black. The back was mottled with splotches of orange, and yellow.

"You can almost feel the heat," she said.

"You can?"

She peered at the title etched in the base. "Hearts and Minds?"

He smiled, an awkward, embarrassed reaction. She waited.

"An expression we had. Black humor actually."

She still waited.

"'Let us win your hearts and minds, or we'll burn down your fucking hut.'"

She raised an eyebrow. "It really is powerful. They all are," she said, as another piece caught her eye. A soldier stood, straddling the supine body of another as he bent to cover his comrade's face with a shiny green sheet. The man on the ground's face was distorted in agony, his mouth opened in a silent scream. The piece was entitled, Purple Heart. She turned to Doc with tears in her eyes. "I had no idea you were so talented."

"It's just a hobby."

"It's much more than that." She continued to peruse the shelves. "The detail is incredible. They're so lifelike. Even the equipment has the feel of realism. The guns look like metal."

"I mix a little silver paint with the black," he said. "Comes out like blued steel. No big trick."

"You should see about exhibiting these."

"Nah."

"I'm serious. It's selfish to keep all this locked in a room."

"We should go."

"What are these?" She stood squinting at a glassed in, shallow mahogany box frame mounted on the wall. White powder on the glass all but concealed two rows of military medals pinned to a sheet of pale blue silk stretched across the backing. She produced a tissue from her purse and brushed away the dust.

"Nothing," Doc said, "just some old medals."

"I recognize the Combat Infantry Badge. My husband was very proud of his. What's the smaller one with the caduceus?"

"Combat Medic Badge. Secondary MOS." Doc shifted from one foot to the other and checked his watch.

"This," she continued, "is a Silver Star, isn't it? A Purple Heart? You were wounded?"

"I zigged when I should have zagged. Just a scratch. Everybody got a bolo badge sooner or later."

She turned to face him, "Bolo badge?"

"It's what we called a Purple Heart."

She turned back to the medals, "What's the one that looks like a cross?"

He cleared his throat. "That's a DSC."

"Oh? What does DSC stand for?"

"Did Something Crazy," he mumbled.

"I thought it might mean Distinguished Service Cross."

"Madeline, we're burning daylight. Let's go."

ꕤꕤ

Madeline watched the sun dip below the dunes as Doc's car rounded the Jones Beach obelisk. It was peaceful at the beach this time of year. The icy grip of winter was gone. Gulls wheeled overhead, their hungry eyes scanning for food. Green was bursting out all over, transforming the bleak, brown desolation of storm battered sand and gnarled bark on stunted scrub brush into verdant life. It might have seemed without purpose had she been alone to balance the hope of spring's wonder against the senseless mayhem of recent days, but with Doc within arm's reach in the speeding car, it was tranquil.

By Memorial Day, Gateway National Park would be awash in humanity. For now, the beach roads were still sparsely traveled byways, used primarily by shore dwellers or those who simply hated traffic enough to drive miles out of their way to avoid it.

"Madeline, stop fussing," Doc said.

She was mildly startled by Doc's sudden command, given as it was in the patient, yet insistent tone one would use to a beloved but vexing child.

"I'm not fussing," she said.

"Yes, you are. Look at the knots in your hanky."

She dropped the twisted cloth as if it were hot, and then sighed, "Well, maybe a little."

"I told you this is perfectly all right," Doc said. "Jack Kobrigian is a good guy and he won't mind us using his place for a few days."

"But you didn't even ask him."

"I don't have to. He asked me to check on the place for him. Trust me. He won't mind if I bring a…a friend to stay for a couple of days."

She saw Doc look for a reaction to his choice of words out of the corner of his eye. Madeline's consternation remained intact. At least she had not flinched. What else could he say? Lover? She had no doubt that the use of that term of endearment would have forced some response, but she was not sure what it would be. It was her ardent hope that by this time tomorrow she would be just that, but she was far too apprehensive to feel confident. She thought she saw just a hint of the same anxiety in his eyes, but she could not be sure.

Madeline tried not to dwell on the inescapable truth that she was about to spend several days—and nights—with a man whom she barely knew. Part of her was as giddy as a teenager on her first date, anticipating a romantic interlude with a man she longed to hold naked in her arms. Then there was the wary, prissy little voice that whispered words of doubt and caution.

The stress of the past several days had left her unsure and vulnerable. Was she plunging headlong into something she was ill equipped to handle? A glance at the sincere, honest man beside her, intent on handling the heavy Cadillac, brushed aside her fears like windswept sand.

Wendell.

She knew she could never see his face in conjunction with that name. He was Doc. Healer. Savior. Warrior. And quite a gifted artist. The depth and humility of the man beside her astonished her. Maybe, she thought, she should rent some old Wendell Corey movies.

"Let's enjoy the time off," he was saying. "I'll have to go back to work in a few days and so will you. We can worry about anything you want then. Okay?"

His devil-may-care smile didn't extend to the look in his eyes. In his heart, she thought, he was worried. It was more than first date jitters, as if something dark and sinister would not stop nagging at him. She thought about the pieces of sculpture—the agonies so vividly portrayed. Were they a cathartic outlet or were they a symptom? Maybe it was post-traumatic stress. Could she handle that again? Was she falling in love? Or was she subconsciously making amends for failing Paul?

ꕥ

The painters were disassembling the last scaffolds in Ron's house and loading their paraphernalia into a paint-splattered pickup truck when a tall, slim man, dressed in a tan, twill shirt and matching trousers, strolled through the front door.

"Glad I caught you guys," he said like a man who fully expected everyone to be pleased whenever he arrived anywhere. The foreman hated him on sight. "Mr. Barbarosa wants the security system checked before he comes back," the newcomer went on as he studied the house, his eyes settling on the lowly workmen in brief glimpses, as if finding them distasteful, yet necessary recipients of his explanation.

Upon completion of his examination of the architecture, he turned to the foreman like a disappointed buyer who is far too polite to inform a would-be seller of the deficiencies in his wares.

"I don't have a key so my boss said I should hustle my tush over here before you lock up."

Tush? The foreman rolled his eyes. The snooty technician with the brand-new toolbox and spotless leather utility belt fit the painter's image of an electronics whiz kid. Nice, clean clothes and shoes. Hair combed just so. Whoops! Make that toupee. God, what a shabby looking rug. And get a load of that scraggly mustache. Like a Fourteenth Street pimp his first night on the job. Vain bastard. No dirt under his neatly trimmed fingernails. Yeah, a real college boy. Probably never worked an honest day in his life and more than likely got paid twice as much per hour as did the painter. He gave him a perfunctory nod to show his disdain for guys who preyed on the vulnerability of the rich.

"Just make it quick," the foreman told the technician. "We're off the clock as of five minutes ago. Mr. Kornberg just called to make sure we're outta here. He ain't gonna be happy if anybody's still hanging around when Ron gets back."

"Oh, shit. Is he coming back tonight?"

"Did I stutter or somethin'?"

"This'll just take a minute. Just have to do a voltage check to see if the sensors are all on line. You guys didn't cut any wires or paint over any of my contacts, did you?"

The foreman snorted and turned his back.

Carl pulled a multi-meter from his pouch and made a show of reading the display as he touched leads to the keypad beside the main entrance before quickly following suit with the doors and windows. He worked his way through the house, memorizing the layout as he went.

In the kitchen, he found what he needed. Working swiftly, he unscrewed the cover from a gang box, snipped wires and attached alligator clips to bypass the sensor on the outside door. He was finished and moving again when the head painter called out for him to, "Get a move on."

"All done," he beamed as he scurried to catch up to the man holding the front door open. "No problems. You guys do nice work."

With a grunt that could have been thanks, but sounded more like a curse, the foreman punched the ARM button on the keypad and pulled the door shut behind them.

Flapping his hand in the air to signify good evening, the pristine security tech loped across the street to his waiting BMW.

"I shoulda gone to college." The foreman sighed as he hoisted a bucket into the bed of the pickup.

"You gotta finish high school to go to college, don'tcha Willie?" one of his painters replied with a mischievous leer and a wink to his comrades.

"Eat shit and die."

Carl heard the men's laughter as he pulled away from the curb.

ꕥꕥ

The Oak Beach Inn was ablaze with light, awaiting the onset of its annual revitalization. It was still too early in the season for the hordes of merrymakers that would descend on the place in the coming weeks, but the old watering hole seemed ready for the onslaught.

"God," Madeline yelled above the racket of the jukebox, "I haven't been down here since I was a kid."

"It seems even louder than I remember," Doc yelled back, pulling a stool away from the bar and offering it to Madeline.

"There were a lot more people then to soak up the noise," she said.

"I'm glad you didn't say I was younger then."

"Perish the thought."

The place did lose some of its charm when you were able to see the worn woodwork, cheap cocktail tables, and mismatched chairs. Still, it reeked with nostalgia and, before long, the two middle-aged people were basking in the glow of fond memories of another age.

Madeline stifled a yawn, cupping a hand over her mouth.

"You must be exhausted," Doc said, realizing neither of them had done more than catnap since the night before last.

"I should be. So should you." She touched his hand lightly. "But I'm still keyed up."

"I know what you mean. It's hard to shift gears."

They wolfed down hot dogs and beer and laughed about the various off-the-wall advertising campaigns the famous Long Island beach club had launched over the years.

Madeline held one finger poised gracefully, and said, "Do you remember when everybody under thirty had a bumper sticker that said: SAVE THE OAK BEACH INN?"

"Of course." Doc laughed. "I had one myself. Never did know what we were supposed to be saving it from."

"Neither did I." Madeline wiped a glob of mustard from the corner of his mouth with a paper napkin.

"The latest craze," he said, "is, GET OUT OF NEW YORK BEFORE ITS TOO LATE."

"That one I understand."

They did not laugh this time. Somehow, the slogan reminded them both of recent horror.

"Want to go?" Doc said softly.

Madeline nodded. The past was suddenly an unfriendly place.

They walked hand in hand across the sand and gravel parking lot. The half dozen cars scattered about the enormous flat space made the isolation of their humanity that much more telling.

"I'm still scared," she whispered as she pulled her knees up when he helped her into the car.

"I know. Don't be. It's over," he whispered, wishing he could believe it.

"Nice car," she said. Her eyes bespoke her yearning to recapture the earlier mood.

"A 'seventy-nine Coupe de Ville," he proclaimed, rolling toward the road. "They don't build chariots like this one anymore. It's getting to be a pain in the ass finding parts for it without getting ripped off, but I can't bring myself to sell it."

"Are you a car nut, Doc?"

Her impish grin made him flush. He hoped it was too dark for her to notice. "Me? Nah. Just a bit behind the times, I guess."

"Never happen. Doc Wiley is a 'nineties man if I ever saw one."

"Thanks, I think."

"You're welcome; I'm sure."

He swung a U-turn at the next break in the median and reversed course, immediately flicking his right hand directional on and turning down a sandy driveway that seemed to pop up out of nowhere. The headlights bounced off a steel I-beam painted a nautical light blue at the end of the road. Beyond the barrier lay a tiny macadam parking lot overlooking a narrow expanse of water.

"Oak Island," he announced.

Madeline stared at the dark silhouettes of houses, spaced like sentries along the length of the low-lying sand bar that formed the well-known haven across the channel.

"Spooky." She shivered.

"Not at all," he said. "Peaceful. Did you know that they don't even have electricity over there? By choice?"

"So I've heard."

"They say it will ruin the Old-World charm of the place or something."

"Jack Kobrigian one of those back to nature fanatics?"

"Hardly. Jack's idea of roughing it is black and white TV. He was one of the first to put in a generator. Some have gone solar. Some even use windmills. Jack went so far as to get a phone."

"Do tell? Cellular?"

"Jack likes convenience, but he's cheap. Land line only."

"How do we get over there?"

"Do you swim?" Her contemptuous glance made him raise his hands in supplication. "Just kidding. There should be a rowboat around here somewhere. Let's get the bags on board and I'll give milady the twenty-five-cent tour."

"I like that."

"The tour?"

"Mmm mm. Milady."

ɞɞ

Ron Barbarosa dropped his house keys for the second time. He stooped to retrieve them and nearly lost his balance. His faithful attorney caught him and scooped the key ring from the step.

"Let me," Kornberg said and opened the door.

Ron staggered inside, slapped at the security alarm, and somehow got the code right on the first try.

"Look, Ron," Kornberg offered, "maybe I should stay until you turn in."

The white-haired barrister suddenly annoyed the ballplayer. He did not need a wet nurse. Madeline's snub at his attempted seduction, that wiseass cop and his snotty mouth, his uncertain future with the team, Natalie's refusal to cut short her tour to come to him in his time of need, and now this patronizing lawyer. He was home in his own by god house. Enough!

"Go the fuck home, you pompous pain in the ass," Ron snapped. "I can take care of myself."

"Ron, you've been under a strain. Let me help you. You'll feel better in the morning."

"Get out of my house, you sanctimonious shit."

"Very well. If that's the way you feel." Kornberg's attempt at maintaining his dignity was lost on the insufferable drunk. He whirled and trotted down the path to his waiting limo.

"Blood-sucking prick," Ron grumbled, slamming the door.

He stumbled into his freshly painted den. All the lights were on. He cursed the painters for their careless waste of his energy dollars and dropped his sports jacket on the carpet before he crashed into the bar. Glassware rattled and he steadied himself with both hands against the black leather bar-rail.

"Just need a little drink," he wheezed. "One more nightcap and ol' Ron's off to beddy bye." He burped, puffed his cheeks, puckered his lips, blew air out in a stream, and started to giggle. "Shit. I don't remember eating that."

He slopped four ounces of Glenlivet into a glass and looked through rheumy eyes into the smoky blue mirror behind the mahogany and brass bar. Something was amiss in mirrorland. He blinked twice to clear his vision.

"Christ. Seeing double," he moaned. Squinting, he peered again at the image in the smoked glass. "Who the fuck?" He spun on his heel, wobbled, and caught himself with his arms outstretched, grasping the bar rail for support with his back against the counter.

"What's happenin', babe?" The mirror apparition, in solid form, stood grinning before him. A baseball bat from Ron's own collection was poised on the slim man's shoulder.

"Who the fuck're you? Get the fuck outta my house."

"Or what? Gonna throw me out? Leave me in the gutter for the garbage men? Again?"

Carl had a sensation like time travel. He saw the slobbering drunk before him as he had been many years ago—young, vigorous, brash, brutal. He saw young Ron's gloating grin above him as he had looked up from the muddy ground on his knees, dazed and helpless. He heard the words that echoed in his memory: 'Nighty night, Ace.' And he saw Ron's fist coming at him in slow motion as he waited, powerless to defend himself.

Ron took an unsteady step forward, bracing himself for a charge. It brought Carl back to the present.

"That's it, Ronny." He smiled, inviting. "Come at me like a fast ball."

With an animal roar, Ron put his head down and launched himself at the intruder.

"Nighty night, Ace," Carl crooned as he swung the bat in a flat trajectory.

Ron, the batting coach, would have applauded the style if not the outcome had he not been the object of the swing. Carl leaned into it, transferring his weight to his lead foot at precisely the right moment, breaking his wrists without affecting the arc of the barrel, following through with poise and grace. The impact of wood against bone sounded remarkably like the crack of the long ball propelled from the stadium.

Carl mimicked the roar of the crowd, pushing air through his larynx in a parody of exultation as the home team hero cranks one into the cheap seats. He did a one-man wave over the collapsed figure on the floor.

Ron Barbarosa died, unaware of his final insult. As the ballplayer's brain swelled to twice its normal size—cerebral hemorrhages erupting like volcanoes—Carl used the corkscrew from the bar to carve a peace symbol on Ron's ballooning forehead.

Chapter 38

The first time they made love was all urgency and heat, a release from longing and physical need. Now, in the afterglow, Doc lay beside Madeline and smiled at the way things had worked out. They had not unpacked; they had not discussed the sleeping arrangements as he had imagined they would. He never got the chance to offer her the master bedroom while he selflessly tossed and turned in the guestroom.

When they first entered Jack's house, Doc started to show Madeline around and admitted that he needed a refresher tour himself. After all, he explained, he had only been there a couple of times.

He made small talk that sounded to his own ears like inane babble and fought burgeoning panic as he blathered on about Jack's family and the island. He was frantic to recall some humorous anecdote to put Madeline at ease and all the while conscious of how miserably he was failing to keep his eyes from her body. Madeline did her best to appear attentive but she seemed to be having a great deal of difficulty controlling her breathing.

They started with the front room, the living room, but never got past the couch. She walked around one end and he the other. They literally ran into each other's arms in the middle of the sofa. Locked in a desperate embrace, they kissed, groped, and tugged at persistent garments. He had barely gotten one leg out of his pants before she was on top of him.

Afterward, they lay panting on the lumpy cushions, bathed in perspiration, inhaling the scent of their passion.

"Does Jack have heat?" she said.

"It is getting a little nippy, isn't it?"

Madeline smiled coyly. "We could get dressed."

"Or finish getting undressed," he said.

"Freedom of movement. I like the concept but I am freezing my ass off."

"That would be bad for both of us," he said, and his hand slid behind her.

She smiled, and said, "What would you suggest?"

"Let's work on the freedom of movement thing. Buck-naked would be my preference. Your ass, of course, must be preserved."

"For posteriority?" She laughed that musical laugh he loved.

"Is that a word?"

"Be still my heart," she said with exaggerated excitement. "He's great in bed and I can beat him at Scrabble."

"Let's save the board games for later—much later—like when you have to visit me in the home. Meanwhile, why don't you move smartly toward our goal of mutual nudity and I will build us a fire to resolve the ass-sickle problem." He pointed out the fireplace just beyond the coffee table with a jerk of his head.

"Now you're talking," she said.

Doc carefully disentangled himself from her embrace and dragged a gaily-colored Amish pattern quilt from the back of the sofa. He draped it lovingly, if reluctantly, over Madeline's semi-nude body and tucked it in around her feet.

The muted glow of a hurricane lamp, with the wick turned low to stunt its radiance, cast tempting shadows on his body. Madeline reached up to rub his hip with her fingertips. She felt the pebble of goose bumps.

"You'd better hurry before you freeze to death," she warned in that husky voice that drove him wild.

"Do you think it's frozen?" He feigned horror as his eyes went to his middle.

Her gaze followed his to his obvious readiness.

"No, but I think we should try our best to find someplace warm for it."

They blushed in unison. He could not believe the ease with which they could drop any pretense at inhibition and he was astonished that he could joke with her after their first time. There was no anxiety, nor was he being flip to bolster a cavalier façade. It was as if they had known each other all of their lives.

He kicked out of his pants and threw his suit jacket on to show some semblance of modesty before he set to work spreading kindling and scraps of newspaper into the fireplace. She threw articles of her clothing at his back, one by one, while he worked.

"This fire may start by spontaneous combustion if you don't cut that out," he said.

"Just keeping my end of the bargain up," she said.

"And mine," he shot back, "in a manner of speaking."

The clothing bombardment ceased and anticipation hurried him. A box of kitchen matches and a can of charcoal lighter fluid, left conveniently on the mantelpiece, allowed him to get a blaze going with all speed.

He piled a stack of dried logs from the wicker basket beside the hearth onto the burning material and slid under the quilt with Madeline, shedding his coat as he did so.

"Now, where were we?" he said.

ଓଓ

Carl had to find Madeline, and soon. The house in Oyster Bay remained unoccupied as the yellow and black Crime Scene tape stretched over the door attested. Imaginary still-photos of the Dietrichs, with mouths agape, necks arched back at impossible angles, blood pooling on bare wood floorboards, with eyes forever wide in eternal shock, played in his mind like a slide show. He did not linger. A quick drive-by was sufficient to confirm that no one was at home. It would not be wise to loiter. This was the first place they would come when Ron's corpse was discovered.

Where the hell was she?

He parked the car on the street beside a pay phone and called the hospital. Mrs. Maclear was on administrative leave, the operator informed him—whatever that meant. He hung up when she asked if there was a message.

He had to think. What would the most likely scenario be? She would be distraught but relieved that the ordeal was ended. Get away for a while? That was logical. But, where? It was a big world and she could be in any part of it.

He ached to finish this. To see the last one go with terror and remorse on her agonized face.

Would he be forced to wait until she surfaced? The odds would begin to shift in favor of the police if this went on much longer. He knew now what they would eventually find in the house in Rockville

Centre. He hadn't missed it until it was time to do Ron. The branding iron. He'd left it in the house. Sooner or later, the Fire Marshal would run across it. No way would they fail to make the connection. He cursed himself for his arrogance and stupidity. He should have known. Computer enhancement would certainly be used to manipulate the file photo on his driver's license. They wouldn't need a sketch artist. They had his landlord to tell them when they got it right. They would have a damned good likeness, a face to plaster on handbills and TV screens. It would limit his mobility. He had to get to Madeline and be gone.

ଓଃଓଃ

"I told you, I'm off duty." Tony Cordova sighed into the telephone. He twisted in the bed and cupped the receiver to avoid waking his wife. Not that there was much chance of that. Phyllis had been a detective's wife too long to be a light sleeper. One cough from the kids or a creaky floorboard that was out of sync with the normal night house sounds and she would be up like a shot. Ringing telephones and hushed conversations in the middle of the night, on the other hand, were as natural to her ear as her own rhythmic breathing.

"Don't you read the papers?" Tony whispered. "The good guys struck a blow for justice today. It's gold star on the report card time. Attaboys all around." Tony was warming to his subject. He was on a roll. The next words he heard stopped him cold.

"What?" Phyllis stirred, but rolled over and drifted deeper into dreamland. Tony dropped his voice to a whisper. "You're sure? Maybe he just walked into an ordinary burglary, tried to play tough guy and got himself offed by some crack-head." He let out a long breath as the desk sergeant explained the circumstances of Ron Barbarosa's demise. "Yeah," Tony replied, shaking his head in the dark "That sounds like our boy all right. Jesus H. Christ, I thought this asshole was history. What? No. Doc's not home. I don't know where he is…Yes, I think the Maclear woman is with him…How the fuck do I know? What Detective Wiley does on his own time is none of my business, or yours, Sergeant…Of course I'll try to reach him. Now get off my damned phone, I've got things to do."

ଓଃଓଃ

The second and third times were less hurried, much less. The two lovers took time to explore and delight in each other's physical mysteries. Finally, sated for the moment, they took a break from their lovemaking.

Doc went outside to start the generator tucked under the back steps in a cinder block enclosure. He found a full five-gallon gas can beside the unit and filled the generator's tank, saying, "I hope you put stabilizer in this gas, Jack." When he pushed the electric start, the engine coughed to life and he said, "Way to go, Jack."

The sturdy Honda soon purred merrily. He had no idea how much fuel the little beast guzzled, but he hoped it wasn't too thirsty. A stiff breeze whipped his jacket around his waist and he felt the icy breath of the night air on his naked buttocks.

"Best duck back inside," he told the machine. "Wouldn't want the neighbors to think I'm mooning them and call the cops." As he climbed the steps he looked toward the nearest dwelling and thought there was little chance of that. The home was nearly fifty yards distant and empty judging by its darkened windows.

When the electric lights came on, Madeline blew out the hurricane lamp and switched on the television to see if she could catch a weather report. If tomorrow was as pleasant as the red hue of last evening's sunset promised, they might drive to Captree and spend the day on a party boat. They might even do some fishing if they could take their eyes from one another.

The eleven o'clock news was just getting under way when Doc returned with a tray, glasses, wine, and some crackers. Adrienne Boyd nodded at him from the TV screen.

"Good evening. And now the news."

Doc winced. "Madeline, please turn that conniving little tramp off. If I ever see that underhanded slut face to face again, I'll lock her up for impersonating a human being."

"Ssh. I just want to catch the weather. Don't take it so personally." She saw the fury in his eyes and looked more closely at the striking redhead on the screen. "Do you know her?"

With a sigh, he set the tray down on the coffee table, sat and hooked one foot around a leg. As he pulled it toward them, he marveled at Madeline's intent profile. She was the most beautiful thing his eyes had ever beheld, sitting beside him with the quilt draped across her shoulders and her legs crossed, revealing a smooth expanse of bare thigh. Little golden hairs caught the glow of the flickering firelight and shimmered like precious gems. Her eyes sparkled with the reflection from the nineteen-inch, color portable sitting precariously on a tray table in the corner. He lifted the quilt, slipped beneath it and heard her breath catch in her throat. He followed her line of sight and frowned at the hypnotic eye across the room to see what had caused the startled reaction.

"It's us," she whispered.

He saw himself, Madeline, Tony, and a flock of uniforms as they marched from the Graille house. In spite of his resentment he was thankful for the sudden distraction. The last thing he wanted to do was to talk about Adrienne. The camera panned to settle on the nemesis reporter as she prattled on about what they were seeing. Madeline's fascination prompted him to grab for the remote. He tapped the OTR button and the VCR on a plastic milk crate beneath the table went into recording mode.

Just like Jack to leave a tape in the machine. He hoped he wasn't taping over some irreplaceable memories. Knowing Jack, it was more likely some National Geographic special or The Yankee Workshop.

"Are you recording this?" she asked, without taking her eyes from the set.

"Yeah. Thought you might like to have it for posterity. Or is it posteriority?"

She threw him a dazzling smile.

"You're famous, you know," he said. "This could be worth millions someday." He laughed at his own joke. She started to turn toward him and froze. Her eyes snapped back to the newscast.

"What?" he asked, before sipping wine.

"I thought I saw something. Someone behind the redhead. He reminded me of something, but I'm not sure what."

"I'll play it back." He reached for the remote.

"No," she said, seizing his hand and pulling it into her lap. "Never mind. It's nothing. I still want to hear the weather." She placed her other hand on his and returned her attention to the show.

Doc secretly hoped it would rain buckets tomorrow. The fish would always be there and he would much rather spend the day in bed. Moreover, he did not plan to do much sleeping.

Adrienne was carping on the Police Department's arrogant treatment of the media in this most harrowing of experiences in the recent history of Long Island. Doc grew impatient with the interruption of his night's ecstasy and nibbled at Madeline's neck.

“You are insatiable,” she moaned.

“Sorry. Can’t help it.”

“I wasn’t complaining.”

They were slipping back down in the cushions. Doc nuzzled Madeline’s ear, pleased to find he was having the desired effect. The news and the wine were all but forgotten when Adrienne Boyd’s quickened tones and raised voice brought their eyes wide open.

“Ladies and gentlemen,” the perfectly coiffured, delicately made-up, and newly installed anchorperson snapped. “This has just been handed me. Ron Barbarosa, the famous hometown ballplayer, was found murdered in his home in Great Neck less than an hour ago. Nassau County Police, in conjunction with the local private police force, are investigating the crime. Initial reports suggest that Mr. Barbarosa was the latest victim of The Terminator, the notorious mass murderer reported killed in a fiery explosion in Sands Point last night.”

Adrienne stopped and the camera zoomed in for a close-up of her trembling hands. She let the bulletin fall flat on the desk. There was no further information to impart. Her eyes dropped to the bottom of the screen, her expression a question. Comprehension dawned. She nodded to someone off camera and her gaze leveled to renew eye contact with her audience.

“Ladies and gentlemen,” she said in a raspy voice, and then loudly cleared her throat. “This reporter has never been at a loss for words but I must confess this development leaves me speechless.” Adrienne immediately contradicted herself and launched into an extended editorial on the mystifying events of the day. While she recounted her eyewitness viewing of the smoldering wreckage of the shattered fuel truck and the blackened bones of the alleged perpetrator, Madeline began to cry.

Doc sat stunned, impotent, powerless to end her shuddering sobs. She fell into his arms and wailed. He sat holding her, rocking her like a baby, dumbstruck.

When the telephone on the end table rang, he picked up the receiver and said woodenly, “Wiley.” Tony’s excited voice sounded a long way off as he reported the awful news in a clipped, precise manner. “I know, Tony, I know. We just saw it on the news.” He sighed like the last breath of the damned. “Film at eleven.”

Chapter 39

In a motel room in Jericho, remarkable only in its rubber stamp duplication of a million motel rooms nationwide, Carl sipped from the second bottle of a six-pack of Corona beer he'd bought at a 7-11 Store and watched, appalled, as Adrienne Boyd betrayed him. There was nothing in her exclusive newscast that would bring him anything but adverse consequences.

Everything had gone wrong. A nosy neighbor had seen Barbarosa's lights on and, unaware he had returned home, called the police. The cops had broken a window to gain entry instead of forcing the door, had found the device he had rigged to the hinges, and disarmed it. A disgusting waste of precious explosives.

Worst of all, they were after him again before the culmination of the operation. Madeline would go to ground. It was conceivable that he would never find her.

He snarled his outrage and hurled the beer bottle. It shattered on the painted beige cinder block wall, spreading a foamy starburst pattern. Spent and in despair, he collapsed on the bed, curled into a tight ball and wept until, exhausted, he slept.

ꕥ

"Run."

"Say again?" Doc thought he had misunderstood Tony's one word of advice on the telephone.

"You heard me," Tony said. "Take off. Bolt. Sky up. Make like a tree and leave. Di-di mau. Vanish. Stop me when you get the message."

Tony's agitated voice sounded foreign to Doc's disbelieving ear. He cast a nervous glance at Madeline's sleeping form on the couch, afraid she might be disturbed by the cowardly suggestion his friend was making on the other end of the line. She did not stir, but his heart ached at the sight of her puffy eyelids and knitted brow. Sleep failed to release her from her waking torment. She whimpered and Doc could think of nothing for the moment beyond ending this outrageous conversation to return to her side. But Tony was still talking. He squeezed the receiver in his fist, glowering at the words he heard.

"You're kidding me, right?" he got in when Tony took a breath.

"Doc, this cocksucker is without a doubt the most diabolical fuck it has ever been my distinct misfortune to run up against. Shit! We saw him fricasseed—what?—twenty-four hours ago? And he's back and rubbing our noses in it. I've been on the carpet at the Puzzle Palace for over an hour. Needleman is going ballistic. Shaw is ready to call out the national guard and start a house-to-house search and destroy. Feds are coming in by the busload. They're expecting to find you and Madeline chopped up like hamburger any minute."

"You didn't tell them where we are, did you?"

"Of course not." Tony did his Sergeant Schultz impression. "I zee nutting, I hear nutting, I know nutting, Herr Commandant." Doc could not help but smile. "And that's the way it'll stay. But, Doc…"

"Yeah?"

"You're isolated out there. You're in Suffolk-fucking-County for God's sake. How can anybody watch your back if your ass is swinging in the breeze in the middle of nowhere?"

"Tony, I told you to keep our whereabouts under your hat for good reason. Think about it. That damned Adrienne has broadcast every move we made from the get-go. Somebody is tipping her. We know that. I won't take chances with Madeline's life."

"I've got to admit, I thought you were plumbing new depths of paranoia when you told me to keep my mouth shut about your little vacation spot. It would now seem, however, that your vision outstrips your neuroses."

"Thank you, Doctor Cordova."

"Don't mention it."

"Regarding your initial suggestion, Tony. No way."

"Your decision to make. Just try not to forget, in your macho pig-headed bravado, that it's not you this creep is after."

Doc clenched his jaw in an effort to hold his temper. Tony was afraid for them. He meant no insult. "Tony, my very good friend, I know you have my best interests at heart, as well as Madeline's." He could almost see Tony nodding on the other end. "And believe me, I understand where you're coming from..."

"But?"

"But where is Madeline going to be safe? If you can answer that one, I'll beat feet so fast the vacuum will suck you into the phone. We don't even know who this fucking screwball is. Where do you hide from the bogeyman?"

"You're right," Tony breathed. "I'm just scared shitless, that's all."

"How would you like to be the lady on Jack's couch?"

"Okay." Tony paused. "You want me to come out there and pull guard?"

Doc thought about it for a moment, and then said, "No. Go home and get some sleep. We'll be all right. Unless this bastard is psychic, he'll never find us here. Just stay in touch and let me know what's happening. Cell phone and pay phones only."

"Gee, I'm glad you told me, I was gonna use Needleman's private line."

"Sorry. Nerves."

"Forget it."

"We'll figure out what our next move will be in the morning."

ꕥꕥ

Carl awoke an hour past dawn. His mouth had turned into a sewer during the night. Bleary eyed, he sat up in the double bed and saw his reflection in the mirror over the dresser. He looked as bad as he felt. The smell of his body, still in the sweat-soaked clothes he had slept in, revolted him. He sprang from the bed, peeled off his garments, threw them in the wastebasket, and marched into the bathroom.

A hot shower and shave did much to relieve his black mood. He wiped the condensation from the bathroom mirror with his hand to examine the image therein. His upper lip was puffy and inflamed from the effects of the glue he had used to fasten the mustache. It altered his appearance. For that, he was thankful. He swished water around in his mouth, wishing he had remembered to pack a toothbrush in the trunk of the Beamer.

That reminded him. Had the painters seen his car? Probably not well, if at all. He had parked well away from the nearest streetlight. Besides, there were more BMWs on Long Island than in all of Bavaria.

Putting on the last of his clean clothes, he thought he had better do some shopping. Retrieving the sports jacket from the floor where he had tossed it last night, he sniffed the cloth and inspected the garment for bloodstains. It was all right. Besides, it went well with the navy-blue slacks and white golf shirt he wore.

He sat on the bed, pondering his next move. An idea struck him and he opened the night table drawer between the beds. There it was, right next to the Gideon Bible—the phone book. He seized it and thumbed through the pages until he found what he sought.

After a light breakfast of sweet rolls and coffee in a bagel shop on Jericho Turnpike, he drove to the town's library. A search of recent newspapers told him what he needed to know. A photo of Detectives Anthony Cordova and W. "Doc" Wiley escorting Madeline from the house in Sands Point was displayed over the lead article on page two of today's Newsday. Barbarosa got page one. He read the page-two story and learned that Cordova was the little guy with the flinty eyes who had stared him down. Wiley was the good-looking clown holding her hand. He tore out the page and stuffed it in his pocket.

Back in his room, Carl let his fingers do the walking again, but threw the phone book down in disgust. Neither name was listed. The idea had been stupid. What cop in his right mind would advertise his home address to all the criminals he met?

There had to be a way. He was certain that these two apes were the keys to the mystery of Madeline. They would know where she was. They were probably with her now. How could he track them? The thought spawned another. He bent to recover the offending pages.

There was a shop in Rockville Centre. He had passed it on several occasions. He found it in the business listings. As he dialed the number, he smoothed the wrinkled pages of the phone book in forgiveness.

"Good morning. Spymasters? Hi. Do you have a Cantrack Three-Sixty with magnetized base plate in stock? You do? Excellent. Would you hold it for me? I'll pick it up in…" Carl glanced at his watch and estimated the time it would take him to reach the south shore. "Say, half an hour. Good. Cash all right with you? Great. I'm on my way." He dropped the phone into its cradle and said, "Those two idiot cops have no idea who they're tangling with. Madeline, honey, you sit tight. Today is the last day of the rest of your life."

Chapter 40

Mitch Numkeena kneaded his brow with both hands. He hated this part of the job—sifting through mountains of intelligence reports—most of which amounted to zip—in hope of finding some scrap of information that would set off alarm bells in his brain. The Anti-Terrorist Unit gathered tons of data. The trick was to make the connection when you saw it.

There were tips from informants that could be anything from a case busting lead to a vindictive attempt to remove a romantic rival. Most snitches worked for cash and Mitch had known a few who should have been writing fiction for a living instead of lying to the cops for pocket money.

Most cases were cut and paste jobs. Snatches of overheard conversations, usually from several sources, were laboriously crosschecked and compared to discern commonality. Financial records and phone bills of known or suspected felons were either subpoenaed or obtained in less civilized ways—such as Dumpster diving, a practice that speaks for itself. Myriad bits and pieces of information were compared for fit, assembled, and analyzed or, as Mitch would say—anal-ized. Anything referring to ongoing investigations, however vaguely, might turn up in the daily avalanche of paper that inundated Mitch's desk.

He lit a cigar and blew a perfect smoke ring at the NO SMOKING sign taped to the glass partition. That small accomplishment made him smile with delight and mumble, "Look, Ma, smoke signals with no blanket."

A sip of the vending machine coffee made him grimace. He had been drinking the stuff since he came into the office at sunup. It was nasty, but he'd be damned if he would clean the carafe in the lunchroom to make a fresh pot. Mitch Numkeena was nobody's maid.

The bored Native American stretched to pull his ashtray closer without taking his feet from the desk and something caught his eye. It was a fire marshal's report concerning the investigation-for-cause of a house fire in a place called Rockville Centre. The list of salvaged items culled from the ashes included the military collar insignia of a full-bird colonel. That particular item was highlighted in yellow and that was why it had found its way to his desk. He had a flag order out for anything related to The Colonel.

Thinking that the Intel guys were going a little overboard, he skimmed the report out of curiosity. The eagles had probably belonged to some retired lifer or maybe a weekend warrior.

The occupant of the burned-out home had yet to be located. That was odd. None of the neighbors had any idea of his whereabouts, nor, for that matter, of his life. He was a mystery to everyone on the block. Even the guy who collected his rent could not shed any light on his tenant. The cause of the fire had yet to be determined, but the fire marshal had labeled it suspicious.

Where in hell is Rockville Centre? The zip code put it in Nassau County, Doc's stomping grounds. He did not envy his friend the insanity that was running rampant out there.

"No offense, old buddy," he whispered, "but better you than me."

Something at the bottom of the page engaged his cerebral gears. The inspectors had found an object they could not identify. Some wanna-be artist had sketched the thing and attached his masterpiece to the report. Mitch studied it, turning the sheet around to look at it from several angles.

Mitch frowned, searching his memory for a tiny kernel recently sown. Still digging, he reached across the desk for the morning newspaper. He had to fold himself in half to avoid taking his feet from the desktop, but he caught the edge of a page with his fingertips and pulled the paper to where he could grasp it.

Pleased, Mitch settled back in his squeaky government-issue swivel chair and perused the front page. The headline article described a carving on the deceased Ron Barbarosa's brow—a peace symbol. Jesus, what a sick freak this guy must be. He looked at the sketch again.

"Whoa," he cried. "Back up the stagecoach and dust off the tom-toms. Big Chief Numkeena's going to town."

This time, his feet hit the floor

ᏋᏋ

Tony was sick of the sight of headquarters. He longed to go back to the good old days when he could work unencumbered, sans brass hats looking over his shoulder. It had never occurred to him, until today, how much he relied on Doc to keep the bosses' myopic scrutiny diffused. While he and Doc had not been partners since their days in uniform, they had worked closely on hundreds of cases since they had earned their gold shields. Tony had been involved in many close encounters with the department hierarchy because of his mouth, but Doc had always been there to thwart their aim when Tony found himself the designated clay pigeon. There was no question as to who was alone in the crosshairs now.

"Detective," Chief Needleman said, with even greater condescension than was his norm, "please explain to me how a serial killer, reported by you and Detective Wiley as having been cornered in Sands Point and killed in a cataclysmic holocaust, returns from the dead to brutally murder another victim. A victim, I might add, who was known to be specifically targeted by the perpetrator."

Needleman's failure to address Tony by name was ominous in itself. The chief was sub-consciously, or intentionally—Tony could not decide—distancing himself from the mistake. He was saying, in effect, Tony who? Never heard of him.

Tony knew this game. It was known as: You-play-ball-with-me-and-I'll-stick-the-bat-up-your-ass. He had been through much the same bullshit with Schiff and his precinct captain last night.

Special Agent Gilchrist of the FBI stood quietly by, dissecting Tony with his eyes. Charlie Schiff sat in a chair beside him, but Schiff might as well have been out of town for all the help he was being.

"Sir," Tony said, shifting in his seat while using his forearms on the arms of his chair to support his weight, rearranging his buttocks to give himself a moment to organize his thoughts. "The corpse in the cab of the fuel truck—hell, there was no corpse. The guy was a collection of blackened bones."

Tony was in no mood to justify himself to Needleman. Sleep, last night, had been as elusive as the whacked-out killer they were trying to outguess. He had had one of those nights when you thought you might have dozed off a few times but you were not sure when. He felt he should be with Doc or kicking over garbage cans and slimy rocks, doing something to locate this nut, not sitting here playing catch-up. "The guy had just shot two cops," he continued, "and lobbed a goddamn bomb at the Graille place." Tony looked at his hands and was surprised to see a tremor. He wasn't nervous, he was angry. "He cut loose with an automatic weapon at the first uniforms he saw when we cornered him in the preserve. Naturally, they returned fire. The truck went up like a Roman candle. There really wasn't time to ask the guy for his ID and I don't think he would have handed it over if we had. When the smoke cleared, we added one plus one and came up with two.

"Who were we to assume this asshole was?" Tony spread his hands and looked from Needleman to Schiff, but neither made any reply. "Is there a waiting list to take a crack at Natalie Graille's picture perfect summer home? How many fucking nuts do you think we've got cruising around out there with the Redstone Arsenal in their hip pockets?"

Schiff gave Tony a give-em-hell look, but they both knew it wouldn't do him any good.

Needleman chose to ignore Tony's profanity and belligerence, even the sarcasm. Tony wondered why, but he knew it would not be forgotten indefinitely.

"And where is the infamous Doc Wiley?" the chief asked.

Tony almost said: It's not my day to watch him. Instead, he bit his lip, shook his head and mumbled, "I don't know."

"What about Mrs. Maclear? Has she disappeared as well?"

"Looks that way." Tony now knew how the perps felt in the interrogation rooms, lying like a rug and trying hard to look as innocent as dog shit.

"What, if anything, do you know, Detective?" Needleman sneered.

Tony had so many wisecrack replies for that question, he could not choose from the list. He thought about his family, pictured Phyllis and the kids in a bread line, and decided he had sounded off enough for one day. His career opportunities were already reaching their outer limits because of his snappy rejoinders. Best not to test the limits of the envelope. Time to shut up and pull the wagon.

He reeled off the details in a monotone, careful to touch on all the salient points, but never allowing any inflection to color his speech. Infuriated by the situation Doc had accurately predicted to occur should things turn sour, he decided to let Needleman do his own thinking for once.

Needleman interrupted when Tony explained how Barbarosa's neighbor's suspicions had been aroused, causing him to call the police. He wanted clarification on that point. It was a silly thing to ask. Talk about looking a gift horse in the mouth. Tony saw it as more proof that Needleman was in way over his head.

"We met this guy when we went to Barbarosa's place the first time," Tony explained. "He's a protective sort. After the scare we put into him, if he didn't expect Ron home, it's logical to assume he would have called us. He's that type."

This seemed to satisfy Needleman. He even gave Agent Gilchrist a knowing nod. Tony went on to give the medical examiner's opinion of the probable cause of death. "Severe cranial trauma caused by a sharp blow from a blunt instrument. They found one of Ron's own baseball bats next to the body. Blood and tissue found on the bat are Ron's. And, of course, there was the peace sign. This time it was carved, not burned, into the victim's forehead. He used a corkscrew from the bar.

"Latents says there are enough prints in the house to keep them busy for a long time. But there are none on the murder weapon or the explosive device, which, according to the Bomb Squad, was a half-pound block of C-4 and some stuff you can buy in any hardware store. They're tracing the C-4 from the serial number on the wrapper. Barbarosa's house, as you know from the preliminary report, had just been painted. The neighbor says the painters were still there yesterday, so they must have finished in the afternoon or early evening. We're trying to find out what contractor he used. There was no name on the truck. That's according to the neighbors, too. Kornberg says Ron hired them himself. Friend of a friend kind of thing. It may take a while, but we'll track them down." Tony spread his hands and asked, "Did I leave anything out—sir?"

"No, Tony," Schiff answered before Needleman could think of anything to say. "Meticulous and professional, as usual."

Cordova was grateful for the compliment. It told Needleman that the lieutenant would stand for just so much punishment of his officers. The chief grunted, thought for a moment, and said, "Can you tell me why the witnesses were so quickly released from custody?"

Tony sighed. "If you will recall, Chief Needleman, the witnesses were in protective custody. The perp was dead as far as we knew. There was no reason to believe our continued support was required.

They were both anxious to get on with their lives. Mister Barbarosa was particularly verbose in that regard."

"And you have no knowledge of Detective Wiley's status or whereabouts?"

"No sir, as I have repeatedly stated."

"In your considered opinion, Detective, do you believe that Mrs. Maclear is with Wiley?"

"That's entirely possible, sir, but I have no way of knowing."

"Very well. What's our next move, gentlemen?"

Cordova and Schiff exchanged embarrassed glances. Even the FBI guy looked at his shoes. The chief should be telling, not asking.

Tony took some measure of satisfaction in knowing that the ivory tower was showing signs of cracking.

Commissioner Shaw, he noted, was conspicuous by his absence. Probably confirming the stash in his Swiss bank account, he concluded, and booking an early flight.

"We're canvassing the victim's neighborhood, of course." Schiff cleared his throat and looked to Tony for assistance. "We are trying to find Doc and the nurse as well."

Tony picked up the thread. "We sent dicks to Oyster Bay Hospital, Doc's apartment, and to Mrs. Maclear's place. She hasn't returned as yet. Neither has he."

"Knowing, as we do," Schiff said, "that the nurse is also a target, we felt it best to concentrate on locating her." The lieutenant had grabbed the ball but it was obvious he had nowhere to run with it. He looked to Tony for support but Tony was also out of gas and they turned, in tandem, to Needleman.

There was nothing to be accomplished by continuing this charade and Needleman seemed to realize it. He stood to signify that the conference was at an end.

"Keep me informed," he said, as he made his exit with Gilchrist on his heels like a shadow. The fed turned for one last pitying glance at Tony but left without voicing the disdain in his eyes.

"Thanks, Charlie," Tony said sincerely, as soon as the door closed behind the dour duo.

"Ahh." Schiff waved it away with a snap of his wrist. "The son of a bitch would have turned on me next." He looked askance at the olive-skinned detective. "You sure you don't know where Doc is?"

"Would I lie, Charlie?"

"For Wiley? In a heartbeat. Now, get the fuck out of here and go catch this son of a bitch."

ཀཀ

The sunlight reflecting on the mirror surface of the flat calm bay stung Madeline's eyes. She let the curtain fall back as she turned from the window.

"He's not out there," Doc reassured her. "No one knows we're here except Tony and he won't tell anyone."

"If you're so positive, why are you wearing your gun?"

He dropped his eyes to the butt of the automatic riding in his shoulder rig. His hand stirred his coffee mechanically and he looked up to find Madeline waiting for an answer, so he shifted his gaze to the worn surface of the rock maple kitchen table, avoiding her eyes.

"I learned to be cautious in Vietnam," he said, at last. "It's just a habit. We're safe here."

"But we can't stay here forever, Doc. Sooner or later we're going to have to go out there." She looked at the window as if out there was the airless vacuum of space.

"They'll get him."

"They already did and he came back."

"Madeline—" He reached across the round table and squeezed her hand. "—don't fall apart now." She looked into his eyes, silently begging for guarantees he could not make. "I need you to be strong a little while longer."

She sat in the chair opposite him. "Only if you promise me a complete breakdown all my own when this is over." The pixy smile lit up her face and his heart melted.

"Scout's honor." He raised the fingers of his right hand in what he hoped was the correct manner. "You may have to draw straws with Tony, though. I promised him first shot."

"You're not supposed to cross your fingers," she said.

They laughed softly and held hands across the table. Doc cast a glance through the separation between the curtains. The big white boat he called a car sat gleaming in the sun on the other side of the water. There were three more cars in the parking lot. That meant there were others on the island. He had no way of knowing whom.

"Tell me about Vietnam," she said.

Doc did a double take. "Now?"

"You just mentioned it. It's a part of you, a part that hurts. The look in your eyes when you say the word, it's like you really don't believe it happened."

He smiled sadly. "Maybe I don't."

"Tell me about the dream, the one you had that night in the hospital when you put the arm lock on Miss Tuttle. Is it awful?"

He started to blow it off, to make light of it and change the subject, but he saw the genuine need in her eyes. She really wanted to know. It was not the morbid curiosity of too many women he had known. He had seen their eyes shine when they asked him if he had killed anyone. It disgusted him, more because he had used it to get into their pants than because of why they asked. It was the ultimate turn-on for some women, and he had been too weak not to take advantage.

Doc had never told anyone the specifics of the dream, not even Barbara, his ex-wife. There was too much pain attached, too much guilt. Madeline sat there, motionless, and for one second, he imagined her listening to his story and then taking him in her arms. In the next second, he saw her turning away from him forever. He had never trusted anyone to understand and look how things had turned out so far. He was about to find out if he had always been a fool or if he was about to become one.

Doc related the sequence of the dream the way he would give an eyewitness report of a crime, details and observations interspersed at appropriate points to form a complete picture. "It was my own, personal horror movie for years," he said at the end. "The longest running fright flick in history. Every night, right here—" He tapped his temple. "—in living color. I thought it was finally over a few years back but that night in the hospital it started again. I don't know why."

"Who was Berryhill?"

Tears clouded his vision. "A friend—a good one—the best."

"The dream. How much is real and how much is not? What happened to Berryhill?"

"None of it's real. It's gothic fantasy, cooked up in the darkest corners of my own little mind." He felt such shame when he looked into those beautiful eyes. "I don't know what happened to Berry."

She reached for his hand, but he recoiled. "Let me finish. I'd been in-country eleven months," he went on. "Berry—that's what everybody called him—for nine. We were Rangers. Worked deep in the jungle in small teams. We were tight. Berry was like my shadow and I, his. You would have liked him. He had the most cheerful disposition of anyone I have ever known. He was also the unluckiest bastard." He shook his head and sighed. "Berry could get his ass in a bind in Saint Patrick's Cathedral at Midnight Mass on Christmas Eve."

She smiled at the image.

"No fault of his own, you understand," he said. "He was a good Ranger. Just born under a cloud, I guess. I felt responsible for him."

He took a deep breath. "I went on R and R to Sydney, Australia."

Madeline gave him a questioning look.

"It's a military acronym for rest and recuperation, like a vacation."

"Sounds weird," she said, "a vacation from war."

"It feels even weirder than it sounds but let me finish. I had waited all that time just so I could get a slot. R and Rs were allocated by time in-country. Sydney was a prime spot. Everybody wanted to go there. The only way to be sure of not getting bumped was to wait until you had so much time in, you couldn't lose your slot."

"Why was Australia so sought after?"

He hesitated.

"Oh," she said, "the women."

Doc flushed. "Tony said you were sharp. Yeah, that was a big part of it. Round eyes, as we used to say."

"It's kind of obvious when you think about it," she said, and Doc marveled at the sophistication the statement showed.

"We were kids in many ways," he said. "Anyway, at the last minute, before I left, I had a premonition, like something was telling me not to go. I told Berry about it. He laughed it off. Said I was getting Asiatic, that it was proof I needed a rest. He practically pushed me onto the plane."

"And you never saw him again," Madeline guessed.

"There's more."

She waited.

"I didn't come back when I was supposed to. I met a girl. She was drop-dead-gorgeous. Long hair, long legs, and eyes like big blue saucers. It's funny. She was so important to me then, and for the life of me, I can't remember her name today." He paused as if contemplating whether to continue, shrugged, and plunged ahead. "The team went out on a mission the day after I should have come back. They got suckered into an ambush in the A-Shau Valley. The enemy blew the ambush prematurely so nobody was hit, but they had the team surrounded.

"We had contingency plans for stuff like that. The guys scattered. One or two men can move faster and quieter than a whole team. The idea is to break contact and rendezvous at a pre-arranged point.

"The guys all found the rendezvous, all except Berry. He's still listed as MIA."

"And you blame yourself?"

"If I had been there, like I was supposed to be, I'd have been with him. I never would have left him alone."

"You think he was killed."

"Alone in the A-Shau? It's a certainty."

"What makes you think you could have changed that?"

"I don't know," he said. "I guess I just would have liked the chance to find out."

"What happened when you got back?"

"Nothing." He said it flatly, a sneer curling his lips. "I was two days late—two lousy days—just long enough to miss that mission. The war was ending. Units were being pulled out almost daily. Nobody wanted to bother with the paperwork to nail one AWOL asshole for two stinking days. I got off scot free."

"But you didn't, did you?"

He did not answer. He just met her gaze, evaluating her reaction, apprehensive, hopeful, and afraid.

"And you never told anyone about this?" she prodded.

He shook his head, unable to speak, as if the telling of his shameful secret had used up all of his words.

"My husband, Paul, had a heart attack," she said.

"You said he had some problems with PTSD."

"Yes. He used to get edgy for no apparent reason. He'd be fine for long periods of time, months on end. And then something would set him off. Most of the time I didn't know what. He would wake up in the morning and be like someone I didn't know, snapping at me for nothing. The silliest things would send him into a rage."

"Did he hit you?"

"Never. But there were times when I thought he would. He always managed to stop himself before it went that far. But he'd shut himself off from me then. Have you ever been with someone and felt like you were alone, like they were physically there, but mentally miles away?"

"Sounds like my daughter."

"Tell me about her."

"One sad story at a time, okay? You were telling me about Paul."

She looked at her hands, nodded, and said, "I couldn't reach him. When he shut me out, there was no way to break in. He'd always come out of it on his own, although the episodes lasted longer each time. I learned to wait it out."

"And then the heart attack?"

"He wouldn't talk about it after he came back." She shrugged. "That's the way I thought of those times. It was as if he went away for a while, as if a stranger occupied his body while he was off somewhere far from me. He'd work harder after each episode, as if making money would compensate for the way he had treated me. He'd swear that he was all right, that he knew what he had to do to get over it, that the last time really had been the last time."

Tears filled her eyes.

"And you believed him."

"No. My training taught me to know that problems like Paul's don't cure themselves. I read up on Post-Traumatic Stress, talked to vets' counselors. He resisted all of my pleas to go for help. The problem was that he was so sweet when he wasn't in the throes of it, so thoughtful and caring that I let myself think that maybe he was right. Maybe I should let him deal with it his way." She sighed. "When he died, I realized how much I had I loved him—more than I ever knew when he was alive—and the pain was so bad I thought I would die. I thought I had failed him, that I should have been stronger, that I should have forced him to get help." She reached across the table and held Doc's face in her hands, and said, "It's called survivor's guilt." Her tears were flowing freely. "You don't have to be a soldier to get it. You just have to lose someone you love. Let it go. I'll help you."

For a long moment, they forgot about The Terminator. They forgot about the world.

"More coffee?" he finally said.

"I'll get it." She rose to get the pot from the stove, and said, "Now, what about Jen?"

"You don't quit, do you?"

"Not anymore."

He smiled. "Point taken. Okay. Jen is in the wind with Barbara, my ex."

"In the wind?"

"Cop slang. They ran away. Barbara is a spiteful woman. This is her way of getting back at me."

"For the divorce?"

"For not loving her."

"Shall I call a dentist? I'm not good at pulling teeth."

"Sorry. Thinking about Barbara brings out a kind of anger."

She cocked her head, her wariness apparent.

"Nothing to do with Nam. Not directly, anyway. That's the problem with self-examination. The deeper you go, the more you find, and the more you find, the deeper you go."

"Forget the dentist," she said, "I need a well digger."

He nodded toward the forgotten coffee pot. "Could I have some of that?"

She poured some into his cup and then topped off her own.

"Barbara and Jen," she said.

He took a sip, nodded several times, and said, "I met Barbara after I got out of the army. She was just what I wanted at the time—cute, sexy, and carefree. What appealed to me most was that she had no desire to get tied down."

"What changed?"

"She got pregnant."

"That will do it."

"I did what I thought was the right thing. It wasn't. To make a long story short, we called it quits before we wound up killing each other."

"How long has she been gone?"

"Almost five years now. We got divorced seven years ago. She made life as miserable for me as she could for a while. Always using Jen like a weapon. Visitation squabbles, that kind of thing. Every time I saw my daughter, she'd be a little more distant. Then, one day, they were gone."

"Have you tried to find them?"

"I did more than try. I found them several times. I'm a detective, remember?"

"And?"

"She'd just take off again."

"So, you gave up."

"If Jen wants to see me, she can. She's old enough now to make up her own mind."

"You gave up."

He narrowed his eyes and set his jaw.

"I can see," she said, reaching across the table to take his hands once again, "you are going to need some serious work."

"Can you fit me into your schedule?"

"No problem."

Chapter 41

Hey! Cordova!" A detective with so much belly hanging over his belt you couldn't tell if he wore one, hailed Tony as he headed for the nearest exit and freedom from Needleman's clutches. "You got a couple messages while you were in with the chief."

He showed Tony three pink slips of paper, one at a time, reading them as he did so.

"Your wife called. Wants to know if she should plan on you being home for dinner."

"Thanks. I'll call her back later." Tony waited impatiently for the other two messages. The detective read the next one while he held the third back, as if to prevent premature disclosure of sensitive information.

"Some guy called, didn't leave his name, just asked if you were here. I told him you was in with the chief. He said he'd call back."

"Fine. Him I won't call."

The detective squinted his puzzlement.

"And the third?"

"Oh, yeah. This one's really for Wiley. Nobody knows where he is. I was wondering if you should take it." He read it to himself, his brows knitting deeper into furrows of contemplation.

"Would you just read me the friggin' thing?"

"Sure. If you think it's all right."

"I promise. Please, read it before Alzheimer's sets in and I no longer give a shit."

"It's from a cop in the city. Guy named Numkee Naster?"

"That's Numkeenaestwa." Tony snatched the slip from the man's fingers. "Thanks."

As Tony stalked off to find a telephone, the portly detective called after him, "What kind of name is Numkeen Naster?"

"Navajo," Tony called over his shoulder.

The detective turned away, mumbling, "Ain't anybody in this country American anymore?"

ᏊᏊ

Carl watched the parking lot from behind the wheel of the BMW, having established that Tony was in the police headquarters building by the simple device of a phone call. When he spied Detective Cordova leaving the building, he twisted the ignition key. He followed the green sedan that Tony drove to the main firehouse in Rockville Centre. Carl now had no doubts as to the meaning of this trip. They were on to him.

Tony left the fire station with something wrapped in brown paper under his arm and a thick nine-by-twelve manila envelope. From there, he drove to his precinct house in Woodbury where he deposited the wrapped package in the trunk of a car. It wasn't a police vehicle. Of that, Carl was sure. It was a brown Chevrolet Celebrity. His personal vehicle. It had to be. Tony went into the building with the envelope in hand.

Carl sat in the BMW, a block away, where he could keep the exits and most importantly, the car, in sight. It was nearly dark when Cordova emerged from the building, still carrying the envelope, and climbed into the Chevy.

Carl followed Tony home.

ᏊᏊ

As the day waned, Doc did his best to prepare for the defense of their island retreat without unduly alarming Madeline. He double-checked locks on doors and windows and set candles that Kobrigian kept on hand for power outages in strategic places around the bungalow.

"In case of a storm," he said in reply to the curiosity on Madeline's face. He divided a box of wooden, strike-anywhere matches between himself and Madeline and instructed her to keep them on her person. Wistfully, he thought of how impossible that might have been had the time spent here worked out as he had hoped. It did not seem likely that they would have their clothes off for anything but a quick shower now, and only one at a time. One more reason to hate this bastard.

Madeline began her own silent preparations. Finding a first-aid kit in the bathroom closet, she spread its contents on the kitchen table before organizing the articles for emergency use. Her sad smile, when Doc stopped to see what she was doing, told him he was not fooling her for a second.

He found a Mossberg twelve-gauge pump action shotgun in a canvas case under the bed in the master bedroom and two boxes of shells in the night table. He would have been surprised if he had not found some sort of firepower. Jack Kobrigian had been a cop too long not to be mildly paranoid. He gave Madeline a crash course in the handling of the shotgun and his service pistol. She followed his instructions, willing and intent. His fears that her professional ethics might cause her to balk at self-defense by firearms proved to be unfounded. He remembered his own instantaneous metamorphosis from healer to killer in a Vietnam rice paddy. His team had been pinned down, the enemy maneuvering to encircle them. They called in an air strike. Napalm enveloped the woods all around them. They charged the nearest tree line before the fires died down, right into a knot of screaming, burning NVA troops. One of them writhed on the ground directly in Doc's path, his tattered uniform smoking, the hair on his head ablaze, blackened fingers twitching, but still trying to raise his weapon.

Doc shot him in the face at point blank range. He could still see the man's brains explode from the back of his head and he could still smell the stink of burning flesh.

Self-preservation was a deep-rooted instinct.

As the sun slipped below the horizon, they ran out of things to do and huddled on the sofa. Doc fed small logs into the fireplace, one at a time, trying unsuccessfully to make light conversation. Paul, Jen, and Berryhill kept coming back. It was night when the phone rang. It startled them and they laughed the way frightened people do when their repressed fear becomes apparent.

Doc answered it on the third ring, spoke in quick, muffled tones and replaced the receiver.

"That was Tony," he told Madeline. "He's got something on our boy and he's coming out to go over it. I'll give him some time to make the trip and then I'll meet him at the dock. He'll never find Jack's place in the dark by himself."

“I hope you told him to bring some food.”

Doc nodded and gave her a sheepish grin, embarrassed that he had not thought to bring anything but cheese, crackers, and wine. Jack’s meager supply of canned goods—one tin of Campbell’s Chunky Chicken Noodle—had been depleted by lunchtime. At least the crackers had come in a handy. In fairness, he told himself, he was not considering a siege when he planned the trip.

ও৩ও৩

Carl ducked behind the Cordova’s aboveground swimming pool and cursed under his breath. He shook the electronic package gripped tightly in both his hands. He should kill the whole family. Wipe out that bitch and the entire litter of whining snot-nosed rug rats. “Daddy! Daddy! Daddy!” Was that all those kids could say? And that cow. “Hi honey, how was your day? Want something to eat?” It was revolting. Infuriating. How could this suburban pack of domestic idiots interfere with his brilliant plan?

The Cordova kids ran around the yard like bright colored orbs caroming off the cushions on a billiard table. Carl only needed a few moments to affix the device to the undercarriage of the Chevy. Didn’t they have to go to bed? Did this cop and his spouse have no control over their offspring whatsoever? Carl slipped farther back into the shadows, to sit in the damp grass with his knees pulled up to his chest and his back pressed against the cold sheet metal of the pool wall. The children’s shrill laughter rubbed his nerves raw. He closed his eyes and willed them to stop.

By the time the kids ceased their juvenile scampering and went inside, allowing Carl to creep within striking distance, Tony emerged from the house. Carl froze and very slowly sank back into the shadows.

“You call me if you’re going to be very late,” a female voice sang out from the kitchen.

Tony nodded absently as he closed the storm door behind him, scowling, preoccupied as he crossed the rouge cinder block patio to the carport. He snapped on the headlights as he started the engine and backed down the short double ribbon of concrete into the street, the picture of a man in a hurry.

The car hesitated at the curb as the driver checked for traffic and then continued into the street where it stopped before it swung into the right-hand lane to accelerate into the night-shrouded streets of Levittown.

If Carl had the time, he would have killed them all. He did not. He had to get back to his own car to follow the cop before he got away. There was no room for stealth. He stood and sprinted on the balls of his feet. Phyllis Cordova saw the backyard floodlights switch on as the motion detector tripped and she caught a glimpse of movement in her peripheral vision.

"Give it back!" She heard her daughter's strident screech from upstairs. "Mom!"

She hesitated, debating whether or not to investigate the cause of the security light's activation. The commotion on the floor above made her decision.

"Anthony," Phyllis bellowed, "don't tease her. If I have to come up there…" The clamor continued. Taking the steps for the umpteenth time that day, she put the motion detector out of her mind.

Carl gunned the BMW around the corner. The car fishtailed and he fought the wheel to regain control. He almost missed his quarry as he raced through the next poorly lit intersection. Out of the corner of his eye he saw the rectangular taillights down a side street and spun the wheel. Bouncing over the curb, he downshifted as he straightened the car and confirmed that his target was indeed ahead of him.

Staying well back, he followed the detective until Tony pulled into a shopping center on Hempstead Turnpike. Carl watched as Tony locked his car and entered Waldbaum's Supermarket. Without hesitation, he pulled up alongside the empty vehicle and checked to see if anyone was taking notice of his movements. The few people he saw ignored him completely. Quickly, he grabbed the gadget from the seat where he had thrown it and slipped out. On the pavement, he slid to the ground and rolled under the back end of the Chevrolet. In seconds, he had secured the device to the forward vertical wall of the gas tank and gotten back into his car. Immediately, he backed out, drove to a spot some distance from Tony's automobile and parked.

While he waited for the detective to return, he tested the gizmo. A flat plastic box with a five-inch screen in its center lay in his lap. Flipping the rocker switch to ON, he watched the ghostly green display glow to life. A crosshatch image, like a sheet of graph paper with a circle at its center, bisected by two intersecting lines superimposed on the grid, cast a faint green light on his face. A blinking red blob at the bottom of the screen denoted Tony's car.

Beside the primary display was another, similar to a bar graph, showing the range of the target from the receiver, as well as its direction and speed. The last, of course, was listed as zero.

The friendly sales clerk at Spymasters had told Carl that the homer was effective on land at one to two miles, depending on terrain and atmospheric conditions. That would be more than adequate for Carl's purposes.

Cordova returned, burdened with two heavy brown paper sacks. He balanced them on his knee while he unlocked the driver's door, stashed the packages in the back seat, and drove out of the lot. Carl waited until he was out of sight to start his engine. He drove with one hand on the wheel and the other bracing the gizmo. To test the accuracy of the readout, he accelerated, weaving in and out of the traffic on the turnpike until he had the detective's car in sight again. Satisfied that the equipment was performing properly, he dropped back, depending on the electronic bloodhound to keep tabs on his target.

The homer indicated a change in direction. Tony's azimuth changed from westerly to northwesterly to easterly to southwesterly. For a moment, Carl was perplexed, almost panicked, until he saw the large green and white sign that informed motorists of the entrance ramp to the Wantagh State Parkway. As he reached the overpass, he saw the cloverleaf roadway that would account for the confusing shifts in direction. He followed the ramp and was pleased to see the display settle down, showing his prey steadying up on a southerly course. By the time Tony left the parkway, heading west on Merrick Road, Carl had to slow down to avoid overtaking him. When the Chevy once more pulled into a shopping center, Carl began to wonder if he had not misjudged the detective's destination.

This time Tony alighted at the door of a take-out Chinese restaurant. Carl parked at the opposite curb to watch. A pair of Zeiss field glasses—purchased at the same shop as the homing device—allowed him to view Tony's transaction at close range. A wolfish grin spread across Carl's face as he observed the quantity of food being packed into a cardboard box by the effusive Asian woman behind the counter. Unless the cop had a ravenous appetite, he was buying enough food for several people. And, unless this was the best Chinese take-out in the county, he hadn't come all the way down here to feed his family.

When Tony got back on the parkway and again headed south, Carl stayed well behind. The road to Jones Beach was all but deserted.

Could this pig be crafty enough to choose such a lonely stretch of highway to ascertain the presence of a tail? Carl doubted it, but took no chances, making sure to stay far enough back to be undetectable.

At the traffic circle surrounding the famous obelisk-shaped water tower he half expected Tony to double back and proceed north, but the display showed the target traveling east.

"Where are you going?" Carl asked the empty road. It lay like a pale gray ribbon, bathed in pools of golden light from sodium vapor luminaires perched atop antique wooden posts on the verges, like an honor guard. The concrete receded into the distance, straight and flat as a rifle shot. Scrub Pines, bent but unbeaten by the incessant Atlantic wind, stood grouped in herds like wandering herbivores, huddled beside the desolate stretch of cement. Salt grass topped dunes stood poised behind them, ready to wander where wind and wave prodded. Broad expanses of black water on his left and occasional glimpses of foaming surf on his right were the only indications that he was on a beach road rather than a stretch of desert.

The tires created a rhythmic beat as the pneumatic cushions thumped the expansion joints—da-dump, da-dump. Carl heard the beat of a marching tune, written for him alone, the drumming of glorious triumph for the conquering warrior. So enthralled did he become with anticipation of his impending victory, he let the speedometer climb to eighty to increase the tempo.

The glow of taillights ahead brought him out of his ecstasy. He yanked his foot from the gas pedal and watched as the needle wound down to fifty. To be stopped for speeding now would be the ultimate joke. He let the Chevy gain and brought the BMW up to fifty-five, matching Tony's momentum. He locked in the cruise control when the gizmo said his target was a mile beyond.

On through the night they rolled, past Tobay, past Gilgo, past Cedar Beach.

"Where in the hell are you going?"

Carl had just decided that the detective would swing north on the Robert Moses Causeway when he saw the glowing dot begin to converge with the center of the screen. The bar graph agreed: Tony was slackening his pace. Carl was approaching Oak Beach when the screen indicated that the hunted was reversing course. Thinking he had somehow been detected, Carl nearly doused his lights but realized in another moment that such action would only draw attention and he resisted the urge to become invisible. Instead, he slowed and watched for the Chevy's headlights on the far side of the greensward separating the east and westbound lanes. He was doing forty miles per hour when he spied the Celebrity turning into a narrow tree shrouded lane on the north side of the roadway.

He braked, nearly missed the turnoff, and skidded into the right lane exit. Bright lights and blaring music surprised him until he recognized the rambling edifice before him.

"I'll be dipped. The OBI," he hissed. Everyone from his generation that had grown up on Long Island knew The Oak Beach Inn.

He cut the wheel, braked, and rolled into the parking lot. It was sparsely populated, but far from deserted. He parked at the east end, facing the sea wall, past the kiddy playground, just short of the boarded-up snack bar. It looked dejected and abused.

He sat for several minutes with the engine off and the lights out, thinking about what was behind him—four lanes of roadway bisected by a swath of trees and grass, bordered by a narrow expanse of sheltered water. Beyond the channel lay Oak Island.

He had them.

Chapter 42

It's us," Doc whispered. "Open up."

Tony stood beside Doc on the porch, huddling against the nighttime chill, subconsciously looking over his shoulder at the silent dunes.

They heard the clunk of a dead bolt being thrown and stood back as the door of the bungalow creaked open on protesting hinges. Madeline lowered the muzzle of the Mossberg and stepped aside to allow Doc and Tony to enter.

"Taking no chances, I see." Tony stepped over the threshold, grinning.

"I'm sorry. Doc said—"

"No apologies, please," Tony said. "Better safe, as they say."

"Do I smell Chinese?" Madeline said.

Tony leaned forward to sniff her shoulder, saying, "Don't think so. What does a Chinese smell like?"

"I meant the food, you idiot." She laughed.

"Hope you like Cantonese."

"Tony, right now cannibal cuisine would tempt me."

"Looks like I got here just in time." Tony opened his mouth to launch into a monologue.

The grim look on Doc's face said that now was not the time for levity. He stepped aside to let Doc lead the way, winking at Madeline as he passed her.

Doc indicated the door with a jerk of his head. Madeline locked it before following the two men into the living room. She busied herself with arranging containers of food on the coffee table while Doc and Tony dealt out paper plates and cans of Coca-Cola.

“I got plastic forks,” Tony said, digging into one of the grocery bags. “I never could get the hang of chopsticks.”

They were shoveling mounds of oriental delicacies onto their plates, attempting to eat with some modicum of civilized etiquette, when Tony broached the subject of the clandestine meeting.

“Couple things have come up,” he said around a mouthful of chow Mein. “Should I wait until you guys have finished?” His eyebrows arched to accent the question.

The starving diners shook their heads in unison, mumbling through full mouths that he should go on.

“Okay, but I warn you, this is not exactly pleasant dinner repartee.” Doc chomped on an egg roll with such ferocity that Tony added, “Remind me not to let my fingers get near your mouth.” He then related the circumstances of Ron Barbarosa’s murder, leaving out the gory details, mindful of his hosts’ appetites. The booby-trapped door and the peace symbol he used as proof that the murderer was indeed their nemesis. He did not dwell on the ghastly method of the symbol’s application. Next, he told them of Mitch Numkeena’s phone call and the subsequent discovery of the branding iron in Rockville Centre. Producing the list of items found in the ruins of the destroyed home, he noted the remnants of several guns and combat knives, which, he concluded, offered further proof that the tenant was of a sinister bent.

“So,” Doc interjected, “you think that The Terminator and this colonel character are one and the same dude.”

“The fire marshal told me, off the record, that he thinks the blaze was caused by an incendiary device of a military nature. Probably phosphorous, but he hasn’t determined the exact accelerant yet. It lends credence to the theory, I’d say. The branding iron clinches it for my money.”

He unwrapped the soot caked object and set it on the table.

“I’d say so.” Doc concurred.

“You never told me about that part of it,” Madeline said, recoiling from the thing.

“In a case like this one,” Doc explained, “where the perp leaves telltale indications—things that will earmark his work—we usually don’t let on.”

“That kind of information,” Tony told her, “can really muddy the waters if word gets out.”

Her frown of puzzlement caused Doc to clarify. “It’s a sick world, Madeline. Sometimes spectacular crimes spawn copycats. Creeps who are dying to get some measure of fame will imitate the crimes to steal some of the limelight. By not alerting the media to the kinkier aspects of the killer's modus operandi, we can compartmentalize our boy's deeds. Makes catching him easier—sometimes."

Madeline shuddered at the implications.

"You think he was figuring on wrapping this up," Doc asked of Tony, "and figured he'd incinerate his nest before heading for the hills?"

Madeline said, "'Wrapping this up'? You mean killing me, too, don't you?" She dropped her plastic fork onto her half-full plate. "I've lost my appetite."

Doc began to apologize but Tony interrupted him with, "Could be. Or maybe something went wrong. One of his toys could have snafued."

"Possible. Too bad he wasn't home if that's the case."

"We should be so lucky." Leaning back in the Morris chair he had pulled close to the table to partake in the feast, Tony lit a cigarette. "By the way, aren't you two curious to know who this turkey is?"

Madeline gasped. "You mean you've identified him?"

Doc's eyes opened wide, dismayed that his emotional involvement had clouded his thinking, and stunned that he had not realized it immediately.

If they knew where he lived, they must have determined who he was. He sat stock still, willing his friend to end the suspense.

"Not only do we know his name, if it is, in fact, his name; we've got his picture."

Carl lay prone at the edge of a stand of pines and searched the island across the narrow expanse of water with his binoculars. He wished for night vision equipment. The absence of artificial light made observation difficult. There was some moonlight, enough to define objects adequately, but it was by no means bright. He had made it to the trees just in time to see the little cop being rowed across, presumably by his partner, but he lost them in the shrubbery when they beached the boat on the far side. In fact, he still did not know with any certainty if Madeline was over there at all.

She had to be. Nothing else made sense.

Residents of the island sanctuary were nothing if not single-minded in their obsession with simplicity and privacy. There were no streetlights. There were no streets. Development of the flat, kidney shaped, Barrier Island was limited to a mixed bag of fishing shacks, bungalows, and plush beach homes. The only way onto Oak Island was by boat, a further guarantee of exclusivity. Swimming across, dressed as he was, was pure folly. The water, at this time of year, was cold enough to give pause to all but the most avid Polar Bear Club bather. There were several small rowboats and skiffs tied to the dock or beached in the sand on Carl's side of the channel, but he would be vulnerable to detection for the duration of the crossing. Surely, everyone knew everyone else in such a tiny community. If detected, he would be hard pressed to explain away his presence. Four cars in the parking lot and lights showing in three of the ghostly structures across the water told him that his prey were not the sole inhabitants of the seaside retreat.

The little detective's car was behind Carl, parked on the side of the road leading to the barred entrance to the parking lot. The killer had left his BMW at the Oak Beach Inn and walked across the double road, tearing his slacks on a rusty bit of wire when he crashed through an unseen section of snow fence in the trees. While concealed in the bushes, he had replaced his white shirt with a black hooded sweatshirt and pulled on sneakers in place of his shoes. The day's shopping spree had been worthwhile. The duffel bag containing his discarded garments and superfluous gear lay in a copse of trees astride his line of march. He would reclaim it, if he could, on his way back. There was nothing to lead the cops to him if he could not. He had the Greasegun, four clips of ammo, two eight-ounce plastic explosive charges with four-second fuses, blasting caps, a Claymore detonator, a small spool of wire, the .25 caliber pistol, and a Bowie knife he had picked up in a sporting goods store. He had left the Browning under the car's front seat. It was probable that he would be moving fast on his return trip and he might have to ditch the sub-machinegun once the locals were aroused, but he would very possibly need a weapon once he got to his car. It had been difficult to choose which to leave. The Browning was the more accurate weapon but the M-2 gave him firepower, something he might need later if they cut his escape route. That, however, was impossible to foresee. Carl knew there would be at least two armed adversaries on the island and there was just so much hardware he could lug around. The Greasegun won the toss.

He would have preferred more time to reconnoiter the enemy's situation. A fast, quiet boat and a silenced weapon would have been nice, but you can't have everything. The hallmark of a professional warrior was his ability to improvise, was it not? He could improvise with the best of them.

Of primary concern was the topography. Oak Island was an excellent choice from the standpoint of defense as well as attack. The enemy was isolated, but able to observe avenues of approach from all sides. Carl was confident in his ability to advance undetected, but his weaponry worked as much against him as it did for him. He would undoubtedly have fire superiority. At the same time, bursts of automatic fire and the thunderous boom of explosives would rouse the few citizens from their beds. The more heavily populated village of Oak Beach, with its substantial compliment of year-round inhabitants, was at his back, just across the road. Considering the tactical reality that there was but one road by which to make his escape and he was as surely in the trap as were his intended victims. The cops could have a nasty reception waiting if he was forced to drive the Shore Parkway back the way he had come. Robert Moses Causeway was minutes away to the east, but they could have the northbound bridge sealed off before he could get over it. Fire Island, to the southeast, was no option at all. There was no way off. He had no doubt they would block the road behind him and stealing a boat with the bay and the ocean blanketed by coast guard and police craft would be suicide. If he went to ground and attempted to evade through the salt marshes and tidal basin, daylight would overtake him. He could hide for just so long. The concentration of manpower they would bring to bear would undoubtedly flush him from cover. At best, he could expect a vainglorious end in the muck among the rushes and Carl did not see himself going out in a hail of bullets.

ೞೞ

Madeline studied the grainy blow-up of the DMV photo, her brow wrinkled in concentration, her memory rewinding through years gone by.

"There's something about the eyes." She put the picture down on the table and stared assiduously as if the increased distance would heighten her powers of recall.

"What about the name?" Doc asked, trying to keep the tension out of his voice, "Carl Esterbrook," he said, as if hearing it verbalized would add something.

“I’ve never known anyone named Esterbrook. Carl is familiar, but I can think of three or four Carls I’ve known, and none of them bear any resemblance to him.” The way she said the last word sounded like an accusation, a condemnation.

“How about the initials?” Tony suggested. “C.E. Ring any bells?”

“No, I—Why?”

Doc stilled her hands, which she wrung in her lap, by holding them with his own in an effort to calm her.

“Most bad guys,” he said, “adopt aliases that resemble their own name, or at least their initials. Sometimes it’s pure ego. Sometimes it’s to avoid careless slips—like monogrammed shirts or a chance meeting with an acquaintance who might call them by name. They very often keep their given name or use something close to it. You may not have known a Carl Esterbrook, but you might recall something similar. Think.”

“I am. It’s just that I thought I’d recognize him immediately when Tony first mentioned the photo. Dammit. I don’t know who this person is.”

Tony and Doc both shrank into their seats. Disappointment relaxed muscles stiffened by anticipation.

“I can’t shake the feeling,” she said, “that I’ve seen this man more recently, not in the distant past.”

“When?” Doc whispered, afraid to break the intensity of concentration in her face.

“I’m not sure. But not long ago.” She sighed. “I’m sorry. It won’t come.” She rested her forehead on her fingertips. “This guy is familiar, but not very. He looks like an aging hippie. That has significance, but I can’t put my finger on it.” The peace symbol branding iron, blackened and bent, lay on the table next to the photo. “This photo,” she said, stabbing the image with her finger, “and this thing—” She pointed to the branding iron. “—together, complete an equation, somehow.” She sighed. “But I can’t solve it. I know there’s something here, but what won’t click. It’s driving me crazy.”

“Have you given this to Schiff?” Doc turned his attention to his friend, embarrassed for Madeline, changing the focus of the conversation to relieve the pressure on the woman he loved.

Tony nodded, eyes downcast, his thoughts running parallel. “Faxed him the whole ball of wax from the precinct. Told him to get this out to every badge in the tristate area, forthwith. Our friend here will have his kisser plastered everywhere by tomorrow morning. The Lab will air brush out the hair and fool around with the face. They'll scare up the guy's landlord and get him to help. I thought I'd bring this all out to you, rather than wait for tomorrow."

"You did right. Besides, we'd have starved to death by tomorrow. What did you tell Schiff you'd be doing?"

"Looking for you and Madeline, naturally. Said I had some leads, but I didn't want to get his hopes up until I checked them out."

"When they nail this prick, you can report our discovery and be the belle of the ball. Nice move, Sherlock."

"Elementary, my dear Watson." Tony fluttered his eyebrows above a wry grin. "I had to have something to make Needleman forget I stepped on my weenie."

"You didn't?" Doc faked surprise.

"Yep. Stomped it flat. Ran off at the mouth in front of Schiff and the effin' BI guy."

Doc winced.

"But—" Tony raised a finger. "—my intrepid detecting, fingering the perp, and finding the missing sleuth and his attractive significant other—" He indicated the couple with spread hands. "—should go a long way toward restoring my fractured reputation."

"You've got the makings of a senior official."

"I'll forgive that slanderous remark."

The banter was wasted on Madeline. She had heard none of it, they saw, as she gazed, transfixed, at the photograph.

"Hopefully," Tony said, "they'll pick this guy up in short order, and you guys can come back to civilization. I think you should consider coming back with me anyway."

"You know how I feel about that," Doc said.

"Yeah, but we can put a blue wall around you in Mineola. No way this guy can get to you."

Doc scowled. "And Adrienne Boyd will give the son of a bitch a blow by blow of—"

"That's it." Madeline snapped erect.

ꕥꕥ

Carl judged the westerly breeze sufficient to take him across. He estimated he should make landfall at a point near the tip of the island. Lying in the bottom of a rowboat, peeking over the gunwale periodically to check the angle of drift, he hoped that any chance sighting would be unremarkable. With luck, it would cause no more of a stir than a loose boat that had slipped its mooring to be hunted down and reclaimed to the chagrin of its careless owner. Once on the island, he would make a stealthy reconnaissance of each of the occupied homes to determine the location of his prey.

ꕥꕥ

"Fast forward," Madeline urged.

Doc complied, at a loss to understand what she was looking for in the tape of the evening news, but willing to go along.

"Here it comes," she said. "There! Pause it."

He thumbed the button so hard that he looked at the skinny black hunk of plastic in his hand to be sure he had not broken it.

"That's him," Madeline cried. "I knew I wasn't imagining it. I did see him recently. Right here. On the news."

"Adrienne Boyd is Carl Esterbrook—in drag?" Tony squinted at the frozen image, incredulous, his expression doing little to hide his fear that Madeline had snapped under the weight of terror.

"No, no, no. Behind her. The guy skulking against the tree." She shoved past Doc to get to the set. "Him!" Her finger stabbed at the face of the man in the background. "That's who I remembered."

"This guy looks nothing like that photo, Madeline," Doc said. "He's a photographer—one more media puke."

"The eyes," she said. "Look at his eyes."

"I can't even make out the color," Doc frowned. "Can you, Tony?"

"No, but we thought The Terminator might have some connection to the media, didn't we?"

"Forget the color," Madeline snapped. "I know those eyes."

"Madeline, honey, do you know who he is?" Doc's rigid posture suggested that the infrared beam from the slim black box had similarly affected him—paused in motion.

"I know this man," she said, "I'm sure of it. Why can't I remember?" The dejection that crushed her exuberance of seconds before was stunning in its totality. She squeezed her eyes shut, clenched her fists and moaned. A second later, her eyes snapped open and she stood rigid. "Oh, dear Mother of God, it can't be."

ꕥꕥ

The prow of the rowboat bumped gently against the sand. Carl peeked over the gunwale to search the bank for movement. Seeing nothing untoward, he got to his knees, balancing his weight as he stood to place one bare foot over the side. The icy water threatened to cramp his arches as he waded ashore. He sat on the beach with the stink of low tide heavy in his nostrils, massaging his aching feet until he felt the warmth of circulation returning. Only then did he put his sneakers back on. The squishing of wet shoes would be a stupid announcement of his presence to anyone listening for him.

With the stubby Greasegun slung across his chest, the magazines in his pockets, and the explosives in a zippered pouch around his waist, he crept forward, the long-bladed knife held loosely in his right hand. Like a wraith, Carl moved soundlessly, flitting from shadow to shadow, pausing frequently to listen, to smell, to taste the salty air.

The first occupied house was two score yards to his front, right on the water's edge.

ᔓᔕ

"It was the last time we were all together." Madeline, seated on the sofa between the two detectives, began her breathless recounting of that weekend long ago. Her eyes glazed over as she remembered a page from her life she wanted to forget. Staring into the fireplace, she began in a whisper, "It was the summer of nineteen-sixty-nine. Woodstock…"

Doc and Tony sat mesmerized by her tale of the Age of Aquarius come to fruition on the rolling hillsides of a poverty-stricken farm in the Catskills and the shameful episode that ruined it for her. In her eyes, Doc saw the sadness of a dream gone sour, the pain of young idealism shattered by the reality of man's inhumanity to man. He thought of another place half a world away, where he had learned the same lesson, where the beads and flowers were carried in the hearts instead of on the bodies of young dreamers trapped in a brutal portrayal of the slaughter of a generation's innocence.

At the end of her story, Madeline said, "I never spoke to any of them again. I couldn't. I was too ashamed."

"So," Tony said, "you picked this guy up on the way to the festival. He was a little weird but he partied hearty and nobody cared. What makes you think he was a soldier?"

"I asked him why he had a crew cut. He said Uncle Sam was his barber."

"Okay. That sounds like a young troop. So then, at the end of the weekend, he dropped a little acid and freaked on the way home. Ron decked the guy on the side of the road, and you all drove away and left him there. Is that about it?"

Tony's concise summation made the teenagers' actions seem more callous.

"Essentially, yes. That's what happened." She looked stricken.

Doc said nothing, but avoided Madeline's eyes, unsure if what he felt was pity or reproach. All he was sure of was that he knew exactly how she felt.

"And he waited almost thirty years to get even?" Doc blanched. The monstrosity overwhelmed him.

"This guy wrote the book on hate." Tony wagged his head. "Hell, he's made it an encyclopedia."

"Mitch is right," Doc thought aloud, "same guy."

Tony nodded. "John Campbell."

"Has to be," Doc agreed. "That's where we look."

"But not Campbell," Tony cautioned.

"No," Doc said. "Campbell's dead. Our boy took his place. We research the rest of the guys in that unit to find him."

Doc and Tony were resuming their detective roles, cataloguing evidence, sorting facts, planning the investigation, beyond their initial shock, non-judgmental, aloof.

"I didn't want to leave him," Madeline croaked. "I tried to help him. I was afraid to be left behind by myself. God forgive me."

Doc took her in his arms and murmured words of comfort, ashamed of his own fleeting pomposity. She was human, nothing more, and he loved her for it.

"It's okay," he whispered. "It's okay. You were a kid. We all were. It wasn't your fault."

"Madeline," Tony said softly, "can you remember his name?"

"It was Carl. I don't think he ever mentioned his last name. It's funny. I couldn't make the connection even when I saw him on TV just a few hours ago. He hasn't changed that much. Still has the same strange look he had in his eyes even then. That's what brought it back. But I simply could not remember until I forced the memory to come. How could I have so completely blocked him from my consciousness? Or should I say conscience?"

Doc took her hands, and said, “You’re going to need some serious work, lady.”

“Think you can fit me into your schedule?”

“No problem.”

Tony frowned. “I must’ve missed something.”

Chapter 43

The first cottage Carl approached sat on pilings to provide stability in the sand and to afford some protection from storm surge. The entire structure fairly vibrated with the sound of snoring. It didn't seem likely that the people Carl had just seen rowing across the channel would be zonked out so soon after their arrival, but he knew that the more he knew of the occupants of the island, the better. He crept to the back, to an open bedroom window, but the window was out of reach.

He stacked driftwood beneath the window until he had built a precarious platform from which to observe the interior. Bracing himself with his hands flat against the shiplap-sided wall, he raised himself up and seized the windowsill with both hands. Slowly, he lifted his head above the sill until his eyes cleared its upper plane.

Harsh light from a Coleman propane lantern on a night table separating two twin beds clearly defined two sleeping forms sprawled across rumpled sheets. Both male sleepers lay flat on their backs, their bulging bellies rising and falling with their breathing, resembling buoys undulating on a rolling ocean swell. They both wore white T-shirts and boxer shorts, one striped, the other plaid. Both slept on top of the covers. Crushed beer cans lay strewn about the room. The density of mangled aluminum cylinders increased with their proximity to the beds. Rods, reels, tackle boxes, nets and assorted colorful plastic ice chests were stacked neatly in a corner. Carl turned to ascertain the best route to the next dwelling.

“Now that we’ve got something to go on,” Doc poured tea into a chipped ceramic mug and placed it before Madeline, “we probably should get you back to the Puzzle Palace. You can help go through the mug shots in case this Carl guy has a record. Tony and I can try to track him through the military. You say you think he was from Queens?”

“That’s right.” Madeline sipped her tea and blew across the rim of the cup to cool the scalding brew. “I think he said Bayside or Sunnyside, something like that.”

“Mitch should be able to help with the city’s files,” Doc speculated. “The colonel connection is thin, but I bet it’ll pan out. That alone will get Numkeena’s juices flowing. He’ll be glad to pitch in.

“Tony, call Schiff. Tell him where we are and get us a nice big escort to shepherd us back to the fold.”

“He may have to get Suffolk involved, Doc, and let’s not forget the feds.”

“I don’t care if he sends the friggin’ army, navy and marines, so long as they pack plenty of firepower.”

“Amen to that. Consider it done.” Tony crossed to the telephone saying, “We may have to hire Indian guides and a canoe. Could you have found a more desolate spot?”

“Very funny. Make the call.” Doc’s genuine smile felt good. For the first time since this nightmare had begun, he had hope that it would soon end. He tried to convey his newfound peace of mind to Madeline with a nod and a wink, but Tony’s sudden pallor as he lowered the receiver from his ear turned the warm feeling in Doc’s stomach to a block of ice.

“Phone’s dead.”

“Kill the lights,” Doc said, as he reached to draw his gun.

Before anyone could throw a switch, the house went black.

“Tell me you did that,” Tony whispered.

Doc could hear the rustle of cloth as Tony whipped back his jacket, followed by the sound of metal sliding on leather. He had not been aware of the hum of the generator until now, when he could no longer feel its comforting throb.

“Madeline,” Doc whispered, “stay put. Get down on the floor. I’ll come to you. Tony, I’m moving.”

“You’re covered. You think it’s him?”

“Don’t you?” Doc felt his way along the back of the couch.

“How?” Tony said. “No one knew I was coming here.”

"Never mind that now. Just stay down and stay ready."

ꕥꕥ

The Bowie knife had parted the telephone wires under the house as easily as slicing bread. The generator was as simple as pushing the OFF button. Staying crouched, Carl eased one foot onto the weather-beaten back steps. When he transferred his weight, the smooth board squeaked. The small sound was like an alarm in the silence. The bottom panel of the door above him erupted. He felt hot wind muss his hair and heard the whine of tiny steel pellets whizzing past his scalp. A blizzard of splinters showered down on his shoulders. He fell over backward in the sand, the blast of the shotgun ringing in his ears.

ꕥꕥ

Doc muttered, "Police officer, freeze," and jacked another shell into the Mossberg's breach.

He had loaded the weapon with alternating rounds—double-ought buck, slug, double- ought, etcetera. It was something he had learned from a point man in Nam. The buckshot was first because you would usually snap shoot the initial blast to get your opponent's head down and, it was hoped, wing him with the widely dispersed pellets. The slug was to finish him off. The theory was: if you didn't get him with the first two rounds, he would probably get you.

No return fire came from the steps outside the kitchen door. Doc listened for all he was worth, opening his mouth and rotating his head slowly to enhance his auditory perception, another trick he had learned in the jungle. He was lying flat on the floor, his shoulder braced against the jam in the living room doorway with the shotgun trained on the shattered back door eight feet away across the kitchen. Willing his heart to slow in order to quiet the hammering in his ears, he waited. Madeline lay against his back, curled up in a tight fetal ball, trembling and biting her hand to keep from screaming. He smelled the salty dust embedded in the rug and heard a cricket chirp amid the faint thunder of the surf.

"Did you get him?" Tony whispered from his position in front of the couch where he laid, gun in hand.

"Don't know," Doc whispered back.

"I hope it wasn't the paper boy," Tony said.

"It's him. I know it."
"Do you happen to know what we're going to do next?"
"Did you bring the cell-phone?"
"Shit."
"I'll take that as a negative."

ശരശര

Outside, Carl rolled under the house, grateful to the builder for setting it on stilts. The pilings raised the floor of the structure approximately four feet above the sand at the rear of the bungalow, graduating upward to what he judged to be six feet at the front. Wood latticework in front and on the sides, broken in several places, covered the gap between the sand and the underside of the house. The back had been left open, probably to allow access to plumbing and wiring.

He could put a few bursts into the floorboards in hopes of hitting the defenders or driving them out. That would expend much of his meager supply of ammunition and bring unwelcome attention to his endeavors. The shotgun's report had aroused no one so far.

There was always the easy way. Rig charges to the pilings, back off behind a dune and blow them to Hell. That would surely arouse anyone within earshot and he wasn't ready to abandon his plan to get Madeline up-close-and-personal.

If he could get inside, he might be able to take them out without further gunfire. Maybe he could kill the few others on the island afterward. The drunken anglers would be child's play. Although he had not checked the last occupied house, he had no doubt that its inhabitants would be less than a match for him.

The thought was delicious. The headlines would be classic. TERMINATOR FELLS OAK.

First things first.

ശരശര

Inside, flickering coals in the fireplace produced a glow causing shadows to dance and attract the eye, as well as backlighting the three people hiding in the living room.

Doc whispered, "Tony, can you douse that fire?"

Sparks whirled and steam hissed as Tony lobbed opened soda cans into the hearth.

"Doc," he said, "we can't stay here, man. We'll be sitting ducks if he's got his toys with him."

Doc nodded in the darkness, gripped the shotgun tightly in one hand and reached back to pat Madeline's hip with the other.

"We're going out after him." He felt her stiffen despite his gentle tone. "We have to. Tony's right. This guy likes to blow things up. He could be setting charges right now. Our only chance is to get outside." The word suddenly held as much terror for him as he had seen earlier in Madeline's eyes.

"I'm so scared," she whimpered.

"I know. Me too. Don't worry. We've done this before." He hoped she did not realize how long ago. He wondered if the old reflexes were still sharp enough to matter. "Just stay down and stay behind me. We'll crawl to the door. I'll go first. You watch me and do exactly as I say. No hesitation. Clear?"

He heard her long quivering breath and felt her hand squeeze his arm.

"Tony, you've got the front. Let's go."

They inched toward the exits. At the splintered panel, Doc craned his neck to peer through the jagged hole, careful not to let his head protrude. His field of vision was limited but the risk involved in sticking his head out was too great. If Carl was waiting beside the door he could be decapitated before he got the chance to react.

He listened. Nothing. Stillness.

ꕥ

In the sand beneath the floorboards, Carl's ears pricked up like a predator hot on the heels of an elusive meal. He heard the creak and crack of old wood above him.

Moving!

Two distinct patterns gradually became evident.

Front and back. Flanking move. Not today, boys and girls.

The shotgun was in back. Deal with the heavier firepower first? Logical, but conventional. Do the unexpected.

Scurrying between the posts beneath the house, he scrambled to the front, to a hole in the latticework big enough for a man to squeeze through. Carl wriggled his body through the breach and crawled on hands and knees to a woodpile twenty feet from the front porch. He took a kneeling shooter's pose behind the stack, leveled his sights at the front door, and hit the magazine release to unseat the thirty-round clip. The weapon had no selector switch. It fired fully automatic. By leaving one round in the chamber, he could fire a single shot. With a tap on the base of the magazine, he could reload and release the bolt in one swift movement and be ready to fire again.

He wanted to avoid firing bursts, if possible. The Greasegun was a blaster with plenty of knockdown power but the recoil made it hard to control and with no flash suppressor, it would advertise his position. His hope of taking them all with the knife was forgotten. The blade rode on his hip.

ക്ക

Doc, sitting with his back to the wall beside the back door, reached up with his left hand, twisted the knob and pulled. The door refused to budge.

Damn! The lock!

His knees creaked as he got slowly to his feet. He slid the bolt back while motioning Madeline to stay down. The scraping of metal against metal sounded inordinately loud. Such forgetfulness did little to bolster his confidence in his ability to do what he was about to attempt. Staring into the blackness, Doc tried in vain to see how Tony was progressing. Ranger School was long ago and his misgivings were innumerable. Tony had had a lot less training. Doc suddenly realized how little he knew of his friend's wartime experiences. Was he setting up his brave little pal to be killed?

"Tony," he whispered, surprised at the dryness of his mouth.

"Yo," Tony whispered back from beside the front door.

"You up for this?"

"We're about to find out. On three. One—two—three."

In one motion, Doc swung the broken door inward and dove over the short porch into the sand. He rolled and came up in a crouch, the Mossberg leveled and swinging in short arcs, his head following the barrel.

Madeline appeared in the doorway, poised to jump. He shot a hand up to halt her and waved her down in the next motion. She dropped to the floor, ducked back, and peeked around the door jam, eyes wide, lips parted, panting.

Doc realized the black cavern beneath the house was the most opportune place for his enemy to hide. As he had learned in the bush, he used the enhanced acuity of peripheral vision to gather any available light and searched its inky depths. With a quick look behind him at the shadowy dunes and brush, he fought panic. Was the guy alone? Did he have an accomplice covering his back?

What else hadn't he thought of? Was his ineptitude going to cost Madeline's life?

His decision made, he beckoned her to follow, keeping the gun trained on the darkness. When he felt her body press close to his back, he waddled into the shadows, the shotgun held firmly in both hands. Madeline matched his movements like a conjoined twin.

Under the house now, he prodded her to move to where her back would be against the generator room. Doc took up position in front of her, kneeling in the damp sand, trying to penetrate the gloom with his senses.

ᘓᘓ

Out front, behind the woodpile, Carl's mind galloped. Seconds seemed like minutes. He was ravenously hungry and he didn't know why. His stomach made him think of a potato. He should have brought one. A spud jammed onto the muzzle of his weapon would make an adequate silencer. It was only good for one shot, but that was all he needed.

Stop it! Concentrate! No time for daydreaming. They are coming for you.

The front door opened a crack and then swung wide. Hinges whined. Carl shuddered, ecstatic. Combat, at long last. He loved it.

ᘓᘓ

Tony slithered onto the porch with his pistol held at arm's length and his head swiveling, trying to see everything at once. He lay motionless for a minute with his heart pounding against the sand blasted wood, breath coming in gasps, mouth like the Sahara. He rose up on his elbows to see past the edge of the boards. There were marks in the sand. They led to a pile of logs that was little more than a gray blob in the quarter-moon light.

A tongue of orange flashed from the woodpile. Something slammed into his chest like a pile driver, lifting him to his knees. He tried to bring his gun up. His vision narrowed as if he were looking through a pipe. Cold sweat burst from every pore in his body. His chest felt like a granite fist had punched through to his backbone. He was nauseated. The steps at the end of the porch were rushing at him. His arm swung reflexively to break his fall and he pitched end over end down the stairs.

ꕥꕥ

Carl ducked back. One down. His head was swimming. He was giddy with euphoria. His penis stirred in his pants. This was the best.

Stop! Think! Not over yet. There's still the shotgun. Draw him out. Bring him to me!

He ran, tucked into a ball, away from the house, toward the fishermen's place.

ꕥꕥ

Doc heard the shot and a heavy clattering sound. Did Tony get him? It sounded like a forty-five. "Tony? You all right?"

He heard a moan, and then, "Medic."

"Tony!"

Doc was up like a track star out of the blocks, dodging pilings that loomed up out of the blackness like hurdles. He saw a shape through the lattice, in stark contrast to the sand, resembling a large sack of cement that had fallen off a truck at the foot of the steps. He crashed through the rotting wood with the force of a college lineman going up the middle.

His friend lay crumpled in the sand. Blood oozed tar-like into the grains. Doc gently eased him on his side to try to see the wound in the darkness. He felt a warm, sticky, spreading stain on Tony's chest and heard a gurgling sound escape his lips. Madeline fell to her knees beside them.

"Sucking chest wound," he told her. "He can't breathe."

"I'll get the bandages," Madeline said calmly. She was gone before he could stop her, running up the steps into the house.

The son of a bitch is still out there. Where?

ꕥꕥ

Carl lay in wait behind a dune for the other cop to come after him. It was what they did. Gotta catch the bad guys. He would take him out as he came. This was great! He slapped the clip into the weapon. A three-round burst would finish the other one. To hell with the noise. Once both armed opponents were down, he would kill Madeline with the knife. His finger tightened on the trigger and he held his breath to hear the approaching footfalls.

After twenty seconds had elapsed, he chanced a look and saw two figures huddled over a third in front of the stairs. A moment later, the woman ran up the steps.

Madeline! Alone? Yes!

He whipped the Bowie Knife from its scabbard, threw the gun onto his back and bolted, running an elliptical path through the dunes to circle behind the house, the submachine gun bouncing on its sling in time with his pumping legs.

ꕥꕥ

Madeline was back in less than a minute. To Doc it was an eternity. She thrust gauze, tape and antiseptic into his hands and snapped on a flashlight she had found by accident. The light worried Doc, but he needed it. He tried to shield it with his body as he worked. She did the same, her eyes darting everywhere, searching for the animal that hunted them.

"Where is he?" she moaned.

"Nearby, I'm sure."

"What is he waiting for?"

"I don't know." He tied the bandage off and said, "There." Blood bubbled from Tony's lips. "Shit! No good. I need to seal the wound. Stop the air from escaping. Gotta be air tight, like plastic."

"I'll get it." She jumped to her feet.

"Take this." He slapped the Mossberg into her hands. "Hurry!"

Again, she ran up the steps. Doc jerked his pistol from its holster and thumbed the hammer back. The solid feel of the familiar iron did nothing to calm him.

"Where are you, you son of a bitch?" He shivered. His shoulders had never felt so broad, his back so naked, his shirt so thin.

ꕥꕥ

Carl shrank into the shadows of the kitchen. Where was she? Gone? So soon? Wait. Someone coming in the front. Madeline? Please.

The light step told him it was she. He could almost smell her. His mouth watered. His loins ached.

ᏋᏜᏋᏜ

Madeline's thoughts stampeded through her brain as she tried to remember the layout of the house. Anything plastic. Flexible. Air tight. And then it came to her. Bread bag! Kitchen! She barked her shin on the coffee table. Why didn't I bring the flashlight?

She nearly ran into Carl's arms.

ᏋᏜᏋᏜ

Euphoria almost overwhelmed him. So sudden. Better than he had hoped for. She was coming right at him. He took an involuntary step back, his sub-conscious wanting to savor the moment. His buttocks struck the kitchen table. Something fell. Smashed.

Carl lunged. Madeline screamed and threw her body aside as his black shape hurtled toward her. He slashed at her; felt the blade stick and glance off. He slipped in something wet, lost his balance and crashed to the floor.

Madeline felt something slice into her side. She fell on her back, dropped the shotgun and flailed at her assailant in the dark, kicking, punching and clawing. Her foot slammed hard into something solid and the jolt sent a bolt of pain from her toes to her knee. She heard him grunt.

Carl saw stars. His temple ached. He was stunned.

Madeline felt the table leg and pulled herself to her knees. She spun, sobbing, and scrambled to her feet to run back the way she had come. Her side was on fire. Just as she threw her body forward, a hand clamped on her ankle.

Dazed, Carl held fast. His free hand scuttled across the floor like a panicked spider, sweeping the area, frantic to find the knife. His eyes bulged in the darkness of the kitchen, rage building with each passing second. He smelled her blood. He would hack her to pieces, butcher her like a cow. He looked up in time to see a dull glint of steel a split second before the coffee pot clanged against the back of his skull. Head throbbing, fighting to stay conscious, he felt more than heard the receding pounding of her feet on the floorboards. He rolled onto his back, groggy, his vision blurry. The Greasegun beneath him brought him sharply to his senses. He threw an arm out to right himself. His fingers brushed the Bowie Knife.

In a flash, he was on his feet, knife in hand. "Now," he rasped, "slice and dice time, bitch." With everything but vengeance erased from his mind, he charged.

Seconds before, outside, at the foot of the steps, Doc thought of Vietnam as he saw Madeline disappear into the house. What did we do in the jungle? Never had enough dressings. He looked down at Tony and thought of the many times this had happened to him before. He mentally snapped his fingers. Cigarette wrapper!

He dug into his shirt pocket, yanked the pack out, tore it open, and neatly covered the bloody gauze with the cellophane. With strips of adhesive tape, he sealed the perimeter. The gurgling stopped. Tony breathed; it was shallow, labored, but breathing. Tears clouded Doc's eyes.

He heard Madeline scream. A crash of glass, a heavy thud. He had just laid Tony's head against the step and gotten to his feet when she hurtled through the doorway, caromed off the wooden railing and toppled into his arms.

A figure crashed through the front window, bounced on the porch planks and leapt to its feet, snarling like a maddened animal. Eyes aflame with bloodlust, Carl reared up, brandishing the knife.

Doc fired. The beast spun, lurched over the railing, and cartwheeled into the sand.

Carl gasped for air and felt sand grate his teeth. The shock of the bullet, followed by the fall, had knocked the wind out of him. He couldn't move. The pain in his chest was intense. He felt as if he had been walloped by a telephone pole. His left foot was cocked at an odd angle. His body wouldn't work. His enemy was behind him. He waited for the slug to slam into his back. It didn't come. He blinked to clear the sand from his eyelids and saw it.

With every ounce of will he could muster, Carl concentrated on his right foot. When the toe of his shoe finally moved, he kicked sand over the Bowie Knife.

Chapter 44

Is he dead?"

Madeline watched the broken heap in the sand, its back twisted, its neck bent at an odd angle, one arm stretched out past its head, its ear to the ground, its face hidden from them.

Doc kept his automatic pointed at the center of mass, at a spot dead center in the small of Carl's back and shifted his position to disentangle himself from Madeline. Her gasp of pain startled him. With the gun still aimed at Carl's spine, he leaned back and examined Madeline in quick glimpses, flicking his eyes away and back as he tried to maintain a bead on the man in the sand.

"You're hurt," he said. "What happened in there?"

"He cut me," she said. "It's superficial."

In the dim light he could see a glistening black wetness spreading on her blouse. Switching the gun to his left hand, he probed the wound with his fingers. He felt warm blood and the edges of a long laceration. She stifled a scream when his fingers entered the wound.

"Superficial my ass," he said. "Your rib cage is slashed. It's practically to the bone." Still keeping the gun pointed in Carl's general direction, Doc helped her to sit on the lowermost step, beside Tony's supine form. Once he had eased her down, he checked Tony's pulse and turned back to her, saying, "That wound needs attention. Just sit quietly and let me patch you up."

Putting pressure on the wound with her own hands, she pulled the skin together and said,

"I'm all right. It looks worse than it is." She winced, jerked her head toward Carl, and said through clenched teeth, "See if he's dead. Look after Tony." She sat back against the steps and pointed to Carl with her chin. "Please. Make sure he can't hurt us anymore."

"Okay, but stay still," he said, getting to his feet. He walked one step at a time, the gun held in a two-handed combat point. As he got close to the still form, it moved. He froze and fixed the head in his sights.

Carl groaned. Doc shuffled closer. His most avid wish was for the guy to make some threatening motion. A little voice in his head was chanting: Kill him. Kill him! KILL HIM!

The eyes fluttered. The beast turned to look into the bore of the pistol inches from his head.

"Congratulations, cop. You hit me. Been practicing?"

An evil sound escaped from Carl's throat. Doc scowled, trying to place the strangely familiar, yet eerie, nerve grating noise. And then he realized that Carl was laughing. It enraged him.

"If anything moves but your mouth," Doc snarled, "I'm going to blow your head off. What's so funny, asshole?"

"I have the right to remain silent." Carl's voice was high pitched. "Anything I say will be used against me in a court of law. I have the right to an attorney. If I cannot afford one, an attorney will be provided me at no cost to myself." Carl was laughing hysterically now. His body shook with it until the pain made him choke. "Not to worry. I can afford my own lawyer. Hell, I might even be able to buy yours."

Doc rammed the muzzle of the nine-millimeter into Carl's jaw, under the ear.

"You have the right to die, motherfucker," he hissed, "right here, right now."

"Humorless," Carl snorted. "Typical."

The killer's utter disregard for Doc's rage and his own fragile mortality was baffling to the detective.

"You're insane," Doc whispered.

"Thank you. So kind of you to notice. But I prefer ex-sane, if you don't mind. Now, call an ambulance, pig. I'm hurt. I think you broke my collarbone. My ankle isn't feeling so hot either."

Doc kept the gun pressed to Carl's cheek and roughly pulled the killer's arms behind his back with his free hand. Carl screamed.

"Dammit," Carl spat through clenched teeth, "I told you; my collarbone's fractured."

"Tough shit." Doc reached for the small of his back, where he kept his handcuffs. They were not there. He had left them in his locker. He grabbed the Greasegun, flipped the sling over Carl's head, and tossed the weapon behind him to land at Madeline's feet. Without regard for his prisoner's comfort, he patted him down hard. The spare magazines he flipped after the Greasegun. The tiny .25 automatic he slipped into his pants pocket. The belly pouch containing the explosives, he gingerly undid and pulled free. With the pouch braced between his knees, he zipped it open.

"What have we here?" he said. "Were you planning to leave another of your surprise packages behind after you killed Madeline?"

"I have the right to remain silent, remember?"

"Oh, I haven't forgotten, and I promise you, you will remain forever silent if either one of those people dies." He jabbed the muzzle of his weapon viciously into Carl's temple. "Where's the knife, scumbag?"

"I must have lost it. It's been a busy evening."

Carl's smug grin infuriated Doc. He tossed the bag toward the steps.

"Don't you move, asshole. I'm going to check on my friends. This gun will be pointed at you all the time. Flinch and I'll put a hole in you your inflated ego would fall through."

"I'll wait. Take your time."

Doc walked backward until he saw Madeline beside him. Squatting, he brushed her cheek with his fingertips.

"How you doing?" he asked.

"A little dizzy. Stomach's queasy. How bad is he?"

"Carl? Humph. Not bad enough. I hit him in the shoulder. His collarbone is broken. Son of a bitch is laughing at me. He's actually blasé about all this. I oughta—"

"Don't. Please." He saw the pain in her eyes, glowing like white-hot coals in the faint moonlight. "No more killing."

His own anger had not subsided enough for the rational man to return until he saw the plea in her tear-filled eyes, her soul-deep sickness of it all.

"Yeah." He let out a long breath. "Enough. Let me patch you up and then we'll see about getting some help."

"Him first."

"What?"

"You've got to stop the bleeding or he'll go into shock with that much trauma."

Doc started to protest, but her eyes stopped him. She had enough goodness in her for them both. He shook his head.

"Where's the shotgun?" he asked.

She looked around as if it might be somewhere in the sand, shook her head and said, "I must have dropped it in the house."

"Take this." He gave her his pistol. "Don't take your eyes off him. Shoot him if he moves. Can you do it?"

Her head bobbed once.

He turned to Tony and scooped up the remains of the medical supplies. Tony's eyes were open. His breathing was ragged.

"How's the boy?" Doc said.

"I'm shot, dammit. Whadya think? I wouldn't want to be in your shoes, though."

Doc stopped, confused.

"Phyllis is gonna kick your ass for getting me hurt."

"Just don't die on me or she'll really be pissed."

"Promise." Tony did a feeble Boy Scout oath with his right hand.

"So that's how it goes."

Tony's gun was missing and he, too, was minus his cuffs. Some ace crime fighters. Madeline stopped him when he eased her arm aside to examine the wound.

"I said, him first." She motioned toward Carl with her head.

"Not a chance."

"Doc, I feel partially responsible for him, for the way he is. I turned my back on him once. Look what happened."

With an exasperated sigh, he set bandages aside on the step for her and took the rest to Carl. As he approached the wounded man, he realized Carl still scared him. Doc sensed that he was not so helpless as he appeared to be. Unblinking, hate filled eyes locked on Doc's face as he ministered to the killer's wound. The bullet had ricocheted off the collarbone, shattering it, but it had not penetrated. There was a ragged gash, a lot of blood, and most certainly tremendous pain, but it was far from life threatening. Doc was sorry he had not hit him squarely in the head.

Fashioning a pressure dressing on the bullet wound and doing his best to leave Madeline a clear field of fire, he looked into that murderous face. The evil was unmistakable, even through the mask of pain.

"You're wondering why," Carl said softly.

"No, I'm not. I know why. Because you're a sick, sadistic asshole. What I don't know is why pond scum like you never seem to quit. There's always another one. You're like cancer. Malignant aberrations."

“Ah, eloquence, oinker style.” Carl snorted. “You’re pathetic”

“Shut your fucking mouth, or I’ll pack this with sand, prick.”

“Excellent.” Carl did a short bow with his head and his eyelids drooped to heighten the effect. “I’ll have to remember that one.”

Doc could see in Carl’s eyes how badly he wanted to kill him. He knew that feeling. He had had it in Vietnam every time one of his team died. It manifested itself in physical discomfort—a burning sensation in the belly that spread to the bowels. So much rage emanated from Carl that Doc could almost feel the heat. He could not resist taunting him. “Don’t get pissed off, laughing boy, you’re liable to get pissed on.”

Carl’s glowering silence gave Doc a minor sense of victory. Finished, he dragged Carl to the lattice and propped his back against it, ignoring the wounded man’s cries.

“Stay put,” he ordered and went back to Madeline.

“Now can I keep you from bleeding to death?” he said.

She lifted her left arm obligingly but kept the gun on Carl with her right hand.

As he painstakingly raised her blouse to dress the wound, he shook his head, saying, “I can’t believe no one heard any of this. I thought there’d be wall to wall cops here by now.” He wrapped a length of gauze around her midriff and said, “Excuse me,” as he lifted one breast with the back of his hand to position the bandage.

She smiled through her pain, and said, “Watch it buster, my boyfriend’s a cop.”

“Wouldn’t you know it?” he said, “just my luck.” He twisted his head and motioned with his chin, causing Madeline to look across the water at the darkened buildings. The OBI had closed. The scene across the channel was serene. “I guess the younger generation doesn’t have the stamina of their predecessors.”

“What time is it?” she asked.

The cracked ice that used to be his watch crystal told him nothing. He shrugged.

“You do nice work, Doc,” she said, admiring the professional job he had done on the bandage.

“Wait right here,” he told her. Bending to retrieve the Greasegun, he added, “Don’t take your eyes off that son of a bitch.” He wiped sand from the sub-machinegun with the tail of his shirt, checked the bolt, blew a puff of air into the chamber to dislodge any grains, and climbed the steps two at a time.

He was back in a moment with the Mossberg.

"I'm going to find a house with a phone," he said. "I hate to leave you two, but Tony sure can't go, and I don't think you should move either. Both of you need a doctor—a real one. Don't take your eyes off our friend over there. He's still dangerous. Remember that. Don't get any closer to him." He jacked the slug from the chamber and loaded buckshot. "Blast him if he twitches," he commanded, placing the gun in her hands and taking back his own.

He figured she would stand a better chance with the shotgun. He did not think she would be able to handle the sub-machinegun and she might miss with his pistol if she had to shoot quickly. The .25 was a popgun. All she would need to do with the Mossberg was point and pull the trigger. A blind man with palsy could not miss at this range.

Carl's grinning leer, as Doc stopped to check on him, made him think again of shooting him, just to be on the safe side. But he knew Madeline would never forgive him. The thought of her seeing him as the same kind of monster as Carl made him dismiss the idea.

There is one way to better the odds.

Snatching the explosives pouch from the sand, he stepped quickly to the wounded prisoner and knelt beside him.

"Let's see what's in the goody bag, eh, Colonel?"

The flash of fury in Carl's eyes told Doc that Mitch Numkeena was going to be a happy camper. He rummaged through the sack with one hand, keeping the Sig firmly in Carl's face with the other.

"Just what the doctor ordered," he said, pulling a little coil of wire from the case.

Carl grit his teeth as Doc wound the wire tightly about his wrists. He would have preferred to bind his hands behind his back but the shattered collarbone would be torture and Madeline was watching. Carl was sweating profusely when he finished.

"Whatsa matter, buddy boy?" Doc whispered. "Hurt? Good."

With Carl's hands secure, Doc shouldered him away from the lattice and set to rigging something behind the wounded man.

"So," Doc said as he worked, "where'd you learn your dirty tricks, Carl? Nam?"

"What would you know about it?" Carl cocked his head and looked at Doc's face. "Hey, you're a brother vet, aren't you, cop? Welcome home, brother."

"You're no brother of mine." Doc worked quickly behind the bound prisoner. "So, what was it? CIA? Mercs?"

"If I tell you, I'll have to kill you."

"Funny man. Special Forces jokes, huh? That it? Green beanie? A snake eater?"

"I have the right—"

"To remain silent. Yeah, yeah, I know." Doc reared back and pulled Carl by the biceps, planting him firmly in the sand with his back against the latticework. Carl moaned.

"Oops. Sorry about that," Doc lied. "I've rigged a little surprise for you this time, Carl. Thanks for supplying the materials. There's a small block of plastique under your tail. Not enough to blow you to smithereens, just enough to vaporize your tailbone and splatter your ass all over the beach. You won't die right away. Maybe not at all. But you'll need a wheelbarrow to get around in for the rest of your life. So, be a good boy and don't move."

As he rose to leave, he said, "Oh, and I know those are four second fuses. Screwed 'em right out of grenades, didn't you? Don't think you can outrun it, smartass. The charge is hooked to your belt. The pin is tied to the fence. If you get up, you'll arm it and take it with you." Doc treated Carl to his most malevolent grin, fluttered his eyebrows and said, "Don't even fart, shithead."

He went back to Madeline and Tony. They were weak, but he would be back soon. Before he left, he kissed Madeline's brow and whispered, "I'd drag him along, but his ankle's banged up, maybe broken. Hang on. I'll be right back," he promised. He set the flashlight on the steps and aimed its beam to bathe Carl in white, halogen brilliance. "Just don't get within his reach."

The anglers' shack was the closest building showing light. He could have broken into any of the nearer dwellings but there was no telephone wire evident to any of the surrounding homes. He threw Carl a wink as he passed and was rewarded with a brooding scowl.

"Interesting fellow, Detective Wiley," Carl said, conversationally, once Doc was out of earshot.

Madeline said nothing.

Suddenly, Carl sucked air through his teeth, stiffened, and groaned.

"Try to sit still," she said. "He'll be right back. Moving around will only make your pain worse."

Carl grinned at her, saying, "Florence Nightingale, I presume."

He grimaced, shut his eyes, and shifted his position slightly. The movement of his heels digging into the sand and the slow thrust, pushing his body imperceptibly backward, was cleverly disguised.

The pain in his ankle made his skull throb. He happily endured it. Sprained, he decided, but not broken.

Madeline leveled the barrel of the shotgun at him, resting the handgrip on her knee, her finger on the trigger.

Carl glanced casually at her weary face, ignoring the menacing pose.

"This is all your fault, you know." He said it so matter-of-fact that her breath caught in her throat. "If you'd dropped that acid like you were supposed to, instead of leaving it for me, none of this would have happened."

Hot tears sprang into her eyes. "I know," she choked.

He felt a rusty nail scratch his spine. Squirming as if to find a comfortable position he felt the wire securing the charge to his belt snag on the point of the steel spike. Relaxing, he felt it pull.

"It must be awful to have that on your conscience," he said.

She spluttered with rage. "You're a psychopath." It came out in a hiss.

"Precisely. That's why I'm going to get away with it." His head bobbed as a wave of dizziness washed over him. He could not pass out. He had to fight off shock, gather his strength. "The bleeding-heart lawyers," he continued, "and the sophomoric media will wring their hands and demand I be packed off to a mental institution for treatment and salvation." The plan was taking shape as he talked, keeping her off balance, teetering between outrage and disbelief. "I'll be the subject of any number of scholarly papers on psychoses and sociopathic disorders. Great men of medicine will study me. They'll cream in their drawers at the chance to interview me." His face twisted up as pain renewed its assault.

Madeline was speechless.

He saw a chance. If he could mesmerize her with his words, he might be able to scoop up the knife and lunge.

No. That wouldn't work. His ankle would not support him well enough to make the leap. He had to disarm her first, and quickly, before the cop came back.

"Do you disagree?" he asked. He knew he had to keep hammering, affronting her morality. "This is the age of blamelessness, you know. No one is responsible for his actions, no matter how gruesome their deeds." He whined, "It's Mommy and Daddy's fault. It's society's fault. It's your fault." He laughed until the pain in his chest brought tears to his eyes.

“They’ll lock you away forever,” she snapped.

“Will they? In time, they will come to know me as a friend, these intellectual men of medicine. They will relax, lulled by my insights. In a few years, if I cannot convince them I am cured, I will simply wait until they drop their guard and kill a few of them when I make my escape. I’ve done it before. I’ll do it again.

“You know something?” His tone changed. He went from kill-crazy animal to conversational companion in a blink. “All through this, I’ve been worrying about an encore. Something at your friend Cordova’s home struck a chord. You look surprised. How did you think I found you?” The beast was back, as suddenly as it had gone. “I bugged the stupid flat-foot’s car. I was in his back yard. I watched his sniveling brats run wild. I saw that dumpy slut he calls a wife wave bye-bye to her idiot mate.”

Madeline was having difficulty breathing. Her eyes went to Tony, searching for support, but he had slipped into unconsciousness. She looked toward the darkened dunes, as if she could will Doc to return. While Madeline was distracted, Carl undid the buckle on his military belt. Palming the smooth rectangle of brass in his hand, he pulled the serrated clasp that fastened it to the canvas belt with his thumbnail and let it drop into the sand between his legs. Now, there was nothing to prevent the belt from sliding easily through the loops when he made his move. If it hung up, he was finished. He’d chance it. Jackknife forward. Ignore the pain. Grab the knife. Fling it in a two-handed arc at her head. She would duck and miss the first shot. That was all he would need. Bad ankle and all, he would be on her before she could reload. Gouge her eyes out. Yank her tongue from her head. Choke the last breath from her body. His wrists were bound but his fingers were deadly.

Then what? Improvise on the fly. They would never catch him. Just keep talking. She’s on the edge.

“The germ of an idea was born in that prefab heaven the working slobs call Levittown,” he said, pontificating, enjoying the utter disgust evident by the look on her face. His eyes shown as the fires of Hell when he said, “You see, the rush is not from the killing. Sure, that’s a kick, but the real mind blower is pain—the delicious agony of the spirit that violent death leaves in its wake. That’s the ultimate high. I didn’t know it until now. The devastation in your beautiful eyes, I can see it even in the dark. It’s exquisite.

“Therefore—” He raised his chin to tell the world, “—The Terminator will target the families of his victims when next he stalks the earth. No more paltry, single kills. I’ll wreak havoc on the innocents and revel in the aftermath.” He turned to stare into Madeline’s eyes, a wild, predatory thing, hungering for sustenance. “And I have you to thank.”

Madeline’s finger tightened on the trigger.

“Oh dear!” The friendly banter was back, but with an edge. “I think your cop friend has stopped breathing.”

Madeline’s eyes dropped to Tony. His eyes were closed. He was very still. She bent to check his pulse. As she did so, the muzzle of the shotgun rose.

ꕥꕥ

The foggy headed fishermen were still sorting out what the wild-eyed guy with the Tommy gun in his hand had been raving about. They popped the ring tops of some fresh suds and watched him slam down the phone and run headlong into the night. The screen door banged sharply closed in his wake. The older of the two scratched his belly, belched mightily, and asked of his friend, “Who’d Rambo say got shot?”

“Wasn’t you or me,” his buddy yawned. “I’m goin’ back to bed. It’ll be in the papers in the morning.”

ꕥꕥ

For Doc, fatigue was setting in. Adrenaline was wearing off. It was over. The chopper would be here in minutes, maybe by the time he got back to Madeline and Tony. There was a hospital just across the bay. They would have a real vacation now, in the Bahamas, or maybe Mexico. He had always wanted to see Chechen Itza. He would marry her if she’d have him. Tony would be his best man. Cordova would get a kick out of that. He might even stop ragging him.

He felt good. At last, his life was turning around.

As he jogged to the crest of a dune, he heard the flat crack of the Mossberg. Cursing the loose sand that slowed him, he ran twenty yards with tears clouding his vision before he heard a muffled explosion and then another shotgun report.

Chapter 45

Doc popped the tab on another can of Miller Genuine Draft and cast a sidelong look at the newly installed adjustable shelves gracing his living room wall. He was weary of this game of make-work, pretending to be doing something that needed doing now that he had the time. It was a habit he had developed in Vietnam that had saved his sanity often since. When the whole world was turning to shit, when the only sensible course of action was to quit, do something. Anything that sparked the tiniest glint of accomplishment would suffice. The most trivial tasks would have worth far beyond their importance. It was simple, really. Create meaning by achievement. His books needed to be organized, which meant a place for them to be so organized, which meant erecting the shelves.

Purpose, that was what he had to have, and maybe another six-pack.

In truth, time was all he had. Life without The Job was proving to be unbearable. The only thing he could imagine that might make this existence—this limbo—meaningful was lost to him, possibly forever.

At least she was alive.

He looked at the book in his hands—a thick volume about sculpture and its place in the modern world—and wondered what had once made him cherish it. His gaze drifted to the dusty plastic drape across the studio doorway. He had not entered that room in weeks. His creative juices had dried up. The ideas still came but gone was the urge to transform thought into substance. Like most things in his life, art had lost its importance.

The doorbell rang. He sighed, dropped the heavy tome back on the pile and went to answer the door.

"Yeah?" He asked the veneer-clad slab.

"It's me, Doc. Ray."

Doc looked at his rumpled khaki slacks and paint-splattered tee shirt, rubbed his chin, and felt the three-day growth beginning to soften with length. He wasn't expecting company.

"Fuck it," he growled, slapped the chain free from its slide, turned the knob, and opened the door.

Ray Beckwith stood with his head poked forward as if unsure of what he would find. His arms held a heavy brown paper sack.

"Come in, Ray. Want a beer?" Doc turned his back on his former colleague and loped into the living room.

"Thanks, Doc. Don't mind if I do. Hot enough for ya?"

"What? Oh. Yeah." He had forgotten about the early heat wave and it dawned on him that he hadn't been out of his air-conditioned apartment since the night before last. The department, thus far, had been able to keep the media from finding out where he lived. By limiting his forays into the outside world to infrequent excursions for necessary provisions—the beer he was drinking, for example—and doing so only at night, he hoped to extend his period of privacy. It would not last forever.

Beckwith stood just inside the doorway, surveying the mess, choosing to ignore the jagged hole in the center of Doc's television screen. Adrienne Boyd's elevation to senior anchor had cost the Sony dearly.

"Doing a little spring cleaning, Doc?"

"Something like that." The apartment looked like the last moments aboard the Titanic. He didn't care. "Have a seat." Doc pulled a sweating cylinder from the plastic carrier in the fridge and joined Ray in the living room.

Beckwith found a clear space at the end of the sofa and accepted the frosty can. "How you holding up, Doc?" he asked, as he took a long pull on the beer.

"I'm okay. You?"

"Fine, fine. Jack sends his regards. He's doing pretty good. Says, 'Why don't you drop by?'"

"Been busy. I'll give him a call." Doc had had enough of hospitals and doctors in the past weeks. He took a sip from his beer and sat on the edge of the coffee table facing Beckwith. He felt obliged to make conversation but found he really did not care to.

"Here's your mail." Beckwith proffered the paper bag full of letters, all opened.

Doc took the sack, glancing at the tattered edges. "Don't they know it's a federal offense to open someone's mail?"

"They're just checking, Doc. You know. Kind of keeping score," Beckwith said. It was an apology.

"And what's the tally?"

Beckwith grinned. "You're slightly ahead in the polls."

"Sure brought the bugs out of the woodwork." Doc grinned back, embarrassed for his colleague. Beckwith could not be very happy with this assignment—mailman to the department pariah.

"That's for sure. How's the nurse?" Beckwith asked.

"No idea." Doc looked at his carpet. Maybe he should vacuum. What for?

Beckwith looked flustered. "I thought—"

"What? You thought what, Ray?"

"You know. You and her, uh…"

"That's in the past, Ray."

"From what Tony told me, I thought you two had a future."

"We might have, but things have changed. Thanks to me, she may lose an eye."

"She blames you, huh? She said that? Did she just blast him, or was he going for her?"

"She hasn't spoken to me since that night. That prick, Carl, says she tried to execute him but he's not the most reliable witness." He took a taste of the beer and sighed. "She was completely hysterical when I got to her."

The image of Madeline—staggering toward him in the sand, blood oozing from between the fingers of the hand clapped over her eye, cursing, waving the shotgun with the other hand—sickened him still.

Doc patted his pants pockets, and said, "I had some cigarettes somewhere." He set his beer down on the coffee table, rose, walked about the room, looking everywhere.

"This them, Doc?" Beckwith pointed to a pack beside the beer can Doc had just put down.

"Yeah. Thanks." He snatched up the pack, pulled a cigarette loose, lit it, and said, "She's surrounded by people who care for her now. That's a really nice bunch at her hospital. Ben Green—he's the doctor she sold her house to…"

"I know, Doc."

"Of course you do. Sorry." He paused. "Where was I?"

"Ben Green," Ray said.

“Right. Ben has reached out to the best eye man in the country. He says that if anybody can save her eye, this guy can.”

“So you’ve talked to Doctor Green, but not to Mrs. Maclear?”

“Yeah. So?”

“I just thought—”

Doc’s glare convinced Beckwith to change the subject.

“—Tony’s going home soon,” he said.

“I know. Phyllis calls every day.” Doc wagged his head. “She says it was a rough way to get him to quit smoking. She’s perfect for him.”

“I know what you mean. I miss the little wiseass. Too bad the way things worked out.”

A feeble nod was all that Doc could manage in reply.

“Any word from Internal Affairs?” Ray asked.

“One of their investigators said that his most optimistic estimate of my future is a permanent posting to the ‘Rubber Gun Squad.’”

“Miserable prick,” Ray said.

“That’s why he’s IA.”

Ray shifted his eyes to the smashed picture tube, and said, “I see your set’s on the fritz. You been keeping up on The Terminator saga?”

“I know he’s not permanently paralyzed and that his face will never be the same.”

“Shotgun pellets do tend to leave a mark,” Ray grinned.

“I also know that the bastard has his choice of top-notch defense lawyers. Hell, they’re fighting over him like piranha in a birdbath. They say my rigging his ass with his own explosives was ‘cruel and unusual’ and that I deprived him of his right to due process.” He poked the burning cigarette toward Beckwith. “What about all the people he killed? Wasn’t that cruel and unusual? What the hell was I supposed to do? Let him kill Madeline and Tony?”

“Take it easy, Doc.”

“Do you know the DA said she might not be able to bring him to trial at all, ‘so grievously had I trampled his rights.’ Can you fucking believe that? The goddamn feds aren’t even sure about the mailbox thing. They say there’s nothing concrete to connect the bastard to the bomb. Shit! They still haven’t proven who he is or if he’s sane or mad as a hatter.” He wagged a finger in Ray’s face. “He’s sane, all right. I thought he must be nuts myself, at first. But no more. He may be the devil himself, but he is as sane as you or me, and the bastard deserves what’s coming to him.”

Beckwith said softly, "Calm down, Doc. It's too hot to get so worked up."

Doc stopped, blinked, and said, "You're right. Sorry, Ray. Want another beer?"

"I never turn down a free drink."

Doc went to the refrigerator and continued talking as he pulled two cans from the box. "I didn't mean to unload on you like that, Ray." He stopped himself. He had no reason to apologize. "At least the mail is easing up." He pointed to the grocery sack as he gave Ray another beer and reclaimed his seat on the coffee table. "A week ago, they had to bring it in those big canvas mailbags. The citizens of America have cursed me as a monster, praised me as a crusading saint, and either insulted my intelligence or congratulated me for it." He took a sip of his beer and riffled through the envelopes. "At least the legal profession gives me equal time with Carl, although none of the esteemed barristers to date have offered to take my case pro bono."

"Don't let them get to you, Doc."

"That's not all, Ray. I get dozens of invitations to speak to and/or join more radical organizations than I knew existed. Of course, there are quite a few special interest groups screaming for my hide. The ACLU is devoting a lot of man-hours to having me drawn and quartered on the headquarters steps."

Beckwith snapped his fingers. "I'm glad you said that. That's exactly what Charlie said would happen to me if I forgot to give you this one." He reached into his breast pocket and produced an envelope. Reaching across the table to hand it to Doc, he said, "Schiff says this is one that's one-hundred-percent on your side."

Doc glanced at the return address. Ms. Jen Wiley was as far as he got before his eyes began to fill up. He wiped his nose with his knuckle, cleared his throat loudly, and said without meeting Beckwith's eyes, "I'll read this later. Thanks."

"Don't mention it."

"And thank Charlie. Maybe he'll stop complaining of being the recipient of my 'fan mail' now that my stardom is waning. The brass are sure dragging their feet. I wish they would get it over with. Either crucify me or sweep it under the rug and let me go back to work."

"Yeah. This waiting around must suck."

"What do you think, Ray?"

Beckwith looked perplexed. "About what?"

Doc's look told Ray stalling would not work.

"About wiring Esterbrook?"

Doc nodded. Beckwith's opinion suddenly mattered a great deal. He would not count Ray among his close friends. Ray was an associate, a brother cop, someone he would socialize with where it related to the job but not outside of it. He'd be a good barometer for the rest of the force. Life would be tolerable if they were behind him. It was, he realized, important to him that he had their understanding, if not their approval.

"Water under the bridge, Doc. What do you care what I think?"

"Don't dance around, Ray. Tell me."

Beckwith squirmed for a minute and then adopted a stern visage. "Piss poor judgment, plain and simple, extenuating circumstances and all. Emotion got in the way of your professionalism. You fucked up."

"That's your considered opinion?" Doc said. Frost crackled on the words.

"Mine and most of the guys." Ray shrugged.

"Thank you for your frank observation, Detective." Doc rose, scowling at the floor, blood pounding in his temples, fists balled at his sides. "You know your way out."

"I wasn't finished." Beckwith looked hurt. He sat as if frozen in time, the beer can poised halfway to his lips.

"Take it with you."

Beckwith shrugged again, took his beer, and walked to the door where he turned, his hand on the knob, waiting to make eye contact.

Doc waited to hear the door close. When he did not, he looked up. The look in his eyes should have chased Beckwith down the hall, but Ray winked, grinned, and said, "Anybody else would have shot the fucker right between the eyes." He toasted Doc with the beer can. "To you, Doc, last of the good guys. I'm proud to know you. We all are."

Doc gaped at the closing door, mildly dazed, unsure whether he had just been insulted or anointed, but it struck him as riotously funny. He laughed aloud for the first time in weeks. He was still laughing, wiping tears from his eyes, trembling fingers fumbling with his daughter's letter when he punched a familiar number on the telephone keypad.

"Hello, Oyster Bay Hospital. Would you put me through to Madeline Maclear, please?"

About the Author

James D. Robertson is the author of FOR GOOD REASON, (Black Opal Books, 2019) a critically acclaimed novel of the Vietnam War. He was also a contributing editor for two non-fiction works, Doc: Platoon Medic, a Military Book Club selection by Daniel Evans Jr. (Pocket Books, 1992) and Steel My Soldiers' Hearts, a New York Times bestseller by the late Colonel David H. Hackworth (Ruggedland Books, 2002). Mr. Robertson served with the authors in Vietnam.

Mr. Robertson is a member of the Mystery Writers of America, International Thriller Writers and Long Island Writers' Guild. He lives with his wife on Long Island where he is working on his next novel.